SHATTERED DREAMS

BOOK TWO IN THE SHATTERED TRILOGY

PHOENIX WOLFE

PHOENIX WOLFE PUBLISHING

CONTENTS

DEDICATION

To my sisters from different misters,

Alyson, Nancy, & Jeana,

who encouraged me

& helped me find my way

with numerous cheese-and-carb-fueled

conversations.

TRIGGER WARNINGS

THIS BOOK CONTAINS REFERENCES to physical injuries, physical assault, sexual assault, kidnapping, PTSD, depression, anxiety, suicidal thoughts, infertility, loss of pregnancy, and graphic violence.

Please read a sample of the first novel in this series for free on my website at **www.phoenix-wolfe.com/sample-of-chapter-one** to see if this book is a fit for you.

CHAPTER ONE

CHARLIE

PALE BLUE EYES ROAM *over my face before halting to stare deeply into my eyes. The smile on Mark's rugged face melts away as he lifts one hand to caress my cheek.*

"Damn, you're beautiful, Baby Girl," he says, his voice husky. One large hand slides behind my neck and tilts my face up to his before he leans in, gently brushing his lips over mine.

"Relax," he whispers against them, and I stretch up on tiptoe to meet him halfway.

I'm startled when he suddenly scoops me up and sets me on the counter, but when I look into his eyes, I forget everything else. He smiles slowly as he dips his head. "That's better," he says as his lips close over mine.

I'm still nervous, though. I feel him smile as he once again mutters against my mouth. "Stop overthinking this. Just let go and feel."

I take the leap and do exactly that.

Mark deepens the kiss, one hand slipping into my hair as his lips touch and tease and taste. When he strokes his tongue across the seam of my lips, I'm all in. Our kisses become hotter. Wetter. Deeper. Excitement spirals through me, and I want more. My fingers somehow end up twisting in his hair, my breasts pressing into the muscled planes of his chest.

He pulls back to kiss his way down my neck before sucking and nibbling his way back up. His perennial five o'clock shadow scrapes over my skin, making me shiver, and I can't help sighing as my head drops back to give him better access.

I need more.

I drag his face back to mine, becoming the aggressor as my lips seek his. A fiery heat engulfs us as our kisses grow more intense. His hand drops from my neck to the curve of my hip, clutching it tightly, pulling me forward. My core grazes his hardness, and heat floods through me.

I tug his hand from my hip and settle it firmly on my right breast. When he squeezes my nipple, my body clenches tightly in response. I wrap my legs around his waist, pulling him closer, arching my hips against him, and my body aches for more. My whimpers of excitement mingle with his deep groan as I grind against him again.

Without warning, he tears his lips away from mine. "Damn, Baby Girl," he gasps, his voice rough. His chest heaves like he's just run a marathon. "You're not broken. Not by a long shot."

Oh. My. God.

What have I done?

Test kiss, my ass. I'm an idiot for agreeing to this.

If I'd taken more than thirty seconds to consider Mark's suggestion, either common sense or my raging insecurities would have kicked in and made me rethink things. I'd never have made such an impulsive decision, possibly ruining the most important relationship of my life.

I made out with my best friend.

And it was hot. Not just hot – electric. Smoldering. Panty-melting. The hottest, most passionate kiss I've ever experienced.

It wasn't supposed to be like that. It was just supposed to be a test, one I passed with flying colors.

Actually, *failed* is probably the more accurate way to view things, because even though it sent my lady bits into overdrive, it wasn't worth screwing up the relationship Mark and I have. He's my best friend, and that's worth more than all the passion in the world.

That panty-melting kiss was last night. Now I'm in my shower, my brain scrambling for a way to fix things while jasmine-scented steam cocoons me in a thick fog. I brace my arms against the spotless white tiles, dropping my head beneath the hot water.

Maybe if I drown myself in here, I won't have to face my screw-up.

What the hell?

It wasn't supposed to be like that.

Mark and I have been best friends since we were kids. Our parents were best friends, too. His mom died from breast cancer when he was thirteen, and his dad committed suicide a couple of years later, too grief-stricken to go on. My parents immediately brought Mark into our home. When they died in a car accident just after my freshman year of college, he and I were alone, a pair of technically-but-not-really-adults, two kids with no one but each other. We floundered a bit before joining the Army. Mark chose infantry and rose quickly through the ranks. I became a medic and loved it, but I missed Mark. I bounced from place to place around the Middle East before I finally scored my transfer to his unit, a platoon embedded deep in a hotspot in Afghanistan.

That's where I met Lila and Tucker. Lila was a fellow medic, and Tucker was Mark's second-in-command and later, Lila's fiance. The four of us became inseparable over our years together, forming our own kinda-sorta-family unit.

Then everything went to hell.

Lila and I were kidnapped by insurgents and imprisoned for eleven days before being rescued. We endured barbaric torture that ended our military careers, and I was left wounded and scarred, traumatized with crippling PTSD.

I functioned on emotional autopilot for years until Mark came to live with me a few months ago. An IED exploded while he was on a mission, leaving him severely injured and missing his right lower leg. After three months in Brooke Army Medical Center, he came here to finish recovering. Lila and I are massage therapists now. We co-own a wellness clinic offering massage, hydrotherapy, and physical therapy for injured veterans. Mark gets PT five days a week, and Tucker, who moved back here and married Lila, spends three afternoons a week helping Mark rebuild his strength.

I brought Mark home with me to heal, but the truth is, he's helped me as much as I've helped him. He's my sounding board, my compass, and my anchor.

After my kidnapping, my persistent male-induced panic attacks convinced me I was too defeated, both physically and emotionally, to feel sexual desire. It seemed obvious I was meant to be alone. Relationships require extensive effort to force myself to be emotionally and sexually vulnerable, and I'd long since run out of energy and motivation. I'd decided the juice wasn't worth the squeeze, particularly given most of the doorknobs I've been out with.

That brings me to last night, when Mark urged me not to give up. I said I didn't know any men I trusted enough to have dinner with, let alone attempt anything physical to confirm my suspicion that I was irreversibly sexually paralyzed. He suggested a test, a kiss between the two of us. I trust Mark implicitly. He'd die before he'd take advantage of me, and we both know it. The idea was to let me safely explore whether I was sexually damaged beyond repair.

Well, I'm not.

Definitely not.

My face grows hot as memories scroll through my mind again. Pale blue eyes holding mine. Rough stubble grazing my neck. Soft lips becoming firm, insistent. Things long forgotten stirring to life. Damp heat. Hardness. Fiery passion.

Jesus, I'm getting turned on again just thinking about it.

No.

I shove my face under the water again to derail my train of thought.

It wasn't supposed to be like that.

It was supposed to be a test, a way to verify my conviction I was too damaged to become aroused. Obviously, I was wrong, and I've screwed everything up.

Mark and I can barely look at each other. We've always curled up on the sofa together to watch movies, but last night we avoided all contact. When I set up for his leg massage to stave off his phantom pains, he pushed my hands away, despite the risk of substantial pain later.

Yeah. Thanks to my overly enthusiastic response last night, I'm not allowed to touch him.

Ever since he moved here, we've spent each night side by side as a trade-off. I help prevent or ease his phantom pain, and he keeps watch so I feel safe enough to sleep. But I didn't sleep last night. I couldn't. I was too busy vacillating between remembering every delicious detail of our kiss and worrying I've ruined the most important relationship in my life.

I'm not willing to give up what he and I have.

I just have no idea how to set things right.

MARK

I'm cross-legged on my bed, my left leg folded beneath me and what remains of my amputated right leg hanging off the edge of the plush mattress. I'm alone. Charlie's already left for work, scurrying out the side door and across the breezeway to her clinic next door. Meanwhile, I'm taking out my frustrations by pounding a squashy gray pillow and cursing enough to make any sailor blush.

I'm a goddamned idiot.

I've fucked everything up with Charlie. I made a spontaneous suggestion without considering the long-term ramifications, and it's strained things between us.

Our relationship is the most important one in my life. Without Charlie, I have nothing.

Charlie's deeply scarred by a past that's entirely my fault. Four years ago, I sent two teams on a medical mission that turned out to be an ambush. Insurgents killed six of my men before taking Charlie and Lila prisoner. The bastards were savages. Charlie endured unspeakable horrors – beatings, branding, mutilation, and rapes, all because I made the wrong call. It took eleven days for me to locate and rescue them, eleven days and nights of hell that left her with unspeakably deep physical and emotional scars.

When she brought me here to recuperate, I had no clue she struggled with night terrors. Unbeknownst to me, she spent every night on a bench in her hall where she could monitor every entrance, dozing in brief spurts until her nightmares hit. She'd awaken in full combat mode, gun drawn, often firing in the direction she believed her attacker was coming from. Things got so dire, Tucker and Lila installed a remote camera system to alert them so they could help reorient her to her surroundings and calm her.

They never said a word to me.

Not one fucking word.

I get it... sort of. I was half a world away, and a split second of distraction worrying about a problem I couldn't fix could literally have meant life or death for me and my men. I understand their logic, and I'd probably have done the same in their position, but it still upsets me. My best friend needed me, and I had no idea. I'm the one responsible for her night terrors. I'm the one who fucked up and sent my team into a trap.

What's more devastating is that she wasn't having regular bad dreams, like falling off a cliff or standing in front of a crowd in your underwear. During her night terrors, Charlie relived what those fuckers did to her. *Everything* they did to her, as though it was happening in real time, every goddamn night.

I discovered this the hard way my first night here. Charlie cried out, trapped in one of her night terrors, reliving a rape by her captors. She was still disoriented when I hurried to check on her. If I hadn't struggled with my bedroom door, she'd have shot me in the head. Instead, she planted two bullets in the wall exactly where my head would have been.

And she's a certified expert marksman.

That horrible night led to a mutually beneficial arrangement. She'd stay with me at night to manage my phantom pains. In return, she'd hand over her gun and trust me to keep her safe so she could sleep without fear.

When her gun isn't with me, it's in a soft belly-band holster around her waist. She doesn't feel safe without it. Night terrors aren't her only struggle. Unexpected male touch terrifies her. Thanks to those bastards, her mind reflexively equates male touch with pain. A mere hug from someone she doesn't trust can instigate a full-blown panic attack, complete with gun drawn. She's only recently begun to initiate affectionate touch with the two males she trusts besides me – Tucker and her friend, Tom. She's working hard to overcome her fears. She was doing really well, even dating one guy for a few weeks until he revealed his true colors.

Trust is unbelievably hard for her, and not just with men. Charlie doesn't trust her own judgment now. I think that's why sexual contact has been so challenging, because she can't relax enough to just *feel*. She'd convinced herself she was too broken to feel desire. We'd talked about it a couple of months ago, before she started seeing Blake. I'd hoped the issue would resolve itself, but it didn't, and when things didn't work out, she gave up. She'd decided she was sexually damaged beyond repair, unwilling to risk dating to confirm or disprove her suspicions.

Enter me and my fuck-up of epic proportions.

A thought flitted through my mind while we were discussing her certainty that she could neither feel desire nor arouse a partner. She and I could test her theory – nothing more than kissing, but lasting long enough for her to relax and let go. Charlie trusts me, so the hurdle of finding someone she could be comfortable with was a non-issue. I can read her better than anyone, and I'd stop at her first hint of anxiety or dissociation.

I didn't really think she'd agree, so I never considered the possibility of consequences. I assumed on the off-chance she did consent, we'd make out for a couple of minutes and she'd realize she could enjoy herself with someone once she let go of her fears.

She startled me by accepting my offer.

She stunned me with her passionate response.

My profound, fiery reaction rocked me to my core.

What the hell?

Where did *that* come from?

Charlie and I have been best friends for nearly twenty-five years. We've been there for each other through everything, from skinned knees to war wounds, bad haircuts to hangovers, losing football games to losing family members. Until last night, we've never once crossed that unspoken boundary, although at sixteen, I'd have jumped at the chance.

Sixteen-year-old me was clapping and cheering last night, rooting for more.

Thirty-five-year-old me is mature enough to understand that while sex with Charlie would be mind-blowing, I can't risk what we have. She's my best friend. I can't lose her.

I let my mind drift back to her fervent response, and my lips curl in a slow grin.

Yeah... she's definitely not broken.

CHARLIE

I wake long before my alarm, the only light coming from the bedside lamp on the other side of the bed. I can tell as I shift positions that I'm alone because there's no weight on the mattress behind me. Still, I snake a hand backwards, hoping I'm wrong but finding only cold sheets. I roll over, scanning the room. Pale blue eyes watch me. Mark is perched on his chaise again. His jaw tightens, and his watchful gaze turns to a glare when our eyes meet.

He's definitely not happy to see me.

He used to be.

He always used to be.

But that was before I ruined everything.

Tears spring to my eyes. I leap from the bed, tripping on the edge of the comforter. He automatically reaches to catch me, but I right myself and pick up my gun from the bedside table.

"I'll get out of your way," I mumble, rushing for the door. After I close it, I hear a crash. I hesitate, wondering if he's fallen, but based on the loud string of curses that follows, he's not injured. His voice isn't coming from floor level. He's just angry.

At me.

God, this week has sucked.

Monday night was the hottest kiss of my life. It was followed by Mark's abrupt withdrawal. He rarely speaks, and if he does, he's crabby. He won't let me massage him at all, not before bed to prevent his phantom pains and not when he's at the clinic, either.

He doesn't want me to touch him.

Maybe I misread things.

Maybe the passion from our kiss was all one-sided.

What if Mark was just trying to prove I still had the capacity to respond?

Oh, God.

It was a *pity* kiss.

And I got carried away.

After that realization sinks in, I can barely make eye contact with him.

At least I've been able to limit my time alone with him. Three evenings a week, Tom and Tucker come over and work out with Mark while Lila and I make dinner, and I've convinced them to watch a movie or hang out afterwards. The other evenings, I've avoided going home. One night I texted Mark that pizza was being delivered so I could go shopping. I'd rather have bamboo shoved under my nails than shop for clothes, so I played solitaire on my phone and ate a burger in my car. Last night, I hung out with Tom and Maya and sent Chinese food to Mark.

I've even figured out how to circumvent the awkwardness of bedtime. I shower and wait upstairs until I hear him in his own shower, then sneak into his room. I leave my gun on his bedside table and climb into bed, feigning sleep when I hear him moving around the bathroom. He climbs in bed next to me, careful not to make contact. When I sleep, I dream of him in ways I wish I didn't. When I wake, he's never beside me. He's always across the room on his chaise, looking grumpy.

This morning was no different, except for the cursing as soon as I was out of sight.

I've ruined everything.

I shower and dress, escaping to the safety of our clinic. The lights are already on when I get there, though it isn't even seven yet. "Hello?"

"In here," calls Lila.

I follow her voice down the hall to my office, an open room with soft sage walls, cherry wood furniture covered in sprawling green plants, and fluttery white sheers over floor to ceiling windows. A fountain on the credenza provides the soothing sound of trickling water. Lila's sorting documents into large piles to fax to physicians' offices and insurance companies. The endless paperwork is my least favorite part of this job. Lila was shocked by the ridiculous amount of redundancy I deal with when she covered for me while I was in Texas with Mark. I've always handled the paperwork because I know she abhors it. Since learning firsthand how much is involved, she's made it a point to help, a task I'm more than happy to share.

"You're here early," Lila greets me. She's cross-legged on the floor, surrounded by precariously high stacks of paper. "I've finally gotten these sorted. We just need to fax those." She points to a pile to her right.

"Thanks. I'll send them and work on invoices today. Tara's covering my clients, so I should have time." I examine her more closely. Her violet eyes are red-rimmed with dark circles beneath them, and her usually perfect blond curls are twisted up in a clip instead of tumbling down her back. I pick my way across the room, stepping between piles to sit down facing her. "Want to talk about it?"

Her eyes flash to mine in surprise before she sighs. "Is it that obvious?"

"Only to me."

She bites her lip, staring at the floor. "I started my period last night."

Oh.

Lila went off the pill in January to pursue her desire to have a baby, and it hasn't happened as quickly as she'd expected it to. She tracks her ovulation days and peak conception windows obsessively, timing her intercourse with

Tucker to increase the odds. Every unsuccessful month seems to take a little more out of her.

"I'm sorry, Lila." I reach out and squeeze her delicate fingers. "What can I do?"

She shrugs lightly. "Nothing. This is on me, I guess."

I don't address the elephant in the room: her fear that the violent sexual assaults by the bastards who kidnapped us caused enough damage to render her infertile.

Like they did me.

But I don't go there, because neither of us is strong enough for that discussion today. Instead, I shake my head. "This isn't on you. Stress makes it harder to conceive, and this has been a hell of a year. I abandoned you when Mark got injured. You managed the clinic, a gazillion goats and horses, your house, your husband, the renovations to my house – hell, I'm exhausted just listing it all. That's a ton of stress." I pause, gazing at her sad eyes. "I know it's easier said than done, but be patient with yourself. You need to recover, too."

She sighs. "Maybe. And you didn't abandon me. Mark was hurt. You did what Tucker and I couldn't do. You were exactly where all of us needed you to be." Then she purses her lips. "Why are you here so early?"

No way in hell can I give Lila one more thing to worry about.

I sidestep her question, tossing my hair and reaching for a piece of paper from one of the piles, pretending to read it. "You know me. Once I'm up, I can't go back to sleep, so I came in to get a head start on this." I gesture around at the stacks of paper. "I had no idea I'd find you here, too." I smile. "I'm glad I did. Makes my day a lot easier."

She eyes me suspiciously, and I'm sure she's going to call bullshit, so I rush to speak before she can. "Why don't you call Tucker and meet him for breakfast? I'll take your morning clients."

"Adam has the flu," she answers, referring to one of our older veterans, a right-sided above-the-knee amputee. "He texted me last night, and Jim has a doctor's appointment this morning, so I don't have a client until noon." She hesitates, and I can tell she's considering my offer. "Maybe I will."

I nod. "Tucker's probably upset, too. Breakfast together will do you both good."

She scoops up her phone. "I hope he doesn't have an early session."

When she's gone, I pull up my knees and tuck my face into them, glad I'm alone so I don't have to pretend everything's fine. I'd give anything to talk to someone about this mess I've gotten myself into.

The problem is, Mark's my go-to person for advice, and he's clearly not an option. Lila's my second, but she's got more than enough to deal with. I could try Tucker, but he'd probably think my kissing Mark was a fantastic idea instead of the giant fuck-up it's become. And Tom is taking the day off, flying to New York with Maya so she can spend the weekend with her mom.

I'm on my own to sort this shit out.

MARK

I'm on the back deck, heaving chunks of charred wood from the firepit at the distant trees lining the lower border of Charlie's property. I'm desperate to expend some energy. Things are getting out of hand.

The night we kissed, Charlie started massaging my leg as usual, but the feel of her hands gliding over me and her scent as she leaned into her strokes made my cock harden. I hurriedly stopped her, not wanting her to notice my erection. The hurt in her eyes almost made me confess, but I held back, not wanting to freak her out.

She laid beside me all night, stiff as a board, not sleeping a wink. Neither did I, not until long after she left for work the next morning. When I eventually slept, I dreamed of her. I awoke irritable, wanting what I can never have.

Charlie.

In my bed.

Crying out my name as she comes with my cock deep inside her.

To my dismay, things aren't getting any easier as the nights progress.

The second night, Charlie does fall asleep. She claims my wrist in her sleep and tugs my arm across her body, anchoring my hand so that her full breast nestles perfectly into it. My mouth goes dry and my body tightens instantly.

The third night, she rolls onto me, her head on my shoulder, both breasts pressing into my chest and her leg slung over my groin. I ease out from beneath her, but she immediately shifts back, clinging to me like ivy to a wall as my cock hardens against her thigh.

Last night, she once again pulled my arm around her so her breast ended up in my hand. Our bodies shifted when she rolled, and her luscious backside slid into full contact with my groin. I grabbed a pillow and pushed it between us to hide my immediate erection.

My only respite comes when she's asleep enough for me to escape to the safety of the chaise, out of her reach. Even then, I'm haunted by the images my mind replays. Our steamy kiss. My hand buried in her silky brown hair. Her lush curves. My stroking hands. Wetness and heat. Her green eyes, dilated with desire. And when she moans or makes soft noises in her sleep, it's almost more than I can take.

I don't let her massage me at all, not at home or at the clinic. I can't. I'm too afraid she'll see how my body reacts to her now. Hurt flashes in her eyes, but she says nothing as I traipse past her down the hall every day with Lila or Tara.

In the daytime, Charlie avoids time alone with me like the plague. As soon as her eyes open, she races to her shower before spending even longer hours than usual at her clinic. She's been at work before daylight every day since our kiss. After work, she keeps a cushion of people around so we're never alone. On workout days with Tom, Tucker, and Lila, she acts as though nothing's wrong, and strangely enough, none of them have noticed she and I aren't speaking or making eye contact.

When the guys aren't here to work out, she evades me. One day, she texted she wouldn't be home because she was going shopping. Did she seriously think I'd believe that? She'd rather face a firing squad than go shopping. And all these visits with Tom and Maya? Okay, fine, she does that at least once a week, but she's doing it more frequently now, and it's not like I don't know why. She's even having dinner delivered to me when she's not here. It's like a giant neon sign flashing, "Don't waste your time waiting for me, because I won't be joining you".

We've got to work this out.

I just don't know how.

Every time I try to talk to her, my words come out like growls. I can't stop it, because it pisses me off that she's pulling away. It's become a vicious cycle. The more I snap, the more she withdraws, and the more she withdraws, the more irascible I become. Her injured expression has me wound so tightly that as soon as she leaves the room, I start cursing and throwing things.

I want Charlie to fight for me. For *us*, for what we have together. She fights every other problem head on – why not this one? The only time she reacts honestly is when she's asleep, wrapping her body around mine. Her authentic response proves she wants more between us, even if she won't admit it out loud. The way she reaches for me in her sleep is a problem, though, because it makes me want more. Much more. I allow myself to savor it briefly, but I can't stay that close to her. It's too torturous. As soon as I'm certain I won't wake her, I extricate myself. I can't act on my feelings, so I flee to the safety of the chaise.

I'm not fleeing the same way she is, though.

Definitely not.

She's giving up. I'm just not giving in. There's a difference.

Yeah, right.

Maybe Charlie isn't the only one avoiding the truth.

CHAPTER TWO

CHARLIE

I DEAL WITH MARK'S ever-increasing bitchiness by surrounding myself with buffers. I know he won't act like an ass in front of Tucker and Lila, especially not if it would require an explanation he won't want to give. Disclosing that he's cranky because I got too amorous for his liking during a kiss that was his idea? He'd never cop to that.

On Friday, I invite Lila to join me in Pueblo for a weekend shopping trip. She accepts without bothering to consult Tucker, not that he'd mind. We do this a few times a year. It's a tradition. We have a specific restaurant we go to for brunch, a set order in which we approach the outlet stores, and a particular hotel we always stay at. We even end each day at the same Mexican restaurant, a place with mouthwatering tacos and bottomless margaritas. The difference is, this time the trip's at my suggestion. That's never happened before. I detest shopping.

Lila doesn't care whose idea it is. Shopping is her favorite hobby. Thankfully, it's fairly easy to keep her distracted from what's going on with me. Every time she asks a question I don't want to answer, I find the perfect pair of shoes for her, or an amazing scarf, or – well, you get the idea. Despite the summer heat, we add to Lila's already overflowing fall clothing collection. She has eight full bags when we return home. When she drops me off, I have my overnight bag and one measly shopping bag. I'd eventually purchased a top at her insistence, a whisper-soft burgundy tunic to wear with leggings when the sultry July weather fades into crisp fall mornings.

Mark glares from his doorway the second I enter the house. "Seriously? You hate clothes shopping. I'm supposed to believe you had a sudden urge to shop for an entire weekend?"

My stomach clenches at the venom in his voice. I close my eyes briefly and take a deep breath. "Hi, Mark. It's nice to see you too. Do you need anything before I go upstairs?"

He whirls away on his crutches, slamming the door.

I have no idea how things got so twisted around. The worst part is, before I agreed to our kiss, I asked him what would happen if it made things weird between us. He said he didn't know any two people, married or otherwise, who had a stronger relationship than ours. He said it wasn't possible for a kiss to destroy what we had.

He believed that. It wasn't just a line to coerce me into kissing him. I believed it, too.

We were both wrong.

I wish I'd never kissed him. All I did was ruin everything.

Every day, the pattern continues. At night, I sneak into his bed when he's in the living room watching TV or in his shower, pretending to be asleep when he comes to bed. The only reason I still sleep in his bed is because I'm afraid my night terrors will return. The last time I had a night terror without him at my side, I nearly shot him in the head. That's not a chance I'm willing to take, so I sleep in his bed and leave my gun on his nightstand. Each morning, I wake up alone to find him glowering on the chaise.

I cope by cutting my time at home even more, staying later at work, even on the days everyone's at my house. Tom returns to the clinic one evening after his workout with Tucker and Mark. When I hear the door open, my hand automatically reaches toward the gun in my desk drawer, stopping when he calls to me. "You still here, Charlie?"

"In my office."

Tom comes in, a white towel slung around his massive shoulders. He's dressed in a gray tank top and shorts, his brown hair damp with sweat. He rubs the towel over his head, then swipes it across his broad chest with a huge hand before taking a seat across from me. He tips his head toward a stack of papers on my desk. "Still working on invoices?"

The pile hasn't budged in the last two hours. I've been agonizing over what to do with Mark, trying desperately to find a way to fix things, but coming up empty. I nod anyway. "How was the workout?"

"Good," he says, sizing me up. "You want to talk about it?"

Shit. I aim for a confused expression. "Talk about what?"

He raises one eyebrow. "What's going on with Mark."

My jaw drops. "Wha – what do you mean?"

He snorts. "Give me some credit. I may be a guy, but I'm not an idiot. You've been avoiding going home, and the only person there is Mark. Obviously, you two had a fight or something. He's not talking, but something's bothering him, and you're clearly upset, too."

I close my mouth, wracking my brain for an excuse.

Tom's warm brown eyes soften. "I know you don't like discussing your feelings. I won't push you. I'm here if you want to talk, and if you need a place to crash, you can always stay with me."

God, I hope I don't have to leave my own house over this.

Of course, that's exactly what I did last weekend.

I smile at Tom, my friend who's as close as a brother. "Thanks. I'm okay. Just working a few things out in my head."

He nods. "If you need a sounding board, I'm here."

I stand and move around the desk toward him. He stands, too, and I slide my arms around his waist. Biceps bigger than my thighs wrap around me in a comforting hug.

I allow myself to revel in my progress. Six months ago – even three months ago – this hug would have been impossible. I'd have had a full-blown panic attack. I was paralyzed with fear at the idea of male touch from anyone besides Mark, even Tom and Tucker. It didn't matter that I'd trust both of them with my life. It's only with the help of a therapist named Willow that I'm now able to hug them without hesitation, and that's huge.

Tom kisses my forehead and releases me. "Sorry," he apologizes. "I'm all sweaty."

I laugh. "I spent eleven years with soldiers in full battle gear in one-hundred-plus degree desert. It takes more than a little sweat to bother me."

He chuckles. "If you were Tucker, I'd shove your face in my armpit and ask if you were sure."

I grin at the image of Tucker flailing, cussing a blue streak. Then his smile fades. "Seriously, if you need to get away for a few days, Maya is staying with my sister this weekend. You wouldn't have to keep pretending everything's fine."

I sigh. "I'm hoping this doesn't drag out that long."

I just don't know how to resolve it.

He nods. "My offer stands." He rubs the towel over his head again. "I'm going to shower here before I pick up Maya. Unlike you, she objects strongly to me being sweaty. I'm supposed to tell you we're doing pasta night tomorrow instead of Friday, since Maya's staying with my sister. Apparently I'm ordering chicken parm and spaghetti and meatballs. I think Skyler's going to be there, too." He grins. "But what do I know? I just live there."

I smile, picturing his amazing daughter with her laughing eyes and impish grin. "Tell Maya I can't wait."

MARK

I like Tom. He's a great physical therapist. He's helped me regain mobility and taught me how to strengthen my changed body, which in turn helps me prepare for the osseointegration surgery I'm hoping to have soon. The surgery involves implanting a titanium rod into the bone of what remains of my right lower leg so I can bolt a permanent prosthetic in place. I despise the idea of a slip-on prosthetic. What if it slipped off and people saw my stump? I hate the thought of a slip-on prosthetic as much as I hate the word "stump". Even the word makes my stomach churn. It brings to mind a dead tree, a useless hunk of wood. That's all my leg is now, courtesy of some asshole in Afghanistan who set off an IED and blew me and half my team to hell.

Anyway, Tom's fantastic at his job, and he's a solid workout partner who helps me adapt Tucker's exercises to fit my physical limitations. He's nice, he's funny – an all-around great guy.

But the more time Charlie spends with him, the more resentful of him I become.

They're just friends. I know this. Charlie told me ages ago she views him the same way she does Tucker, like a big brother. Tom once broke Blake's nose for causing her to have a panic attack, and he beat the crap out of him – as did I – after he hurt her several weeks ago. Tom's very protective of her, and I'm glad he's looking out for her.

They're just friends.

Of course, she and I were just friends, and look what happened. A few more minutes on that kitchen counter, and we might have gotten too carried away to turn back. My mind drifts to our bodies arching together, her legs around my waist.

Returning to reality is painful.

It's even more painful when I think about Charlie and Tom.

Because the worse things get between Charlie and me, the more time she spends with Tom and Maya. I can't fault her for wanting to be around Maya. She's amazing. I've never met a kid like her, not that I've spent a lot of time around kids. She's funny and witty, perfectly comfortable being the only kid in a roomful of adults when we all have dinner together a few nights a week. She joins in conversations and gives thoughtful, intelligent responses.

I can't even fault Charlie for wanting to be around Tom. He's genuinely a terrific guy.

But something happens when I see Charlie and Tom together, with Maya tucked between them.

I see Tom's healthy body, twinkling eyes, and warm smile.

I see Charlie's head tilting down to listen to Maya, her green eyes sparkling with laughter at whatever Maya's excited about.

And I see Maya's huge smile and springy copper-streaked curls as she gazes at Charlie with open adoration.

They look like a happy family.

And it makes something inside my chest roar with anger.

Tom's handsome, strong, virile. He's not half a man. He can be to Charlie all the things I can never be. Things she deserves. A whole man, not one with a stump for a leg.

And I'll be damned if she doesn't spend evenings with him and walk in the front door happy, only for her smile to evaporate as soon as she sees me.

Yeah. Fine.

I'm jealous.

Because Charlie used to smile with me. Now she can't get away from me fast enough.

The fact that I'm growling like a pissed-off grizzly bear all the time doesn't help, I know, but still, she doesn't have to rub his perfection in my face.

Fuck.

I wish I'd never kissed Charlie.

That's what I tell myself, anyway.

Maybe one day I'll believe it.

LILA

I carry two canvas bags down the hall past Charlie and into her kitchen. "Nachos," I announce. "They're the perfect Friday night food and they don't take much time, so we only need twenty minutes to cook." I pull out a bottle and grin. "I also have margarita mixer, and I know you've got tequila." I unload the raw ground beef, cheese, and margarita mix into her refrigerator and leave the bags on the counter.

I'm startled when I turn to Charlie. Under the kitchen lights and without her fake smile, I can see the deep gray shadows under her eyes. She's not sleeping. Her face is pinched and tense, her forehead creased.

That fucking Blake. This is all his fault. I shouldn't have stopped Tom from beating his ass in the parking lot, even if it was at work and Mark had already laid into him. Tom pounded the hell out of him later anyway. He also dismissed Blake as his assistant boxing coach at the youth center. He said he wouldn't have someone he couldn't trust influencing his boys, even if it meant coaching alone.

Charlie summoned the courage to be completely vulnerable with Blake, showed that jackass her scars, and he freaked out. When she called him on his behavior, he said unforgivable things – that she looked like something out of a horror movie and that she was too fucked up for anyone to ever want. She's not been herself since then, and it's been well over a month.

From down the hall, Mark laughs at something Tucker's said, and the pain that flashes across her face startles me.

Wait. Charlie's upset because of *Mark*?

What the hell?

Things slowly slide into place.

Last week was an off week for me. Finding out for the sixth month in a row that we haven't conceived definitely knocked the wind out of me. But as soon as Charlie wanted us to go on a weekend shopping trip, alarm bells rang in my head.

Charlie loathes shopping. I normally have to drag her along to essentially be my caddy, holding outfits and carrying bags and following along while I shop my little heart out. I always have to prod her into making a purchase, and her favorite part is the end-of-day celebratory taco and margarita extravaganza. I waited all weekend for her to tell me what was up, but she never said a word. It was obvious something was bothering her, but I'd assumed she was still upset about Blake. Her eyes were tired, her face pale. She had no appetite and drank more than usual.

She's bright and cheerful at work, though, chatting with clients and co-workers alike. I figured the distraction was good for her. The only time I've seen her smile falter is when Mark has requested Tara or I do his massage.

Oh my God.

Mark doesn't want Charlie to massage him?

Little things suddenly click. Charlie keeping us here unusually late after dinner. Her staying at the clinic really late on non-workout nights. Her exhaustion. The shopping trip. Mark not letting her massage him. And the pain on her face when she heard him laugh just now.

There's a problem between her and Mark.

And judging by her expression, she and I need to talk, even if she's reluctant to.

I grab a bottle of red wine and two glasses and take Charlie's hand, pulling her to the living room. I nudge her onto the overstuffed beige couch and pour us each a glass, setting the wine bottle within reach on the huge reclaimed wood coffee table. I wait until she's taken a few sips before I begin my interrogation.

"Are you going to tell me what's going on?"

Her eyes flare briefly before she clamps an innocent expression in place. "What?"

"Between you and Mark."

"What do you mean?"

"You're both acting weird. You won't look each other in the eye and you're both keeping your distance. You're behaving like you're uncomfortable with each other, and I've never seen you two like this. Did you have a fight?"

Charlie shakes her head. She won't meet my eyes, instead rubbing her finger around and around the rim of her glass. "No. Nothing like that."

"Then what?"

She hesitates. "I think I've really screwed things up."

"How?"

Charlie still won't look at me, staring instead at the rock fireplace. Finally she describes, with numerous tearful stops and starts, the conversation she and Mark had last week that culminated in a mutual agreement to try a test kiss.

She looks miserable. I'd bet my favorite goat that their kiss brought up feelings neither of them was expecting. "I'm guessing it went well."

"How did you know?"

Her stunned look makes me smile, and I shrug. "A hunch."

She sighs heavily and nods, drying her eyes. "Yes, it went well. Too well. And now things are awful, and I don't know how to fix them. We aren't speaking. If he does say something, he bites my head off, so I'm avoiding him, but that only makes him angrier."

I reach over and cover her hand with mine. "What do you want to do, Charlie?"

"I want to go back to how things were. I mean, I guess it's good to know I can become aroused, but it wasn't worth losing our friendship over."

I study her, observing her reaction. "If you can't go back, what about going forward?"

"Forward how?"

I sit silently, waiting for her to catch on. Her green eyes widen as she grasps my meaning.

"I can't do that, Lila," she splutters. "Things are awful now because we kissed. If I – if we – we wouldn't even be able to look at each other."

"Or your relationship could progress to the next level," I point out. "The reason you both responded like that was because of something already simmering between you. It's just that neither of you realized it was there before."

"But what if things didn't work out? If we can't act normally around each other after kissing – if we took things further and they didn't work out – I'd lose him completely, Lila. It's not worth that. I can't take that chance."

"Then I suppose you need to figure out how to go back to how things were."

"How?"

"You're going to have to talk to him. Tell him that the way things are right now is painful, and you need to figure out how to move past it together. You guys have helped each other deal with truly horrible things. Dealing with an amazing kiss should be easy by comparison."

She looks at me like I've lost my mind. "Easy? We're barely speaking. How the hell do I have a conversation like that with someone who won't even talk to me?"

I refill her wineglass and push it toward her. "A little liquid courage can't hurt."

TUCKER

It's Friday afternoon, and I'm helping Mark with his workout. Tom's at his sister's with Maya, and Lila and Charlie are down the hall. I have to keep getting Mark's attention because he's making stupid mistakes. He's completely unfocused.

"What the hell's going on with you?" I finally demand, snatching the dumbbell from his hand. I've just corrected him for the third time on an exercise he's executed perfectly for two months.

He shakes his head. "Sorry. I'll pay attention."

"I didn't ask you to pay attention. I asked what the hell's up."

"I've got a lot on my mind, that's all."

Mark reaches to take the dumbbell back, but I extend my arm past his reach. "I'm waiting, Chandler."

He scowls and leans closer, but I move my arm again. "If I punch you in the face, I bet you quit moving the damn weight," he grumbles.

"I'll quit moving it when you start talking. Let's hear it, Princess. What's got your panties in a pucker?"

He turns to get his crutches to leave, but I react faster, snatching them away before he can grab them. "Stealing crutches from a cripple is a dick move, Maxwell," he mutters.

I snort. "Cripple, my ass. Don't try your pity-bullshit on me. I can wait all night, and you aren't going anywhere without these, so you might as well spill it."

His jaw tightens as his face reddens. "What's with your sudden urge to talk about feelings? Can't we just work out?"

"If you were working out like you're supposed to be, we wouldn't be having this conversation, so start talking." I pause a second before adding, "Unless you'd rather I asked Charlie."

"No," he snaps.

I grin knowingly, and his shoulders slump as he recognizes defeat.

"Fine," he grumbles. I wait expectantly until he raises uncertain eyes to mine. "I kissed her," he confesses, dragging a hand through his short sandy hair.

My face splits in a huge smile. "It's about damn time."

He glares.

"What? You two've been dancing around this for as long as I've known you. You're crazy about her, she's crazy about you. Everybody can see you belong together."

"It's not that simple, Tucker. It's screwed everything up between us."

"How?"

He takes a deep breath. "Because I want more."

I raise one eyebrow. "You say that like it's a problem."

He stares at me, incredulous. "This is Charlie. She's my best friend. We live together. She's not some random woman I can walk away from if things don't work out."

"No, she's not, so you'll be invested. Besides, who says it has to be more than a fling?"

He shakes his head firmly. "With everything she's been through, a fling isn't an option."

"Fine. Friends with benefits," I suggest. "You add another dimension to what's already there with the understanding that it's just sex."

He gives me a doubtful look. "Kissing her has already fucked everything up between us. I'm not sure adding sex will make it better."

"It's fucked up because of all the sexual tension. Sex would relieve that," I point out.

"Or make things worse."

I shrug. "You've only got two options here. Either you let it go and forget wanting more, or you go for it. But you can't keep ignoring it, because all that's done is make everything awkward. Decide what you want."

"What I want and what Charlie wants may be very different."

"Guess you'll have to talk to her, then," I reply with a broad smile. "Lila and I were going to see if you guys wanted to catch a movie after dinner, but it sounds like your evening is full."

"No, let's go out," he says hastily. "Anywhere you want. My treat."

I laugh. "I don't think so. As a matter of fact, I think you and I need to cut things short here. It's not like you're accomplishing anything, and you two have things to settle."

He glares. "What happened to 'Whatever you need, we'll be there, Mark'?"

I grin. "That's why we're leaving. So you two can figure out what you need." I pass him his crutches and jump up. "You know, I think I feel a headache coming on. I should go home." I stride to the door and pull it open.

"Tucker, I swear to God," he mutters.

I catch Lila in the hall and tell her we need to leave. I wink when I tell her I think I'm getting a headache, and she grins. Apparently, she and Charlie have been talking as well. I hear Mark's crutches ticking on the floor behind me as Lila apologizes to Charlie, telling her she needs to take me home. When I glance back at Mark, he glowers. I grin and blow him a kiss. He flips me off, quickly moving his hand to rub the back of his neck when Lila reappears.

I look at Lila when we're outside. "It's about damn time," I tell her, tipping my head toward Mark and Charlie.

She grins. "Be patient. They're not there yet, but they will be."

CHAPTER THREE

CHARLIE

I CLOSE THE DOOR behind Lila and Tucker and take a deep breath, wishing my buffers weren't leaving so soon.

I can do this.

Steeling myself against rejection, I fake-smile and turn to Mark. "Looks like we're on our own tonight. Want to grab dinner somewhere?"

His jaw tightens slightly. "No."

No excuses, no explanations, just "no".

I take another deep breath. "Alright. How about we sit down and talk instead?"

He exhales sharply, refusing to meet my eyes. Then he shakes his head, whirls around, and heads into his room. When he shuts his door, it's not exactly a slam, but it's close.

That's when it sinks in.

We've ruined things beyond repair.

His anger, his icy chill when he looks at me, his refusal of my massages even to ease his pain – I can't take any more of his blatant, unrelenting rejection. When I hear his shower turn on and know I can escape unnoticed, I collect my pillow and my things from his bedside table and take them upstairs. Fuck the night terrors. I survived them before. I'll survive them again.

I'm starving, and since I don't feel like cooking, I need takeout. I slam my car into drive and speed to the closest restaurant. It's a pizza place, the kind where you can buy huge wedges of hot pizza by the slice. I pick up some sausage and olives for Mark and Hawaiian for me. As I let myself back into the house, I hear his shower cut off. I deposit his pizza and a bottle of beer on his bedside table before he can finish toweling off, then scurry to the living room for the bottle of wine and my half-full glass. I take my wine and pizza to my room upstairs. Mark can't manage my steep stairs, at least not very well. He'd probably have to crawl, which is actually an appealing thought. I'm hit by a momentary stab of guilt for my pettiness. Then again, he's the one refusing to speak to his so-called best friend.

Maybe ex-best friend if we can't figure this out, and it doesn't seem like he wants to.

For the rest of the evening, I eat pizza around the giant lump in my throat and sob between glasses of wine. I drink the entire bottle, knowing I'll hate myself for it in the morning, but I don't care. I need to numb tonight's pain. I'll deal with tomorrow's pain tomorrow. Before bed, I remove my handgun from my soft belly-band holster and place it in my top dresser drawer, accessible in a true emergency but not within reach if I freak out with night terrors.

I lay atop my covers, crying until I fall asleep.

MARK

Charlie wants to talk? *Talk?* After ignoring me all week, now she wants to talk? What's the point? I glare at her injured expression and escape to my shower, mad as hell with no idea why. I stay in there longer than usual, avoiding her while trying to sort out my jumbled thoughts.

I had difficulty managing my emotions after my injury. That's shrink-speak for, "I acted like a complete dick." My entire world had shifted, and I had to recalibrate my life. Meds, my psychiatrist, and a support group for new amputees were all beneficial, but Charlie's really the one who helped me find my footing in my new reality. She keeps me grounded. She always has. The problem is, now that things are rocky between us, I'm backsliding into an emotional mess.

We have to sort things out. I know that. This impasse is hurting both of us. Unfortunately, I can't seem to stop acting like an ass long enough to sit down and talk with her.

When I step out of the steamy bathroom, I'm greeted by the smell of sausage and pizza sauce. My eyes follow the scent to its source – my bedside table. There's a pizza box and a beer. But something's different. I scan the room.

Charlie's pillow is gone. So is her lotion, her brush and her hair tie. Even her book is gone, leaving her bedside table empty. Sterile. Cold.

No. NO. NO NO NO NO NO!

She can't leave me. I can't do this without her.

I haul myself as fast as I can on crutches into the hallway, jerking open the front door, breathing hard. Her silver SUV is in the driveway. I stop short, listening. The house is silent. Where is she? Did she leave with someone? Did she go off with Tom?

Then I hear it. Muffled sounds upstairs, from the direction of her room, or at least, where I presume her room is. In all the months I've lived here since my injury, I've never attempted to climb her stairs. Crutches combined with a missing leg and a steep staircase has the potential for a rapid descent and a trip to the emergency room.

It slowly sinks in that Charlie's moved upstairs.

Away from me.

The icy panic I felt moments ago morphs into scorching anger. She won't even stay downstairs now? She wants to get away from me, to go somewhere she thinks I can't follow. She wanted to talk? Fine. I'll talk. I'll give her a damn earful.

I climb the sharply-inclined stairs cautiously. It takes forever, because my crutches force me to forego the handrail to stabilize myself. By the time I pass the halfway point, I'm wobbly as a newborn foal. I'm forced to lower myself to my ass and scoot backwards up the last four steps. Thank God no one's here to see my humiliation.

That's when I lose my grip on one crutch. It glides gracefully down the stairs, landing with a soft thump at the bottom.

Perfect.

Just. Fucking. Perfect.

The effort involved in mounting the stairs has downgraded my anger to bristling annoyance. I stand, tucking my single remaining crutch under my right arm and bracing my left arm against the wall. I glance around. There are six closed doors, but only one has a strip of light shining beneath it. I hobble toward that one.

Then I hear Charlie crying, harsh, gut-wrenching sobs.

Because of me.

She's in there crying her eyes out because of me, because I'm stubbornly clinging to my frustrated sexual desire instead of my promise to her that kissing me wouldn't damage our friendship.

Fuck.

The sound gouges my heart, filling me with shame. I want to go to her, to console her, but I don't, because she came up here to escape my open hostility. I sink to the floor in the hall, my back against the wall outside her door, bending my left knee up and wrapping my arms around it. I bury my face in my arms, trying to drown out the sound of her tears.

I'll talk to Charlie tomorrow. We'll sort this out.

We have three options, at least as I see it.

Go back to being friends and forget this ever happened.

Decide we can't move past it and call everything quits – not an option for me, and, I hope, not for her, either.

Or explore the possibility of more.

Her screams awaken me just after three-thirty, when her night terrors begin.

CHARLIE

Pain. So much pain. My wrists burn from the bite of the barbed wire around them, chewing into my bones. The wire loops over a pipe in the ceiling, suspending me several inches above the floor. My shoulders scream for relief. My head pounds from the Chihuahua's beatings, and my cheek and nose are taut from the swelling that closes my left eye. Fire blazes across my back and hips where he's torn them to ribbons with his leather and razor-wire whip and seared my flesh with his goddamn brand. My breasts sting where he sliced them with his rusty knife, and low in my belly, the deep ache echoes the internal violation of his filthy blade between my thighs. Despite my nudity, I'm burning up.

Angry male voices approach from behind. Boots clomp discordantly on stone floors, out of step with each other, moving closer. Keys jingle behind me. I wonder why they even bother locking my cell when I'm all trussed up. It's not like I'm a flight risk.

I fight to clear my foggy mind. It feels like I've been here for months, but it can't have been much more than a week, can it? There are no windows, no way to distinguish between day and night. I measure time by torture sessions, not by hours or days.

I blink rapidly, trying to focus. *Sharpen up. Game face on. No weakness.* I grit my teeth, dreading what's to come.

The metal door screeches, clanging into the stone wall behind me. Sharp pain rockets through me as a booted foot slams into the small of my back. My body swings, the barbed wire digging deeper into my wrists. I bite back a groan as my entire abdomen throbs. I struggle to focus, shifting into medic-mode to clear my mind.

Internal bleeding – a leak, not a full-blown rupture. And sepsis setting in from open wounds in squalid conditions.

Either one can kill me, though, regrettably, not immediately. Death, even a painful one, is preferable to this torture.

I've tried pushing him hard enough to goad him into killing me, but he enjoys playing with his new American toys too much. Still, he's insecure and hot-tempered, and that makes him easy to manipulate. I'll keep provoking him. Eventually, he'll snap and kill me, ending my torment.

The Chihuahua steps in front of me, dark eyes glittering. He's the ring-leader of this fucked-up circus. I've nicknamed him the Chihuahua because he reminds me of a hate-filled ankle biter, bullying others because of his own cowardice. His stubby body is full of rage and loathing, and he unloads it on me.

Based on the laughter of the men behind me, I can guess they're here to torture me. Rough hands grind a gritty substance into the raw flesh of my back. I struggle, recognizing the fiery burn of salt. Four males jeer as I silently writhe in my restraints. When they fail to elicit cries from me, the Chihuahua holds out a hand for the whip, and the real pain begins.

"No!"

My own cry awakens me, and the room around me slowly comes into view. I'm alone on a bed, upright against the headboard, my back still burning with remembered pain. My bed. My room. I scan the reclaimed wood dresser and bedside tables with clear glass lamps, both lit because I can't handle darkness. My beige recliner sits in the corner with a red blanket draped across it. The closet and bathroom doors are closed. I shut my eyes, panting, breaking out in a cold sweat.

I can get through this.

Four things I can see. I open my eyes and silently name them. The wall-mounted television. A print of a bright red cardinal in a monotone birch forest. My empty pizza box. My equally empty wine bottle.

Three things I can touch. The white comforter beneath me is soft. My yoga pants feel slick to my touch. I reach for my aqua glass lotion bottle on the bedside table. It's cool and smooth under my fingers.

Two things I can hear. I strain, listening. A light breeze rustles the leaves of the maple tree outside my window. The rest of the house is silent, except for my rapid breathing. I'll count that as the second sound.

One thing I can smell. I open my lotion bottle and inhale its soft jasmine scent, exhaling slowly, deliberately.

Four, three, two, one.

I'm fully present.

And awake. Fully fucking awake.

Dammit, it's not even four in the morning. Mark is probably still awake. I can't go downstairs until after daylight, when he normally goes to sleep.

I may not have slept up here in years, but I still remember my old hiding places. I slide off the bed and pad across the plush carpet to my closet. A bottle of rum perches on the top shelf.

Just enough to get back to sleep.

It takes four shots to stop my trembling. Three more to get sleepy. I push the bottle, still open, onto my bedside table and lie down, praying for dreamless sleep.

I'm not that lucky.

Loud voices advance, speaking Dari too quickly for me to grasp individual words. I glance up. Wire digs into my wrists, which are lashed together above my head. Blood drips from the raw wounds encircling them, warm ruby liquid rolling over brown trails of dried blood. I'm thirsty, so thirsty. My lips and tongue are parched and cracked.

The cell door shrieks open on rusty hinges, banging into the wall. I try to count feet as they file in. Four men, I decide.

Game face on. No weakness. I clench my jaw and wait.

The Chihuahua moves in front of me. His soulless black eyes shine with hatred. He rattles off something I don't understand, and the others laugh. He leers, reaching a hand up as if to stroke my face, but I know better. He slaps me hard, and I taste blood. Without hesitation, I spit on him. It lands on his cheek, more blood than saliva, and he drags his sleeve across his face, glaring. He grabs my face in an iron grip, crushing pudgy fingers into my bruised and swollen flesh.

I can't spit, but I can still kick. I glare at him, and he laughs. While he's celebrating his manly prowess in battering a restrained woman, I drive the solid bone of my shin into his soft groin. He releases me and groans, dropping to his knees. It's not the first time I've done so. A smarter man would learn situational awareness. I laugh rudely, and he shoots me a contemptuous look.

When he can stand, he beats me until I lose consciousness. When I wake, I wish I hadn't. Each man takes a turn raping me, and there are five of them, not four. When they finish, one of them grabs a section of rusty pipe and shoves it inside me. It rakes my torn flesh, and I suck in a sharp breath. Raucous laughter echoes around me as blood trickles down my inner thighs. *I will not cry. I will not show weakness.* I fight the bastards with everything I have, but it's not enough. There are too many of them.

When I wake, I'm on my knees on the floor, screaming, drenched in icy sweat.

Fuck.

I fall back onto my backside, panting, as I lean against the bed and allow myself to cry.

MARK

Charlie's screams and subsequent sobs are nearly my undoing. It's all I can do not to burst into her room, but (a) the last time I did that during one of her night terrors, she nearly shot me in the head, and (b) she came upstairs to get away from me. I don't blame her, but I'm also not sure I'd be welcome.

Only when I hear her shower turn on shortly after daylight am I reassured she's okay.

Well, relatively okay.

That's when I hop my crippled ass down the stairs, gripping the handrail tightly as I take it one step at a time. It's a relief to reach the bottom and retrieve my second crutch. I return to my room, gently closing the door. I crawl into bed, but sleep is my enemy, evading me at every turn.

CHAPTER FOUR

CHARLIE

AN ENTIRE BOTTLE OF red wine plus seven shots of rum plus minimal sleep interrupted by graphic night terrors equals an exceptionally shitty morning.

My head throbs like there's a bass drum pounding inside my head. The room spins when I change position too quickly, and I'm nauseous. At least I'm not vomiting. I start with a cold shower to clear my head and eliminate any remaining buzz. Then I switch to hot water, letting it buffet my neck and shoulders, trying unsuccessfully to loosen the knots.

After dressing, I go downstairs, where I nibble on a toasted cinnamon bagel as my queasiness fades. I follow that with two large glasses of ice water and aspirin.

I pace aimlessly, too restless to sit and too jangled to focus, until inspiration hits. I need to go to the woods. They soothe my soul. I swap my yoga pants for jeans and lace up my boots, loading a backpack with water and my journal before texting Lila where I'm headed. Regardless of how crappy things have been lately, I'm safety conscious. Lila, Tucker, and I have been on too many search-and-rescue teams for lost and injured hikers in these mountains.

It's a little over a mile to my favorite spot. The trail cuts up the mountain, unmarked but well-used. It winds through wooded areas so thick, the trees obscure the sky. I haven't been here since last fall, when the leaves were glorious reds and oranges and golds, and the ground was thick with pine cones and acorns. I'd watched a family of porcupines, three deer, and two bears that day. They were busy eating berries and snuffling for acorns and paid me no attention.

I reach a break in the climb, a flattened shelf-like area on one side of the slope. I follow the path deeper into the woods. Bushes and trees form thick clusters on either side. The leaves are dozens of different shades of green – pale chartreuse, soft jade, bright emerald, cool sea glass, and deep evergreen. Sunshine filters through the thick canopy above. I can't see the sun, but its dappled light splashes the ground. Moss and pine needles carpet the trail, silencing my steps.

I hear trickling water before I reach the opening. It grows louder when I step off the trail into my spot. Water flows down the mountain in a stream less than ten feet wide. In summer, like now, it tumbles gently over algae-slicked rocks. In spring, it's a rushing torrent, engorged by melting snow from the Sangre de Cristo mountains.

It's cool here. Empty. Quiet.

This is my happy place. The silence of the woods soothes my ragged soul like nothing else can. I'm an introvert, and dealing with people all day every day leaves me drained. I need a little time alone each day just to function. Coming here allows the solitude of this space to recharge my spirit as it peels away the layers of emotional noise.

But nothing quiets my emotional noise today, not the breeze sifting through the leaves, not the brook babbling merrily, not the chattering of the squirrels or the singing of a lark on a branch above me. All I can hear is the cacophony of my pain.

I reach for the journal in my backpack. My psychiatrist, Dr. Linda Martin – Linda – encourages me to "brain dump" my feelings when things are hard. Essentially, I write down anything and everything, letting my mind release some of the clutter inside so I can more easily identify the emotions buried beneath the chaos.

But the words won't come. I sit in my favorite place, completely miserable, unable to work through my pain. It's a good thing I have tissues, because the only thing I manage to do is cry. Again.

In the end, I pull out my phone and play one sad song on a loop – "Something In the Way" by Nirvana. Its words resonate with me, a song of loss and isolation and being cast aside by those who should care. I spend hours letting my soul bleed while listening to lyrics that remind me how unwanted I am by the person I care for most.

The roll of thunder in the distance breaks through my despair, and I immediately pack up my things. Being surrounded by trees in a lightning storm is something I'd like to avoid, no matter how bad the last week and a half has been. I jog down the mountain, but I'm not fast enough. I beat the thunderstorm, but not the downpour. I'm soaked to the skin when I reach my house.

Unfortunately, I'm still full of pent-up emotional energy. My dash down the mountain wasn't enough to relieve it. If it weren't storming, I'd go for a long run. Running usually clears my head and drains excess energy.

Guess it's the treadmill for me.

I swap my drenched clothes for shorts and a tee shirt, push earbuds in, and dock my phone, putting the same depressing song on a loop again. The music combined with the steady thump of my feet on the treadmill provides enough background noise to drown out the clamor in my mind, but it doesn't help my mood.

It's my own fault I've lost Mark. I allowed my desperate desire to feel normal, to *be* normal, to affect my behavior, and I made a stupid decision.

Newsflash: I'm not normal.

After the horrors those bastards inflicted on me, normal isn't possible.

And if I'd never admitted my longing to feel normal, Mark wouldn't have felt compelled to "fix" me. Nothing would have happened between us. We'd be fine.

Instead, my train wreck of a life derailed the only relationship that gave my life meaning. Now I'm alone.

No.

I'm worse than alone.

I'm living in a house with someone who can't stand to be around me.

Being alone wouldn't hurt nearly as much as being blatantly rejected by the most important person in my life.

I don't even try to stop my tears. I just keep running, hoping to either outrun my pain or exhaust myself enough to no longer feel it.

MARK

I don't sleep at all, tossing and turning all day before moving to the chaise. The sound of Charlie's sobs rings in my head, and my guilt over not interceding during her night terrors is suffocating.

My shame over why we're in this predicament is even worse.

Why did I stalk away last night? Why did I refuse her when we obviously need to talk?

My questions are rhetorical, of course. I avoided her because I hate myself every time I see the pain in her face and the sorrow in her eyes, knowing I'm the cause.

I have to make things right. I'm already the reason for most of her pain. I can't add this to the list.

Charlie runs up the steps in the pouring rain, soaked to the bone. She left hours ago on foot, following a path that snakes off the edge of her backyard and down before rising sharply up the mountain. She spent all day in the woods, probably trying to find some peace. She finds the lush greenery and tranquility soothing. She goes upstairs, then returns a short time later. When I hear pounding on the treadmill, I know she didn't find solace in the woods. She's running to escape her pain.

Tucker's advice drifts through my mind. *Just sex.*

But there's no such thing as *just sex* in our situation. Adding sex to our relationship isn't something to be done lightly.

Charlie isn't like any other woman I've ever had a relationship with, friend or otherwise. Even ignoring her past, mixing sex into our deep friendship would alter things in a way that could never be undone.

But there's no way to ignore her traumatic past, and adding sex to our relationship would require an even deeper emotional commitment on both our parts to help her heal enough to take that step – if she would even want to.

And what if we did, and things didn't work out?

I shake my head. One amazing kiss has made things so awkward we can't even carry on a conversation. A failed sexual relationship could destroy everything.

Yet despite my misgivings, I'm plagued by the possibilities.

What if we tried and it didn't fail?

What if this is the path we're meant to take, a path my mind wandered down nearly twenty years ago?

I amble to the weight room and open the door, drawn to her as always. She's facing away from me, her sneakers drumming a rhythmic beat as she runs. I sidle in and take a seat on the weight bench on the far side of the room to watch her.

God, she's beautiful. Her light brown hair is pulled up in a ponytail that bounces with each step. She's slim and petite, a full head shorter than me, with long legs and lush curves. Though she runs with her eyes closed, I can easily picture their emerald depths. High cheekbones, full lips – she's gorgeous. But it isn't just her beauty that draws me in – it's her strength. Few people could survive the hell she did and still function, let alone emerge fighting.

I'm both surprised and saddened by the tears rolling down her cheeks as she runs, lost in her own thoughts, unaware of my presence.

That's when it hits me, as solid as a body blow. Charlie won't want to risk taking things to the next level. She thinks we've already done too much damage.

Maybe she's right. Maybe I have.

Another wave of guilt washes over me, followed by an urgent need to repair things between us. I pull out my phone and place an order for Italian delivery. Pasta and wine and an apology. That's what Charlie needs from me.

For almost two weeks, I've been strictly focused on what I want. The kiss was my idea, and she went along with it. I promised Charlie nothing would change between us, but *I* changed. I've acted like a complete ass because she tried to keep our friendship the same as it had always been. I'm the one who wanted more, because what we shared that night was incredible.

But our relationship isn't about me and what I want. It's about both of us.

I've just returned my phone to my pocket when her cadence abruptly stutters. She reaches down and grabs her right calf, stumbling as she hits the emergency stop button. She winces and groans as it shudders to a stop. I grab my crutches and hurry toward her. Her eyes widen when she sees me, and she snatches her earbuds free.

"What's wrong?"

"Cramp," she gasps. She steps off the treadmill, clutching her leg, limping a few steps before collapsing to the floor, trying to flex her foot and rub her calf.

I ease to the ground and reach for her leg. "Let me," I murmur, my large hands finding the knotted muscle easily. She leans back on her elbows, wincing again.

"It's my own fault," she says, panting from exertion. "I stopped for a few minutes and didn't warm up again." Sweat trickles down and mingles with her tears, and her damp shirt clings to her heaving chest.

I don't look at her, instead focusing on untangling the bunched muscle. "I ordered Italian food. I thought maybe some pasta and wine would be nice tonight." I feel her eyes on me, confused by my abrupt shift in behavior, but I concentrate on her spasming calf.

"Flex your foot up," I instruct. She does, groaning as it seizes up again. I massage more deeply, my fingers probing further. I work in silence for a couple of minutes, feeling her muscle gradually soften under my touch. "Flex up again." She complies without pain. "Now down." The muscles try to tighten against my hands, so I continue to knead until they relax again.

"Flex up." She does, then flexes down automatically. The muscle remains pliable. "How does that feel?"

"Much better," she says, her eyes cautious. "Thank you."

I nod, pulling myself upright with one hand on the treadmill before helping her to her feet and collecting my crutches. "You have time to shower before dinner gets here."

She smiles. "Is that your way of telling me I'm sweaty and gross?"

I chuckle. "No, it's my way of suggesting warm water to keep that muscle loose."

She returns as the delivery guy is dropping off a large paper bag. She's dressed in form-fitting black yoga pants that hug her legs and a loose Army tee shirt, her damp hair twisted up in a clip. She takes the bag when she sees me struggling to carry it while maneuvering my crutches.

"What did you order? These are the big containers." She peeks into the bag.

"Chicken parmesan, Alfredo chicken pasta, spaghetti with meatballs, big salads, and lots of garlic bread. And I opened red wine, but there's also white if you prefer."

"There's so much food in here," she says happily. "How hungry did I look?"

I laugh. "We can eat this for the rest of the weekend. Neither of us has to cook."

She smiles, the first real one I've seen in twelve days. "It's adorable that you assume there will be leftovers."

We sit down at the table, both of us taking some of everything and digging in. I wait till she's finished eating and pouring her third glass of wine, her cheeks pleasantly flushed, before I look across the table at her.

"I owe you an apology."

She looks up in surprise. "For what?"

"For everything. I suggested the kiss. I promised it wouldn't change anything. I talked you into it. I enjoyed it more than I should have, and I've been a jerk ever since. I'm sorry."

Her eyes fly to mine. "You enjoyed it?"

How can she ask that? I know she felt my erection – I clearly remember her grinding against me.

Then it dawns on me. Charlie's still convinced she's broken – not that she can't feel aroused, but that she's too damaged for anyone to desire her. "I enjoyed it very much. Too much."

She wrinkles her forehead in confusion, considering my words, then carefully puts down her wineglass. "You didn't talk me into anything. I chose to kiss you, and I obviously enjoyed it, too. But I should have known better than to risk screwing up what we have. That's on me."

I shake my head. "No. You and I have literally been through hell together. We were there for each other when we both kept losing family members until we were the only two left. We've had each others' backs for almost twenty-five years. I pulled you out of that hellhole in Afghanistan, and you've dragged me out of mine. You're my best friend, Charlie. What we have means everything to me. I should never have let a kiss come between us." I hesitate for a moment. "I can pretend it never happened if you can."

"Maybe what we should discuss is why kissing each other created issues," she says slowly.

I raise my half-full wineglass to my lips and drain it, avoiding her gaze.

"Do you want to talk about that?" Wide eyes await my response.

I know damn well what issues that scorching kiss created for me, but volunteering that information probably isn't a great idea, at least not yet. "What are your thoughts?" I ask instead, reaching for the wine bottle and watching her closely.

She toys with her wineglass as she takes a deep breath. "I think maybe it exposed something neither of us was aware of, and we didn't know how to handle it." Her voice is quiet, and she keeps her gaze focused on her glass.

My heart leaps. *She felt it, too. It wasn't just me.* Even though she reaches for me in her sleep, hearing her admit it aloud makes my breath catch.

"An attraction," I murmur.

She nods, still looking down.

I refill my glass and lean back. "Then I guess we should figure out what to do about it."

She glances up. "What do you mean?"

I choose my words carefully. "Pretending neither of us felt anything hasn't gone well. I think it's safe to say neither of us wants to end our friendship over this. That leaves two options. We can acknowledge the attraction and consciously decide not to act on it, or we can explore what it would mean if we did."

She reaches for her wine again and takes another large sip, her cheeks turning pink. "Define acting on it."

Here we go.

I hold my breath, not taking my eyes off her. "Adding a physical aspect to our relationship."

She pales noticeably. "Sex?" she whispers, her fear palpable.

Shit. I don't want Charlie to be scared of me. I'm the only one she's completely comfortable with.

I keep my voice calm. "I'm not suggesting sex. I know physical relationships scare you. I'm simply saying one option would be to add a physical aspect to our relationship in whatever capacity you choose. Or you can decide you're not interested in that, and we'll move on."

She chews her lip. "I don't know, Mark. Look how things have been these last two weeks from just a kiss. A really good kiss," she amends, "but look how badly it screwed things up."

I measure my words, speaking deliberately. "I never expected things to be so intense between us. It made me want more of that with you, and it created this — this sexual frustration. Maybe you felt it, too. But because we've never had a physical aspect to our relationship, it made things awkward. I responded by being an ass, and I'm sorry. Neither of us knew what to do with our attraction, so we avoided each other in the daytime. But at night, we're close, and it built up this tension, this longing. At least, it did on my part." I study her, watching her reaction.

"Mine, too," she admits.

"But it hasn't ruined things between us. It's taken time for each of us to figure out how we feel individually so we can decide how we want to handle it together. It hasn't changed who we are. You and I have been through too much to let one kiss mess up what we have."

We sit without speaking for long moments.

"So what now?" she finally asks.

"Now we talk about what you want."

"Why not what you want?"

I smile. "Because I'll do whatever you want, Charlie. If you decide you aren't interested in a physical relationship, we'll keep things exactly as they were before. And if you do want to explore a deeper relationship, I'll gladly take that chance with you."

And just like that, Charlie clams up, leaving me with my soul exposed and my emotions laid bare.

CHARLIE

Lila was right. Mark and I needed to talk, and I'm glad we're finally talking, but these are deep, scary waters.

Mark wants to know what I want, and he says whatever I want, he's with me.

I'm silent for a long time. A *really* long time.

Part of me is thrilled at the idea of a physical relationship with him... and part of me is terrified. There's so many what if's. What if we tried, and it made things even worse than they've been these past two weeks? What if we became a couple and then broke up? Based on what happened after our kiss, I'm not sure we could work through a break-up without lingering hard feelings.

I'm honest enough to admit I want him. After what those bastards did to me, I thought I'd never have those feelings for anyone, let alone the gorgeous man across the table.

I'm also honest enough to know I can't risk losing him. He's too important to me.

I go for so long without speaking that Mark finally reaches across the table and links our fingers, his eyes tight. I realize he's essentially said he wants more, and I've not responded at all.

I look up at him, my eyes damp with unshed tears. "I'm scared," I confess.

An exquisitely sad expression crosses his face as his shoulders sag. "Please don't be afraid of me, Charlie," he says quietly.

"I'm not afraid *of* you," I correct him. "I'm afraid of losing you."

He wraps both my hands in his large ones, his gaze intense. "If you don't want anything to change, it won't. We'll keep things exactly as they were. But please don't let the fear of losing me be the only thing keeping you from considering something more. You won't lose me, Charlie, not ever. You've been the best part of my life for as long as I can remember, and nothing could make me walk away from you. Nothing," he promises, holding my gaze.

I believe him.

"I don't know what to do," I confess, fighting back tears.

"So let's not do anything," Mark says gently. "Let's keep everything exactly the way it was. And if the time ever comes where you want to try something more, we'll talk about it."

I want to bury my face in a pillow and cry. All the pressure of what to do rests on me, even though I know by suggesting we leave things as they are, he's trying to remove that pressure.

Why does this have to be so complicated? After all this time, we've finally admitted that there's something more between us than just friendship. Why does that have to be this insurmountable problem?

I know the answer even as I pose the question.

Because with my trauma-related issues, any physical relationship is problematic.

I hate my scars, so I hide my body. Physical contact sometimes makes me panic, though never with Mark. Still, we've never touched in a sexual context before. What if that changes? What if things progress between us and I freak out? I pulled my gun on a guy for kissing me without warning. Panicking during sex is a distinct possibility. I close my eyes, fighting the urge to cry.

"Talk to me, Charlie. Tell me what you're thinking." His voice is calm, but his face is tight with anxiety.

The fears I'm wrestling spill forth like water from a burst dam. "I'm scared, Mark. Part of me wants to try more, but the rest of me is terrified. My issues aren't something to take lightly. I hate my body because of my scars. I panic sometimes at male touch. I never have with you, but that's when we were just friends. What if I panic with you? What if you and I are touching and I shut down or have a meltdown?" A soft sob escapes me. "Why do I have to be so screwed up? I'd give anything to be like every other person on this planet." My eyes brim with tears I'm barely holding back.

Mark still holds my hands, and he gives them a light squeeze, his tone gentle. "Charlie, it's okay. Nothing has to change."

"It already has," I reply sadly. He shakes his head, but I keep talking. "I can't go back to how things were, and I'm afraid to move forward."

I tug my hands back, and he releases them immediately. The look in his eyes is something akin to panic, but Mark doesn't panic, not ever.

I meet his gaze wearily. "I'm so tired of being controlled by fear. Fear of letting someone get close. Fear of being intimate. Fear of losing you if things go wrong. Fear of missing something incredible because of my fear of losing you."

His words are soft as his eyes search mine. "If you weren't afraid, Charlie – if fear wasn't a factor at all, what would you want?"

I study his light blue eyes. My eyes roam over his sandy hair, his rugged jaw, his full lips, the dark shadows beneath his eyes. These last twelve days have been awful for him, too. I try to forget my fear and just focus on him.

I think about the boy from nearly twenty-five years ago, a boy who snatched a bully off a girl he barely knew, then held him for me to punch squarely in the mouth. A bully he'd then warned against ever bothering me again.

I recall the teenager who took me to my prom when my sleazy ex dumped me for another girl two days before the prom. I remember a night of slow dancing, giant cheeseburgers, and lying in the bed of his truck, staring at the stars until the sun came up. Once again, he cemented his place in my life as my hero.

I vaguely remember worried blue eyes gazing into mine and lips close to my ear, whispering to me and holding me while someone cut me free from my barbed wire shackles in a filthy cell in the basement of a bombed-out mosque. Those same worried eyes showed up at Walter Reed weeks later, determined to help me stand on my own two feet again.

I remember a few nights ago, standing in the kitchen. His lips. His hands. The heat. The passion.

Mark's been there every time I've needed him. The closeness we have, the trust we share, is so rare, so beautiful.

But what if it could be even more?

And in a flash, I know.

Icy fear grasps at me like thick tentacles, pulling me back and reminding me of the potential pitfalls, but I twist free and plunge headlong into the unknown. I take a deep breath, meeting his gaze without wavering. "More. I would want more."

He smiles a slow, sexy smile. "Me, too, Baby Girl. So let's try more."

CHAPTER FIVE

MARK

WE'VE MOVED TO THE living room, where Charlie's clutching her glass of wine for dear life. "So what does 'more' mean?" she asks, facing me on the couch. "What does it look like?"

"I don't know. This is new territory for us."

She pauses. "Well, like you said the other night, we're already closer than a lot of married couples. We just don't have a physical relationship. So maybe we just add that. Not the couple part," she hurries to clarify. "I'm not pushing that on you."

I grin. "I didn't think you were. This is just you and me, thinking out loud."

We both fall silent, and Tucker's phrase "friends with benefits" floats through my mind. I wonder if it would sound as tacky out loud as it does in my head.

"I don't think we should go into this looking for romance," Charlie blurts.

I look up, startled, as she continues.

"I mean, if we approach this like a dating relationship and things don't work out, I'm afraid it will feel like a breakup, and I don't want to lose you. If we keep everything casual and it isn't working out, it will be easier to change course if there aren't romantic entanglements."

I scrutinize her cautiously. "So like... friends with benefits?"

I brace myself for a slap that doesn't come. Instead, she hesitates. "Kind of. But with my issues –" her voice trails off.

"I'm not pushing you to have sex, Charlie," I say gently. "I wouldn't do that. You know that, right?"

"I know," she says, but I hear the doubt in her voice.

Time to come clean.

I take a deep breath. "You aren't the only one uncomfortable with the thought of sex, Charlie."

She stares at me like I've sprouted another head. "What are you talking about?"

I raise an eyebrow and gesture down at my body. "The missing leg. The scars all over me. I'm not the guy I once was. I'm not comfortable with my body, either."

She takes my hand, her gaze unwavering. "I don't see any of that when I look at you, Mark. I only see you."

I lift her hand to my lips and kiss her knuckles. "That's one of the million things that makes you incredible."

She blushes. "Well, if neither one of us is comfortable thinking about sex, that should take the pressure off."

"There isn't supposed to be any pressure," I remind her.

She sighs. "When it comes to a physical relationship, for me, there's pressure. Not from you," she adds hastily. "From myself."

I observe her closely. "Did you feel pressured when we kissed?"

Pink tinges her cheeks. "No. It was actually very... freeing."

I shrug. "So let's stick to kissing."

She thinks for a moment and reddens further, and I know exactly what she's remembering. My eyes close briefly as I remember her legs around my waist, her soft whimpers driving me wild. I swallow hard.

"We can always add more if it's something we both want," I tell her, striving for calm in my voice. "But for now, we leave it at kissing. Does that sound reasonable?"

"It seems weird, discussing this like a business arrangement."

"We've both been miserable because we didn't discuss things. Hopefully, establishing some loose guidelines will prevent that."

She's quiet for a minute. "So kissing."

I nod, unsure if it's a statement or a question.

"When?"

I can't help chuckling. "I don't know. Let's keep things relaxed, with the understanding that if we decide to kiss, it's okay. We've merely adjusted our boundaries of what's acceptable. Kissing isn't a requirement. We'll figure this out as we go."

She grins sheepishly. "I'm sorry. I know I'm being stupid."

I stop her with one finger on her lips. "The last two weeks have been hell for both of us," I say quietly. "We took a big step without thinking it through and didn't know how to handle the fallout. We're just trying to keep that from happening again. If that means having awkward discussions now, let's have them, instead of not talking for days or weeks later."

Charlie studies me, then sets her wineglass down and slides over. She leans against my chest and wraps her arms around me. I hold her close, my face resting on her hair, inhaling her warm scent. I've missed this so much. Charlie's part of me.

The best part of me.

She looks up. "I'm sorry it's been so rough."

"Me, too, Baby Girl." I kiss her forehead. She leans her head on my shoulder, and we stay like that, content to be comfortable in each other's arms again.

She looks nervous at bedtime. I'm in bed already when she comes in. She goes to the closet and removes the mirror and massage oil. She sets up the mirror and hesitates. "Is it okay for me to rub your thigh again?"

I grin. "It's fine." She warms the oil in her hands and begins to massage in firm, even strokes. The sight of her touching me sends my mind wandering, and I struggle to distract myself before my body reacts. I shut my eyes and mentally recite everything I know about osseointegration surgery, ignoring the feel of her hands so close to my groin.

I'm relieved when she moves from my right thigh to my left lower leg. "Is the mirror angle right?"

I glance down to ensure my healthy left leg is reflected where my right lower leg should be and nod. I close my eyes and visualize my missing lower leg being massaged as she kneads my left calf and shin. When I open my eyes to refer to the mirror again, I find Charlie staring intently at my mouth.

I can't help the smile that forms on my lips. She looks up, flustered at being caught, and drops her eyes, biting her lower lip.

The sight of her biting her lip sends an electric jolt through me. I have a desperate urge to grab her and kiss her senseless. Once again, I'm left struggling to distract myself. Whatever happens between us needs to be on Charlie's terms. She has to take the lead.

She finishes my massage and returns the mirror to the closet. She washes her hands and climbs into bed, scooting in and pressing her back against my left side as usual, facing the door. "Good night, Big Guy."

Instead of lying on my back as usual, I curl behind her, draping my arm loosely around her waist, the way I sometimes do after she's had night terrors. My mouth hovers beneath her ear. "Good night, Baby Girl."

Charlie freezes, a marble statue in the bed beside me.

I smile, my mouth almost touching her smooth skin. "Relax. I've held you while you fell asleep before."

"I am relaxed," she lies, and I laugh softly against her neck. This time, she shivers.

"You're stiff as a board. Do you want me to roll back over?"

"No," she says, and I can hear her reluctance.

"Good," I whisper just below her ear, my warm breath caressing her skin. This time when she shivers, she moves her neck against my lips instead of away.

I smile slowly, nuzzling her neck with my stubble, inhaling the coconut scent of her hair. She arches closer as my nuzzling turns to nibbling. Her breath catches and she drops her head back. I press my mouth against the base of her neck, nipping and nuzzling my way back up to her ear. She bites her lip again. That's my cue.

I slowly pull back and cuddle her warm body, my mouth poised just below her ear without making contact. "Sleep well."

Frustration and indecision radiate from her. I wait patiently, my breath warming her neck. It feels like forever before she turns toward me.

Her deep green eyes capture me. She bites her lip a third time, and it's nearly my undoing. My gaze locks with hers. "Did you want something, Charlie?"

She hesitates for the briefest of seconds before raising up on her elbow and leaning forward, sliding her small hand behind my neck and pulling my face to hers. Our kiss is gentle and soft, lips barely brushing lips, until I brace my right arm against the mattress and lean forward to deepen it. She tastes like clover honey, and our lips meet again and again as she presses closer.

She wants more.

She clutches the front of my shirt and I ease her back against the mattress, holding myself above her. I don't want her to feel trapped.

I slide my tongue across her lips, and they part immediately. I slip inside, exploring her mouth, caressing her tongue with my own. She moans softly, her fingers in my hair, and the sound nearly pushes me over the edge.

God, I want her.

Fiery heat builds rapidly between us. It's like nothing I've experienced with anyone before, an intense blaze that could easily burn out of control. It takes every bit of my willpower to tamp down my desire. I transition back to languid kisses, easing space between our bodies. I pull back, looking into her eyes as I stroke my thumb across her cheek.

"So beautiful," I murmur.

"You said that when you kissed me the other day," she says shyly.

"Because it's true."

She's always been beautiful.

Charlie could never not be beautiful to me.

I kiss her again lightly before drawing back and shifting to my side. I curl my arm around her waist and pull her against me.

"Good night, Baby Girl."

Her tone is tender when she answers. "Good night, Big Guy."

CHARLIE

I sleep well, and when I wake, I'm still in Mark's arms. It's amazing the difference twenty-four hours has made.

"Good morning," he says, his stubbled face nestled against my neck.

His whiskers tickle deliciously. "Mmm. Good morning."

"Want me to start the coffee?" His lips graze the curve of my shoulder.

What I really want is for him to keep nuzzling, but as I haven't brushed my teeth yet, I simply nod. He slides off the bed and heads for the kitchen.

When he returns, I've brushed my teeth, and he catches me finger-combing my hair.

He smiles. "Leave it. You look beautiful."

Pffft. I know better. I just saw my reflection.

He stops in front of me, raising a hand to tilt my chin. "Good morning," he murmurs.

I smile. "You said that already."

He leans down and kisses me. "Did I do this, too?"

My breath catches. "I'd have remembered that." He kisses me again, longer this time, his lips firm yet gentle, lingering, tasting, teasing. He leaves me breathless, clutching his shirt.

"Damn, Baby Girl," he says when he pulls away, his voice gruff.

The effect his touch has on me is surprising, given my plethora of issues. The fact I affect him similarly is utterly inexplicable.

We share a quick breakfast of scrambled eggs and toast with orange wedges. When Mark goes to bed, my mind drifts to last night.

Mark's confession that he's not sure he's comfortable having sex because of his body leaves me speechless. The man is incredible in every way. His scars and injuries don't even register with me. I'm appalled someone as beautiful as he is can't truly see himself. He only sees his scars, and he's convinced they diminish his value.

My brain chimes in with her two cents. *The way you only see yours? The way you're convinced they detract from your worth?*

I dismiss that annoying inner voice. That's different.

I was memorizing his features last night when he caught me staring. He's so good-looking, he steals my breath. Pale blue eyes framed by too-long-to-be-legal-on-a-man eyelashes, sandy blond hair that curls at the nape of his neck, a strong jawline dusted with soft stubble. And that mouth. God, his mouth. Butterflies spiral through my stomach just thinking about it. I was totally focused on his full lips when he caught me gawking at him.

I pause, remembering. When he stopped nuzzling my neck, I was torn between wishing he'd never started and begging him not to stop. Desire fought with fear as I debated turning to him.

My stomach does somersaults at the memories. Nuzzling. Nibbling. Suckling. Kissing.

And I was aroused almost immediately, my body burning with need.

It's never been like this, not even before Afghanistan. I've never responded so intensely to anyone.

I'm still torn, but things have completely shifted from a mere twelve hours ago, and I don't even know how it happened. Last night, my conflict was between fear and desire. Now I'm conflicted about the pace of progression.

Because I definitely want things to progress.

Mark's touch makes me want more, a lot more, and my body longs to say yes – the big yes, the yes I never thought I'd say because the mere thought of sex held such a negative connotation. That's definitely one for the win column.

But despite my newly-raging libido, my mind is pumping the brakes. Logic says it's much too soon to even consider such a significant step with someone so important. It's too risky. Rushing into a kiss left both of us reeling. Racing into sex would be disastrous.

As though he sensed my inner turmoil last night, Mark took control, slowing things down, being cautious when I couldn't. It reiterates how much I can trust him.

Mark won't hurt me.

I stay cocooned in my delicious memories all morning, smiling throughout my shower, light housework, and errands – a typical Sunday. I'm unpacking groceries when Mark enters the kitchen. He's freshly showered, his hair still damp. His shirt hugs his tautly muscled chest and arms, and my mouth goes dry as my eyes linger.

Down, girl.

"How did you sleep?" I ask, hoping my voice doesn't betray my wayward thoughts.

He smiles slowly. "Very well. I had exceptionally pleasant dreams." His husky voice sends tingles down my spine, and his eyes fix steadily on mine.

Butterflies whirl in a flurry through my stomach. I like Suggestive Mark very much. "What did you dream about?"

He leans back against the island, moving his left crutch away so he's only leaning on the right one. "Come here and I'll show you," he murmurs.

I'm scarcely in front of him when he hauls me against him, his mouth meeting mine in a kiss that's instantly explosive, all lips and tongues and heat. My fingers slide into his damp curls and I tug him closer, arching upward, my breasts pressing into his chest.

I know I need to slow down, but damn, I don't want to. There's a delicious ache building in me, and I want more. I need more.

I need *him*.

Mark slows his kisses, gentling them. I nip his lower lip as he moves to pull away, and he chuckles. "We don't need to rush things," he says against my mouth as he kisses me again. "I want to enjoy every second of this."

"I am," I whisper.

His blue eyes hold mine. "Me too. But I don't want things to go further than either of us is ready for because we got lost in the moment."

He's right, and we both know it. I sigh. He caresses my face and gently kisses me once more before sitting on a barstool and unpacking the canvas bag closest to him.

My phone buzzes on the counter. It's a text from Lila. "Well??? I've tried 2 b patient, but ur KILLING me with this radio silence!"

I send a kiss emoji in response. She answers with several smiling emojis, followed by hearts, champagne glasses, and party hats.

I've barely laid the phone back on the counter when she calls. "Do you guys want to come over? We're taking the four-wheelers up the trail for a picnic. Mark can use Joey's four-wheeler." Tucker bought a special ATV utilizing strictly hand controls after his brother's spinal cord injury left him without the use of his legs.

"Let me check." I turn to Mark. "Want to ride four-wheelers and go on a picnic?"

"Sounds fun." Then he frowns. "What about my crutches?"

I smile. "Gotcha covered." I turn back to the phone. "We'll be there. What do we need to bring?"

"Just yourselves."

"Let me put up groceries and we'll head over."

Mark finishes unpacking the bags while I put the food away. "I'm going to change into old jeans and a different shirt. Tucker's like a ten-year-old, splashing through creeks and slinging mud."

He grins. "I'll change, too."

I return with my hair in a ponytail, wearing an ancient pair of soft jeans, a baseball-style shirt, and old running shoes. I'm surprised to see Mark in faded jeans. He's sitting on the bench, trying to cut off the lower right leg of his pants while wearing them.

I chuckle. "You really should have done that before you put those on."

He shoots me a crooked grin. "Are you laughing? It's rude to laugh at cripples."

I roll my eyes. "Nice try. First of all, the preferred term is 'amputees' not 'cripples', and second, I'm laughing at your lack of common sense. Do you want some help, or would you prefer to keep mangling them with those dull scissors?"

"I've got it."

I watch him struggle with the thick denim for a few more seconds before I can't stand it. I pull fabric scissors from a drawer and hand them to him. "At least use these. Otherwise, we'll be here all afternoon while you hack away."

He sighs. "Fine. Would you give me a hand?"

"Gladly." I take the scissors and kneel in front of the bench. "Where did you find these?"

"In my stuff the Army finally shipped. They're probably ten years old."

"That's when they're just broken in." I cut his jeans off evenly. "How's this?"

Disgust flickers briefly across his face. "As long as it covers everything, it's good."

I wonder if he'll ever stop hating his changed body, but say nothing. Instead, I collect a backpack from the hall closet and a zip-top bag from the kitchen.

"What's that for?"

"Your crutches. They're held together in the middle with a bolt and a wing nut. So before we ride, we take them apart and put the hardware in this." I hold up the baggie. "Then we put the disassembled crutches in the backpack and zip them in place."

"Pretty smart."

I wink. "That's me. Pretty *and* smart."

"Beautiful and brilliant," he corrects me, and I can't contain the stupid grin that spreads across my face.

When we get there, Tucker's already pulled the four wheelers out. Lila dances out to meet us.

"Where are these magnificent goats you've bragged so much about?" Mark says as she hugs him.

She beams. "Come see my girls. Just watch your step. The ground's uneven and the animals like to leave deposits."

She leads Mark around the side of the house to the pasture, gushing about her hooved hellraisers that are all named after supermodels. Tucker steps out of the shed and grins knowingly in my direction.

"So..." The word hangs in the air.

I raise one eyebrow but say nothing.

He walks closer, stopping directly in front of me. His big muscled body might seem imposing if we weren't like siblings. He crosses his arms. "Are you really going to make me ask?"

I blink innocently.

He sighs. "Well? Are you two together now or what?"

I pause, suddenly uncertain how to describe our situation. "It's complicated," I finally say. "We're keeping our options open."

Tucker stares at me, his dark blue eyes registering confusion. "What does that mean?"

"It means... well, we aren't dating, but we're open to things changing."

He looks at me blankly. "I still don't know what that means."

I sigh. "We decided we're okay with trying more."

"More what?"

"I don't know, Tucker," I say in exasperation. "You know things are hard for me. But we're willing to explore the possibility of being more than friends."

"You're already more than friends," Tucker scoffs. I start to protest, but he waves me off. "You know it's true. You guys are as close as Lila and I are, just without the sex."

I take a deep breath. "I know that. But neither of us wants to screw up what we have."

He shakes his head. "You two are meant to be together." He looks down, his eyes softening. "I was with him when you were kidnapped, Charlie. It nearly destroyed him. If we hadn't found you guys, it would have. Mark loves you with every fiber of his being. Trust me."

I wrap my arms around his waist, resting my head on his broad chest. "Thanks, Tucker."

He returns my hug and kisses the top of my head. "You two are meant to be," he repeats.

Lila and Mark return a short time later. Mark is complaining about one of the goats giving him the cold shoulder. "All the others were friendly, but not that tall skinny one with the long legs. She's awfully pretentious for a goat."

Lila winks. "Chele," she says, and I grin. When Lila named her, we had no idea Tom's haughty ex-wife – Maya's mom – was the exotic, mocha-skinned supermodel Chele, but the name perfectly fits the goat's snooty personality. We've never mentioned it to Tom or Maya. Tom would be amused, but Maya might not. Luckily, it's never come up.

Tucker explains the hand controls for the four-wheeler before Mark climbs on and hands me his crutches. I dismantle them and tuck them in the backpack, then slide behind him. He looks over his shoulder in surprise.

"You're riding with me?"

I cock my head. "I was planning to."

"You trust me?"

I snort. "I've ridden with you in places way more dangerous than this."

"Yeah, but not since – I mean – I've never used controls like this before." He stumbles over his words.

He's nervous. He doesn't trust himself.

No. He doesn't trust his changed body not to disappoint him.

Mark has always been a natural at everything he tries, but his changed body has damaged his self-confidence. I hand him a helmet and put mine on, then wrap my arms around his waist. "I trust you. Now shut up and drive."

Tucker laughs. "You heard the lady. Let's go."

Tucker and Lila lead the way up a winding path into the mountains. The trails are little more than deep ruts in some places, but thankfully, it's dried enough since yesterday's brief downpour that we don't get stuck in the mud. Mark is hesitant and tense at first, but after a few minutes, he relaxes. We bounce along for what feels like an hour, splashing through three small streams before finally reaching our destination.

The scenery is spectacular. Sprawling oaks and weeping willows spread their low limbs wide, shading the ground with curtains of green leaves. The summer heat is absent here. Instead, it's cool and refreshing. A narrow creek babbles quietly in the background. I hop off the back of the four-wheeler, and Mark and I quickly reassemble his crutches while Lila spreads out a blanket and pulls sandwiches and bottled water from her backpack. Tucker and Mark discuss the four-wheeler and how it felt using the hand controls.

It's a wonderful afternoon. The four of us lie around on the blanket, eating and talking and laughing. It's relaxing. Serene. Perfect.

At one point, Mark moves closer to me and slips an arm around my waist, drawing me against him, never pausing in his conversation with Tucker. It feels so natural, so right. From my peripheral vision, I see Lila smile.

The sun is starting to dip in the sky when Tucker glances up. "We should head back. Those trails are a bitch in the dark."

We gather up our things and break down Mark's crutches once again. "Want to drive on the way back?" he offers.

I shake my head. "I'd rather hold on to you." Tucker's chuckle turns quickly to a grunt when Lila elbows his ribs.

It takes longer to get down the trail because the setting sun is blinding, shining directly in our faces. When it finally drops below the ridgeline, shadows obscure the path, making it more difficult to see the dips and ruts. I'm relieved when we arrive back at their house.

Lila hugs me before we leave, leaning close to whisper in my ear. "Details. Tomorrow morning. I'll bring the coffee."

I have no doubt that Tucker is muttering something similar to Mark behind me.

MARK

Night has fallen when we get home, and Charlie stays beside me as I climb her front steps in the dark. She's scarcely locked the door when I pull her against me. "I've been wanting to do this all afternoon," I whisper between hot, wet kisses.

"Why didn't you?"

I move my lips to her neck, my hands low on her lush hips. "I wasn't sure how you'd feel about me touching you in front of Tucker and Lila."

She shivers as I nuzzle her ear. Her words are more breathy when she gasps, "You put your arm around me in front of them."

I graze her jawline with my teeth before nibbling her earlobe. "They've seen me with my arm around you plenty of times. They've never seen this."

She turns her head and catches my lower lip in her teeth. "You talk too much."

I smile and kiss her thoroughly, deeply, until we're both breathless. I pull away reluctantly, leaning my forehead against hers. Only then do I notice she's pressed me against the wall, and both of my crutches have tumbled to the floor. She realizes what she's done in her ardor a split-second later and blushes to her hairline.

"Sorry," she mumbles, making sure I'm balanced before grabbing my crutches for me.

I catch her by the waist. "I'm not," I tell her, staring into her gorgeous eyes.

A shy smile flits across her face. "Me neither."

Both of us are mud-spattered, so she heads upstairs to shower. The bumpy ride down the mountain has my leg throbbing fiercely, something that hasn't happened in a while. I down a couple of aspirin in my room and hope a hot shower will help.

It doesn't.

By the time I'm out of the shower, my pain has escalated so much I can scarcely breathe. I wonder if I've damaged something with all the jostling. I don't bother drying off. I drag on clean shorts and barely make it to the bed.

The agony keeps intensifying. My entire leg feels like it's on fire.

Long minutes pass before I hear Charlie on the stairs. I'm draped across the bed, rummaging through the bedside table for the pain medication I haven't needed in months. I spot it and reach for it with shaking hands, but the bottle slips from my fingers and tumbles to the floor. I let loose a string of curses as the door opens.

"What's wrong?" She's at my side instantly, her hand on my shoulder.

"My leg."

Charlie helps me back onto the bed before picking up the bottle. "Phantom pain?"

"Yes. No. I don't know. It's my whole damn leg," I groan. Excruciating pains shoot like fire from where my toes would be if I still had them, all the way to my upper thigh.

I toss back the two pain tablets and muscle relaxer she hands me. She pushes the leg of my shorts all the way up, her touch gentle, her voice soft. "Close your eyes."

I squeeze my eyes shut and fist my hands in the blanket as waves of pain wash over me, making me nauseous. She places her small hands just above my knee, massaging the length of my quad muscle, slow and deep. She pauses, and when she resumes, her hands are slick with oil. Her fingers glide across my skin as she works in silence. My quad starts to loosen, but the pain continues.

"Roll onto your stomach," she murmurs several minutes later, and I comply. She oils her palms again and rubs my hamstring with long, measured strokes. My body eventually begins to relax, but I'm not sure if it's from the massage or the medication.

About fifteen minutes later, Charlie has me roll onto my back again. She nudges my legs apart and kneels between them, pushing both legs of my shorts all the way up.

"I'm wondering if the rough ride on the four-wheeler has agitated the nerves in your leg," she says, oiling her hands. "I'm going to massage both thighs at the same time to see if it will interrupt the pain loop, sort of like what I do with your lower leg. If that works, we'll try mirror therapy for the lower part."

Once again, she starts just above my knees, her hands sliding across my skin before beginning a deep-tissue massage. I groan, and she pulls back.

Please don't stop touching me. The thought pops unbidden in the forefront of my mind.

"I'm okay," I mutter. "Keep going."

"You sure?"

I nod. "I'm alright. It's helping."

And it is. Charlie keeps working her magic, and the pain in my right thigh gradually eases. The phantom pain in my nonexistent lower leg has dulled as well, though I can still feel it. She follows the thigh massage with mirror therapy for my missing limb, and after a twenty-minute mirror session, I'm finally pain-free.

"How do you feel?" she eventually asks.

I love the feel of your hands on me.

"You're incredible."

She smiles and puts away the mirror, then curls up next to me on the bed. I pull her closer, and she rests her head on my bare chest.

"Thank you," I whisper, kissing her damp hair and inhaling its coconut scent.

"I'm sorry."

"For what?"

"Suggesting the trip. I didn't mean to hurt you."

"There was no way of knowing that would happen. I guess the nerves are still healing."

"I still feel bad."

"I'm just glad you have a magic touch."

She lifts her head and grins. "I could add that to my business cards."

"I'm not sure you should hand out business cards for a massage with a magic touch," I tease, and she swats me before laying her head back on my chest. I lace my fingers through hers, my lips on her hair.

Everything about this, about her, about us, feels so... right. So perfect.

The only thing that could make this any better would be if I were the old me. The whole me.

The undamaged me.

I suddenly can't wait for my osseointegration surgery so I can be normal again.

CHAPTER SIX

CHARLIE

MARK HAD THREE ADDITIONAL phantom pain episodes overnight after bouncing around on the ATV. I was able to temporarily relieve them with massages, but they kept returning. By morning, I text Lila and tell her I've got to call the VA to work Mark in for an urgent appointment. I drive him to Pueblo mid-morning, having to pull over once to massage his leg from another attack. The doctor takes one look at Mark's pale, sweaty face and taut jaw and shakes his head.

"I suspect you've pinched or agitated a nerve bundle from jostling around on rough terrain."

"So I'm stuck like this?"

Dr. Patel shakes his head. "A course of steroids and pain medication should do the trick." Mark frowns, and the doctor raises an eyebrow.

"He doesn't like pain medication," I explain, "but if he needs it, I'll make sure he takes it."

Mark shoots me a look, but when I give him a pointed glance, he nods reluctantly. "Fine. Just make it stop. I'd almost stopped having phantom pain attacks until yesterday."

My cell phone rings on the drive back, and I answer it without looking, assuming it's Lila wanting an update on Mark's condition. Instead, a deep voice booms over my car's speakers. "Green Eyes!" bellows the man.

I grin, though he can't see me. "Stubbs! How are you?"

"Black and beautiful, baby. How are you?"

"You're on speakerphone. I'm in the car with Mark. We're driving back from the VA."

"Pretty Boy! How the hell are you?"

Mark shakes his head at Stubbs' nicknames for us. "I've been better. I had a rough night last night."

"What happened?"

Mark explains how the bumpy ride on the ATV revved up his phantom pains again while I drive and listen, smiling. Stubbs is Mark's mentor from the hospital in San Antonio where he spent three months recovering from his IED attack. Stubbs is huge, with rich mahogany skin and a voice like Barry White. He's easily six-five and built like a tank, and the only thing bigger than his muscles is his personality. The man is a unique blend of Zen and swagger, with a healthy dose of profanity and a sprinkle of wisdom for good measure. He's a Marine (never use the phrase "former Marine" around him unless you want an earful) who lost both legs in an explosion similar to Mark's.

The mentorship group at Brooke paired experienced amputees with newbies to help them adjust to their new reality. Stubbs was Mark's mentor. The first time I met him, I immediately stuck both feet in my mouth. He'd introduced himself as Stubbs, and in my exhausted and shamefully unfiltered state, I'd cocked my head and asked if he was serious. A double amputee whose name was Stubbs seemed appallingly unfair. He'd laughed and asked if I really thought he looked like the sort of fellow who'd tolerate name-calling. Then he'd explained that his name was actually James Mackey, but that he went by Stubbs, "with two B's for black and beautiful, baby."

Stubbs has helped both of us deal with the aftermath of Mark's injuries. He taught Mark what to expect from the perspective of both a patient and someone dealing with the often disability-unfriendly outside world. Stubbs helped me understand Mark's mindset and how to best support him. We email or call a few times a month and text regularly, and occasionally, we video chat, though not as often. Last time, I was folding laundry with my laptop on the coffee table while we skyped. He caught me off-guard with his sudden wolf whistle when he spotted me folding a pair of lacy black panties. I'd flipped him off and threatened to disconnect the call until he sheepishly apologized.

Stubbs chats with us the entire drive back. We've just pulled into my driveway when he clears his throat. "I'm thinking of coming up to Cedar Ridge for a week or so. Would you guys mind showing me around?"

"Not at all," I exclaim. "You can stay with us."

"I don't want to inconvenience you," he says quickly. "I can stay at a hotel."

"Don't be silly. I have a five-bedroom house, and it's just me and Mark. We've got plenty of room. When are you coming up?"

"In August," he says, "after graduation. I'm rewarding myself for my hard work." Stubbs is finishing his master's degree in mental health counseling.

He wants to work with vets with PTSD and those struggling to accept their combat injuries.

"Come when you're ready and stay as long as you want," I tell him. "If you give me a few days' notice, I'll see if I can get a couple extra days off work."

Mark grins as he slides carefully from the car. "It'll be good to see him again. I can't wait to introduce him to Tucker and Lila. They've heard so much about him, it'll be good for them to have a face to put with the stories."

"He'd be good with some of our newer clients, too. Maybe I can sweet-talk him into meeting with a few people. And I know Tom would love to meet him."

Mark has one more phantom-pain attack right before bed, but it eases with massage and the pain meds. I wipe his damp forehead with a cool cloth afterwards. "Hopefully, the steroids will start working their magic soon, and you won't have any more of those."

"I hope so," he mutters. "No more ATVs for me." He catches my guilty expression and tugs my fingers to his lips, kissing them. "Not your fault," he says firmly. "We didn't know that would happen. Now we do."

A very impatient Lila is waiting in my office with coffee and strawberry cream cheese croissant bites when I arrive at work early on Tuesday. Our tell-all chat was postponed because of Mark's visit to the VA. She pats a spot on the sofa beside her and grins. "Start talking."

I join her, my face growing warm as I reach for the coffee. Her grin widens. "You're blushing. This must be good."

"I'm not sure exactly what to say."

"Why don't you begin with when we left," she suggests. "Did you guys go out to dinner?"

I shake my head. "No. Friday was terrible. I asked if he wanted to go to dinner and he said no. When I asked if he wanted to talk, he stormed into his room and slammed the door." She gasps. "He got in the shower, and while he was in there, I moved upstairs." Lila and Tucker understand our non-traditional sleeping arrangement.

"Then what?"

I shrug. "I spent the night holed up in my room, eating pizza and crying. And drinking way too much," I add. "I woke up with night terrors twice. I spent all day in the woods Saturday, but it didn't help, and then I got caught in the rain. When I got home, my brain still wouldn't shut up, so I ran on the treadmill until I seized up with a leg cramp." My voice softens. "Next thing I knew, he was on the floor, massaging my calf. I don't know what changed between Friday night and Saturday, but he'd already ordered Italian food so we could talk."

She smiles. "Tucker said Mark was struggling."

I nod. "We had dinner and wine. I had a lot of wine," I admit with a rueful grin. "And then he apologized."

Her face lights up. "Tell me every word."

I chuckle at her eagerness and replay our conversation for her. She grins and holds out the pastry box. "Keep talking, and I'll give you more of these."

I take a bite of the warm croissant. It's warm and flaky and sweet and tangy all at once, and I moan at how good it is.

"Less moaning, more talking," she demands.

I oblige, describing our discussion about discovering our mutual attraction. When I confess my fear, her eyes turn sad. "Charlie, you don't need to be afraid of Mark. He won't hurt you."

I frown. "He thought that's what I meant, too. I'm not afraid of Mark. I never have been, not even at my worst. I'm scared of losing him. I'm scared I'll freak out with him, or that it'll screw up what we have if things don't work out. I'm just —" I stare down at my lap. "I'm a mess, Lila. I don't want to ruin the most important relationship in my life."

"You're not a mess," she says. I snort in disbelief, and she seizes my free hand. "You're not," she insists. "You're healing, and you're making progress. That's all any of us can do." She studies me with gentle eyes. "I've been where you are, Charlie, exactly where you are. Shattered and scared and crazy about someone, torn between desire and fear, afraid to risk intimacy. I promise you, I understand. I've lived it, too."

Tears fill my eyes. Lila does understand my struggles. She was captured with me and endured similar horrors. "But you were strong enough to move forward," I whisper.

Lila takes the croissant from my hand, puts it down, and wraps me in a warm hug. "I keep telling you, you're much stronger than you believe."

I pull back. "You're the strong one, Lila. I'm still stuck."

She shakes her head and gives me a tender smile. "You aren't stuck. I saw the way you two looked at each other."

My cheeks grow warm.

"I need more details," she declares, handing me back my croissant. "So you were talking about being afraid," she prompts.

I nod. "I told him I was tired of fear controlling my life. He asked what I would want if fear didn't enter the equation. That's when I knew. I want more."

Lila smiles, and I see tears in her eyes. "Oh, Charlie," she whispers, hugging me again. "You're not stuck. You're choosing to move forward."

I laugh. "Well, kind of."

"What do you mean?"

"We still aren't really sure what 'more' entails. We don't want to 'date' in case things don't work out, and sex — well, I know I'm not ready for that." *Even though my body seems to feel otherwise.* "And I nearly passed out when Mark said he's not comfortable enough with his body for sex, either."

She doesn't look surprised, merely thoughtful. "I think in time, the situation will resolve itself. Did you set any ground rules?"

"We agreed kissing was safe territory. And we left ourselves the option to add more later if we get more comfortable."

She grins saucily. "And are you comfortable kissing him?"

My face flames, and she chuckles. "It's intense between you two, isn't it?"

I can't speak, so I simply nod.

"Just be careful," she cautions. "I don't think Mark is someone you can be casual with for long. You're already so deeply connected." Then she grins. "I knew it would be spicy if you guys ever got together. There's been heat simmering between you two for years. You were the only ones who couldn't see it. It won't take much for that simmer to become a rolling boil."

I shake my head. "We've already agreed – no romantic entanglements. This is just adding a physical aspect to our relationship."

Then I think about Mark's panty-melting kisses.

Lila's more right about the heat than she knows.

LILA

It's fantastic to finally see Charlie happy again. There's a light in her eyes I haven't seen in years. She's always smiling, humming to herself at work. She's got it bad. If it were anyone else, I'd vomit from the overload of cuteness. Tom and Tara smile when she's not looking. She and Mark may not be "dating", but they're clearly involved, and she's falling fast.

"I'm worried Charlie's falling hard for Mark," I tell Tucker one evening.

He grins. "It'll be fine, Lila. They're soulmates. He'll fall even harder for her."

I run a finger down his chest, catching his belt loop and tugging him toward me. "Speaking of harder..."

He winks. "I'd love to, Sweetness, but I can't. I promised I'd help Joey this evening."

"You can't go out tonight," I protest, reaching for his arm. "Today's the day. We're in our peak conception window right now. You can see Joey any time."

Tucker cocks his head at me. "He's my brother, Lila. We made plans."

I bristle. "Cancel them. You knew this was our best window of opportunity."

Tucker pulls his arm away. "How the hell would I know that?"

"It's on the calendar in the bedroom, and I put it on the calendar on your phone."

"I don't use the calendar on my phone, Lila, and who puts a calendar in the bedroom?"

"People who are trying to conceive," I snap.

Tucker looks at me with an unfathomable expression. "Come on, Tucker," I wheedle, and even to me, my voice sounds whiny. I move closer, sliding my hands into his back pockets and rubbing against him. "I'll take good care of you."

When he doesn't protest, I take his hand and lead him upstairs. I undress him, kissing his neck, touching him all over, seductively peeling off my clothes while peeking over my shoulder and biting my lip. His thick cock stands at attention long before I'm done. I nudge him back toward the bed and take the lead, riding him like a porn star, giving him one hell of a show. When he climaxes and empties his seed into me, it feels like victory. I collapse beside him, quickly elevating my hips with a pillow to encourage his semen to move north. When he gets up a few minutes later and says he's going to Joey's, I just smile. "Hurry back, Stud."

TUCKER

I leave Joey's house much sooner than planned, but I don't immediately go home. Instead, I find an empty parking lot and sit silently in my truck.

No one – well, no guy – would give me the time of day if I talked to them about this problem at home.

Frankly, referring to it as a "problem" sounds ridiculous, even to me. At most, it's a situation.

My "problem"? My hot wife wants sex, and she's going to want it multiple times a day for the next couple of days.

Every guy I know would revoke my man-card and laugh me out of the room for complaining. Hell, once upon a time, I'd have laughed at a guy complaining about his woman wanting sex.

That was before, though.

And the thing is, it isn't a request. It's an expectation, whether I'm in the mood or not.

Don't get me wrong – I'm fully consensual. It's just that the loss of spontaneity and fun when it comes to sex is taking a toll. There's a strain between us that's never been there before. Where sex was once us-focused, it's become very goal-focused, and it's changed the mood and emotion of our encounters.

She feels it, too.

Lila has certain sexual "tells" when she's lost in sensation. The dilated pupils, her flushed cheeks and chest, the way her head drops back just so and exposes her throat, her throaty moans when she's close to coming. I can tell when she's caught up in the moment.

Her performance earlier?

That's exactly what it was – a performance.

And calling me Stud? Reminding me that my services will be required again this evening?

That chapped my ass, but of course, I didn't say anything.

What could I say?

My smoking-hot wife is demanding sex, and I'm complaining?

Maybe I *should* turn in my man-card.

MARK

"You're gonna love this," Tucker promises as he, Lila, Charlie, and I trudge across the huge parking lot outside a nondescript warehouse. "It's a fantastic upper body workout."

I frown. "It's not my upper body I'm worried about."

I've finished my course of steroids for my phantom pain, and the attacks have finally calmed down. Tucker informed me yesterday that now that I'm recovering, I need to be "more active". When I pointed out that I exercise a minimum of three hours every day between PT, workouts with him and Tom, and Pilates with Lila and Charlie, he'd shaken his head. "There's more to life than working out."

I'd cocked my head at him. "Isn't that blasphemy, coming from a personal trainer who owns his own gym?"

He'd grinned. "You need to get out more. I love Charlie, but she's an introvert and a homebody. It takes a Herculean effort to keep her from spiraling happily into hermit-hood."

"There's nothing wrong with staying home in her off-time if it makes her happy. Being around people drains her. She needs to recharge."

"Absolutely," he agreed. "But you're working toward a full recovery, and that includes getting out and functioning in the outside world."

"So you're taking me out for a playdate?"

He'd grinned again. "More or less. Wear something sexy, and don't forget, I'm an ass man."

I'd punched him just hard enough in the gut to make him grunt.

That's how I find myself following Tucker and the girls into a brightly-lit building Saturday afternoon. I pause, taking in the scene around me. Sixty-foot-high walls wrap their way throughout the vast interior of the building. Some are short, straight sections unto themselves, while others connect and weave in a serpentine fashion. There's even a section along a back wall that has an overhanging vertical face like a cliff. The walls are studded with randomly-shaped fluorescent climbing holds. I watch as a lean, wiry man ascends the wall, paying careful attention to how he places his feet.

I purse my lips. Toeholds could be a problem. I study the patterns of climbing holds on the wall nearest me, mentally mapping out a route I can manage with one leg.

I'm so busy scrutinizing the wall that I don't notice the man approaching from my right until he speaks. "Hi. Welcome to The Goat Path. Have you guys been here before?"

Tucker sticks out his hand. "I've been here a few times with my brother. I think he and I worked with you before. My brother's a paraplegic. You're Craig, right?"

The two of them launch into a discussion about Tucker's brother, Joey, while I stare at the walls with new fascination. If Joey could do this without the use of either of his legs, surely I can manage with one.

Indoor rock climbing is fantastic. It's nothing I'd ever have thought about on my own, probably because I'd have assumed I couldn't do it. Don't get me wrong — it's challenging as hell, but finding a path I can navigate using a single toehold or by pulling myself up using only my upper body is exhilarating. I start off on the practice wall to get used to the harness, ropes, and techniques. Once I'm comfortable, the four of us tackle a beginner's wall. I glance over, watching Charlie nimbly scale the wall like she's done it a thousand times before, even though I know she never has. My eyes linger on her long legs and perky ass, clad in sleek black yoga pants. My mouth goes dry, and I look away, forcing myself to concentrate on the wall in front of me. We end our adventure by completing a full-scale course, including hanging slabs, vertical faces, and a man-made cave.

"You're going to be sore tomorrow," Lila warns me as the four of us head into a casual restaurant for dinner. "That's a really intense upper body workout."

I shrug. "I work out a lot. I'm sure it'll be fine."

Tucker laughs. "I'll remind you of that tomorrow. Remember how I said I'd push you to your limits? This is one of those times. All of that work was done over your head, Princess. You're going to hurt in muscles you didn't even know you had."

Charlie leans close. "Don't worry. I'll give you a good rubdown after a hot shower tonight."

For the rest of dinner, all I can think about is Charlie's hands all over my body.

CHAPTER SEVEN

CHARLIE

THESE LAST TWO WEEKS have been incredibly hot. I'm spending every night in the arms of a man whose rock-hard body fits like a puzzle piece against mine, a man who's gorgeous and sexy and the best kisser I've ever known. Just thinking about him makes my mouth water and my panties grow damp.

I'm glad Mark is a pillar of control, because I'm the farthest thing from that, at least where he's concerned.

My newfound sexual desires leave me wanting much more than is prudent, and I keep finding myself wordlessly encouraging him to go further. Putting his hands beneath the hem of my shirt. Wrapping my legs around him when we make out. Rubbing my core against him.

When I get carried away, Mark always manages to dial down the intensity in a way that makes me feel respected, not rejected. Maybe it's because I can feel the evidence of his own arousal, and I know he's consciously choosing not to do something we haven't discussed and might end up regretting. I have to admit, though, I'm toying with the idea of talking to him about advancing our physical relationship beyond kissing.

I arrive early at the clinic one morning and find all the lights already on. I follow the sound of sniffles. Lila's in her office, red-eyed and clearly miserable, surrounded by a pile of crumpled tissues. I rush to her side. "What's wrong? Did something happen?"

She shakes her head, waving me off. "I'm fine."

I perch on the edge of her desk. "Try again."

"It's nothing."

"Third time's a charm." I meet her eyes steadily. She remains silent, staring off into space. "I know where you live, and I'm not leaving, so you might as well talk."

She draws a ragged breath. "I got my period again."

Damn. I reach for her hand. "I'm sorry, Lila."

She shakes her head. "I was so sure this time would be different. I just... I don't know. Maybe it's not meant to be."

"Make an appointment with your gynecologist. I'll go with you if you want," I offer.

She shrugs. "I'm starting to think maybe motherhood isn't in the cards for me."

"Don't say that. You guys have only been trying for what – seven months? It hasn't even been a year. Seriously, make an appointment. I'll come along. We can make a day of it."

A faint smile crosses her face. "My feet up in stirrups, followed by margaritas. Sounds like a winner."

I grin. "We could always have the margaritas first."

She does smile then, before sweeping the tissues off her desk and into the trash can. "Enough about me. How are you and Mark?"

I feel a stupid smile crawl across my face. "Amazing," I admit. "It's like nothing I could ever have expected. He's just – he's amazing," I repeat.

Lila studies me carefully. "Be careful, Charlie. You need to take things slowly."

Her remark puzzles me. "I am. This is just – you know, casual."

Her violet gaze pins me. "I don't think you can do casual with Mark. It'll be too easy for you to fall for him." She bites her lip. "I don't want either one of you to get hurt."

"I know. Don't worry. I'm keeping my heart out of this."

She doesn't say anything, but her skeptical look speaks volumes.

A funk falls over me as the day wears on. It's only after I'm home alone, with Mark and Tucker at a sports bar, that I realize what's lingering in the back of my mind, troubling me.

Lila's worried motherhood isn't in the cards for her.

She still has a chance, though.

I don't.

It's not in the cards for me at all. Those fuckers made sure of that.

It wasn't even that I'd necessarily wanted children. Honestly, I'd never given it much thought. I joined the military after my parents died at the end of my first year of college. I was medically discharged from the Army after the kidnapping, and by then, all possibility of motherhood had been ripped away.

I had an epiphany just after the first of this year. I realized – while standing in Maya's kitchen, hugging her – that I'd give anything to settle down with an incredible man and have kids and dogs and cats and all the beautifully messy chaos that comes with a family.

But that's not possible.

Not for me.

A deep, intense loss for things I never had and never will have drowns me in a flood of pain.

I work my way through an entire bottle of wine, staring at the flames dancing in my gas fireplace despite the summer heat. I'm still in the same spot on the couch when Mark comes home to find me tearstained and more than a little drunk.

"Baby Girl? What's wrong?" Worried blue eyes search my face as he pulls me into his arms.

But I can't tell him. I can't explain why I'm devastated even though nothing *happened* today. Nothing's actually changed. This has been my reality for the past four years. I just don't let myself think about it, because it hurts too much.

Which is why I need a distraction.

I kiss him instead of answering, converting my pain to passion. Before I realize it, I'm straddling him, pressing my breasts into his chest, gripping his shoulders and arching into him. My mouth slants over his again and again, kissing him deeply, trying to numb my pain with physical pleasure. He groans deep in his throat as I grind against the erection pressing into my inner thigh. His hands spear my hair, holding my head, pulling his lips away and leaning his forehead against mine.

"Easy, Baby Girl," he murmurs.

"I don't want easy," I protest, seeking his mouth again. He kisses me, but he's gentle.

"Twenty-four hours," he says, his lips on mine. "Give us twenty-four hours to think this over. No more hasty decisions. You're too important to me for us to screw things up with something we'll regret later. Besides, I won't take things further when you're drunk and upset. Whatever happens between us needs to be for the right reasons."

Even in my state of mind, I know he's right. I crawl off his lap and curl up in a miserable ball on the couch. "Come on, Baby Girl," he says gently, tugging at a lock of my hair. He pulls my hand until I stand, leading me to the bedroom. He turns down the covers, nestles me into his chest, and holds me until I cry myself to sleep.

For the first time in weeks, I awaken in a panic with night terrors.

LILA

It plagues me all day. The telltale bloody stain. The proof of my failure.

Charlie considers herself broken, but the truth is, things are pretty messed up here, too.

Maybe I'm not meant to be a mother. Maybe I've lost that chance forever. Charlie did. Why should I be any different? I don't deserve anything better. If anything, she deserves motherhood more than I do, because those bastards did horrible things to her that they never did to me.

What they did to me was bad enough, though.

After I killed the first man that tried to force me – a feat that still fills me with pride, given his size advantage – they shackled me so I couldn't fight. They chained me to a table edged with iron rings, its wood stained black with old blood. My arm restraints were looped through the rings, my legs chained to the table legs. I was face down, spreadeagle, nude from the waist down.

Even then, they never came to my cell alone, not after I left the first man drowning in a pool of his own blood. They came in groups, each one taking a turn with me, hour after hour, day after day.

Eleven days is an eternity when measured by rapes.

When we were finally rescued and hospitalized, I was diagnosed with pelvic inflammatory disease. In layman's terms, my rapists had caused an infection that had spread past my cervix and into my uterus. The doctors cured the infection, but they warned me I could have problems later on. I assumed they meant something like hepatitis or HIV, neither of which I developed, thankfully. Maybe they'd meant fertility problems.

Charlie had offered to go to the gynecologist with me, but I didn't want to talk about it anymore, so I shifted the subject to her and Mark. There's so much between the two of them already that it won't take more than a nudge to push them into a full-blown relationship. She insists she's taking things casually, but anyone can see she's falling for him. Mark's been half in love with her for years, so as long as he accepts that, they'll be fine. Her initial statement about him not being comfortable enough for sex still troubles me, though. They both have body image issues that only complicate an already-delicate situation.

I pick up the phone three different times to make an appointment with my gynecologist, but I can't do it. I'm not strong enough to hear her say those bastards won after all.

I dream of the rapes in detail, waking up screaming for the first time in years.

TUCKER

Lila's shrieks startle me into alertness. I sit up quickly, reaching for her, stopping myself just in time. She's having a nightmare, thrashing violently after kicking the covers off the bed. Her negligee is twisted around her hips from her flailing. Heart-wrenching wails echo off the walls as she screams over and over, "No! Don't touch me! Stop!"

The lamp is on beside our bed. Like Charlie, Lila can't tolerate darkness. My chest grows tight as I helplessly move away, feeling her pain and fear. I can't touch her. She's disoriented, and she won't know it's me. Physical contact now will only make it worse for her.

My clear, calm tone masks my own pain. "Sweetness, it's Tucker. You're safe. No one's going to hurt you." I repeat myself over and over until her screams turn to sobs.

"Sweetness? You with me?"

Lila flings her trembling body against me. I wrap my arms around her and stroke her back, her tears soaking my bare skin. After several minutes, I lay us down, tugging the comforter up before brushing her damp hair out of her tear-stained face. "What can I do?"

"Hold me," she begs. I tighten my arms around her, kissing her temple.

"What if they won?" she asks a few minutes later in a small voice.

I pull back to look down at her. "What if who won?"

She swallows hard. "If – if I can't have kids. What if they took that from me, too?"

Understanding dawns. Another month without conceiving has her remembering what happened, wondering if those bastards are the cause of that misery, too.

Lila's broken expression makes my heart clench. She's worked so hard and come so far. When I first came home, she was terrified of my touch. It took a lot of work, tears, and therapy to get to where we are today.

My frustration from a couple of weeks ago evaporates. If Lila needs to use me as a stud, I'll do it. I'll do anything for her, and sex with her is a pleasure, not a hardship.

I cup her face in my hands, looking her in the eye. "As long as we have each other, Sweetness, they didn't win. Even if you can't carry a baby, we have options. We can foster, adopt, whatever you want. Family isn't just blood. Look at us and Charlie and Mark. We're not related, but we're definitely family." She nods as another tear falls.

I hold her tightly long after she falls asleep, until night has bled into sunrise.

MARK

Two weeks.

It's been two weeks since Charlie and I decided to try "more", whatever that means, and it's been the best time of my life. This newfound ability to be openly physical is freeing. Most nights, after the sun sets below the ridgeline, she and I retire to the back deck and light a fire in the stone firepit. We cuddle on a lounge chair together and sip wine, listening to tree frogs, crickets, and cicadas as the sky grows dark. Her house is set back far enough from the main roads that there are no street lights to pollute the view. We bask in the cool evening air, watching the stars appear in the inky night. When we go to bed, I'm no longer standing guard all night while Charlie sleeps. Instead, we sleep together, tangled in each other's arms.

We're teasing, flirting, dancing around the inevitable.

And I want more.

Kissing her is amazing, but it's getting harder and harder –no pun intended – not to give into the urge to go further, especially when she wants it, too.

At the same time, though, I'm uncomfortable with the thought of having sex. Not because of Charlie – my body aches to be buried deep inside her, skin to skin. I want her like I've never wanted any other woman.

I'm uncomfortable because of me. Because of my body.

I used to be a good-looking guy. Sandy hair, blue eyes, nice smile. I'm tall and muscular, with broad shoulders and a narrow waist. I wasn't arrogant, at least I don't think I was, but I knew my looks and athleticism distinguished me from the crowd. Then an asshole with an IED literally blew my world to hell. Now my body is a roadmap of scars. Pale pink ones of various shapes and sizes are scattered all over my upper body from shrapnel punctures, chest tubes, and surgery to repair free-floating broken ribs. A lavender line spans the width of my abdomen from another surgery to stop internal hemorrhaging. Purple scars track down my right thigh to my knee, courtesy of multiple surgeries for my femur fracture. One scar runs down the center of the thigh; two others run down the outside. A circumferential pattern of pale white dots highlights where external fixators pinned the bone fragments together. Pale patches – some textured like a cheese grater – disfigure my left inner and right outer thigh from second and third degree burns.

And lest we forget, there's the amputation. I lost most of my right leg below the knee after it was ripped to shreds by that goddamn bomb.

Now I have a stump.

God, I hate that word. The PC term is "residual limb", but most people, even amputees, still call it a stump. Even my stump is scarred, with a thin line crossing the end where they "refined" the shape after sawing off the damaged part of my leg.

I don't talk about it to anyone, especially not Charlie, but when I look at my right leg – or what's left of it – it literally turns my stomach. A knot forms in my stomach, a chill runs up my spine, and a queasy sensation washes over me. I'm not squeamish. If I were, I'd never have lasted fifteen years on the battlefield. But the sight of that weirdly rounded appendage on my body disgusts me.

That's why going any further with Charlie is problematic. I'm fine removing my shirt. I'm scarred, but I've worked out enough that I've got the full six-pack and visible inguinal muscles that vee toward my groin, aka the "sex lines". My body right now is as toned as it's ever been. After three months in a hospital, I was weak, but with little to do besides heal and work out, I've been pushing myself, so even my right thigh is thick with muscle.

But below the knee, there's just this... unmuscled, soft *thing*, like a large pale worm.

And I fucking hate it.

So going further with Charlie?

I have no idea how to pull that off without exposing my scars and my stump.

And the thing is, Charlie-my-best-friend has seen it all before. She dressed my wounds, and she's massaged my leg for months, and it never bothered me, because she's my best friend.

But Charlie-my-possible-lover?

That's different.

My fucked-up body isn't something my lover should see. I can't even turn out the lights, because Charlie can't handle darkness after what those bastards did to her. Her surroundings have to be well-lit so she can feel secure, so no one can sneak up on her. Besides, if she and I ever reach that point, I want the lights on. I want to drink in the sight of her luscious body and burn it into my mind forever.

God, I can't wait for my osseointegration surgery. I need to be normal again.

CHAPTER EIGHT

CHARLIE

It's been a few days since I accosted Mark on the couch while drunk, and neither of us has brought it up. I'm finding myself more and more in favor of taking things further between us. Making out with him is amazing, but we've reached the stage where it leaves both of us aroused to the point of discomfort. One evening while we're watching a movie together, I struggle to find what I want to say. The movie's half over before I find enough courage to broach the subject.

"So, um... I was thinking about maybe adjusting the parameters of what we consider acceptable touch."

So much for courage.

The hands that have been stroking my back go still, and his eyes flick to mine. "How so?"

Here we go. Deep breath.

"Well, I'd say things are going... well."

Smooth, Charlie, really smooth.

I wait until he nods.

"And I think it's safe to say we're both... um... aroused by what we've been doing."

Why is this so hard to talk about?

Another nod.

"I think it's also safe to say that if either of us were in the same situation with a different partner, we wouldn't deny ourselves... um... pleasure. We'd go further."

He frowns and nods a third time, though I don't understand the frown.

Is he going to say anything at all?

"We're only denying ourselves because we're friends. And I'm not sure punishing ourselves is doing anything besides causing a lot of – sexual frustration." My words tumble out in a rush.

A smile of amusement crosses his rugged features, but he still says nothing. Not one damn word.

Humiliation washes over me as I realize I'm essentially begging for more while he's sitting there laughing at me. Tears sting my eyes. "Never mind. Forget I brought it up," I mutter, turning away. I reach for the remote and turn up the volume on the television.

Mark takes the remote from my hand and mutes the sound. "What just happened? I thought we were talking."

"No, *we* weren't. I was talking. You never said a word. You just frowned and then looked like I said something really funny while I was baring my soul, which is quite humiliating, by the way. Thanks for that. Forget I said anything. I've changed my mind."

My face burns, and I push off the couch to leave, but he grabs my arm. "I'm sorry," he says.

"Forget it," I repeat, trying to twist away, but he's too strong.

"Will you let me explain? Then if you want to leave, I won't stop you."

I stop struggling. "Fine."

"Will you look at me?"

I can't. I'm too close to tears. There's a lump in my throat, so I simply shake my head.

"Fine," he says, curling his arms around me and pulling me onto his lap, my back to his chest. When he speaks again, his voice is low against my ear. "Charlie, I find you extremely arousing. I didn't think I needed to tell you that. Just sitting this close to you makes me hard." He shifts slightly, and his erection pushes against my backside. "I didn't realize I was frowning. You said if we were with other people, we wouldn't deny ourselves. I don't like the thought of you being with anyone else. You're mine."

My eyes widen. Mark's never said anything like that before.

"And as far as acting like you said something funny, that wasn't it at all. I'm glad you're sexually frustrated, too. I'd hate to think I'm the only one suffering. And yes, it's selfish, just like me frowning at the thought of anyone else ever having you is selfish." He nestles his lips just below my ear, nuzzling my neck, his breath hot. "Forgive me?"

I sigh and tilt my head in answer, giving him my neck to nibble and kiss. Shivers run down my spine as he complies with my unspoken request.

"So about these parameters," he says, his warm breath tickling my skin. "What are you thinking?"

"I'm not sure," I admit. "Not sex. Not yet, anyway. But more."

"Pleasuring?" His lips graze my ear.

"M-maybe." His hands skim down my sides to my hips before sliding back up and brushing the sides of my breasts, and I suck in a breath.

"Touching?"

I can only nod as his hands lightly cup my breasts through my clothes before closing over them, squeezing.

"Under clothes?"

"Yes," I gasp. Long fingers splay across my bare stomach, moving slowly. Too slowly, and I arch toward his fingers. He chuckles softly in my ear as his hands slip beneath my bra, kneading and massaging. My nipples harden immediately as I strain into his touch. His head nudges mine and I turn my face to his. He captures my lips possessively, his tongue delving deep, and I whimper and arch back against his hardness. He groans.

"I want my mouth here," he murmurs, rolling my nipples between his fingers.

I freeze, hesitant for the first time. "I – I'm scared to take off my shirt."

He scoops me up suddenly, turning me to sit astride him, his mouth on mine, driving me wild. I wrap my arms around him, tracing the thick muscles of his back. He pulls away to focus his attention on my neck, trailing kisses down to the collar of my shirt. I cup the back of his head. "What scares you?" he asks, his lips against my skin.

"Scars," I say breathlessly. His tongue dips beneath the neck of my shirt as I yank it lower to give him more access.

"I've seen your back," he reminds me, returning to my mouth. Our kisses grow heated, and I moan. Electricity courses through my veins.

"But not my front. It's scarred, too, and I –" I break off, swallowing hard.

His lips pause just above mine. "I don't see your scars. I only see you. My beautiful Baby Girl." He dips his head again, kissing me until I can't think straight and my entire body throbs with need.

When he pulls away, I whimper, and he smiles, kissing me lightly. "Go put on shorts and a thin tee shirt. Nothing else. Then meet me in my room. I have an idea."

"Wha- what?"

He leans forward, kissing me again. "Trust me," he says, his hand cupping my ass and squeezing lightly.

I'm upstairs rummaging for one of my filmiest shirts when I hear his shower cut on. I cock my head at the sound. *We're getting in the shower? Dressed?*

I bounce down the stairs a couple of minutes later, my hair in a messy bun. I'm wearing a white shirt and shorts that hug my ass. The shirt is thin enough that my hard nipples are clearly visible.

Mark's in his bathroom, the door open, the shower on. His walker is shoved out of the way in the corner. He's sitting on the shower bench, wearing only a pair of shorts. His bare chest and arms glisten, water droplets covering his muscled body.

Oh. My. God.

Broad shoulders. Bulging pecs. Thick biceps and forearms. The six-pack. Taut muscles veeing at an angle into the waistband of his shorts. Hard thighs.

My gaze lingers on his wet shorts. His pecs aren't the only thing bulging.

If I were wearing panties, they'd be sopping wet. I've never wanted someone so badly in my entire life. Even though my head knows I'm not ready, my body screams for more.

Mark's eyes roam possessively over my body, halting at my perky nipples. He utters something under his breath and runs his hand through his wet hair. Then he holds out his hand. "Come here, Baby Girl."

I step inside the shower, closing the glass door behind me, and he reaches for one of the handheld shower heads. I gasp as he sprays me with warm water. My clothes instantly cling to me like a second skin. Then he returns the shower head to its mount, angling it so that it continues to spray toward us. "Can't have you getting cold," he murmurs, then pulls me toward him. He slides forward so he's sitting on the edge of the bench before patting his lap. "Face me."

I straddle him, and though we're both clothed, our bodies fit snugly, my folds surrounding his hardness. He sucks in a breath and closes his eyes briefly. "The things you do to me, Charlie."

My pulse throbs between my legs. "That goes both ways."

He leans toward me, his lips pausing just above mine. "Do you trust me?"

I nod wordlessly.

"Our clothes will stay on, but you've been sexually frustrated long enough, Baby Girl, and I intend to rectify that."

Before I have time to ponder what he means, his mouth finds mine with deep, languid kisses, like there's nowhere he'd rather be than enjoying the taste of my lips. My hands leave his shoulders to roam his back, feeling the muscles ripple beneath my fingers. His hands cup my face, long fingers gentle on my neck, as he explores my mouth, learning every part of it like it's the first time. I squirm against his erection, and he chuckles.

"Patience," he whispers against my lips.

But I don't want to be patient.

His mouth finds the hollow beneath my ear, nibbling and licking a scorching trail down my neck before nipping my collarbone. I moan, pressing my breasts into his hard chest.

"Up on your knees," he murmurs, his hands lifting my hips up and away from his erection, and I groan in protest. "I'll make it worth your while," he promises.

Kneeling brings my breasts level with his face, and I understand this a split second before his mouth closes over my peaked nipple through my shirt. The tension between my legs skyrockets. One arm behind my ass holds me in place while his other hand works the opposite breast, squeezing, plucking my nipple between his thumb and forefinger. His suckling sends impulses directly to my core, making the ache between my legs more fierce. He swirls his tongue around my nipple before nipping it lightly with his teeth, and my moans echo off the bathroom walls. I weave my fingers through his damp hair as he moves his mouth to my other breast. My head drops back and my hips rock desperately against nothing as I whimper, my body taut with need.

When he moves his hand and mouth away from my breasts, I groan in frustration. He tilts my face to look at his, and his pale blue gaze sears into me. "I'll take care of you, Baby Girl." His hands grasp my hips as he pulls me back onto his lap, centering me so that his erection presses directly against my core. Strong hands grip my waist. "Lean back," he murmurs, shifting the angle of my body, causing his thickness to press against my clit. I suck in a breath at the sensation, and he smiles slowly. "So fucking hot," he murmurs, and then he helps me move, rubbing against his hard shaft.

"Ohhhh," I gasp, arching my hips forward as I lean further back. I reach behind me and clutch his knees for balance, using them for leverage as I slide back and forth against him. The pressure inside me builds, but as it does, so does my desire to be closer to him.

I sit up, bringing us chest to chest, and this time, he's the one to gasp as my breasts press into the hard planes of his chest. My mouth closes over his, and I moan against his mouth as I roll my hips, grinding against him. His hand slides into my hair, holding my head in place as he claims my mouth, his tongue keeping time with the movement of my hips.

I'm so close, right on that knife edge of agony and ecstasy, and I whimper.

Mark tears his mouth from mine and grips my hips firmly, pulling me harder against him as his pelvis arches into mine. My nails dig into his shoulders as I ride him. His mouth finds the curve of my throat. "That's right, Baby Girl. Take what you need," he growls against my neck.

I grind frantically against him, his thick shaft massaging me into a violent explosion of pleasure. I cry out, my head thrown back as he continues to drag me over his length, riding out the storm of sensations overwhelming me. Only when I collapse against him, breathing hard, does he release my hips and still beneath me as I slowly come back to earth.

Damn. That was white-hot.

Mark presses his lips into the top of my shoulder. "So fucking hot," he murmurs again.

That's when I remember he's still rock hard. I shift my hips and roll against him. He lifts his head and grins. "Ready for round two?"

I smile. "You're still on round one," I say pointedly. "We need to rectify that sexual tension we were talking about earlier."

He surprises me by shaking his head. "Not tonight," he says.

"Why not?"

"Tonight was about you."

"That's not right," I protest.

"Sure it is. Besides, I want to remember the sight of you coming apart in my arms when I fall asleep tonight."

My cheeks grow warm as his eyes hold mine. "I wouldn't have done that if I'd known –"

He silences me with a kiss that goes from light to deep in a millisecond. When we finally break apart, he lifts my chin to look into my eyes. "We're not going to rush things, okay? Tonight was about you. Believe me, I enjoyed myself. I'm going to carry that memory forever."

"Me, too," I murmur, suddenly shy. I ease off his lap, not wanting to cause him any further sexual tension, avoiding looking at the massive bulge in his shorts.

He chuckles. "I'm going to need a really cold shower."

"I feel guilty," I confess.

He grins, his eyes twinkling. "Really? I'm feeling quite pleased with myself."

I smile in spite of my embarrassment. "I see that." I get to my feet. "I'm going to borrow a towel and find some dry clothes before the water gets too cold for me. I'll meet you in the bedroom."

Only when I dash upstairs in a towel do I let myself linger on the thoughts of what's just happened.

Mark and I have definitely moved into the friends-with-benefits category.

MARK

Hearing Charlie peel off her wet clothes and knowing she's naked on the other side of the shower wall does absolutely nothing to relieve my sexual tension. The steamy air still carries the scent of her arousal. When I'd pulled her off her knees and down onto my body, she'd been dripping wet, and not from the shower. The wet fabric had done nothing to hide her full breasts, bouncing up and down as she rode me through our clothes. And her orgasm... Jesus Christ. I could feel her pussy shuddering along my cock as she cried out my name.

So. Fucking. Hot.

I could strip out of these shorts and jack off – it would only take about ten seconds, she's got me so wired – but I won't. As stupid as it sounds, I'd rather wait until I'm balls-deep inside Charlie to come.

Because after tonight, I have zero doubt we're going to get there.

So instead of relieving my own tension, I take an icy shower, realizing too late I neglected to bring dry clothes. I wrap a towel around my waist and awkwardly use the walker to hop to the door, a task made infinitely more difficult by trying to keep my towel on. I peek around the door, hoping Charlie's not there so I can grab some shorts.

Naturally, she's waiting in the bed for me.

I sigh. "Can you toss me a pair of shorts? I forgot to bring a dry pair."

Her eyes twinkle. "You were a boy scout. Isn't there some rule about being prepared?"

I wink at her. "I was too distracted by your breasts."

She blushes and gets up to retrieve my shorts. When I'm dressed, I join her in the bed, spooning behind her as usual. My cock hardens again instantly, and since it's nestled snugly against her ass, she notices.

"Are you sure –"

"I'm positive," I say firmly. "We're going to ignore him."

She giggles. "Him? He's his own entity?"

"Obviously. My brain thinks he should lie down and go to sleep. This is all his doing."

She tosses an impish look over her shoulder and repeats my words back to me. "Really? I was just feeling quite pleased with myself."

"You should. The mere thought of you makes him stand up and salute."

"I do appreciate a good soldier," she murmurs, twitching her ass against me.

Long after she's fallen asleep, I'm still hard as a rock. Every time she moans softly in her sleep, I instantly remember our shower. When I roll onto my back to put some space between our bodies, she follows, throwing her shapely leg over my waist and pressing her luscious breasts into my chest, and I can't stop recalling her breasts bouncing and her thighs squeezing my hips.

It takes every drop of my willpower to let her sleep instead of waking her up, but I do, and eventually I fall asleep.

Of course, I dream of Charlie, coming all around my cock, crying out my name.

LILA

I've admitted to myself and Linda, my psychiatrist, that I can't handle hearing my gynecologist tell me I'll never be able to carry a child. However, as Linda points out, there's a big difference between having difficulty conceiving and being infertile. She also reminds me that there are a plethora of options my doctor can offer to help improve the odds of conceiving, so I square my shoulders, put on my big girl panties, and make the appointment.

Even though both Tucker and Charlie have offered to go with me for moral support, I go to the office alone. This is something I need to face by myself.

Dr. Krakowskyvych – who insists her patients call her Dr. K – is a petite woman with dark hair and a matter-of-fact personality. I've seen her for my yearly pap smears and birth control since moving here, but this is the first time we've ever really discussed anything substantive.

I'm sitting on the paper-covered exam table dressed in a pink gown while she sits on her rolling stool, perusing my chart. "I understand you'd like to discuss your difficulty conceiving. Is that correct?"

"Yes. I've been off birth control since January, and even though we're tracking my ovulation and trying on my peak days, it isn't working."

Dark eyes study me. "Seven months isn't that long, and you're only thirty-two. Let's talk about why you're worried."

I take a deep breath and lace my fingers together. "Four years ago, while I was in the military, I was kidnapped and gang-raped for eleven days. By the time I was rescued and transferred to Walter Reed, I had an infection that had spread beyond my cervix and into my uterus. The gynecologist there did a D&C and treated the infection. She said there was significant uterine inflammation and that I might have difficulties in the future."

Her face softens, and she rolls her stool close enough to lay a soft hand on mine. "I'm sorry," she murmurs, and for a split second, I see a flash of pain in her eyes. It disappears so quickly I think I must have imagined it, especially when she returns to the desk and rifles through some pamphlets.

"It's not uncommon for women who have had pelvic inflammatory disease to have difficulty conceiving, but conception is certainly still possible. I'm going to do some bloodwork and a pelvic exam to look for any obvious causes. I'd also like to do an ultrasound to get a better look at your uterus and ovaries." She hands me several pamphlets about fertility treatment options and stands. "I'll give you a moment, and then my nurse and I will return and we'll get started."

Two hours later, I'm driving to the pharmacy with a prescription in hand for hormone injections.

My bloodwork and pelvic exam were fine. The ultrasound showed some scarring of my uterus, but otherwise, it looked fine, so we're going to try ovulation induction, a fancy term for flooding my body with hormones. I'll give myself injections to stimulate my ovaries to release multiple mature eggs each month instead of just one, thereby exponentially increasing my chances of conception.

Dr. K mentioned side effects from the shots – breast tenderness, nausea, irritability, fatigue, blah blah blah. I don't care. I'll gladly deal with it if it means a chance at a baby.

Those fuckers didn't win. I'm not broken.

God, I hope this works.

MARK

It's a workout day, which means after work, Lila, Tucker, Tom, and Maya gather here with Charlie and me. The girls hang out and cook dinner while the three of us do the caveman thing and work out. We aren't being sexist — we all can and do cook. When we're all here, though, Lila usually claims the role of head chef.

The food is great, the company is great, but I'm too distracted to pay attention to any of it. All I can think about is them leaving so I can drag Charlie off to my shower again. At the dinner table, while everyone is laughing and talking, I lay my hand on her thigh and draw slow circles with two fingers. I hear her sharp intake of breath and know she understands I'm imagining what I'd like to be doing between her legs.

She smiles before turning the tables on me, sliding her hand across my thigh to stroke my groin. In my shock, I knock over my water glass. There's a rush as Lila jumps up before it splashes into her lap and Tucker snags a dish towel to mop up the mess. Charlie winks and squeezes my thigh before removing her hand.

I look forward to tormenting her for that later.

It's nearly nine before the leftovers are put away, the dishes are done, and everyone's finally cleared out. Charlie's locking the front door when I come up behind her. She turns, and I flatten her against the door with my body. My left crutch tumbles to the floor as I cup her ass with my left hand, pulling her against me. I'm already hard from thinking about what I want to do to her. Her hands slide under my shirt to caress my back. Her touch licks over my heated body like flames. I kiss her aggressively, our mouths crashing together. When her hands slide to my ass, pulling me forward as she curls one long leg around my hip, I growl into her mouth.

I drag my lips from hers and brace my left arm against the door. "Go change and hurry back."

She slips under my arm and retrieves my crutch for me before climbing the stairs. I watch the sway of her perfect ass as she goes. When she disappears from sight, I head to my room, ripping off my clothes and pulling on the thinnest pair of shorts I can find. I remember to take dry clothes with me this time, as well as snagging a couple of towels for inside the shower and two more for afterwards. Satisfied, I hop into the shower with my walker and turn on the water. When it's warm, I douse myself, remembering Charlie's hungry gaze last night.

She comes into my bathroom wearing skimpy shorts and a shirt so sheer it ought to be illegal. My cock surges at the sight. She stares at me, drinking in my body the same way I'm drinking in hers. She's left her hair down tonight. Her green eyes almost glow in the dimly lit shower. I commit it all to memory – perky breasts, legs for days, and hips I want to grip as I bury myself inside her.

I smile slowly, holding out my hand to her as I did last night. She enters the shower without hesitating, pulling the door closed. I scoot to the edge of the bench as she points beside me. "What's with the folded towels?"

"Your knees were red last night from kneeling on the bench."

She blushes then, a gorgeous pink. "I didn't notice," she admits.

I noticed everything about her last night.

She straddles me immediately, keeping her body slightly above me and wrapping her arms around my neck. "Hi," she says, suddenly shy.

I grin and move forward, my lips barely brushing hers. "Hi." I distract her with my lips while reaching for the showerhead, spraying her clothes, and she gasps. "Too cold?" I murmur against her mouth.

"No."

I return the showerhead to its holder, angling it to keep the warm mist splashing in our direction, then pull back to look at her. The wet cloth is so sheer, she's almost naked before me.

Almost.

Rosy peaks stand out sharply as the fabric melts against her full breasts and flat stomach. Her shorts leave nothing to the imagination, clinging to her folds, molding to her ass.

"So beautiful," I murmur, brushing her hair back. She bites her lip, and I can almost hear her internal dissent. "Fucking gorgeous." I pull her to me and kiss her until she's breathless, her fingers gripping my hair, her body pressed tightly to mine. She tastes like honey and mint and smells like summer, like coconut and sunshine, jasmine and ocean breezes. I trail hot kisses down her neck, and she clutches my shoulders, moaning as I suckle along her collarbone, grazing her with my teeth before rubbing my stubble against the curve of her throat. My hands slide down her body to cup her firm ass.

She kneels above me, surprising me, thrusting her breasts toward me, and I'm happy to oblige. I reach for them, massaging them through the filmy fabric, and she moans. My mouth closes over one rosy peak as my fingers find the other, sucking and tugging simultaneously. Her breath comes in gasps as I work her nipples mercilessly.

She pulls back suddenly, her hands gripping the hem of her shirt an instant before she peels it over her head, baring her breasts.

Fucking. Gorgeous.

My cock throbs a steady drumbeat, aching to be inside her.

Not tonight.

She pulls my head toward her chest, and I know she doesn't want to think about her scars being exposed. Not a problem. I can distract her. And I do, caressing and tasting, teasing and licking, nuzzling and grazing them with my soft stubble until she's ready to combust, and for that matter, so am I.

Only then do I ease her down onto my lap, adjusting her until my thick cock slides between her soaked folds. There's fabric between us, but her heat and moisture are unmistakable, and the perfume of her arousal only makes me harder. My hands cup her perfect ass, sliding her back and forth over my cock, and she moans and bites her lip. She hangs onto my shoulders for balance, swirling her hips, rubbing her pussy all over my cock, and I groan, aching to be inside her. She spreads her legs wider, giving me better access. I can feel her entrance even through her clothes, and my hips arch against her of their own accord.

"Yes," she moans, her fingers digging into me. I'm arching and thrusting, while she's rolling her hips and grinding her clit against me. Pressure starts to build deep inside my body. I grip her hips tightly, watching her beautiful face. She's panting with desire, biting her lip, one long moan after another escaping her as she rides me, her breasts bouncing. She opens her eyes then, green and glazed with desire, and she cups her breasts in her hands, pushing them toward my face. My cock surges against her core, and she holds my gaze as she rapidly approaches her peak.

I pull her down hard, grinding my pelvis against her, circling, and she comes undone. She lets go of her breasts, instead grabbing my hips and tucking my body even closer against hers. I'm teetering on the edge of control when she pushes her core firmly against me, crying out my name. Her mouth drops to my shoulder and she sinks her teeth in, gasping, her nails digging into my hips. Her pussy convulses so hard that even through our clothing, it grips my cock, and the sensation pushes me over the edge. I explode with a growl, my cock pulsating as the storm of pleasure rushes over me.

So much for waiting until I was balls-deep inside her.

My musky scent joins hers in the humid air.

So. Fucking. Embarrassing.

I feel like a fumbling teenager with zero control. I drop my head onto her shoulder. "Dammit," I mutter, my chest heaving.

She raises her head. "What?"

I gesture toward my groin, and she looks confused. "I enjoyed that more than I'd planned to," I hedge.

She smiles. "That was the point."

"What do you mean?"

"I have no intention of being the only one enjoying things," she says pointedly, "so I took off my top."

"For me?"

She grins. "I've seen my breasts before. You needed a push to make you let go."

I'm speechless. Instead, I plunder her mouth, letting my body say what I can't put into words. I can't tell her how I feel, but I can show her.

I've never been happier in my life.

My trip to the VA in Pueblo to get ready for my osseointegration surgery is in a few days, and if all goes well, a few weeks after that, I'll have the surgery. Normalcy is in my future – my near future.

After Charlie falls asleep, I let myself think about what I want after my surgery. Who I want. Forever.

The next morning, instead of taking my antidepressant, I shove the bottle into my night table drawer. I don't need it anymore. I'm the furthest from depressed I've ever been. I have Charlie, and life is fucking awesome.

TUCKER

If I've ever complained in the past about Lila having PMS, whether honestly or in jest, I'd like to formally retract every word.

Seriously.

Whatever she had before was nothing compared to this.

Holy Mother of God.

She's a damn roller coaster of emotions now. Anxious and then frustrated, weepy to instantly pissed, followed by horny as hell and insatiable, all in the space of an hour.

Everything I say is the wrong thing to say. Everything I do – well, you get the idea.

It's okay. I'll ride this out with her for as long as it takes.

But dear God, I hope these shots work.

CHAPTER NINE

MARK

IT'S LATE AT NIGHT, and I'm in bed with Charlie. She's got one exquisite leg slung over my waist, and her knee grazes my groin. Her breasts nestle against my chest, and her silky hair spreads over me like a curtain. She's wearing a tee shirt and lacy boyshort panties; I'm in my boxer briefs. She curled half-atop me after our now-nightly routine of heavy petting in my shower. She's currently in and out of a light slumber, and I'm rock hard, remembering the feel of her skin on mine, slick and wet, water sluicing over her full breasts as she trailed kisses along my collarbone.

If anyone had told me that fooling around without penetration could feel this good, I'd never have believed them. Charlie and I haven't had sex – not yet, anyway – but I've come harder with her than with anyone else I've ever been with.

She stirs with a soft moan, and I nudge her head back a bit, exposing her throat. I drop my mouth to her neck and nuzzle, rubbing my soft whiskers over her satiny skin, something that drives her wild.

"Mmmm," she murmurs with a shiver, then rolls off me and away, onto her stomach.

The invitation of her delectable curves draws me like a moth to a flame. I stretch my body out above hers, nosing her head to the side again to kiss her neck. She sighs contentedly. I slip my hands beneath her and cup her full breasts through her thin shirt. Her nipples pebble against my fingers, and I tease them through the fabric. She sighs again, and I lean into her, my hips pressing against her lush backside. My clothed cock grazes the hollow between her thighs. Charlie writhes beneath me. Her breathing quickens. I roll my hips into hers, and she writhes again.

A sudden sharp elbow to my ribs is followed by a panicked, "No!" I freeze, startled, then quickly move off her. Charlie scrambles across the bed, her fists clenched as she flings herself back against the headboard. Her eyes are wide, her pupils dark pools.

She's guarding her back?

From me?

What the hell?

Charlie was enjoying herself – at least, I thought she was. Soft moans. Contented sighs. But one look at her anxious face tells me I couldn't be more wrong.

She's scared.

Of me.

And I have absolutely no idea why.

My eyes linger over her face, confused by her distress. I don't understand. I kissed her neck and caressed her breasts through her clothes. We did far more than that just a few hours ago.

Then I look more closely at her eyes. Despite the fear, she looks disoriented. And groggy.

My stomach clenches. Charlie *was* awake... wasn't she?

Jesus Christ.

Did I grope her in her sleep? Was I touching her without her consent?

The truth hits me like a bullet as I realize that's exactly what I just did.

Horror washes over me, and I shove myself backwards, putting as much space between us as I can. "Jesus, Charlie, I'm so sorry," I stammer, my voice hoarse. "I thought you were awake. I thought –" My throat closes, and I can't speak, can't explain how badly I misread things. I turn away, grabbing my crutches and hauling myself across the room to the chaise.

She won't want me anywhere near her, not after what I've just done.

"I'm sorry, Baby Girl. So fucking sorry. I won't touch you again, I swear." Her breath still comes in short bursts, but her panicked expression is fading. "I'll call Tucker to come get me so you don't have to be around me. My phone's on the bedside table. I just need to get it."

She shakes her head quickly, but I'm not sure if she means, "No, don't come near me," or "No, don't leave," and I'm too afraid of her response to ask. I watch her close her eyes and breathe deeply. I recognize the pattern – inhale for four, hold for four, exhale for four. The psychiatrist at Walter Reed encouraged her to try it when she felt a panic attack coming on.

Fuck.

I manhandled her to the verge of a panic attack.

"Do you need Lila?" I ask quietly. She shakes her head without opening her eyes. After another minute or two, her breathing's returned to normal. She hugs her knees to her chest and buries her face in her arms.

I lie back, my arm over my eyes, hating myself for hurting her.

Again.

CHARLIE

I don't sleep a wink for the rest of the night, and I don't say a single word to Mark. What *can* I say? "Sorry I'm such a fuck-up," maybe? Or "I didn't mean to freak out over literally nothing," perhaps? Or how about my personal favorite – "Sorry I confused you with an asshole rapist." The wounded look in his eyes is almost more than I can bear. It's almost a relief when he throws his arm over his eyes so I can't see them. Still, I feel pain and frustration pulsing from him in sharp waves. I spend the rest of the night with my knees drawn up, hiding my face in shame.

As soon as I'm sure Lila will be awake, I slip from the room and hurry upstairs. "Come 2 work early? REALLY need 2 talk," I text, then turn on the shower. Before the water's had time to warm up, she's answered.

"Can be there in 15m. 30 if u want sugar and caffeine."

"Definitely 30," I reply, climbing under the warm spray.

My shower is brief and perfunctory, because showering makes me think of Mark's shower, which in turn, makes me recall our recent shower play, inevitably leading to me replaying last night's fiasco. I hurry to finish, quickly dressing. I don't bother drying my hair, and my attempt at makeup goes no further than foundation and lip gloss.

I'm curled up on the white sofa in my office when I hear keys jingle down the hall. "It's me," Lila calls. The paper bag of pastries in one arm rustles as she enters, balancing a cardboard tray with two large coffees. At the sight of her, I burst into tears, startling myself as much as Lila. She deposits her cargo on the nearest surface and rushes to me, gathering me into her arms. "What the hell, Charlie? Are you alright?" She pulls back long enough to scan me for injuries – a holdover from medic life – then wraps her arms around me again and lets me cry.

"You should have called me sooner," she admonishes when my tears finally subside. "Tell me what happened."

"I'm not sure," I admit, sitting up and wiping my eyes. "I thought I was dreaming at first. I was sleeping against Mark's chest. I think he kissed my neck, but it's all kind of fuzzy. I had a flashback or something. I don't remember what he and I were doing, but I guess – I guess we were fooling around. I don't know. All I know is that all of a sudden, I wasn't there. I was back in that cell, and –" I stop, swallowing hard. "Anyway, the next thing I remember is fighting to get away. I came around with my back against the headboard and my hands in fists, and Mark looked confused as hell. And then appalled," I added. "He apologized. He said he thought I was awake, and I'm pretty sure

I was. I don't know what happened." I rub my hand wearily over my eyes. "Mark deserves someone he doesn't have to go through this shit with."

"Charlie, I love you, but shut the fuck up," she says kindly. "This isn't about anyone deserving anything. You had a flashback. You didn't have it on purpose, and Mark certainly didn't try to cause it. As shitty as it is, this is part of the recovery process."

"So this is going to keep happening?" Dismay tinges my voice.

"Not necessarily, but it might. It happened to me a lot when Tucker and I first started being intimate again," she reminds me. "We got through it, though."

I sigh heavily. "So what do I need to do?"

"Is this the first one you've had?"

"Like this, yeah. I had a few early on, but never when I was with someone."

"You haven't *been* with anyone since then," she says pointedly. "I think your best bet might be to give Willow a call and see if she can see you."

Of course.

Willow Entwein, sex therapist extraordinaire.

I say that in jest, but it's actually not far from the truth. I saw her earlier this year after scoffing when Lila first suggested it. At the time, I couldn't even be alone with any male besides Mark without fighting the urge to panic. Why on earth would I possibly need a sex therapist?

But Willow turned out to be an invaluable help. By following her recommendations about intentional vulnerability, I was able to move past my fear of male touch with Tom and Tucker. I gradually relearned that not all male touch is bad. Six months ago, I'd have gone into a full-blown panic and broken out in hives at the thought of hugging either of them, despite the fact that I trust both men with my life. Now I can hug them without a second thought.

I get up from the sofa, suddenly desperate for large quantities of sugar and caffeine. "Tucker went with you to see Willow, didn't he?" I ask, retrieving the coffee and doughnuts.

"Doughnut holes," she says, gesturing to the bag. "Chocolate cake with clear glaze, plain glazed, and brown sugar-pecan. The coffee is medium roast with vanilla. And yes, Tucker and I went together."

"How did that work?"

She reaches into the bag and pulls out a handful of napkins, passing a couple to me before selecting a couple of pastries. "In the beginning, it was mostly discussing what we were doing that triggered a flashback. In detail," she adds. "Then we'd work on those scenarios in her office." My eyes widen, and she chuckles. "Not like that. We didn't have sex in front of her or anything," she says. "But one of my biggest triggers was being approached from behind. You remember when I had to get stitched up," she says, her eyes shadowing, and I nod.

At the time, Lila and I shared an apartment, and Tucker hadn't been home from the Army for more than a couple of weeks. He'd come up behind her when she was at the kitchen sink and slipped his arms around her waist, and she'd had a flashback. She and I endured similar tortures at the hands of our captors, but one thing specific to Lila was that every rape she endured was from behind. The bastards chained her facedown on a table, and though she couldn't see them, she knew what was coming. Tucker's innocent hug transported her back to that horrendous place and time. She'd smashed a glass in the sink and jerked free, brandishing a shard and lunging at him. He was quick, and he caught her wrist before she'd stabbed him, but she'd sliced her hand up pretty badly and ended up with stitches. That's when she'd started seeing Willow.

"Willow would have us practice over and over in her office. I'd stand across the room from Tucker with my back to him. He'd start talking to me from across the room, moving one step at a time under her direction. Sometimes it would take him half an hour to walk ten feet. We'd stop when he was right behind me and hold our positions, not touching. It was terrifying. I knew it was him, but that didn't keep me from having panic attacks," she admits, shaking her head. "It took months before I could let him touch me when I couldn't see his face, even with both of them coaching me."

I gulp, hoping it won't take that long to sort things out for me. I've got more than enough issues as it is. "Do you think I need to take Mark with me?"

"Talk to her one-on-one first and see what she thinks. If it's the only time it's happened while you two've been fooling around, maybe not. If it becomes a pattern, you might." She points at me with a pastry. "Eat. I'm sending Tucker over to talk to Mark this morning."

"Why?"

"Because I'm sure he's as upset by what happened as you are." Guilt floods over me for letting my fucked-up life spill over into his again. "Tucker's been where Mark is. He can help."

I call Willow at eight o'clock, surprised when she answers on the second ring. I'd expected to get her voicemail, but her sultry voice slides through the phone. I'm even more surprised when she tells me she has an opening, and at five minutes to four, I find myself ringing her doorbell.

When I'd originally agreed to see an intimacy specialist named Willow, I'd expected someone different – a hippie, maybe, with long graying hair and flowy bohemian dresses. I certainly didn't expect an exotic beauty. Today, she's dressed in a white dress with cap sleeves, a narrow waist, and a full skirt. On first glance, it looks innocent and demure. Then I notice that the narrow neckline vees almost to her navel, and both sides of the skirt are slit to her upper thigh. Golden hazel eyes meet mine, and she smiles before leading me down the hall. Her dark tresses brush the small of her back, and brilliant red stilettos click on the hardwood floor. I take a seat in one of the plush red chairs in her office, facing her.

Willow smiles, her voice like warm honey when she speaks. "It's good to see you again, Charlie. You sounded distressed earlier. Tell me what brings you to see me."

I recount my overnight experience to her, avoiding mentioning Mark by name. Last time I was here, I'd said Mark was the one male I was comfortable being affectionate with because we'd been best friends for so long. Willow's skeptical expression indicated she didn't believe we were merely friends, though at the time, it was true. Our recent discovery of our attraction to each other isn't something I want to disclose, mostly because I don't want to admit she was right.

Willow leans forward when I'm done speaking. "What do you recall from just before your flashback? Do you remember him kissing you, or did you just find yourself panicking beneath him?"

I close my eyes, thinking back. "I remember him kissing my neck. I remember liking it." I think harder, then shake my head. "After that, it's a blur."

"Would you say you were fully present during the kissing?"

I rub my hand over my face. "I'm not sure. I'd been sleeping across his chest. I remember the kiss, but it's hazy. Sort of like trying to remember what happened the morning after you've had too much to drink. I have flashes."

"That indicates you weren't fully present. Was the encounter consensual?"

I stiffen. Mark would never touch me without consent. "Yes," I say firmly.

"So it began consensually, when you were fully present, but at some point, that changed, and you had a flashback." She tilts her head, waiting for my assessment.

"It was definitely consensual," I say slowly, "but I'm having trouble recalling being fully present. I'd fallen asleep on top of him. I moved, and he kissed my neck, and I liked it. I remember rolling over and feeling his body against mine and liking that, too. But the next thing I knew, I was sure I was back in Afghanistan with a man trying to rape me from behind."

"Your lover was behind you last night when this happened?"

I nod.

"During your captivity, were you always violated in that position?"

I swallow. "Most of the time. They could control me more easily from behind."

"There are two possibilities," she says, her clear gaze holding mine. "It could be that you were half-asleep and willing, but not fully in the moment. That would allow your mind to slide more easily into traumatic memories. The other possibility is that by being behind you, your lover triggered your flashback."

I consider her words. I enjoy having Mark at my back, especially when his hot breath tickles below my ear or his whiskers graze my collarbone as he nuzzles my neck. "The first option," I decide. "I was still groggy. It was consensual," I repeat, "but I'm not sure how much was me thinking I was dreaming about fooling around with him, as opposed to being aware we were actually fooling around."

"Have you experienced flashbacks before?"

"Not like this," I admit, "but this is the first man I've had a physical relationship with since my trauma. The other flashbacks I had were pretty early on. Loud noises behind me or strong body odor would trigger them. Body odor still does, though not as badly as it used to."

"What happens?"

"I have to get away," I reply. "Immediately. If it's a client, I claim their muscles are overly tense and send them to the whirlpool. I tell them it will loosen them up, which is true, but really, it's because the menthol soak we use will mask their scent. If it's someone in public, I leave."

"What happens if you don't?"

"I used to have full-blown panic attacks. Now, I mostly feel trapped. My heart pounds and my chest gets tight. Sometimes it makes me queasy. Once I get away from the smell, I'm okay."

She nods, her golden gaze steady. "Have you had intercourse yet?"

I feel my face heat, but I don't drop my eyes when I shake my head no.

Willow nods again. "The most important thing for you to do is to talk openly with your partner. He needs to ensure you're fully present during your physical encounters, and not just after you've been sleeping. Because this is your first relationship since your rape, it's possible you may find yourself dissociating if things progress. You may find that certain activities or positions trigger you. It's critical to maintain an open line of communication during sex. He needs to pay close attention to your responses, particularly if your physical relationship advances to intercourse.

"Another thing that can help," she continues, "is something we've discussed before, and that's creating fantasies. The more you visualize healthy sexual encounters, the more you prepare your mind to enjoy them. Start slowly. Utilize all of your senses. What do you see? Are the lights on or off? What is he wearing? What are you wearing? What do you smell? What sensations do you feel? Where is he touching you, and what does that feel like? Think of it as traveling a familiar path. If you've already enjoyed something in your mind, there's a good chance your body will respond in like manner."

The last time she'd mentioned fantasizing to me, I didn't follow her suggestion. In part, it was because I spent every night next to Mark, and I couldn't imagine fantasizing about Blake while lying beside my – at that time – platonic male best friend. Now? I have no doubt I can work up a few fantasies.

Our recent showers together have given me quite a bit of material to work with.

Of course, that's assuming I didn't scare Mark off by freaking out on him. Again.

At least I didn't try to shoot him this time. If he forgave me for that, he'll probably forgive me for last night.

Right?

MARK

I'm at the kitchen table with my head in my hands when the doorbell rings. I frown. I'm not expecting anyone, and honestly, I can't think of anyone I want to see. I'm too busy beating myself up for hurting Charlie last night. The doorbell peals again, one quick ring after another without letting up. I only know one person who'd be that obnoxious at this hour.

Sure enough, when I open the door, Tucker's standing there in shorts and a black polo with the name of his gym across his chest: Press On. "Brew the coffee," he says, holding up a bag. "I brought breakfast burritos."

He pushes past me into the house, leaving me to close the door and follow him. "I already made coffee. What are you doing here?"

He grabs a couple of napkins and puts the bag on the table near my half-empty coffee cup. He glances at it, then takes it to refill while pouring his own cup. "Weren't you listening? I brought breakfast. This little Mexican place on Highway 160 has the best spicy burritos you'll ever taste. Eggs, chorizo, fried potatoes, peppers and onions, roasted jalapenos, cheese, and salsa, all rolled up in homemade tortillas." He brings his fingers to his lips in a mock chef's kiss. "They're life-changing."

"Lila called you, didn't she?" She must have. Why else would he show up here out of the blue? "Save your breath. You don't need to yell at me. Believe me, I feel bad enough."

He frowns, carrying both cups back to the table. "Why would I yell at you?"

Huh. Maybe he doesn't know. "I caused Charlie to have a flashback last night."

He pauses, his unwrapped burrito halfway to his mouth. "What do you mean, you caused it?"

I explain what happened, feeling guiltier by the second. "She was terrified of me, Tucker. As long as I live, I'll never forget her expression."

Sadness flickers briefly in his eyes. "Believe me, I get it."

Tucker told me once that Lila had flashbacks when he returned after his deployment. They'd been engaged before her kidnapping. After her rescue, Lila was flown to a field hospital, then transferred stateside to Walter Reed. Tucker had been granted leave to see her, but because she was in the hospital, they hadn't been intimate. He was discharged a few months after her release from the hospital, and their renewed physical relationship triggered her flashbacks.

His visit suddenly makes sense. Lila didn't send him over here to yell at me. She sent him over to teach me what to do and, more importantly, what not to do.

"Tell me you have advice for me," I say heavily. "I can't stand putting her through that."

He shrugs. "The first thing you have to do is stop blaming yourself. More than likely, you didn't put her through anything. The bastards guilty of that are long-since dead. It might have been that she wasn't fully awake, or maybe she was more tired or stressed than usual. Stress made Lila more likely to have flashbacks, and at first, everything we did was stressful. Hell, just being in the same room with me could send her into a panic attack because she felt guilty about having flashbacks with me."

"Those fucking bastards," I mutter. "I swear, if I knew then what I know now –"

"I'd have tortured every goddamn one of those fuckers," Tucker quietly agrees, his deep blue eyes glittering with something dark he hasn't let slip in a long time. The last time I saw that expression was when we'd found two of our men gutted and beheaded on a routine patrol.

The bastards responsible for that incident had paid, too.

He inhales deeply and rubs his hand over his face, drawing himself back to the present. "As far as what to do, you already know a lot from dealing with her night terrors. Don't touch her when she's disoriented. Give her space. If you touch her, she'll believe it's them, not you." He waits for me to nod. "Talk to her in a calm, soothing voice. She won't register your words, but your tone of voice will eventually get through to her."

"So I just do the same stuff I do when she has night terrors?"

"It will eventually help, but Mark, waiting it out is hard. For me, it was harder than Lila's nightmares, because her flashbacks would happen when she was with me, awake. I had a hard time not blaming myself. The key is to do what you can to prevent flashbacks in the first place."

"How do I do that?"

"When you two are – you know, together – you've got to make sure she's fully present."

I frown. "Like the whole 'tell me four things you see and three things you can touch' spiel I use to make sure she's oriented after a nightmare?"

He shakes his head. "No. It's more about her engaging and interacting with you. She needs to make eye contact, say your name, stuff like that. Not just making sounds, because those can be misleading." I recall how badly I mis-interpreted Charlie's soft moans last night. "If you know there's something that's difficult for her, make sure she's with you, in the moment, the entire time." He takes a deep breath before glancing at me. "Lila and I have a safe word. If she starts to feel overwhelmed, she says her word, and everything stops. You and Charlie might consider that. Have her choose a word that grabs your attention, not something like 'Don't' or 'Stop' that she might say when she really means the opposite. Pick a word that's out of place in a sexual context, but easy to remember."

I nod, thinking. "Does she need to maintain eye contact the whole time?"

Tucker chuckles. "No. Charlie staring at you the entire time like a pigeon would kill the mood for both of you. You just need to be sure she's in the moment with you." He tilts his head. "Think about last night. At the time, it seemed normal, right? But looking back at it now, does anything strike you as being a bit off?"

"She never made eye contact," I admit. "She'd been asleep on my chest, and I kissed her. She rolled over, and..." My voice trails off. It feels wrong, sharing details with Tucker. "She sighed when I kissed the back of her neck, but she wasn't as engaged as she usually is."

He nods. "That's the stuff you have to watch for. I don't know if Charlie's verbal when you guys – uh – well, you know. And I don't want to know, because she's practically my sister. Follow her lead, and remember, active participation will keep her grounded in the present and keep you from worrying."

His words are reassuring, but I'm not sure anything will keep me from worrying about causing another flashback.

CHARLIE

"Pull," I instruct Tucker, my feet planted and my gun firmly mounted. Tucker hits a button on a remote control, and a four-inch clay disc – also known as a "pigeon" – rockets skyward from a launching station ahead on the right. I track the disc, staying slightly ahead of it, squeezing the trigger when it reaches the pinnacle of its arc. I follow through with my swing, smiling in satisfaction as the clay explodes into tiny shards.

It's the day after my visit with Willow. Tucker called last night and suggested the four of us go skeet shooting today. He knows a guy named Preston – because Tucker knows a guy for everything – who owns a hundred acres of land and has a private shooting range on his property. It's not – and I quote – "competition approved", but it's pretty nice. The skeet-shooting area is a large half circle, with painted lanes indicating the individual firing stations. To the left is a standard outdoor range with pop-up targets, hay bales, and bulls-eyes. Unlike the majority of shooting ranges, however, these are fully paved, making them wheelchair-accessible. "Preston's son is a paraplegic," Tucker had told me over the phone. "He's always loved shooting. He built his own range so John could shoot from his wheelchair."

Mark had agreed when I'd asked if he wanted to go, and that's how I find myself firing an over-under double-barrel shotgun at flat clay discs. I haven't missed a single shot. I had a passing familiarity with guns before entering the Army, but after their marksmanship course, I was hooked. I earned my expert badge and am proficient in a multitude of weapons, though handguns are my firearm of choice. I'd be ecstatic if Mark weren't having such a hard time.

Normally, skeet-shooting is done from a standing position. You stand with your feet shoulder-width apart and shift most of your weight to your dominant foot. Then you shoulder your gun, making sure it's comfortably mounted and your stance is solid. Only then do you call for the skeet to be launched into the air.

Unfortunately, Mark requires crutches to stand, and crutches aren't conducive to mounting a shotgun against one's shoulder. To participate, he's been forced to use a wheelchair, something he hasn't done since his time at BAMC. The wheelchair is throwing off his balance, frustrating him. When he swings his upper body to follow the skeet with the gun, he's tipping sideways onto one hip, and his shots are going wide. The more frustrated he gets, the worse his aim becomes.

When Mark's next turn comes up, I stop him before he raises his gun. "Can I make a suggestion?"

He shrugs, his face impassive. "Can't hurt. I haven't been able to hit the broad side of a barn today."

I squat in front of the wheelchair. "You've got the brakes set to ensure the chair won't move, but you're still off balance."

"No shit," he mutters, but I ignore him, instead placing one hand on each of his muscled legs. It catches him off guard, and his eyes widen. They grow wider still when I slide my hands to the inside of his thighs.

Tucker half-snorts, half-coughs behind me with a muttered, "Get a room." I grin, then push Mark's legs apart, pressing them into the sides of the wheelchair.

"Brace your outer thighs against the sides of the chair to stabilize your lower body. That should help your balance and leave your upper body free to move with the targets."

He studies me for a moment, then nods. I stand back up and wait as he maneuvers himself into position and tests it, turning his upper body side to side. Only when he's satisfied does he raise the gun, tucking it into his shoulder. "Pull," he says after a moment.

His shot turns the clay into a cloud of dust, and his mood improves, as does his shooting. When we progress to having two clays launch simultaneously from opposite sides of the range, I'm in my element, though this is my first time skeet-shooting.

"How are you so good at this?" Tucker grumbles good-naturedly.

"Expert marksman," Lila reminds him.

"Geometry," I tell him. "Their trajectories will be in the same area at the peak of their arcs. If you're patient, they'll be close enough together that you don't have to chase them."

We spend all afternoon on the range, and when we head home, I'm slightly sunburned. I'm quiet on the drive, remembering last night. I'd come home after my visit with Willow, anxious to talk to Mark, yet worried about facing him. He'd been waiting for me at the dining room table.

"No workout crew?" I'd asked, a little surprised to find us alone.

"Tom's taking Maya and Skyler to dinner and a movie, and Tucker and Lila decided to give us space to talk."

"Oh." I'd stood there awkwardly for a moment. "Let me just go change out of these clothes."

When I'd returned, he was accepting a bag of food from the delivery guy of my favorite Chinese place. I took the bag from him and led the way back to the table. Then I'd poured us each a glass of tea, and we'd dug into the meal. In my experience, food often defuses tense atmospheres, making discussions less difficult by providing a distraction.

"I talked to Tucker," Mark said finally, twirling lo mein noodles around his chopsticks. "He had some suggestions for me about helping you deal with flashbacks."

I nodded. "I went to see Willow today." He'd glanced at me in surprise, noodles halfway to his mouth. "The sex therapist," I'd confirmed. "She had some suggestions for us as well."

"Like what?"

"Talking, for one thing. Not just now, but when we're – um – together. Communicating. To make sure I'm fully present." I'd hesitated. "I'm really sorry about last night, Mark."

He'd put down his chopsticks and reached for my hands across the table. "You have nothing to be sorry for. Nothing," he'd repeated fiercely. "It wasn't your fault."

"It wasn't yours, either."

He'd drawn a slow breath. "Maybe not, but I should have been paying closer attention."

"We learned from it," I'd said quietly. "That's the important part."

"Charlie, I don't want to make things harder for you than they already are. If being with me is bringing up bad memories –" He'd trailed off, but his meaning was clear.

I'd frowned. "So that's it? I have one bad moment, and you're ready to throw in the towel?"

Pain flickered in his eyes. "I don't want to hurt you."

I'd leaned back, my hands still in his, studying his troubled expression as I scrambled for an analogy. "Do you remember having your burns cleaned when you were in the hospital?"

His hands tightened noticeably. "Of course."

"It looked very painful."

His jaw flexed. "It was."

"Burns are one of the most painful injuries a person can endure. One of the worst things about them is that you have to cause more pain to help the person heal. You have to scrub away the damaged tissue to allow the healthy skin underneath to flourish."

He'd kept his expression blank. "What are you saying, Charlie?"

"Sometimes, healing is painful. I'm okay with that, because the benefits are worth it." I'd squeezed his hands lightly. "I'm not ready to call it quits because of one flashback."

"You were terrified of me," he'd said softly. "I saw it on your face."

I shook my head. "I was afraid, but not of you. I was afraid of things in my past."

"I don't want to hurt you," he repeats.

I'd stood up then, pushing back from the table, gathering our half-full containers and sticking them in the refrigerator.

He'd watched me, his brows furrowed. "What are you doing?"

"Communicating," I'd answered. "Making sure you know I'm fully present." Then I'd peeled my shirt off and tossed it on the floor, meeting his surprised gaze. My leggings followed as he'd watched with hungry eyes. I'd paused, dressed only in a white lacy bra and panties. "I'm going to get in your shower now," I'd announced, unfastening my bra and letting the straps slide down my arms. "I'd like it very much if you'd join me." Then I'd turned away, slipping my bra the rest of the way off and holding it on one fingertip before dropping it to the floor as I walked away. I hadn't even cleared the kitchen when his chair scraped backwards across the floor and crutches thumped rapidly across the floor behind me.

We'd spent a long time in the shower. A deliciously long time.

Mark's deep voice from the passenger seat breaks my reverie. "What are you smiling about?"

"Thinking about last night," I answer, glancing at him, and he winks.

"What's the wink for?" I ask, turning into our driveway.

"The shower I'm about to take. You're more than welcome to join me."

I shut off the engine. "That's a very tempting offer."

He grins. "Believe me, I'll make it worth your while."

He does.

Twice.

CHAPTER TEN

CHARLIE

BLISSFUL. FOR THE FIRST time ever, that's how I'd describe my life. I'm floating on air, cocooned in perfection.

My days pass as usual – work, workouts, group dinners, movies, music, and weekend outings.

My nights? They're exquisite.

Once I'd made it clear that mutual enjoyment was my requirement for our shower sessions, Mark succumbed, and though it's – by his own description – like being a teenager in the back of a station wagon, neither of us gives a damn. It works for us. Mark wears his boxer briefs, and I wear lacy boyshort underwear, removing my shirt before stepping into the shower. I dim the bathroom lights so I can't see my scars, but as soon as our bodies tangle together, I forget about them. We haven't actually had sex yet, but I've had more orgasms with Mark than I've had in my entire life.

Yeah. I said *yet*.

Because I'm pretty sure we're close to taking that final step.

The last Thursday in July dawns hot and muggy. A gloriously bright sunrise greets us as Mark and I head for the VA in Pueblo for two days of pre-op tests and consults. Ribbons of pink, orange, and gold peek through lanky fir trees and craggy peaks as we wind our way north. Traffic is light, which is good, because it's going to be a long day. Nothing ever moves quickly at the VA. If all goes well, though, he'll be approved for surgery.

We arrive in Pueblo in plenty of time to enjoy a delicious pancake breakfast. At one point, Mark grins, leaning over and licking the syrup off my lips. I wrap my arms around him, returning the favor. Only when cheers erupt around us do I remember we're in public and dial down the PDA, blushing furiously.

Mark chuckles when he leans back, clearly pleased with himself. "You're sexy when you blush." When I feel his hand grazing my inner thigh, my face gets even hotter.

"You're only doing that to make it worse," I hiss.

"Come sit on my lap. I promise I'll fix what ails you," he winks.

A voice at his shoulder startles him, and I watch as our waitress, a plump woman in her sixties with a nametag reading Hazel, leans over and cups his cheek. "You promise, do you? Cuz I'll take a seat on your lap, Sugar. I've got a lot of things that need fixing."

Mark's mouth opens and closes like a fish on a riverbank, and I burst out laughing. He looks like a deer caught in the headlights. "Sorry, honey," she says to me, "but he needed his jets cooled." She pushes her glasses down her nose and bumps her ample hip against him. "But if your offer still stands, I have a break coming up in a few minutes."

I'm still giggling when Hazel winks and sashays into the kitchen.

"It's not that damn funny," Mark says, trying to hide a smile.

"Please. If it happened to Tucker, you'd laugh till you passed out."

"Oh, God," he groans, "you're not going to tell him, are you?"

I shake my head, and he looks relieved until I continue. "I'm telling Lila. You'll only pray it was Tucker harassing you."

Our first appointment at the VA clinic is with Dr. Walters, the orthopedic surgeon who will review Mark's studies and determine if he meets surgical criteria. He's tall and thin, with sparse hair and dark eyes. He peruses Mark's records before turning his attention to his residual limb. He runs his hands all over it, pressing, inspecting the end. He asks about sensitivity, pain, and range of motion. Finally, he slides his rolling chair back to the desk and takes off his glasses.

"I agree with Dr. Paxton's assessment. I think you're an ideal candidate. You're young, so your bones are solid and strong, and you'll have much better proprioception with an integrated limb as opposed to a socket prosthetic."

Mark's eyebrows pull together, and Dr. Walters smiles. "Sorry. I get used to writing in medical terminology and it just slips out. My wife says that's why I'm no fun at cocktail parties. Proprioception is the ability to sense vibrations from the ground in your natural bone. A socket prosthetic slips on over your residual limb, but there's no physical connection to your body. Because your implant will be grafted to your bone, as you walk, you'll be able to sense differences in terrain. It won't be as sensitive as your intact limb, but you'll still feel it and be able to adapt to changes in walking surfaces. It gives you a more natural gait because you're able to transfer all of your weight to the integrated prosthetic as you move."

Mark nods. He's read more about this than I have.

"The surgery is fairly straightforward," he continues, reaching for a lower limb model on his desk. The limb ends just below the knee and has a metal tip protruding from it. He tugs the metal tip, and the titanium rod pops free from the model. "Yours won't do that," he chuckles. "This is for demonstration purposes. This model has less bone remaining than you do, so your residual limb will be longer than this. I'll make an incision across the tip of your lower leg to expose the bone. Then I'll drill out the center of your bone to make room to implant the rod." He passes the rod to Mark. "You'll notice the rod's surface is grooved and porous. That allows it to fully fuse with your bone in about three months. By that time, you'll be walking on your own with your integrated implant and no crutches."

Mark's face lights up at those words. Disappointment washes over me at his reaction. He's counting on the implant to conceal his altered body, rather than accepting himself as he is.

Not that I have a lot of room to talk.

Dr. Walters takes the rod from Mark and returns it to the model before reaching for a skeleton on a rolling pole. The skeleton is wearing a fishing hat, complete with colorful lures, and a nametag that says, "Hi! My name is Bob!" is plastered to his sternum.

"Now, your tibia bone ends right about here." He indicates the area on Bob's bony form. "The implant will be inserted to about here. I'll know for sure after we take a look at your CT and X-rays." He rolls Bob back into the corner. "During surgery, a plastic surgeon and a neurosurgeon will refine the end of your limb. Do you have phantom sensations?"

Mark nods. "Not as much as I used to, but I still have them."

"While we adjust your limb to accommodate the rod, we can refine your nerve endings and remove scar tissue. That may help relieve them."

He asks if we have questions, and when we don't, he sends us back to the waiting room with a lengthy list of tests and consultations. Mark has bilateral leg X-rays to check bone density and ensure the prosthetic and rod are designed to fit the height and shape of his body, followed by a CT scan to get a closer look at the internal structures and their precise measurements. Blood is drawn to make sure he's healthy enough for surgery. He meets with a psychiatrist to evaluate whether he's emotionally prepared for the procedure. He's even scheduled to consult with a prosthetic specialist to review his options and decide what model suits his needs.

It's an all-day affair. The prosthetist is his last appointment, and he shows us into his treatment room. It's very similar to the rehab gyms Mark is familiar with. It has parallel bars, wooden stairs, bright orange cones, and a ladder in one corner for agility training.

"I'm Chris," he says, holding out his hand. "I understand you're here for an integrated right lower extremity implant. I'm here to help you decide on all the bells and whistles. Let's talk about what you want."

I've spent years around veterans with amputations and artificial limbs, but even my head is swimming at all the available choices. Once you get into the more modern prosthetics, the options are limitless. Robotics. Bionics. Hydraulics. Carbon-fiber. Waterproof. Bladed feet. Foot-shaped feet. Colors. Patterns. Skins, with and without tattoos. It's overwhelming, but Chris narrows the options to fit Mark's desired lifestyle and activities.

Mark finally chooses a carbon-fiber leg with a hydraulic ankle for everyday use, and a Caucasian-skinned shower leg with a non-slip sole.

"I'm this close to being normal again," he says excitedly as we exit the building, holding his fingers barely an inch apart.

I stop walking. "Mark, you are normal."

He frowns. "You know what I mean. I won't have to look like this." He gestures down at the end of his residual limb peeking out from the bottom of his shorts.

"You know what? I like you like this. You're you. You're real. And you're perfect just the way you are."

He makes a face and turns toward the car. After a moment, I follow him, climbing in.

Since we have to see Dr. Walters again tomorrow morning, we've opted to stay in Pueblo overnight rather than drive home and back again. Our drive to the hotel is silent.

When we pull into the hotel parking lot, he reaches for my hand. "I'm sorry. I know you meant what you said. I love that you see me for me. It's just – I'm not there yet. To me, my leg is a reminder of everything I've lost." He swallows hard and his jaw clenches.

I reach out and stroke his face. He closes his eyes, pushing his face into my palm. I wait for him to open his eyes and look at me.

"Do you remember the night I showed Blake my scars?"

His pale blue eyes flare instantly at the reminder of the asshole I went out with a handful of times. "I remember beating his ass," he growls, and I smile.

"I was talking about what you said when we were in the dining room. Lila told me to stop defining myself by my scars. You said even though they were a part of me, they don't define me, that they were proof of my strength." I study his face. "Did you mean it?"

"Of course I did."

"Then listen to your own words." I push my hand against his chest, right over his heart. "You're not defined by what you've lost, Mark. You're defined by who you are."

He pulls me to him, kissing me tenderly, deeply, before resting his forehead against mine. "Thank you," he murmurs.

"For what?"

"For being you. For being my person. For keeping me grounded. For all of it." He kisses me again, and when we finally enter the hotel lobby, my car windows are steamy.

MARK

Even though it's only four p.m. when we check in, we're both starving. The pancakes from seven o'clock this morning have long since disappeared, so we opt for an early dinner. We stop by a wine shop and pick up a couple of bottles before choosing a steakhouse. The steak and salads are good; their house cabernet is better.

We return to the hotel, where we open another bottle of wine and drink it from clear plastic cups in our room. I need Charlie relaxed for what I have planned for this evening. She's on the menu, and I plan to devour every inch of her body until she's trembling and screaming my name.

We meet in the shower as usual, both of us in our underwear. However, even though this is a disabled-accessible room, the shower bench's sturdiness is sketchy at best. We relocate to the bedroom, our damp bodies briefly chilled by the air conditioner.

"Do you trust me?" I murmur against her lips.

"Always."

"Then take off your wet underwear. I'm going to do the same. I want to kiss you all over."

"Sex?" she whispers, though she doesn't sound alarmed.

"No. I just need to taste you. We'll ignore him."

She smiles. "Your entity?"

I nod, kissing her firmly. She reaches for her underwear, but I catch her hand. "Wait. Turn down the bed." When she does, I shuck my briefs and sit, tugging the sheet over my hard-on before leaning my crutches against the wall. "May I?" I ask, my hand grazing her lacy boyshorts.

She bites her lower lip and nods.

It's like opening a Christmas gift I've waited twenty-five years for.

I slip my hands inside the waistband at the back to cup her perfect ass, pulling her forward. I dip my head, nuzzling the apex of her thighs through her panties, and she gasps. I rub my soft whiskers up her inner thighs until she gasps again.

Mine.

The thought appears out of nowhere. I ignore it. I have more important things to do.

I move my hands to the sides of her panties, slowly peeling them down her toned legs. I pat the mattress behind me. "Come here, Baby Girl."

She climbs into the bed faster than I expected, but she sits with her arms around her knees, hiding her body.

She's nervous.

"I promise you, Baby Girl, even if you beg, my entity won't misbehave."

"It's not that. I trust you. It's just..."

"Just what?"

She sighs before meeting my gaze. "I know it's hypocritical after what I said earlier, but letting you see my scars up close is... well, scary."

I shift toward her, careful to keep my "entity" covered by the sheet while I consider her concerns. "Well, we have three options. You could blindfold me. We can turn the lights really low. Or we can challenge your fears."

"Challenge them how?"

I love how she immediately zeroes in on the choice that takes the most courage. My Baby Girl is strong. She always has been.

I study her face. "You let me pay individual attention to each and every one of your scars. Kissing. Licking. Touching. I'll taste every single inch of you tonight, scarred or otherwise. I'll make tonight better for you than it's ever been in your entire life."

Her eyes widen.

"It's just me, Baby Girl. If it's too much, all you have to do is tell me. We can stop now if you want, just lie down and go to sleep. I'll never do anything you don't want me to."

Charlie takes a deep breath before rising up on her knees. Her bare breasts press into my chest as she kisses me. "Okay. Let's challenge them," she says breathlessly.

That's my girl.

I remember Tucker's advice about having a safe word, especially for situations Charlie might find challenging. This certainly fits that criteria. "I want you to pick a safe word, Charlie. Something you can say to let me know you're getting overwhelmed, and I'll stop immediately."

She frowns. "Like a BDSM thing?"

Charlie's endured enough bondage and sadism for a dozen lifetimes, and I don't want that association anywhere near our bed. "No. It was one of Tucker's suggestions. It's something he and Lila started when they were dealing with her flashbacks. Willow recommended it."

"Okay," she says, followed by, "What word should I pick?"

I grin. "Something easy to remember that doesn't have any sexual connotations."

She purses her lips. "Daffodil," she says firmly. "My favorite flower."

They were her mother's favorite flower, too, but I don't mention that since we're both naked and I'd rather neither of us were thinking about her mom right now. "Okay. Daffodil it is. If things get too intense, say your word, and everything stops. Alright?"

When she nods, I smile slowly. "Lie down on the bed on your back."

She moves to the center of the bed, lying down. When she's settled, I crawl toward her, careful to keep the thin sheet between my cock and her bare flesh. I pause to admire the view. Her golden-brown hair fans out around her. Full breasts await my touch, her nipples already pearled. Her hips are perfectly curved to fit my grip while I bury my cock deep inside her. I feel like a man in the desert staring at a bottle of ice-cold water. I need Charlie like I need air.

"So fucking beautiful," I murmur.

She tilts her head, an odd look on her face.

"What?"

Her voice sounds confused. "You really mean that, don't you? You're not just saying it."

"Of course I mean it."

"I've never watched your face when you've said it. You're being sincere."

She seems surprised by this revelation, surprised I would find her beautiful. I lean on my elbow, hovering above her to stroke her soft cheek, waiting for her to look into my eyes. "Yes, Baby Girl. I mean it from the bottom of my heart. You're so beautiful, you take my breath away."

Small hands curl around the back of my neck, pulling me down, and my lips meet hers in tender kisses. My tongue traces the seam of her lips, and she immediately parts for me. I angle my head to kiss her more deeply, exploring every part of her mouth. She's sweet like honey, and I can't get enough. She touches me, running her fingers through my soft stubble, holding my face to hers, sighing softly as our lips mold together again and again.

Eventually, I sigh and pull away. "Don't leave," she complains, and I smile.

"I'm not going far." I slide down the bed, pausing mid-thigh. "I promised to taste every square inch of you. I think I'll start right here." I nudge her legs apart, settling myself between them. I lift her left leg up, hooking it over my shoulder, and she sucks in a deep breath as my mouth closes on her thigh.

"Tasting me – all over – won't take long – if you start there." Her words come in sharp bursts as I nibble and lick her inner thigh. I stop, rubbing my whiskers against her soft skin, feeling her arch toward me.

"You misunderstand. It's a round trip. I start here –" I lift her right leg up as well, nipping at her thigh, " – and move down to your toes and up your back. Then I work my way down from the top of your shoulders and finish here." I reach up to stroke her damp flesh with my fingers. Her essence coats them, and she groans and chases my fingers with her hips as I pull away.

"All in good time," I promise. "I'm going to make this perfect for you."

I take my time and do as promised, licking and tasting, nipping and nibbling, nuzzling and grazing. Inner thighs. Outer thighs. The dimples of her knees. The curve of her calf. The bony part of her ankles. I suck her toes, and she moans. I bite the arch of her foot, and she rocks her hips.

"Turn onto your stomach," I murmur, and though she hesitates for a second, she complies, moving her hair away from her back without me having to tell her to.

I make the same trip north I just finished on the front of her legs, paying special attention to the hollow behind each knee before nudging her thighs further apart.

Charlie has several scars between her thighs, some of which extend to the back, and I devote extra attention to these, pushing her legs apart, kissing them, tracing each scar with my tongue, all the way to the edge of her folds. She's restless, fraught with tension as my face moves closer to her glistening pussy without touching her.

This is where I want her. Too focused on her pleasure to give a damn about her scars.

Then I move to her luscious peach of an ass, kissing and nipping, grazing her with my teeth, making her gasp. The scars here begin along the upper third of her perfect buttocks and continues all the way up her back, but I don't want her thinking about that.

My hand slips between her thighs, tracing the scars my lips just traced, my fingers hovering just outside her reach. She whimpers and arches toward them. I ease one finger into her folds, tracing them. She's so hot, so wet. She rolls her hips, straining toward my hand, and I let my fingers slowly caress from her clit to her entrance. She moans again.

My mouth returns to her back, tracing her scars with my tongue, kissing, licking, suckling. She arches toward me as I drag my whiskers over the textured flesh, moving closer to the worst of her scars. When I reach the brand below her shoulder blades, I softly kiss all the way across it. Her body stills, even with my fingers stroking between her legs.

She knows exactly where I am. This is the scar she hates most of all.

"My Baby Girl," I murmur over and over as I rub my soft stubble over it. Then I kiss it again, laving it with my tongue, lavishing as much attention on it as I intend to give her breasts and pussy.

My fingers slowly circle her clit, pulling her attention away from her scars, and she groans, rocking against my hand. I keep working my way up, kissing and tasting, until I reach her neck.

Time to give my Baby Girl some relief.

I nuzzle her neck below her ear, an area that's particularly sensitive for her, and she gasps and tilts her head to give me better access. I move my fingers faster as she pushes into my hand, adjusting my pressure and speed to match her movements.

I speak low, just beside her ear, letting my hot breath emphasize my slow words. "You're so wet for me. So fucking hot. Maybe one day soon, it'll be my cock inside you instead of my fingers." She moans at that, bucking against my hand. "That's right. Come for me, Charlie. I want to feel you come for me."

She cries out, desperate for release, and I work her scorching flesh until I wring her orgasm from her, feeling her spasm around my fingers. I kiss the back of her neck and shoulders while she comes down from her state of euphoria. When I feel her body go limp, I nuzzle her neck. "Turn over, Beautiful. We're not done yet."

"I don't think I can take any more," she mumbles, but she turns over anyway.

I take my time, kissing her temples, her forehead, the little crease between her eyebrows, the tip of her nose. Every time I get close to her lips, she tries to capture my mouth, but I move just out of reach until she huffs in frustration. I nuzzle her ear, and she shivers. "Something wrong?"

"Kiss me," she commands.

"I've been kissing you."

"Kiss my mouth."

I find the sensitive place between her ear and her collarbone, suckling and nuzzling, and she squirms. "Are you sure that's what you want?"

"Y-yes."

I move to the opposite side of her neck and repeat my actions, and she moans and shivers again. "You don't sound very sure."

She groans. "Kiss me, Mark, please."

It's her "please" that does it, and I return to her mouth, intending to get her fully worked up before I move to the scars on her breasts.

But Charlie has other plans.

I'm holding myself above her on my elbows when she spears her fingers through my hair and kisses me thoroughly, a blend of heat and tongues and moans and need. Her legs wrap around my waist, her ankles hooked together so I couldn't escape even if I wanted to. The only thing between her beautiful pussy and my rock-hard cock is a thin sheet, now damp from her essence.

That's when she arches against me, and I suddenly realize I'm about to lose control. Intense pressure is building inside me, and I need a distraction, right fucking now.

I drag my lips from hers and rest my head on hers. "Stop moving for a minute. You're too fucking hot and I'm on the edge."

"Mutual pleasure," she reminds me.

"Not until I'm done with you."

Her electric green gaze pins me. "Promise me." When I don't answer her as quickly as she'd like, she rubs against me again, and my cock throbs in response.

"I promise. Just please, let me do this. Let me show you what I think of your scars."

She releases me then, unhooking her ankles but leaving her bent legs on either side of my hips. I draw a ragged breath.

And here I'd thought I was the one in control.

I take a second to gather myself before returning to her neck. "You're driving me crazy," she groans as I nuzzle and kiss the hollow at the base of her throat and the spot where her neck and collarbone meet. I lift her arms and worship every inch of them, from her tricep to the area inside her elbow to the underside of her wrist where the scars hide beneath her bracelets. I suck her fingers, and she reaches for my hand in response, sucking deeply on my index finger. My eyes close as images of her full lips tight around my cock flood my mind.

Focus.

I work my way back to her chest, and once again, she stills. I pretend not to notice as I run my tongue over the scars on her breasts, lapping at them, suckling and pulling away with soft pops. When I finish with the scars on her right breast, I move to her left, bringing my hand up to continue teasing her right breast while I trace every scar on her left breast with my lips. I graze them with soft whiskers and lick every pale white line. Charlie's panting and writhing beneath me long before I'm done, her scars forgotten. Only when I've traced each scar do I turn my attention to her nipple, closing my mouth over its rosy peak as I work its twin with my fingers. I bite down gently, smiling when she gasps. "So fucking beautiful," I murmur.

I keep teasing her breasts with my hands as I kiss my way down her flat stomach, grazing her ribs, tracing her surgical scar with my lips, swirling my tongue in and around her navel, gradually working my way lower. I lick and nuzzle each and every scar on her inner thighs, moving closer and closer to my prize.

By the time I reach her satiny pink folds, she's glistening with need, and I growl deep in my throat at the gorgeous sight. I prop myself on my elbows between her legs, staring at her face. She's panting, biting her lip, arching toward me.

So. Fucking. Hot.

The first swipe of my tongue laves her from her entrance to her clit, and she cries out. I repeat the movement, lapping up her juices, loving her tangy nectar. Her fists tangle in the bedsheets. I focus my attention on her entrance, licking lightly at first before full-on tongue-fucking her. She gasps unintelligible sounds, pushing her delectable pussy against my face, and I can't get enough of her. When I replace my tongue with my fingers and curl them inside her to caress her sweet spot, she bucks hard against me.

I bury my face in her, sucking her clit in time with the thrusts of my fingers. Her heels dig into the mattress as her cries grow louder. She's so close to her climax that I can feel the tension in her inner walls. "Please," she begs, her fingers in my hair. I give her what she needs, working her damp flesh over with my fingers, lips, and tongue.

Her thighs clamp tight around me as her orgasm hits her like a hurricane. She rides wave after wave of pleasure, crying out my name. I don't stop until her thighs fall open and her body relaxes. Only then do I crawl up the bed and lie down beside her.

"So fucking beautiful," I murmur, stroking her hair away from her face.

She turns to me, pulling my face to hers for a slow, deep, lingering kiss. When I draw back, I'm startled to see tears in her eyes. I start to sit up, afraid I've hurt her, but she places a finger over my lips. "I'm fine," she assures me. "Just overwhelmed, that's all."

I look at her doubtfully, and she raises up on her elbow to kiss me again. "I promise I'm fine. Better than fine. I'm amazing. No, you're amazing. You play my body like a musician plays his instrument." Then she grins. "Speaking of playing with instruments," she says suggestively, licking her lips. "Your turn."

I chuckle. "No oral. You're the only one getting that tonight."

She rolls her eyes. "You can't keep making up rules after the fact."

"Watch me."

"Fine. Any other rules?"

"Same as before. Pleasuring but no penetration. And..." I hesitate. "My right leg stays covered, at least the lower part."

She nods, unbothered by my request. "I can kiss you other places, though, right? Just not your 'entity'?" She makes air quotes with her fingers.

I nod. "Dealer's choice."

She looks thoughtful. "I can work with that. Can you follow directions?"

I grin. "I'm a soldier. Of course I can."

"Then roll onto your back, Soldier. Hands at your sides."

And just like that, I'm at her mercy. She covers both of my legs with the sheet, tucking it so it rests just above my knees as requested. Then she kneels with her legs on either side of my thighs so that her core is past my cock. She leans down, her perfect ass in the air, sweet as a Georgia peach, pressing her lips to the muscles in my lower abdomen, tracing them with her tongue, kissing her way up my chest. As she moves up, her full breasts graze my skin, burning a path toward me. By the time she reaches my face, I'm already breathing hard.

Charlie shimmies her shoulders, making her breasts dance on my chest, and I groan. "Do you want to touch?"

"God, yes," I burst out.

"Go ahead." The words are barely out of her mouth before my hands are cupping her breasts, squeezing, teasing her already peaked nipples.

She leans forward, kissing me aggressively, her tongue swirling over and around mine, biting my lip lightly before drawing it into her mouth. The heat between us builds quickly, and she moans into my mouth as I knead her breasts. She arches closer, and as her abdomen dips down, my cock makes skin to skin contact with her. I suck in a deep breath as the intensity between us immediately rockets to another level.

That's when she sits back on her heels, still straddling my thighs, my cock at full attention. I watch, unable to tear my gaze from her as she slowly licks her hands. When she takes my cock in her wet hands and caresses my shaft, I groan in pleasure. I revel in her touch, awaiting a handjob from the sexiest woman on the planet.

What I get is so much more.

"Eyes up here," she instructs me, using one hand to indicate her face and breasts.

Then she begins to bob up and down, her ankles hooked over my thighs to help her move. It looks like she's riding my cock, using her hands to simulate sliding in and out of her warm, wet pussy.

"Oh, fuck, Charlie," I groan. "You're so fucking hot."

When I feel her damp heat graze my balls as she moves, I nearly come on the spot.

"I need to touch you," I say, my voice gruff. She nods, and I reach for her, one hand cupping a lush breast, the other sliding between her legs to firmly circle her clit. She moans in response. I feel her body throbbing with desire, but my control is slipping fast as her hands stroke my cock like they were made for it.

When she pauses to reach between her legs, I can only stare, mesmerized. She pulls her fingers out, wet with her arousal, and uses them to lubricate my cock, stroking with each bounce of her body on my thighs, her gorgeous breasts rebounding with each thrust. She throws her head back, moaning as I massage her clit. She cries out my name as she comes again, and that's when I lose all control, thrusting forcefully into her hands, my eyes fixed on her face. "Mine," I growl as I climax, exploding all over her chest and abdomen.

I'm breathing as hard as if I'd run ten miles, but I can't take my eyes off Charlie. Her eyes have that sated look, her chest is flushed from her orgasm, and her lips are swollen from my kisses. Her green eyes stare directly into mine as she rubs her hands over her body, painting her breasts with my seed.

"Yes. Yours."

Damn right.

CHARLIE

After that mindblowing – I don't even know what to call it – Mark reaches for my hand, dragging me against his chest, not caring the least bit that I'm covered in his semen. "That's the sexiest fucking thing I've ever experienced in my whole life."

I smile. "I was about to say the same thing to you."

"You're so fucking hot," he says for the umpteenth time tonight before capturing my lips in a searing kiss.

I've only ever felt this way with him.

We shower together again before spooning naked in each other's arms for the first time.

I wake before him to find his erection nestled against my ass. Just thinking about it makes me wet. When I hear him stir behind me, I slip my hand between our bodies and stroke him. I hear his sharp intake of breath just before his hands reach around and cup my breasts. His mouth nuzzles the hollow beneath my ear.

I want to feel him as close as he can be without penetration.

I shift my body and guide him between my folds, arching back against him. I gasp at the feel of him. Mark groans, his hand moving to my hip. Wetness surrounds him as he glides against me, sliding past my entrance to my already swollen clit.

"God, you feel good." His voice is ragged.

I arch back against him in response. "More," I beg, and he raises up on one elbow, moving faster, his erection massaging my clit with each firm stroke. He thrusts purposefully, his breathing harsh against the side of my neck, his hot breath driving me wild.

"Fuck," he groans, dropping his head to my shoulder. "I'm already close."

"Oh, God." My whimper becomes one long moan as he picks up speed. I'm on the precipice, my orgasm just beyond my reach. "Please."

His mouth pauses at my ear. "Come for me, Charlie. I want to feel you come against me. Let me feel it." His rumbled words, his breath on my neck, his thick cock sliding against my clit, all combine to propel me over the edge, and I climax hard, crying out, my contractions squeezing his shaft. Mark follows immediately, sinking his teeth into my collarbone as his body shudders and spasms against me.

Afterwards, I'm sure. Next time, I want him inside me.

I'm ready.

LILA

I'm out in the barn, feeding my goats, when the door opens and Tucker's brother, Shepherd, comes in.

"Sorry I'm late," he mumbles. "I overslept."

I shrug. "Late night?" I'd never say it, but Shepherd looks rough this morning. His hair sticks up like he threw on a hat with wet hair, and he has deep circles under his eyes. He's got at least three days' worth of dark stubble, and that's not like him. He may spend his days working in the barn and riding horses, but his grooming is always immaculate.

Shepherd looks nothing like the rest of the Maxwell boys. They all look like their mom, with light brown hair that turns to unruly waves if it gets too long and dark blue eyes framed by lashes I'd kill for. Tucker, Joey, and Ethan are solidly built, with broad shoulders and chests. Marie, their mom, says Shepherd looks like his paternal grandfather. He's as tall as Tucker, but his build is long and lean, his hair and eyes dark brown. They have opposite personalities, too. Where Tucker and his other brothers are outgoing and gregarious, Shepherd prefers to keep to himself.

"Something like that," he mutters.

I try again. "Hot date?"

He reaches for Carol Alt's halter. "You know it."

He silently leads my matriarch out to the pasture, and all the others trail behind her. Goats are often matriarchal in herds, and Carol Alt is the queen of this one. All my girls are named after supermodels, including (but not limited to) Cindy Crawford, Kate Moss, Heidi Klum, and Chele. It was only after working with Tom for a couple of years that he disclosed that Chele was, in fact, his ex-wife and Maya's mom. I don't think he knows I have a goat named after her. Funnily enough, she's my most hard-to-please, finicky goat, traits she apparently shares with her namesake.

I help Shepherd lead the horses out. I have four mares: India, a gorgeous black Morgan; Aruba, a beautiful white Orlov Trotter; and Paris and Madrid, a pair of striking chestnut thoroughbreds. Paris has a white star on her forehead, and Madrid has a white stripe down her face. All my horses are show or racing rescues. When horses can't perform to the standards the equine world demands, many are put down. I can't rescue all of them, but I can do my part.

Shepherd's land butts up to ours on the opposite side of our barn and pastures. When Tucker and I bought our land, we purchased a huge plot with a pair of barns, four pastures, a cabin, and a house. We realized afterwards it was much more than we needed, even taking our animals into account. Shepherd was looking to buy property that would eventually accommodate horses, so we sold half our land to him, including one of the barns and the cabin. We then hired him to run our farm. It works out well. Shepherd prefers solitude, and working with horses fits his personality. Besides, he's a nature photographer, so his hours can flex to accommodate his needs, and he can ride the horses up the mountain trails to capture truly spectacular images. All the canvas prints of nature photographs hanging in our clinic were from photos Shepherd took, and they're absolutely stunning. He truly has a gift.

"We're grilling tomorrow night. Want to come over for dinner?" I offer as we lock the fence behind the last horse.

He shakes his head, the same way he always does. "Thanks, but I've got plans already."

I don't get it. He always declines. I'm pretty sure he doesn't dislike me. Otherwise, he'd never have bought the land behind us and decided to spend his days running into me on a regular basis.

Then again, maybe I'm just too stubborn to take a hint.

"If you change your mind, we're doing ribs with all the sides. You can bring your friend."

He looks puzzled. "My friend?"

"The one you have plans with."

When his expression freezes, it hits me. Shepherd doesn't actually have plans with someone else. He just doesn't want to come over. And since he stops by to see Tucker at the gym three or four days a week, maybe the problem really is me.

I step backwards, averting my eyes. "I'm late. I've got to go shower before work. See you later, Shepherd."

"Lila, wait," he calls, but I turn and almost run to the house in my haste to get away.

I'm not sure how much of it is embarrassment, how much is hurt feelings, and how much is from the damn hormone shots, but by the time I step inside my foyer, I'm in tears.

It's the shots.

I'm not a crier.

It's definitely the shots.

I just hope all this crying means they're actually working.

CHAPTER ELEVEN

CHARLIE

LILA AND TUCKER JOIN us for dinner at my house when we return to Cedar Ridge.

"So everything went well?" Lila glances at Mark as she places a platter of grilled chicken on the table.

"Dr. Walters said everything looked good. They've submitted the measurements for the titanium rod and the prosthetics to the fabricator. If everything goes according to plan, I'll have my surgery by the end of August," he says.

"Do you have to go back to San Antonio?" Tucker asks, helping himself to pasta salad.

"No. I'm having it at UC Health in Aurora. They have a specialty orthopedics program."

"That's only a couple hundred miles from here. You can make that in three, three and a half hours, depending on the traffic outside Denver," Tucker muses.

Mark nods. "At least we don't have to fly. I don't really want to deal with crowds right after surgery."

Lila says, "Take the red-eye," just as I say, "Trust me, we'd take a red-eye flight."

Mark raises an eyebrow as Tucker chuckles. "They aren't fans of crowded, noisy flights."

My mind drifts from their riveting conversation, instead replaying the one Mark and I had on our drive back earlier this afternoon.

THE conversation.

I'd been restless, fiddling with the music, adjusting the AC vents, shifting in my seat. Finally, Mark had reached over and laid his warm hand on my thigh. "Spit it out."

"What?" I'd flicked a glance toward him.

"Whatever you're wrestling with. Just say it."

I'd hesitated, not sure how to broach the topic.

"It was too much for you this morning, wasn't it?" His voice was quiet, serious.

A strangled sound somewhere between a cough and a laugh escaped me. "No. Quite the opposite, actually."

I'd peeked over at him. He'd been watching me intently, so intently that I honestly wasn't sure he was breathing.

I'd taken a deep breath and steeled myself for a negative response. "When you and I first discussed – um, more – we both agreed neither of us was comfortable with the idea of sex at the time. We said if things progressed, we'd revisit the topic and see how we felt." I'd paused, my pulse bounding so hard in my throat that it bordered on painful. "Well, I – I'm okay with it now. I don't know if you are, and I'm not pushing you or anything. I'm just saying, if it – if we – you know – got to that point again, I'm – um – ready. But if you aren't ready, or you don't want to, that's fine."

Eloquent, I was not.

When he was silent, I'd stolen another glance, startled to find his pale blue eyes swirling with blatant desire.

"There's nothing I want more," he'd said, his hand tightening on my thigh.

Tonight.

Tonight, we'll take that last step. And as Willow advised, I've been fantasizing about it all day. Rustling silk. Hot kisses. Languid touches. Tangled bodies.

It seems like an eternity before Lila and Tucker leave. They're scarcely out the door before I look at Mark. "I'm going upstairs to shower. I'll be back in a few minutes."

Surprise crosses his chiseled features, probably because we've been showering together at night, but he merely nods.

I pin up my hair and race through my shower. When I'm dry, I brush my teeth and don a black silk chemise that barely reaches my thighs. I fluff my hair and glance in the mirror one final time before heading downstairs.

When I enter Mark's room, he's on the chaise, holding a book as though he's calmly reading.

Except his book is upside down.

He's nervous, too.

As soon as he sees me, the book tumbles to the floor. He sucks in a deep breath as he gapes at me. He's bare-chested, wearing shorts, not the boxer briefs I've grown accustomed to.

I pad across the soft carpet, stopping beside his chaise. "Want some company?"

His hand smooths the fabric over my hip, his fingers curling around the slit on the side before gripping the silk, breathing hard. I smile at his sudden inability to speak. "I'll take that as a yes." I straddle him on the chaise, kneeling above him, running my hands over the planes of his muscled chest before resting them on his shoulders.

"Jesus, you're beautiful." When he finally speaks, his voice is rough. He's still staring, an expression of wonder on his face. He sits up, his hands moving to cup my face lightly, and I'm startled to feel them trembling. He pulls me toward him, his mouth closing gently over mine, his kiss almost reverent.

It doesn't stay gentle between us for long.

Kisses turn hot and deep, his mouth insistent, seeking. Long fingers tug the top of my chemise below my breasts, framing them above the black silk, the taut fabric pushing them up. Full lips close over my hard nipples, eliciting a moan from me, the first of many to follow.

I pull back, reaching for his shorts, dragging them down his body, letting my fingertips skim over his body as I do. I watch his shaft spring free before resuming my place, kneeling above him just beyond the reach of his thick cock. His mouth finds my breasts again, and when he clamps down on my peak, I feel an answering throb between my legs. His hands cup my ass, squeezing, and he groans.

"You're fucking perfect," he murmurs, his mouth moving to my neck. My head drops back as his stubble rakes over my skin, his lips sending shivers straight to my core. One of his hands glides over my hip and moves between my legs, and I gasp at the contact.

"So fucking wet," he rumbles. "So hot." His fingers stroke me, rapidly intensifying my need, to the point that I pull his hand away, instead settling myself against his thick cock, nestling it between my folds.

His hands grip my hips, sliding me back and forth over his length, angling my hips forward so his cock is constantly massaging my clit. The pressure builds rapidly inside me. I'm panting with need, moving faster, and I push his hands away.

"Oh, God, I'm so close," I gasp, rocking against him.

"Give me a second," he groans, reaching to still my movements. I lift my hips off his, breathing hard, my body aching so fiercely for release that it hurts. His hands drop to his sides, fisting as his chest heaves. He squeezes his eyes closed.

His cock twitches, flexing against my entrance in unspoken invitation.

And I accept.

I shift my hips and sink onto him, taking his full length inside, moaning at the fullness. Mark's eyes fly open, his startled gaze finding me. His thickness stretches me deliciously, and every nerve ending in my body is on fire.

My body takes over, and I ride him hard and fast. His shaft strokes my sweet spot, and his pelvis massages my clit with each descent.

"No," Mark groans. "Wait. I can't –" His hands grab my hips to slow me, or maybe stop me, but I couldn't stop if my life depended on it.

"Oh, God," I wail, and then I'm sobbing as my climax overtakes me, white-hot fire and exploding stars filling my vision. My inner walls contract ferociously, squeezing him, and he bucks into me and shudders, spasming inside me as jets of his hot liquid trigger aftershocks deep inside me.

I collapse against his chest, breathing hard, utterly satisfied.

"Dammit," Mark groans. "I didn't want that. It was too soon."

I hear his words, and suddenly, I can't breathe as hot guilt suffocates me.

He didn't want that.

He didn't want that.

I scramble off him, horrified.

"I'm sorry," I say, my hand over my mouth, backing away. "I'm sorry."

The tears are falling before I run out of the room.

MARK

Charlie walks into my room in a silky black negligee, looking like every man's wet dream, and I very nearly come all over myself right then and there.

I'm literally that close to losing control, and I haven't even touched her. I've been wound up ever since we talked about sex in the car. The fact that I nearly blow my wad at the sight of her doesn't bode well.

My control doesn't get any stronger.

Hands and lips. Wetness and heat against me. Her sweet nectar coating me. Soft hands push me back as she moves above me, sliding her silken flesh along my cock. Her perfect breasts bounce with every movement. Her eyes close.

It feels so good.

I try to ignore the soft moans coming from her, because I'm barely hanging on as it is. I try to distract myself, but it doesn't work.

Fuck, I'm too close.

I'm about to come.

No.

I have to make this good for her.

Jesus, I'm not even inside her yet. I'm not sure I'll last that long.

"Oh, God, I'm so close," she gasps, her sweet pussy grinding along my shaft.

"Give me a second," I beg, reaching to still her hips, and mercifully, she stops, lifting herself above me, giving me space, though her desperate need is evident. I breathe deeply, my hands clenched, fighting for control, trying to back down the intensity raging inside me.

Then my cock throbs, twitching against her entrance.

My "entity" takes matters into his own hands, nudging her, and she complies, her hot wet pussy sheathing me, burying me to my hilt.

Oh, fuck.

She feels too good. Her tight pussy grips me like a wet silk glove, squeezing, and I gasp. My hips roll of their own accord, even as my mind screams at me to stop.

I have to make this good for her.

She moves above me, taking me deeper, moving faster.

"Wait. No," I groan, trying to pull back, to stop my body's response. It's too soon. I'm so fucking close.

Too close.

"Wait. I can't –" I grab her hips to stop her, but she's panting, already lost in pleasure.

"Dammit," I grunt, and her orgasm seizes her. She cries out, her head thrown back in ecstasy, and her pussy convulses around me, gripping me tightly as I thrust hard once.

One. Fucking. Thrust.

And I'm done.

"Fuck!"

Her inner walls clench around me, milking every drop of my essence as I explode inside her, all pleasure drowned out by my mortification. "No," I groan in frustration.

Fuck.

Charlie collapses against my chest as I berate my lack of self-control. I shove my hand in my hair.

"Dammit, I didn't want that. It was too soon," I mumble, furious with my performance, or more accurately, the complete lack thereof.

As soon as I see the stricken look in her eyes, I know she's misunderstood. She backpedals away, looking appalled, apologizing, running from the room like a frightened deer.

I call out to her, but she doesn't stop. She's so upset, I'm not even sure she hears me. Her feet pound up the stairs, and I hear crying before her door closes.

Fuck.

I wanted our first time to be perfect.

This? This is a disaster.

I hurry after her on my crutches, but the steps are a fucking nightmare to navigate, and when I nearly lose my balance trying to rush, I'm forced to slow down.

I don't bother knocking when I finally reach her room. She's facing away from me, crying. When I approach, she sits up, red-eyed, her expression crushed.

"I'm sorry," she says, a fresh rush of tears overtaking her. "I'm so sorry. After we talked, I thought –"

I silence her with a kiss, a slow deep kiss that both calms and confuses her as I lay her back on the bed, stretching out beside her, letting my hand trace down her lush curves as I slowly kiss away each tear.

"You misunderstood my meaning," I murmur against her lips, kissing her again. "I've imagined our first time over and over, but in my fantasies, I had some semblance of self-control." I pause, tasting her, fitting my lips to hers. "I was upset with myself, not you, Charlie. Never you. You're so fucking hot, I barely lasted that long. It's embarrassing as hell," I admit.

She pulls back, her green eyes bright with tears, studying my face. "Really?"

"Really."

I claim her mouth, tasting, teasing, caressing, until she whimpers and arches her hips. I nuzzle her ear, and she shivers. "How would you feel about a do-over?"

She wraps her legs around my hips in answer, and round two is fucking perfect.

I'm able to take my time with her body now that my desperate desire has been slaked. I linger over her lips, worship her breasts, and drive her wild, waiting until she's vibrating with need before I bury myself inside her. I fill her over and over with slow, deep thrusts as she arches, urging me on. Her nails rake my back, her heels dig into my ass, and she cries out her pleasure again and again before I finally let go, my body convulsing in spasms of pleasure that leave me weak and panting, utterly bewitched by her.

I can never get enough of this woman.

Mine.

CHARLIE

Once the sex hurdle has been breached, things between Mark and me completely transform. This is the ideal relationship – hot sex with my best friend, the man who knows me better than anyone.

And damn, is it *hot*.

I'm not sure if this is how regular relationships are. I've never had anything that compares to this. All I know is that we can't keep our hands off each other. Morning sex before I go to work. Occasional quickies on my lunch break – a definite perk to working next door. Sex on the chaise, the couch, the bed. Oral sex on my counter, the dining room table, and his bathroom sink. And even when we aren't having sex, we're always touching. He mindlessly rubs my back or strokes my hair, or I find myself leaning into him, wrapping my arm around his waist.

We've even started sort of – dating, I guess, going out to dinner and the movies, things like that, though in some ways, it's a little pointless, because we already have dinner and watch a movie or listen to music together every night. Sometimes when we're out, I see him staring off into space with an odd expression, but he insists he's fine. We double-date with Tucker and Lila occasionally, and when we do, I don't see that look in his eyes. It's only when we're out alone.

A few nights ago, he and I went to a dimly lit restaurant, and I skipped wearing panties. When his hand slipped beneath my dress to skim my thigh at dinner, I leaned over and whispered my secret to him. We didn't make it home. I found a pull-off along a mountain road and we leaned his seat back. I pushed his pants down past his hips, and he unbuttoned my dress to the waist and guided me into place.

That's the night we'd discovered that men could be multi-orgasmic as well. White. Hot.

It's become so easy between us, so natural, the kissing, the touching, the sex. I never knew a relationship could be this perfect.

I never knew *our* relationship could be this perfect.

The only shadow hanging over us is Mark's lingering disgust with his leg. Maybe as soon as we get him through his surgery, his life will be perfect, too.

MARK

Charlie is incredible. Our friends-with-benefits arrangement is going better than I'd dared to hope. Adding sex to a relationship as deep and complex as ours merely completed the circle. She's unafraid again – like the woman she was five years ago. She's confident. Self-assured. She's becoming what she deems "normal", but Charlie was never abnormal. She never realized it, but she's incredible.

And she's a fucking sex goddess.

Jesus, the things that woman does to me.

After work yesterday, Charlie went upstairs and changed into a strappy little tank top and pulled her hair up in a messy bun. That wouldn't be a big deal for any other woman on the planet, but for Charlie, it was huge. She's kept her back hidden for the last four years. Yesterday, on a workout day, she left the upper part bared for everyone to see. Tom kissed her on the cheek and told her he was proud of her. He knew about her scars, but he'd never seen them. He slipped his arm around her shoulders without a second thought, and her face lit up, pleased that he wasn't put off by them.

Something dark twisted deep inside me then. I recognized it when I heard the silent snarl deep within my chest.

Mine.

I can't wait to get this surgery, to get my permanent prosthetic so I'm not always hopping around with half a limb. I want to be good enough for Charlie. I want to be the man she deserves. I want to be more than her friend, more than her lover. I want to be her forever, and I want her to be mine. I want every day, every night, from now until the end of time.

But not until I'm fixed. Not until I'm whole.

My surgery is in a couple of weeks. I'm *this* close to everything being perfect, and as soon as I get this osseointegration surgery, it will be.

TUCKER

I step out of the shower to find Lila crying. She's gotten her period. Another unsuccessful round of attempts. I kiss her lightly on the head, wrap a towel around my hips, and step into the bedroom to grab my clothes for work. When I've dressed, I meet her in the bathroom doorway and lower my lips to hers. "As long as we have each other, Lila, that's what's most important."

She pulls back, her violet eyes suddenly flashing. "You're an unfeeling asshole, you know that?" She shoves me away and slams the bathroom door, locking it.

Yeah. These hormone shots are really... yeah.

I make the bed and sit down on it, grabbing my phone and texting my morning clients to tell them I need to reschedule, that something's come up. Then I sit down on the bed to wait for the storm to pass.

When Lila emerges from the bathroom, she's pale and red-eyed. She looks devastated. "I'm sorry, Tuck. I didn't mean it." Tears slip down her cheeks. I stand and pull her into my arms before she's done apologizing, kissing her soft lips.

"I know this is hard, Sweetness. But our family only works if you and I are solid, and whatever you need, I'm in – timed sex, fostering, adopting, kidnapping." She smiles, and though it's faint, it's real. "Whatever it takes, I'll do it. But we have to keep this –" I motion between us "– you and me, strong. I love you, Lila, more than life itself."

"I love you, too, Tucker." She stands on tiptoe, kissing me lightly.

I tighten my hold when she moves to leave, leaning into another kiss, deepening it. I tug her toward the bathroom, taking off her shirt, pulling mine over my head. I pull us together, chest to chest, my intent clear against her hips.

Lila looks up at me demurely from beneath long lashes that frame her stunning eyes. "I don't think this is on our sex schedule."

"Fuck the schedule," I say, capturing her mouth, sucking her lower lip.

"I'm bleeding," she reminds me as I peel her leggings down her perfect legs.

"That's why you'll be screaming my name in the shower. Now shut up and kiss me."

LILA

Another month. Another crushing failure.

But Tucker's right. No matter what, when it comes down to it, our relationship is about the two of us. Maybe one day we'll be lucky enough to have a child, but whether we do or don't, at the end of the day, it's still the two of us standing together, and we can't allow our struggle to conceive to drive a wedge between us.

We make love in the shower, and it's spontaneous and wonderful and somehow freeing, because it's about setting things right between us, not about trying to get me pregnant.

But as soon as I get to the clinic, I call Dr. K's office to set up my next ovulation induction.

CHAPTER TWELVE

CHARLIE

THE FIVE OF US are on my back deck, sipping beers and grilling burgers – myself, Mark, Lila, Tucker, and Stubbs. Stubbs flew in this afternoon to stay with us for a week. Tucker and Lila insisted on coming over. They couldn't wait to meet the man they've heard so much about.

Tucker's reaction when he saw Stubbs' six-five, massively-ripped body was nothing short of comical. His mouth had fallen open, and in an awe-struck voice, he'd said, "Jesus, you're a fucking tank." Stubbs had thrown his head back in laughter.

Lila shook her head, her lips twitching. "I apologize for my husband's lack of manners. He owns a gym, and he's a personal trainer. Please excuse him for lusting after your body."

Tucker flushed. "I'm not lusting after his body. The only body I lust after is yours," he'd said, kissing her. "I just find his musculature extremely impressive."

Lila lifted one eyebrow. "You know you're kissing me while staring at him, right?"

"It's a lot like looking at a supermodel," I'd told Tucker. "Once the initial shock at his perfection wears off, it's easier."

Stubbs had chuckled when he looked my way. "You've never looked at me like that, Green Eyes, and neither did she." He'd tipped his head at Lila.

Lila grinned. "I'm sorry. Have I wounded your man-pride? Should I swoon and fall at your feet? I could if you like, but I thought Tucker was doing enough of that for the both of us."

"No more swooning," Mark had pronounced with an exaggerated eye roll. "He's big, he's muscled, we get it. Stop gawking at him like a hunk of meat."

Stubbs batted his long lashes at Mark. "You're my hero, Pretty Boy," he'd crooned. Mark had thrown a dishtowel at him, and just like that, Stubbs assimilated perfectly into our little tribe.

"It's beautiful here," Stubbs says, lifting his beer bottle to his lips from his perch on a deck chair. His eyes travel over the mountainside, admiring the view. "So green, I can smell it. So many trees." His gaze halts on the gigantic tree with its low-sprawling limbs in my backyard. "You've got an angel oak."

I nod. "I love that tree."

"I haven't seen one since I lived in Charleston," he says.

I glance toward Mark, remembering my flight to San Antonio a few months ago to bring him home with me. Severe weather caused the pilot to change course mid-flight. I'd watched as pink lightning illuminated the purple midnight sky. The lightning had reminded me of my angel oak and a lesson about damage and scars. I'd meant to share the story with Mark, but in the excitement surrounding his discharge, I'd forgotten all about it.

"Come take a look at it with me, Mark. You, too," I say to Stubbs. "That tree has a very important story." They both stand and follow me, Stubbs taking long, powerful strides on his carbon-fiber prosthetic legs, Mark following determinedly behind him on his crutches. I stop at the base of the tree, running my hands over its rough bark.

"A couple of years ago, I was home during a spring thunderstorm. It was a nasty storm – the winds were howling, and the rain was coming down in sheets. I was making soup in my kitchen when I heard what sounded like a rifle shot. I dropped to the floor." I look at Mark, then Stubbs. "Habit," I explain, and both fellow combat veterans nod. "Then I realized the sound was a lightning strike. I looked out the window and saw smoke rising from my tree, but no flames."

I move my hands to one side, tracing a healed, barkless gash with my fingertips. "I came outside after the storm passed. The lightning had carved a path from its upper trunk–" I point, though thick leaves obscure the area where the lightning struck "–all the way to the ground. Bits of bark that had exploded off the trunk littered the ground. I was afraid I'd lose my tree. Thousands of trees die from lightning strikes every year."

I turn to Stubbs. "But it was amazing. Over the summer, the bugs ate away the charred wood. The opposite side of the tree stayed green, and when autumn came, its leaves changed color like always and fell to the ground. In the spring, my tree fully leafed out, just like always. The only evidence anything ever happened to the tree was its scar." I look at Mark, finding his pale blue eyes watching me, his jaw tight. He knows where I'm going with this, and he doesn't like it. "The lightning could have killed it, but it didn't. The damage is a permanent part of the tree, but it doesn't limit it. My tree thrives despite it, because it's more than its damage and scars."

Stubbs moves beside me, pulling my gaze away from Mark as he lays one huge dark hand against the trunk. "It was beautiful to me before," he murmurs, "but knowing its story makes it even more so. The truly strong are those who persevere through challenges."

Mark doesn't speak, and the silence goes on for so long that it becomes awkward. It's almost a relief when Tucker yells, "Quit fondling that tree and get up here. The burgers are ready."

A rude remark about exactly what Tucker could go fondle pops into my head, but I manage to contain myself. No sense traumatizing Stubbs on his first night here. Then again, he's a Marine. I doubt he'd be so much as bat an eye at my juvenile comments.

Mark's tension eases over dinner. The five of us swap military stories till long after the sun's gone down. Stubbs talks about some of his more colorful commanding officers, and Tucker regales Stubbs with stories of pranks we'd pulled on each other overseas. I light a fire in the circular stone firepit, and we move to the chaise lounges to gaze at the stars. There's a meteor shower tonight, and the skies are clear. With any luck, we'll see some shooting stars.

"There," Mark says a few minutes later, pointing. I follow his finger to see a white streak race through the sky.

"There's another one," Lila says. That one leaves a green trail in its wake.

"The crickets and tree frogs are loud tonight," Tucker says. "You know, I never knew I even liked listening to the damn things until I spent eight years in the desert without them."

"It's peaceful here," Stubbs says in the darkness as another meteor streaks across the sky. "A kind of peace I can feel all the way in my soul. How did you guys end up here together?"

"Tucker's mom and brothers live here," Lila says. "Charlie and I moved here because we didn't have any other ties when we got out of the military, and we knew the four of us would always be close. It made sense to go where Tucker had roots."

"Neither of you had any other family?"

"None of us do," Lila replies. "Charlie was an only child, and so was Mark, and their parents had been dead for more than a decade. I've lived in more foster homes than I can count. Tucker was the only one of us with a family."

"You guys are my family," I tell her.

"We've formed our own family unit," she agrees, glancing back at Stubbs. "We may not be blood, but the ties are just as strong."

"Family is more than blood," Stubbs agrees. "It's in here." He lightly pounds his chest with his fist twice. It reminds me of the way Mark and I used to thump over our hearts twice, a wordless "love you" when one of us was heading into something dangerous.

We stay on the deck watching the colorful streaks race across the sky until almost midnight, when Lila yawns. "I have to get home," she apologizes.

Tucker stands and pulls her to her feet. "Come on, Sweetness. I'll drive."

We make our way indoors and say our goodbyes. "I'll bring the coffee in the morning," I tell Lila.

"Make it a double," she says. "Tara's making a cinnamon-crumb coffee cake."

I return to the kitchen, surprised to find Stubbs rinsing the dinner dishes while Mark loads the dishwasher. I lean against the doorframe. "It does my heart good to see men doing dishes," I tease them.

Mark snorts. "I help with the dishes most nights."

I shrug. "Doesn't mean my heart is any less thrilled to see you two cleaning up."

Stubbs grins. "I don't just do dishes. I can cook, too. Maybe I'll show off when we go camping this weekend."

Yep. Camping.

It started off innocently enough. Lila and I were discussing renting a big lakeside cabin for all of us. We thought Stubbs might enjoy the time in nature. Tom overheard and suggested camping instead, because he's a boy and doesn't care about pesky things like indoor plumbing. The next thing I knew, Tucker, Tom, and Mark had reserved several adjacent lakeside campsites for us. We're closing the clinic at noon Thursday and not reopening until Monday. We've told our clients we're going on a team-building retreat, which is sort of true. The entire crew is going – Stubbs, Tucker, Lila, Mark, me, Tom, and maybe Maya and Skyler – the girls are still undecided. We tried to convince Tara to join us, but she'd laughed merrily and announced that if God intended for her to camp, he'd miraculously plunk her down at our campsite.

Lila's made lists of everything we could possibly need. Tucker has researched and planned all the activities. Tom's been amassing his camping gear. I had no idea he had so much of it. I knew he liked to camp, but since it's only him and Maya, I'd assumed he had maybe a tent and a pair of sleeping bags. Nope. Tom takes his sister and her family camping, and Tracy and her husband have four kids. At last count, we're taking five tents and possibly a sixth, plus enough gear for an expedition to Everest, because no matter how old they get, men never stop being boys.

At least it'll be easy to identify us. We'll be the only campers with a U-Haul.

MARK

The day after Stubbs' arrival, we spend the morning hanging out in the work-out room of Charlie's house. He's running on the treadmill while I work on my quads. I pause between sets, trying not to stare as I watch him run.

"Like what you see, Pretty Boy?"

I flip him off. "I was looking at your prosthetics, smartass."

He laughs. "That's what they all say." Then he slows the treadmill before stepping off completely, wiping his sweaty face with a towel. He sits on the floor beside me. "Look all you want." Then he winks. "If you're nice, I'll even let you touch them."

"You're not my type," I say dryly as I examine his prosthetics more closely. His carbon-fiber legs are smooth, with an almost-iridescent snakeskin pattern of black on black. Silver hydraulic knees and ankles are at either end. He's got cocoa-colored silicone feet, but they're concealed by the white ankle socks that disappear smoothly into his running shoes. I won't need the hydraulic knee. Stubbs' amputations are just above where his knee would have been. I'll only have the carbon-fiber shin and hydraulic ankle. Sweatpants or jeans will conceal everything, and no one has to know I'm missing a leg. I'll look normal again. I'll *feel* normal again. No more crutches or hobbling. No more women rushing to get a door for me instead of the other way around.

"Was it hard to get used to wearing them?" I ask.

He shakes his head. "They're a lot lighter than the slip-on prosthetics I used to have. I wore those for a couple of years, but they were too hard on my delicate skin." He grins. "I'd get blisters, and they'd slip if I got sweaty or my legs changed shape throughout the day when I was up and active. These are a massive upgrade. I just attach them and go, then take them off when I'm ready to go to sleep."

"So you're glad you had the surgery?"

"One hundred percent," he says firmly, "but there's an emotional and physical learning curve that goes along with it. It's not all sunshine and roses the second you come out of surgery. There's a lot to it."

I nod, but really, I don't care. This entire road has been nothing but a learning curve. Getting a permanent prosthetic will let me be normal again.

Only thirteen more days.

Stubbs joins me when I head next door for PT, where I take him over and introduce him to Tom. Tom greets him with a big smile just outside his office area. It's more like a half-cubicle, to be honest. There's an actual office tucked in behind the seating area, but he didn't want it. Tom prefers having his desk in one corner of the gym, facing the rehab area. He says it helps him set goals for his clients, because even if he's at his desk, he can monitor their progress. I've never seen him at his desk, though. He's an in-the-gym-with-you therapist.

A low bookcase about eight feet long separates Tom's desk from the rest of the gym. The top of the bookcase is lined with photos of Maya. There's one of her with her overgrown puppy, Bella. In another, she's holding her highly disgruntled three-legged cat, Eddie, whom she's stuffed into an unfortunately bright sweater. I glance down the row of pictures. Maya with her red-haired friend, Skyler. Maya leaning back against Tom's chest. Maya between Charlie and Lila, all of them laughing. Maya with her mom. That one's new. I notice it at the same time Stubbs reaches for it.

"Holy Mother of God," he murmurs. "Do you actually know this gorgeous woman?"

Tom glances at the photo Stubbs is holding. "My ex-wife and our daughter?"

"Your what?" Stubbs taps the photo of the exotic beauty with rich brown skin, golden eyes, and high cheekbones. She's standing beside Maya against the backdrop of a New York skyline. She's wearing an outfit even I can tell is designer and probably costs more than most people's mortgage payment.

"Tom was married to Chele," I offer, "and they have a daughter, Maya." Maya has the beautiful skin color that's the perfect blend of her mother's warm brown tones and Tom's ruddy complexion.

Stubbs looks at Tom. "You were married to a world-class supermodel in this town?"

"Briefly. We met in New York and moved here. When her career took off, so did she." Tom's voice holds a bitterness I've not heard from him before.

"So you two aren't together? No lingering feelings?"

Tom snorts and shakes his head.

"It would probably be very poor form of me to ask you to introduce us," Stubbs hints with a smile, though I'm pretty sure he's only half-joking.

Tom laughs. "Talk to Maya first. I don't care if you hook up with Chele, but you might want a more realistic view of her."

Stubbs raises an eyebrow. "You want me to ask your daughter if I can have her mom's number?"

Tom shakes his head. "I'd rather not involve Maya in any more dating drama than necessary. Just ask her about her mom without hinting that you're interested in Chele. It's likely to be rather eye-opening."

"I have absolutely no use for that woman," Charlie announces to the three of us as she appears from around a corner. She slips her arm around my waist. "But I'm biased. She completely ignores Maya fifty-one weeks out of the year and then pretends for the camera that she's mother of the year when Tom takes Maya to see her in New York every Christmas."

Stubbs frowns. "She only gets to see her mom once a year?"

"Chele only agrees to see Maya once or twice a year," Charlie swiftly corrects him. Her tone is sharp, but it's not aimed at Stubbs. "She's always busy – fashion show this, on location that, shoots coming up, blah blah blah. She's completely focused on her career. Nothing work-related ever falls off her radar, but she can't be bothered to remember her own daughter's birthday, holidays, or anything else of any significance. She never calls or texts or emails. She has an amazing daughter that she completely ignores."

Stubbs returns the photo to the bookcase, grinning at Charlie. "Is that the filtered or unfiltered version?"

Charlie snorts. "Definitely filtered. The rant I went on after she told an interviewer how hard it was to juggle a career with being a single mom? That was unfiltered. But only to Tom and Lila. I'd never say anything like that to Maya."

Tom sighs. "She wasn't always like that. We had some good times in the beginning. But her modeling career took off when she was in the late stages of pregnancy, something unheard of in that line of work. It went to her head, and she became a completely different person."

Charlie frowns. "I'd be willing to bet the signs were there all along, but you were too caught up in your shiny new romance to see them."

"Maybe," he admits, "but I hate the way it's affected Maya."

The guy I usually work out next to, Terrell, walks into the clinic then, and I make my way to the table next to his. He and I have similar injuries, though he's further along in his recovery than I am. We haven't been working out long when Stubbs settles on a chair between our tables and starts chatting with Terrell. In no time at all, he's got him baring his soul, talking about survivor's guilt. Two of Terrell's buddies didn't survive the blast that damaged his left leg and arm. I've worked next to Terrell for four months, and I never knew that. I've gotta hand it to Stubbs – he's good. When our hour is up, he's jotted down his cell phone number on the back of a card with instructions for Terrell to call him anytime he needs to talk.

The next morning, Stubbs catches my eye over coffee. "Do you mind if I go hang out at the clinic? Maybe talk to a few of the guys in rehab?"

I grin. "Of course not. Tom would probably love it. You and your Zen thing – you'd be perfect. I'll come, too. There's this hot chick that works there that I've really got a thing for."

He smiles. "I see you and Green Eyes finally figured things out."

I shrug. "We're still figuring it out."

He laughs. "A blind man can see how you feel about each other. Don't let that woman get away. You two have something special."

Stubbs spends the entire day in the clinic. He mostly hangs out in the rehab gym, but also makes sure to greet clients as they come in for massage therapy.

He introduces himself as "First Sergeant James Mackey of the 15th Marine Expeditionary Unit, but you can call me Stubbs," and he returns the salutes of those who offer them. I'm amazed by his talent for instantly connecting with strangers. Four different people invite him to accompany them to their massage session so they can keep talking to him. He hands out card after card to veterans, encouraging them to feel free to reach out anytime they need a listening ear.

He couldn't have picked a better day to visit, either. Mid-morning, an unfamiliar man in dress blues stops by to speak with Charlie. It was an unscheduled visit, so he has to wait about fifteen minutes for Charlie to finish the massage she's performing. Stubbs introduces himself, chatting him up the way he's chatted with everyone else. When Charlie comes out, Stubbs stands, shakes the captain's hand, and passes him a card, encouraging him to call if he ever needs someone to talk to. As it turns out, the captain is Dr. Reed Martinez, the medical director of the Pueblo VA. He'd stopped by to arrange for Charlie to come to Pueblo and discuss further services her clinic might be able to provide for veterans in this area. Dr. Martinez was extremely impressed with Stubbs, especially when he learned he was scheduled to take his boards to be a counselor to work with veterans. Charlie was grinning from ear to ear when she told Stubbs.

"Dr. Martinez said he'd love to hire you to help vets through our clinic. You'd be perfect here. I know you'll have plenty of offers, but keep us in mind. We'd love to have you."

Stubbs hangs out with me and Terrell during our PT today. Tom joins us, and the camaraderie between the three of them reminds me so much of the guys in my platoon that it makes my chest ache. I miss my guys. I miss the brotherhood, the teamwork, the sense of accomplishment when we succeeded on missions. I love Charlie and Lila and Tucker, but I miss having a sense of purpose. I'm like an old boat in the middle of the ocean, worse for the wear and without a functional navigation system. I'm drifting, tossed by the sea, with no agency of my own.

Twelve more days. Just twelve more days, and then I'll be normal. I can do whatever I want after that.

I can manage for twelve more days.

CHARLIE

Late Sunday afternoon, I admit to myself that Tom was right. I wish our outdoor weekend didn't have to end. I was skeptical about staying in tents instead of a cabin, but the weather has been gorgeous, and the scenery is nothing short of spectacular. The lake is nestled in a valley surrounded by tall peaks, the highest of which still has a dusting of snow. Tall birches and narrow pines surround the water. The lake was formed when a glacier carved out a bowl-shaped dent in the landscape. The water is crystal clear, reflecting the bright colors of the surrounding trees and shrubbery. In the daytime, the temperatures have been in the seventies; after dark, it's in the upper forties. Chilly, but nothing we can't handle with a light jacket and a campfire.

The six of us – Tucker and Lila, me and Mark, Stubbs, and Tom – have had a blast these past three days. Maya and Skyler opted to stay behind with Tom's sister Tracy when they discovered she was taking her kids to an amusement park. We drove up Thursday afternoon and immediately started setting up camp. We didn't need a U-Haul, but it was close. Our vehicles were stuffed to the gills. Mark and I quickly assembled our tent and inflated our air mattress. Stubbs and Tom worked together to put up their tents in short order, too, and the four of us stowed our belongings and mattresses in our tents while being thoroughly entertained by our lone married couple. Lila and Tucker squabbled relentlessly over the proper way to erect their tent. The rest of us finished before Tucker even hammered in the first tent peg. He and Lila were still grumbling by the time the rest of us had put up the large fifth tent to hold our (theoretically) bear-proof food containers and outdoor gear. Lila and Tucker were both sweaty and red-faced when they were done.

"Problem?" Mark had asked innocently.

"Only if you consider a man being too stubborn to read the damned directions to be a problem," Lila muttered, glowering at Tucker.

Stubbs grinned. "Just think of the quality time spent making memories." When she'd rolled her eyes, he added, "If that doesn't work, you can always push him in the lake."

Our campsite ran parallel to the water's edge, so we spent our first evening relaxing in camp chairs and fishing from the shore. Tom, Mark, and Stubbs caught an impressive haul of rainbow trout, which we cooked with butter and lemon and served with potatoes baked in the coals of our campfire. Lila and Tucker both caught several huge catfish which they released, agreeing it seemed wrong to eat animals that had lived in the lake for so many years. My sole catch was someone's old waterlogged sneaker. I didn't care. It was enough to be there, smelling the fresh damp air and green trees and listening to the friendly banter.

When we'd gotten up Friday morning, Tucker announced our itinerary: hiking up one of the easier trails, having a picnic lunch, and hiking back down. Mark had raised an eyebrow as he gestured to his crutches. "Relax," Stubbs said with a shake of his head. He'd headed for the tent with our extra gear. "I've got you covered, Pretty Boy."

Tucker turned to Mark with a huge grin. "I think that's my new favorite nickname for you. I just love the way it rolls off the tongue. Pretty Boy..."

Mark had rolled his shoulders and cracked his knuckles. "It won't sound the same without your teeth," he'd said, and Tucker laughed.

Stubbs reappeared with a pair of black forearm crutches. Instead of resting under one's arms, these fit around the wrists. "These are more user-friendly for hiking than those," he'd declared, tipping his head toward Mark's usual crutches. "Stand up. I'll help adjust them for your height."

That was the end of any worries about scaling a mountain on crutches.

We didn't hike far, maybe a mile or so at a leisurely pace, and we stopped often to admire the scenery, surreptitiously giving Mark a chance to rest. Tucker had one of his brother Shepherd's cameras. Shepherd is a well-known nature photographer, and I couldn't fathom him letting Tucker drag one of his expensive cameras out here. Tucker caught my curious look and grinned. "Yes, he knows I have it. He picked this one for me to use. He swears it's idiot-proof."

Lila muttered something that sounded suspiciously like, "So was assembling our tent." I'd hidden my giggle with a cough, but not before Tucker made a face at both of us.

The wildlife was active, and during our frequent breaks, Tucker captured pictures of deer, moose, and even a mother bear with her three cubs (from a safe distance, with a zoom lens). I'd sat on a log and patted the spot next to me. When Mark sat down, I'd tugged him toward me by his shirt front for a kiss. What started as a quick peck ended up being a lot more substantial. The whirr of the camera eventually broke through my bliss, and I blushed when I saw Tucker scrolling through what were obviously multiple photos of us kissing.

"You have serious voyeurism issues," I'd grumbled, but he'd simply smirked.

"He's not the only one with an issue," Mark murmured in my ear, his warm breath tickling my neck and making me shiver. "How long till we're alone again?"

My voice was quiet enough that only he could hear me. "Too long."

When we'd reached our destination, Lila removed her backpack and spread a waterproof blanket on the ground before passing out sandwiches, fruit, and water. We all sprawled on the ground, soaking in the sunshine and fresh air, and I remembered again why I'm happiest in nature. After lunch, Tucker unearthed cards and colorful chips from his pack, and the guys played several hands of poker while I laid my head on Mark's lap. I dozed off, only to wake when he'd ruffled my hair and stroked my cheek.

"Hey, Sleepyhead. We're going to head back down soon," he'd said quietly.

I sat up and stretched. "Sorry about that. Didn't mean to use your lap for a pillow."

He'd leaned in and whispered, "I have a much better use for it later."

I was certain he did, but unfortunately, we'd discovered last night that the air mattresses squeaked every time one of us moved. There was no way we'd be able to have sex without everyone hearing the squeaks, knowing exactly what we were doing mere feet from them.

"Monday night," I'd whispered back. "Stubbs flies home Monday evening."

The trip back to our campsite was easier for Mark, likely because we were headed down the mountain. When we got there, I'd glanced at our pile of firewood. We'd need more before nightfall. "I'm going to get wood," I told Lila. "I'll be back."

Mark had grabbed his rucksack from our tent. "I'll go with you. I can haul a lot in this." I'd nodded and grabbed my empty pack as well.

We were several minutes away from the campsite when he'd veered off down a side path. "Where are you going?" I asked.

"Just over here," he'd replied. "Give me a hand."

I'd added another dry log to my pack before trailing after him. When I followed the path he'd taken, I found him tossing a blanket on the ground beneath a tree. "What are you doing?"

He sat on the blanket and leaned back against the tree. "You can't kiss me like that and expect me to wait till Monday," he'd growled. "That's three more days." He'd reached for me then, pulling me onto his lap, and I was more than willing. His mouth closed over mine, hot and possessive. I moaned and straddled him. Strong hands cupped my breasts through my clothes, and I'd arched against him. He'd dragged my shirt up, pushed my bra aside, and clamped his mouth over my nipple, and I'd sucked in a sharp breath, praying none of our friends wandered this way. I rocked against him and he'd groaned, then reached for the zipper of my jeans.

There wasn't a lot of finesse in our coupling – no soft bed or warm shower — but finding this stolen moment in nature more than made up for it. Our lovemaking was heated and frantic, clothes pushed down and out of the way as our bodies fit together perfectly. I sank onto his thick shaft, and he guided my movements. When I came, I buried my face against him to muffle my cries. He sank his teeth into my collarbone as he spasmed inside me a short time later, wringing a second orgasm from me.

"I can't believe we did this. I've never had sex outside before," I said breath-lessly, raising my head off his chest.

"This was all your idea."

I'd shot him a glance. "It most certainly was not. You told me to follow you."

He'd grinned wickedly. "You'd said you were going to get wood." He wiggled his hips teasingly beneath me. "I gave you wood."

I'd groaned. "You did not just say that."

His sinful grin had widened. "Don't look at me. You were the one talking dirty."

I'd brushed the bits of bark off his shirt and he'd pulled the leaves from my hair, and we'd straightened our clothes before filling both our rucksacks with wood – *actual* wood, not teenage euphemisms. We'd returned to the campsite, and as soon as Lila had looked at me, I'd turned beet red. She'd given me a questioning glance, opened her mouth, then closed it and smiled knowingly. We'd been in the tent collecting food for dinner later when she'd grinned. "Tell Mark not to leave bite marks if you don't want us to know what you were doing," she'd murmured, tugging the collar of my tee shirt closer to my throat.

I wanted to crawl under the tent, but she'd just laughed. "I don't think anyone else noticed."

"You couldn't hear us, could you?"

She'd laughed again as she shook her head. Then she'd looked thoughtful. "Next time, *I'll* go get wood... with Tucker."

Saturday was nearly as much fun as Friday had been. We'd rented canoes and paddled around the lake. The water was so clear, you could see everything along the bottom of the lake. Tucker took picture after picture, not just of the wildlife, but of all of us. Finally, Lila took the camera from him. "Get out from behind the camera and enjoy this," she'd said, then snapped a few pictures of him as well. He'd rolled his eyes when she said, "I want to remember the gorgeous scenery, too."

Now it's Sunday afternoon, and after spending a relaxing morning exploring another trail, it's time to break down our campsite. Tents disassemble faster than they go up, but packing them in their storage bags is a much slower process. The same goes for rolling up and repacking sleeping bags and air mattresses. Still, with six of us, it goes relatively quickly, and before long, our campsite is as clean as it was before our arrival.

We're getting ready to climb into our vehicles when Stubbs speaks. "Let's mix things up for the ride home. Green Eyes, how about I ride with you?"

Mark's eyes flick curiously to mine. "Okay," I say, shrugging.

"I'll ride with Tom," Lila announces, and Tucker turns to Mark. "Okay, Pretty Boy, you're with me."

"You say the sweetest things," Mark says with a wink.

Tucker flips him off. "It's a long walk home on those crutches," he teases.

"Is that a cripple joke? You know those are in poor taste, right?"

Tucker rolls his eyes. "Just get in the car. Stubbs and Tom get to ride with beautiful women, and I get stuck with a smartass."

"Better than me. I got stuck with the dumbass," Mark quips.

The drive with Stubbs is pleasant. He's a great conversationalist, and the more we talk, the better I understand him. Yes, he has a larger-than-life persona, but beneath that beats the heart of a true Renaissance man. He loves full-contact sports, action movies, and military biographies, but he also loves art, poetry, and music. He's complex, a mysterious enigma wrapped in a riddle.

We're halfway home when he turns to me. "I asked to ride with you so we could discuss Mark's upcoming surgery."

"What about it?"

"It's not going to be easy for him."

I remember what I've read about the process. "I have no doubt about that. Any surgery involving drills and hammers won't be a walk in the park."

But Stubbs shakes his head. "I'm talking about the psychological aspects of the surgery."

I glance at the man in my passenger seat, drumming his huge hands on thickly muscled thighs. "What do you mean?"

There's a long pause as Stubbs carefully chooses his words. "This procedure requires a certain level of self-acceptance that I'm not convinced Mark has achieved."

I furrow my brow. "I don't understand."

"I hope I'm wrong," he says vaguely, "but if he's anything like me..." He trails off, leaving me hanging with his incomplete thought. I wait for him to go on, but he doesn't.

"So you had a hard time with the surgery?" I prod him.

He nods soberly. "I wasn't always the Zen type, you know? I eventually found myself, but not until after I spent a long time fighting."

"Fighting what?"

"The doctors. Friends. Family." He hesitates. "Myself, mostly."

Stubbs' nebulous responses leave me struggling to grasp his point. "You're giving me a lot of non-answer answers," I complain, and he laughs.

"I don't really have an answer to give you. More of a warning, I suppose. Don't expect him to suddenly be the Mark you knew a year ago just because he's had the surgery."

I frown. "I don't. Besides, I know him even better now than I did a year ago."

"Do you really?" he asks cryptically. "Or do you only know what he's letting you see?"

I huff in exasperation as I toss one hand up and glance at him. "Do any of us really know more about someone than they let us see? If you're going to get all philosophical on me, this discussion will have to wait until we got home, because I'm going to need a drink."

He chuckles, but it's a humorless laugh. "I'm probably just projecting my old feelings," he says, then adds, "but if you need me, I'm here."

"I know," I say quietly. "Thanks, Stubbs." The car falls silent, and I'm left wondering what exactly he thinks is going to happen after Mark's surgery.

CHAPTER THIRTEEN

MARK

THE DAY BEFORE MY surgery, we leave for Aurora around midday. It's a suburb of Denver, and the closer we get, the heavier the afternoon traffic becomes. Still, we're able to check into our hotel room around four.

"Out or in for dinner?" Charlie asks me after we get to the room.

She's leaning over to take toiletries out of her travel bag, and my eyes zero in on her perfect peach of an ass. "In. Definitely in."

She looks back over her shoulder and catches me staring, then grins. She slowly walks to where I'm perched on the edge of the bed before pushing me back. I lean up on my elbows, watching as she crawls up my body, sitting astride my hips. Her full lips hover just above mine. I watch as she bites her lower lip, her eyes wide and innocent. "*In* is definitely better," she murmurs against my lips before grinding against my already-hard cock. "I definitely like it in."

Sex. Goddess.

I take her hard and fast. She's on her back, her right leg against my chest, her ankle over my shoulder. I claim her mouth as my hands roam her body. It's fucking hot. No – *she's* fucking hot. She's so wet, her body beautiful and glistening, and the harder I thrust, the more she cries out, her breasts bouncing as I pound into her again and again, skin slapping skin. I'm like a man possessed, unable to get enough of her. "Mine," I growl as I bottom out inside her. "Mine."

"Yours," she moans. "Always yours."

When she climaxes, she screams my name. The spasms deep inside her pull me over the edge, and I empty into her with one final growl. "Mine."

I lay there afterwards, our fingers threaded together, spooned against her luscious curves, marveling at the way this siren beside me was convinced a mere two months ago that she was unable to feel desire or become aroused.

Sex. Goddess.

We spend most of the evening and night in bed, tangled in each other's arms. Being in this hotel room and knowing I'm going to be incapacitated after surgery compels me to take her while I can. Somewhere around seven, we order Chinese food and eat takeout on one of the two queen-sized beds while watching a movie on her laptop. Later, we shower together, and thankfully, this hotel has a sturdy shower bench, because we make excellent use of it. She climaxes in the shower, but I hold back. I'm not done with her yet. We return to the bed, where I feast on Charlie – her delectable mouth, her lush breasts, and her sweet pussy. I taste and lick and suckle her tender flesh until she detonates against my face with her hands fisted in my hair. Only when she's feeling the aftershocks of her orgasm do I stretch out above her and slide my ready cock inside her tight depths. She digs her heels into my ass, clutching my sides, begging me not to stop. Her body rises to meet me with each thrust, pulling me in deeper. When she tightens around me a third time, I bury myself deep, my cock pulsing within her.

We hold each other till dawn, speaking very little. My mind keeps drifting to all the things I'm going to do once I'm normal again, and at the very top of my list is telling Charlie how I feel. She's my past, my present, my future, my everything, and I want her to be mine forever.

I'm lost in thought when she speaks quietly, her head nestled into my shoulder. "I'm scared."

I tilt her face up to mine, startled by the anxiety in her eyes. "Why?"

She swallows hard. "Every time I wait while you're in surgery, my mind always goes to 'what if'." She pauses. "Do you remember in Afghanistan when we talked about what we would want if one of us was badly injured?"

I remember.

The four of us were talking after several of our guys had been critically wounded in an IED blast. One ended up with a brain injury so severe, the doctors said he'd be a vegetable if he survived. Tucker posed a question to each of us: if we were too badly injured to be what we were before, would we want to survive? Charlie's answer had been slow and deliberate. She said if she couldn't survive without machines, or if she was completely oblivious to everyone and everything, an empty vessel, she wouldn't want to be forced to go on that way. I'd promised her I'd make sure she didn't have to, and she promised me the same. I still recall my words to her. *There's a difference between existing and living. If I'm merely existing, I'd rather die.*

I don't say the words aloud now, but I nod, watching her face.

"The flight to Texas when you'd first been hurt was hell," she admits. "All I could think about was that conversation, wondering how I'd find the strength to keep my promise if that's how things turned out. I'd do it, because I'd said I would, but I was terrified. And now there's another surgery, another chance for things to go wrong, and it scares me, because I can't do this without you, Mark. I can't." Tears fill her eyes and she bites her lip, trying to blink them away.

I roll to my side, taking her with me, looking into emerald eyes so deep I could drown in them. I lift one hand to stroke her face, rubbing my thumb over her cheekbone. "Everything's going to be fine, Baby Girl. You aren't going to lose me. I made you a promise too, remember? You won't lose me, not ever. You've been the best part of my life for as long as I can remember, and I'm not going to let anything ruin that."

The words "I love you" are on the tip of my tongue, but I manage to swallow them back. God forbid, if something does go wrong, I don't want her crushed by thoughts of what could have been, and if things go as planned, I want to tell her when I'm normal again. When I'm whole.

"I need you to keep that promise," she says, her hand caressing my face.

"Always, Baby Girl. Always."

We make love once more as the sun peeks over the mountains. It's slow, tender, full of deep yet unspoken emotions. Charlie's my drug, my addiction, and I have to have her.

She's mine.

Always.

I shower again, and it's far less fun because I shower alone with surgical soap that doesn't lather. Charlie's dressed when I emerge, her eyes tight with worry. She refuses food or coffee, saying she's too nauseous, promising to grab something later.

The hotel is literally almost across the street from the hospital, so finding a parking place takes longer than the actual drive. Charlie slings her backpack and my overnight bag over her shoulder before we go inside.

It's like déjà vu – an unpleasantly familiar blend of bright lights, strange smells, and incessant pokes and prods. The cacophony of overhead announcements and ringing phones never ceases. I put on a gown that exposes my ass, and Charlie smiles as she tells me the view has added a definite perk to her morning. I wait on an uncomfortable stretcher as a nurse starts two IVs, one in each arm, and administers something to "relax me" that turns the white fluorescent lights pink. Charlie's in a chair beside my stretcher, her head on my shoulder and her hand gripping mine. I catch myself dozing and startle awake repeatedly, but Charlie keeps telling me to relax and rest, that she's with me.

I need her with me.

I wake again when another nurse says my name as an orderly unlocks the brakes on my stretcher. "We're taking you down to surgery now, Mr. Chandler." My eyes flit to Charlie's. She leans over, smiling and cupping my cheek as she kisses me. She's trying to appear calm, but I can almost smell her fear.

"I'll be waiting for you."

"I'll be back soon, Baby Girl. I have a promise to keep." I squeeze her hand tightly before she's forced to step away. The blur of lights as I roll beneath them makes me dizzy, and I close my eyes as the stretcher travels down the hall. I picture Charlie, her green eyes smiling up at me as I stand before her whole. Normal.

It's the last image in my mind before I drift into unconsciousness.

CHARLIE

Sitting in a cramped waiting room brings back stomach-clenching memories of Mark's injuries earlier this year. My fear and anxiety mushroom, threatening to overwhelm me. After all we've been through to find happiness together, what if I lose him now?

My chest grows tight as the familiar iron bands wrap around my ribs and it gets hard to breathe. *Fuck.* I haven't had a panic attack in months.

I need to get away.

Desperate to be alone, I find a quiet spot in a chapel just off the waiting room. I close my eyes, striving for calm, listening to Mark's voice in my head from years ago at Walter Reed.

Breathe.

Slow and easy.

I'm right here with you, Baby Girl. I've got you.

Just breathe.

My deep breathing combined with the memories of his soothing voice calm me enough to stop my trembling. I return to the waiting room and drink terrible hospital coffee that sits like an anchor in my stomach as I wait for news.

Dr. Walters emerges several hours later, pulling off his surgical cap and running a hand through his thinning hair. I jump to my feet, my heart in my throat until he smiles. "Everything went beautifully," he says. "The implant seated well, and the plastic surgeon refined his limb to accommodate the external abutment. There was a significant amount of scar tissue that had entangled a bundle of nerves. The neurosurgeon was able to excise a good deal of it, so I'm optimistic his phantom sensations will improve."

"How is he?"

"Stable but groggy. We've just moved him to the recovery area. He'll rest today. Tomorrow we'll start his PT and load-bearing exercises. He should be able to go home in a few days."

"When can I see him?"

"As soon as he's a little more awake, they'll take you back."

I call the clinic to update Lila, but Tom answers the clinic phone. "Lila's in a massage," he says apologetically. "Do you need me to get her?"

"No. Just tell her Mark's surgery went well, and I'll call her back after I see him."

"Will do. If you guys need anything, call me, okay?"

"I will. Thanks, Tom."

Now that I know Mark's okay, I'm restless. I won't feel better until I see him with my own eyes. I drink another cup of coffee that tastes like motor oil, pacing like a caged cat and counting the minutes.

MARK

I'm still woozy when Dr. Walters comes to talk to me in the recovery room. "You did great, Mark," he says. "The surgery was a success. The fixture is in place, and tomorrow, we'll start you working with a rubber footie in physical therapy."

"Footie?" I mumble.

He nods. "It's the first stage, before your prosthetic. It only lasts a few weeks."

He leaves, swishing the curtain closed behind him, and I'm alone in the cubicle.

Curiosity overwhelms me, and I tug back the sheet to stare at my leg.

What the fuck?

No, seriously, what the fuck?

The tip of my – I might as well call it what it is – my *stump* – is swathed in white gauze, though I can see some bloody drainage around one end. It's what's beyond the gauze that captures my attention. A silver rod protrudes about two and a half inches from the end of the stump. It's round, then square, with a specialized screw tip.

Screwed.

Like me.

Like my life.

It looks like a too-short, goddamned pirate's peg leg. All I need is a fucking eye patch and a parrot for my shoulder. I thought I was going to be normal. Whole. How the fuck is this normal?

I stare in disgust at the metal rod extending from my leg. I'm even more of a freak now than I was before, and that's saying something.

Normal isn't an option for me. It never will be. Now, unbelievably, I'm even more abnormal than I was before.

Every hope I'd had for a forever with Charlie melts away, leaving a bitter residue in its place.

Fuck.

CHARLIE

It takes forever for a nurse to come out to take me to see Mark. "Mrs. Chandler?"

Something unfamiliar spirals through my body at her words, and my heart skitters like a jackrabbit. Images flash rapid-fire through my mind. Mark and I laughing. Kissing. Him tenderly brushing the hair from my face. Lying in his arms. Making love. Standing before him in a wedding dress while he leans down and lifts my veil.

It's my dream, the one I didn't even know I had until that night in Tom's kitchen with Maya. My dream of a husband who loves me and a house full of big dogs and cats and chaos – well, everything but the kids.

And the man who fulfills my dream of a happily-ever-after?

It's Mark.

My chest is suddenly tight, but not like earlier. I freeze for a split second before remembering the nurse is staring at me, waiting. I slowly shake my head. "Just Charlie. We aren't married."

"If you'll come with me, I'll take you to see him." I follow the woman in green scrubs through a maze of halls and whooshing double doors before she stops and parts a curtain for me. The lights are dim, but my eyes go immediately to him. I can't see much of his face. One muscled arm is draped over his eyes, as though blocking out what little light there is; the other lies atop the sheet, fluids dripping into the IV in his hand. His breathing is even. I glance at the bedside monitor out of habit. His blood pressure and heart rate are good, as is his oxygen level, and his cardiac rhythm is perfect.

My eyes linger on the lower part of his face, the only portion visible, and the heavy sensation in my chest grows stronger.

Oh my God. I've fallen in love with him.

The realization hits me out of the blue, and for a second, I can't breathe.

This wasn't supposed to happen. It was supposed to be just sex. We agreed – no romantic entanglements.

Then Mark takes a deep, shuddering breath, and all my attention shifts to him.

I step close and lean over, kissing his cheek. "Hey, Big Guy. How are you feeling?"

"I've been better," he says, his voice hoarse. I slide my hand into his and squeeze his fingers, but he doesn't squeeze back, and he doesn't move his arm away from his eyes.

"Are you hurting?"

He laughs darkly. "You could say that."

"I'll get the nurse. She can give you something for pain."

He shakes his head. "Medication won't touch this pain."

Something's wrong, and I don't know what. Fear shivers up my spine. I reach for the arm over his face, lightly touching him. "Please look at me, Mark."

"Why?"

Panic rises inside me. "Because you're scaring me."

He moves his arm away then, looking directly at me, and I almost wish he hadn't. Pale blue eyes study my face with a flat, emotionless look.

This isn't the Mark who held me so tenderly just hours ago. My chest tightens again, the iron bands squeezing, and my breathing picks up speed. *What's going on? What's happened?*

His eyes travel over my face before softening slightly. "I'm just tired and hurting. You don't need to be afraid, Charlie."

I squeeze his hand, but his fingers remain motionless within mine. He draws a deep breath and moves his arm back up over his eyes again.

Tears burn my eyes. Something's terribly wrong. He's pulling away, and I have no idea what changed between this morning and now. I press the button for the nurse, and she injects his IV with something for pain. His breathing becomes more even.

He's just tired and hurting.

Pain meds and rest. That's all he needs. Pain meds and rest.

Everything's fine.

CHAPTER FOURTEEN

MARK

THIS WASN'T SUPPOSED TO happen like this. The surgery was supposed to fix me, make me whole again.

I mean, obviously, I wasn't going to wake up with a brand new leg, but this definitely isn't what I'd envisioned.

In my mind, I'd pictured myself standing tall, without crutches. I'd wear pants so no one could see my prosthetic. It would let me walk with a natural gait, so no one would know I was half a man unless I wanted them to — which I wouldn't.

I'd be able to dance and run and ride ATVs and do – well, anything Charlie wanted to do. Like stand in front of a minister in a tuxedo. Like ride zip lines in South America on our honeymoon, or maybe snorkel in the Caribbean, or go rock-climbing.

But once again, reality is a heartless bitch. I feel like I've lost my leg all over again, except this time, there's no hope, nothing to look forward to.

Just a lifetime of never being good enough for the woman I love.

Fuck.

I wish that goddamned explosion had killed me.

CHARLIE

Everything's fine. He just needs pain meds and rest.

It becomes my new mantra.

They move Mark upstairs to a private room after a couple of hours. I keep the blinds closed. I text Lila rather than calling because I don't want to disturb him. I don't mention his behavior to her. I'm hoping he'll feel better after some sleep.

Although he wakes up occasionally, he keeps his eyes closed and doesn't speak. He declines food every time it's offered, though I do get him to take a few sips of water now and then. Just before midnight, the nurse gives him pain medication along with something for sleep.

It works. I stay in the recliner beside his bed, wide awake and anxious. I'm haunted by the emotionless look in his eyes. He's withdrawing from me, or at least, that's how it feels. It doesn't help when he begins talking in his sleep. "No," he mutters. "No." He thrashes his head back and forth, and I place my hand on his chest.

"It's okay. I'm here," I murmur, and his body instantly relaxes.

It happens over and over, all night long, nightmare after nightmare, always the same anguished "No!" on his lips. Nurses come in and out, changing his IV fluids, emptying his catheter, administering IV antibiotics, checking vital signs. They give him pain shots two additional times, and he doesn't balk like he normally would.

I don't think it's a good sign.

For the second night in a row, I'm awake all night at his side, but the difference between his behavior last night and tonight leaves me shaken.

MARK

Nightmares plague me all night, the same dream, over and over.

Charlie and I are standing before a minister. She's in a beautiful white gown, and I'm in a tuxedo. She's breathtaking – her hair down, her green eyes sparkling.

The minister, whose face I can't see, asks if anyone knows any reason we should not be wed, and tells them to speak now or forever hold their peace.

Someone, a male, yells out, "Because he's only got one leg!"

And every time, Charlie looks at me, her eyes angry. "You don't have two legs. How could you think I'd ever marry you?"

My subconscious is a real asshole, but he's right.

I was a fool for thinking I'd ever be good enough to find forever with someone as perfect as Charlie.

CHARLIE

Mark really is out of bed the day after surgery. His first visit with a physical therapist takes place in his hospital bed. "I'm Shane," announces a kid who could pass for a blond surfer headed to Florida for spring break.

Mark eyes him skeptically, but says nothing.

"I know what you're thinking. I'm too young to be a real physical therapist. There's no way I know what I'm doing, right?" He grins. "I started college at fifteen and got my master's at twenty. I've been doing this for six years. You're in good hands, I swear."

This guy's a little too perky for this hour of the day, although, to be fair, it could be that I've been awake for over forty-eight hours and my stress level is off the charts.

He tugs Mark's covers down without asking, exposing his leg. It's the first time I've seen it. The abutment extends past the gauze bandage over his stump. There's a little serous drainage and old blood on the dressing, but no fresh bleeding. His leg above the dressing doesn't appear red or hot, only swollen, which is normal under the circumstances.

"Alright," Shane says, "I'm going to explain everything as I go. Some of it you may already know, but this way, I can be sure you have a baseline understanding about your procedure. Your surgeon reamed out the center of your bone to create a hollow to insert your implant. He drilled the hole slightly smaller in diameter than the rod. Then he hammered the implant into place for a tight fit. That implant is called your fixture, because it's fixed in place. An adaptor mounts to the external end of your fixture. That adaptor is called a dual cone. It's the go-between for your internal and external hardware. The abutment connects directly to the dual cone. The abutment is your external hardware. It's the piece you'll attach your prosthesis to with an Allen wrench." He points out each part of the metal extending from Mark's leg. "Fixture. Dual cone, which you can't see. Abutment over the dual cone."

Mark remains silent, but I nod.

Shane produces an odd-looking walker and pulls out a plastic bag, withdrawing a foam-bottomed rubber pyramid. "This is your footie." He grabs an Allen wrench from his pocket and proceeds to slip the pyramid onto the abutment and tighten it into place with the wrench. "Snug, but not too tight," he says, glancing at Mark. Then he straightens. "The footie is to get your bone used to bearing weight again. Bone that's used is bone that's fused," he quips with a grin. "Light weight-bearing helps the bone fuse more quickly to the fixture. We start with a footie because the fixture needs to be partially fused before we add the weight of a prosthesis."

Mark glares, but Shane is undeterred, whipping out a tape measure and measuring from the bottom of the footie to Mark's heel on his intact leg. Then he reaches for the walker. I realize it looks different because it has an adjustable shelf with a computerized display. Shane adjusts the height and rolls the walker to Mark's bedside.

"Okay, Mr. Chandler, time to get you on your feet." Shane directs him to turn and slide to the edge of the bed. "Mrs. Chandler, if you could come help for just a second."

My eyes fly to Mark's face as he clenches his jaw, clearly displeased by Shane's words. His expression slices my heart like a knife.

Is the thought of being married to me that appalling?

"It's just Charlie, not Mrs. Chandler," I say, hiding my hurt as I move to Mark's side. "What do you need me to do?"

"When he stands, I'd like you on his right to help him balance while I move the walker into place and adjust the scale's height if needed." He grins. "Can you be his crutch?"

I remember laps around the halls at Brooke where I did just that, when the shrapnel injury to his upper arm kept him from being able to use a crutch. "Sure." I sit beside him on the bed, careful not to bump his leg, ducking beneath his arm so it's over my shoulder and sliding my arm around his waist. "Grab the bedrail." I nod toward it and wait for him to grip it. "Up on three? One, two, three." He stands more easily than I expected, and I help him balance as Shane kneels down, fiddling with the walker. I rest my head briefly against Mark's chest and feel him press his face into my hair. Tears spring to my eyes at the unexpected touch.

Maybe things aren't as bad as I fear.

"This walker is yours," Shane says from the floor. "Go ahead and move so that your footie sits on this scale. Don't press down yet – just rest it there."

Mark moves his right leg into position, grimacing as he does.

"Good. Is the height right for you?"

Mark nods, one terse movement. "Okay. This readout –" Shane gestures to the small display "– shows you how many pounds of pressure you're applying to this built-in scale. Your goal today is to apply twenty pounds of pressure for ten minutes, for a total of four times. Tomorrow you'll do it six times. The next day you stay at six sessions, but for fifteen minutes at a time. After that, we'll begin incrementally increasing the weight. If all goes well, you should be able to attach your prosthetic limb in about three weeks. Now you won't be able to fully bear your weight for at least twelve weeks," he cautions, "so you'll still need crutches for a while. But this baby here?" He gestures to the footie. "She may not look like much, but she's your ticket to freedom." He grins. "I like to name the footies. You know, like pin-up girls. This one here? She looks like an

Ava to me." And before either of us realizes what he's doing, Shane's whipped out a silver permanent marker and scrawled the name across the black footie.

Mark scowls, but Shane's irrepressible mood can't be dampened. "Okay, big guy, let's get you to bear some weight." Mark tenses noticeably at Shane's inadvertent use of my nickname for him. "Push down and hold when you get to twenty pounds. Then we start the stopwatch."

It's harder than it sounds. Being able to consistently apply enough pressure without going too far takes a lot of muscle control, and those muscles are hurting from surgery. By the time ten minutes is up, Mark's thigh is trembling, and beads of sweat dot his forehead.

"Alright, big guy, sit back down on the bed," Shane says.

"My name is Mark," he snaps.

Shane just grins. "I knew Mr. Strong and Silent would talk sooner or later." He helps Mark back into bed and pulls the covers to his waist. "I'll be back in about four hours. I'll have the nurse bring you pain meds before I come so it won't be as bad next time. You did really well. You pushed through the pain. You're strong and determined. You'll be walking before you know it."

I'm at the sink before the door even closes, wetting a face cloth with cool water and pressing it to his head. He closes his eyes while I gently stroke the cloth over his damp skin. Then I pull his covers up. "Thanks," he mutters.

It's literally the first word he's said to me all day.

"Can I get you some water? Are you hungry?"

He shakes his head. "I just want to be left alone."

By midafternoon, I'm exhausted and hungry. I slip out of the room and call Lila while making my way to the cafeteria.

"How's he doing?" she asks immediately.

I hesitate. "Physically? He's doing alright. He's had PT twice today. He's got some swelling, but nothing compared to when he first got to Brooke. And he has pain, but the pain meds seem to take the edge off."

"No phantom pain?"

"Not so far."

"You said he was alright physically. What does that mean? What's wrong?"

Tears form in my eyes, and my throat gets tight. "Charlie, talk to me," she says, and I hear the worry in her voice.

"He's pulling away. Not talking, not eating, barely drinking. Before surgery, he behaved one way, and now – now it reminds me of his emotional roller coaster at Brooke. He's not volatile," I hasten to add, "but he's distant. There's a chill in his eyes, and before, he was –"

Warm. Loving. Tender.

"Different," I finish lamely.

"Tucker said he'd have a hard time accepting the external rod. He said Mark kept talking about being normal again and being whole. He was worried when Mark woke up and saw that abutment sticking out of his leg, it would hit him hard."

I remember the day we left the VA in Pueblo, when he told me he was "this close" to being normal. "That's what's wrong," I say softly. "We discussed it a few weeks ago. He was talking about being almost normal. I told him he wasn't defined by what he'd lost, but by who he was." I sigh. "He'd seemed so happy lately, I thought he was starting to see himself differently."

"He's happy because of you."

"He was. Now... something's changed, Lila, and I'm worried." A thought occurs to me. "Maybe if he talked to someone again."

"Like a therapist?"

"He saw a psychiatrist at Brooke, but only because it was mandated. I'm not sure he'd be willing to go now. Maybe he'd go to an amputee support group. That might help. I'll text Stubbs. I don't want Mark hating himself again."

"Let me work on it. I have a couple of clients that could probably recommend a psychiatrist, or at least steer me in the right direction."

"Thanks, Lila."

"If you think he's up to a video call later, let me know and we'll be there."

"I will. Love you guys."

The cafeteria has a section dedicated entirely to deli sandwiches and paninis. When Mark was at Brooke, I frequented a nearby deli several days a week. I'd bring Mark lunch most days. It was a way to help him feel less like a patient stuck eating hospital food and more like a guy hanging out with his best friend. I decide to try the same approach today. The cafeteria makes a pressed Cuban panini here that reminds me of the Cuban sandwiches from the deli in San Antonio. I purchase paninis, chips, and chicken soup, the world's greatest cure-all. It's still hospital food, but at least it's not the bland stuff they send up on his trays.

I return to the room just as Shane is leaving. "He's doing great, Mrs. – uh – Charlie. He's determined. That's a good indicator of success." He frowns. "I'm pretty sure he's hurting more than he lets on, though."

He is. In more ways than one.

I push into the room, my arms laden with food. I put it down on the bedside table. Mark doesn't even open his eyes.

But I can be stubborn, too.

He opens his eyes when I sit on the bed at his waist. I lean across him, my chest brushing his. "I thought you might be hungry for something." I let my gaze linger on his mouth, hoping to pull him back to me.

He looks at me, his eyes cold. "No. I don't want anything."

"You're sure I can't tempt you?" He turns away from my double entendre, literally shifts away from me. Stung, I stand and reach for the bags. "I brought you a Cuban panini and chicken soup."

Mark exhales sharply. "Leave."

My head spins, and I can't breathe for a second. "What?"

"I don't want you here. Leave."

"What changed?" I burst out. "Yesterday I felt like you –"

Like he loved me.

"And now you don't even want me around? Why?"

Mark never answers my question. He shifts further over in the bed, turning his back on me. "Close the door on your way out."

I stare at his back for a full minute before realizing he's not going to answer me or change his mind. Finally, I pick up my backpack from the corner of the room, wiping tears away before he can see them, and leave, quietly closing his door as he requested.

CHAPTER FIFTEEN

MARK

CHARLIE'S SHOCKED GASP AND the tears she didn't want me to see replay in my head on a loop.

I steel my resolve. Better to hurt her a little now than a lot later. I can't let her get in any deeper with me, not now that I know I'll never be whole.

I assume she'll come back in a couple of hours, but she doesn't. She doesn't call, doesn't text. Nothing.

What did you expect? You told her to leave. You told her you didn't want her here.

Lila and Tucker try to video-chat with me, but I make excuses, telling them I'm hurting. When they ask for Charlie, I tell them she's sleeping at the hotel after being awake for nearly sixty hours. I hope she is, but the truth is, I don't want them calling her and finding out I sent her away. I'm not up to hearing about it from them.

I don't sleep at all. The nurse gives me something for pain and something else for sleep, but when I close my eyes, all I see is Charlie's hurt expression.

I'm startled when my cell phone rings late in the night. It's the front desk of the hotel. "I apologize," the woman on the other end says, "but with the screams coming from your hotel room, I wanted to be sure you were alright. Miss Emerson said it was the television, but other guests said it sounded like someone was being attacked, and I wanted to make sure I didn't need to call the police."

My stomach clenches. *Charlie's screaming.*

I realize the woman doesn't know I'm not at the hotel and scramble for a response. "No, you don't need to call the police. We fell asleep with the tele-vision on. Charlie woke up and tried to turn it off and hit the volume button by mistake. I apologize for the disturbance." I thank her for her concern and hang up, running my hand through my hair.

Fuck. Charlie's having night terrors. The same thing happened when she slept upstairs after I acted like an ass after our first kiss.

Instead of relying on her gun, she trusts me to keep her safe.

I close my eyes in frustration. How am I supposed to stay away from her when I know what happens when I do?

CHARLIE

Black, soulless eyes glitter, leering at me in the darkened room. The only light comes from a small lantern flickering in the far corner of my stone cell. I hang suspended by my wrists, the rusty wire looped around them gnawing all the way to my bones.

The Chihuahua sneers, gripping the huge blade tightly in his hand. It's oxidized as well, old and scarred from use. He steps forward, dragging the tip lightly across my skin before using the razor-sharp edge to slice into my left breast. It stings, but it's a shallow cut. He won't plunge the blade into my chest and kill me. Not yet, anyway. He's having too much fun playing with his newest toy. He continues carving up my breasts, one slice after another, not too deeply, but enough to cause blood to crawl in slow trails down my abdomen.

I grit my teeth and close my eyes, and it irritates him that I'm dissociating from his torment. He backhands me, smashing my lips. The metallic taste of blood coats my tongue.

Then he moves his knife lower, between my thighs.

He laughs coarsely as he simulates the sex act with his knife, driving it deep inside me. Every thrust feels like fire, and when I suck in a deep breath, he twists the blade as he pulls it out. The more I struggle, the more it hurts, and I stop fighting, clenching my jaw, refusing to make a sound, unwilling to give him the pleasure.

When blood runs freely down my thighs, he throws the knife down, unzipping his pants and moving behind me. He grips my hips roughly. I kick back, but he's already between my legs, and I can't get any leverage. All I can do is try to shift my hips away, but he only laughs, grunting as he thrusts like a rutting animal. The pain inside me intensifies as he forces his way deeper into my bloodied flesh.

The loud ringing of the telephone beside the bed startles me. I'm on my knees beside a dresser, panting, my heart pounding in my chest. I stare around, momentarily confused before recognizing the hotel room.

I'm safe.

I get to my feet and answer the phone.

"Miss Emerson, we've had calls about screaming in your room from several other guests. Do you need an ambulance or the police?"

"No," I say hoarsely. "No, it was – the television," I stammer, casting about for a plausible excuse.

"Alright, ma'am. If you could keep the volume down for our other guests, I'd appreciate it."

I apologize and hang up, damp with sweat and trembling. I sit on the edge of the bed, dropping my head into my hands.

Fucking night terrors.

Breathe.

I'm safe here.

Breathe.

When my heart rate has returned to something close to normal, I get to my feet and stumble through a shower. After dressing, I go downstairs to the lobby. A young woman sits at the front desk, twirling a lock of her dark hair, reading a paperback novel.

"May I help you?" When she looks up and speaks, I recognize her voice from the phone.

"I was wondering if you had a night manager I could speak with."

"Is there a problem with your room?"

"No, nothing like that. I just wondered if there was someone I could talk to."

"Hey, Gus!" she calls over her shoulder without taking her eyes off me. "Can you come out here?"

An older gentleman pokes his head out of an office door behind her. When he sees me, he straightens and comes to the desk. He's dressed in khakis and a crisp white shirt, with rolled-up sleeves that reveal tanned forearms and a hint of dark ink. He looks to be in his late sixties, with thick white hair and dark eyes that see everything. He glances toward the girl behind the counter.

"She asked to speak to the manager."

He smiles when he steps out to meet me. "How may I help you?"

The lobby door opens and a couple of obviously-intoxicated frat boys stagger toward the elevators. "Is there somewhere we could speak privately?"

He looks at me curiously before nodding. "Come on back to my office." He leads the way to a small room not much larger than a janitor's closet. He gestures to a chair and closes the door.

"Wait," I say, unable to keep the panic out of my voice, still shaken by my dream.

This man isn't going to hurt me.

His eyes flash to mine, and his face softens at my expression. He pulls the door half open and takes a seat behind a desk stacked with papers and gnawed pencils.

"What can I do for you, Miss –?"

"Emerson. Charlie Emerson. I – I'd like to pay for the hotel room for the guests on either side of me and below and above me for tonight."

White eyebrows raise sharply. "Why?"

"For disturbing them."

"Why?" he repeats, pushing up his sleeves further and leaning back in his chair. The action reveals more of his tattoo, and I recognize it.

"Airborne?"

"The 187th Airborne Infantry. Korea." He studies me carefully. "You served."

I nod. "Eleven years as a frontline medic." I swallow hard. When I look up, those dark eyes that don't miss a thing are staring right at mine.

"That wasn't the television they were hearing, was it?" After a second, I shake my head. "Flashbacks?"

"Night terrors," I murmur. "I was captured. It was... hard." I look up and find him still watching me closely. "I was wondering if you had another room I could move to, maybe a ground floor corner room where I won't bother your other guests."

He turns to his computer, pulling up a screen, clicking and typing rapidly. "Not disability-friendly, no," he says finally.

My shoulders sag. "Then I'd like to cover the bills for the rooms on either side of me and above and below me for the remainder of my stay."

"That's going to get expensive."

I shrug. "They shouldn't have to be disturbed because I'm – because of me."

He studies me carefully before reaching for a stack of papers, flipping through them.

"We're updating the D-wing on three floors," he says, pushing two large pages toward me. One is the schematic of a floor of the hotel; the other appears to be a schematic of the exterior of the building showing the levels. "A pipe burst on the seventh floor and flooded all the way down to the fifth. We're reopening the rooms next week. The remodeling is finished on the fifth and sixth floors. They smell like fresh paint, but the rooms are ready to go. They're still painting and papering on the seventh floor and moving furniture in, so it's noisy in the daytime, but I have a disability-friendly room on the sixth floor that's ready. You can have it, if you like. But there won't be anyone else on that floor," he says, "so if that would make you uncomfortable –"

"That's fine," I say quickly. "Can we look at it?"

He gets to his feet and pulls a key card from the top drawer of his desk. I follow him out of the office. "Back in a minute, Trudy," he tells the girl at the desk. She doesn't even look up from her book.

The room does smell of fresh paint, but it's not overpowering. It's the mirror image of my current room, with two queen-sized beds, a refrigerator and microwave, a corner desk, and a walk-in shower with rails and a bench. It's crisp and clean and quiet. "When can I move in?"

"Whenever you and your companion are ready," he says.

My smile falters. "He's actually in the hospital. He had surgery."

"I'm sorry to hear that."

I shake my head. "It's a good thing." *At least, it was supposed to be.* "He's Army, too, or was, until he lost his leg from an IED. The surgery was to set him up for his permanent prosthesis. He'll be released in a few days, but we may stay here a day or so after he's released, depending on whether he feels up to traveling."

Gus shakes his head. "Service comes at a high cost," he muses. "Please consider yourself and your companion guests of the hotel as thanks for your service."

My jaw drops. "I can't let you do that."

He grins and taps his gold name badge. "I'm the manager. You can't stop me. And I'll knock a chunk of the bill off for the ones who were woken up."

"I don't mind paying," I protest.

His smile turns sad. "I believe you and your companion have paid more than enough." Then he holds out his arm toward the door. "Let's go downstairs and I'll get you a key to this room and a trolley for your luggage."

An hour later, I'm checked out of my old room and into the new one under the name VIP GUEST at Gus' insistence. Trudy looks mildly impressed when Gus shoos her away from the computer and handles the details personally, especially when she sees the name he puts in. I catch her studying me with interest, trying to figure out if I'm someone famous.

It's a long day without much to do. Mark not wanting me around means I basically have nothing to do but sit around waiting for him to be released. I don't feel like sightseeing or going out. Instead, I order takeout and stream movies on my laptop for background noise, hoping to drown out his voice in my head.

"I don't want you here. Leave." His icy blue eyes glare at me, his lips curled back.

I jolt awake, knocking my phone to the floor as a chill runs up my spine.

I've not let myself dwell on the fact that I've fallen in love with Mark. Honestly, with everything going on – his surgery, his abrupt shift in attitude, my night terrors – I've managed to push it from my mind. I've also tried to forget the way he jerked his head back in revulsion when his overly enthusiastic physical therapist called me Mrs. Chandler. The only thing I've not been able to chase from my mind is the realization that I need Mark much more now than I did before.

I was afraid of losing Mark during his surgery after all we've been through to find happiness. Things go wrong. People have reactions to anesthesia or antibiotics. People bleed out. Hearts stop for no apparent reason. I was worried about the plethora of medical complications that might take him for me.

It never once occurred to me that I might lose him because his surgery was a success.

MARK

Charlie didn't come in this morning, even after her night terrors. I was sure she would. I reassure her when she has them. I dry her tears and hold her until she stops trembling.

But I haven't seen her since I told her to leave.

Since I told her I didn't want her here.

The sharp loss of her presence invades every corner of my soul. Charlie and I have always been close, linked in a way that transcended friendship. We understand each other without words. We ground each other. Since we tried "more", that closeness has only deepened. I've shared more with her than with anyone else on this planet. My mind. My body. My soul.

My heart.

She deserves so much more than I can give her, but my desperate need for her overpowers my resolve. By late afternoon, after my fifth grueling PT session with Shane, I break down and call her cell phone. It goes to voice mail.

"Hey, Charlie. I was just checking on you. Call me."

Two hours later, I call again. Voice mail. "I haven't heard from you. Just checking on you."

Eight in the evening. Voice mail. "Charlie? Are you okay? Call me."

By ten that night, I'm going out of my mind. I look up the number for the hotel and call. "I need Charlie Emerson's room, please. I can't remember if it was 312 or 321."

I hear the clicking of keys and breathing into the mouthpiece. "It looks like Miss Emerson checked out of the hotel."

That can't be right.

"Are you sure?"

"She checked out of room 312 a little after five this morning, sir. Will there be anything else? Sir?" I end the call, my mind whirling.

She left me?

My eyes close as the truth rings loud and clear in my mind.

You told her to, dumbass. She did exactly as you asked.

You said, "I don't want you here. Leave."

What did you expect? You told a woman who shared every part of herself with you that you didn't want her around. You hurt her, asshole, badly enough to make her leave, and she didn't do that even after that bullshit you pulled in San Antonio.

No. She can't leave me.

Please, no.

I need her.

I try her phone again, but it goes straight to voicemail. "Charlie, I'm sorry. I didn't mean it. I didn't mean to hurt you. I —"

I love you.

"I miss you. I'm sorry, Charlie. Please come back. Please don't give up on me."

But there's no answer. I text, but there's no response.

The pain in my body is nothing compared to the pain in my heart.

CHARLIE

It's three-thirty in the morning, and I'm standing at an all-night big box store, staring at a rack of phone chargers, trying to figure out which one fits my phone. After knocking it under the bed earlier, I forgot about it. When I went looking for it to call Lila, the battery was completely dead, and my charger was nowhere to be found, presumably lost when I changed hotel rooms.

I stare back and forth from the tip of the packaged charger to the little port in my phone. Finally, I pry open the package to check. It fits, and I make my way to a register.

As soon as I plug my phone in at the hotel, it lights up. Voicemails, missed calls, and missed texts chime like a casino in Vegas. I let it charge while I shower, hoping the hot water will ease some of the tension from my neck and shoulders.

It doesn't.

I pad across the newly carpeted floor and sit down on the bed, still in my robe, rubbing a towel through my hair. I have seven voicemails. I'm surprised to find the first four are from Mark, each one progressively more anxious, until in his fourth one, he says the words I needed to hear. *I miss you. Please come back.* His last phrase seizes my heart.

Please don't give up on me.

Those are the same words he spoke after his epic eruption on me in Texas, the words that made me return to his hospital room.

I won't give up on him. His behavior is driven by his injury. We – myself, Tucker, Lila, and Tom – supported him through his initial injuries and recovery, and we'll get him through this stage, too. He just needs time to recalibrate.

The next three voicemails are all from Lila, beginning yesterday afternoon. "Hey. I didn't call last night because Mark said you'd been awake since Sunday, and I was hoping you were asleep. Call me when you have a minute and let me know how things are going." The second is from ten-thirty last night. "Hey, Charlie. Mark called asking if I'd seen you. What's going on? He said you'd checked out of the hotel this morning. Call me." Her final message is from well past midnight. "Charlie, I'm getting worried. Are you alright? I don't care what time you get this, please let me know you're okay. I love you."

I glance at the clock. It's four-thirty in the morning. I'm not going to call and wake her up to tell her I'm fine. I send a text explaining why I changed rooms and giving her my new room number under "VIP GUEST". I also tell her I haven't seen Mark since Tuesday and why.

It's now Thursday.

I haven't had his lips on mine since Monday morning before his surgery, a situation I'm hoping to rectify in the very near future. I pull on denim shorts and a loose white sleeveless blouse, stick my feet into flats, and run a comb through my hair before tossing a few things in my backpack and grabbing my keys.

There's a twenty-four-hour McDonald's near the hospital, and I pick up breakfast and coffee for us on my way in. When I reach his room, I pause outside his door, quietly opening it in case he's asleep.

He's not.

He's sitting up in bed, wide awake, and he looks like hell.

He's pale, and he has dark circles under his eyes. His hair is a mess from running his hands through it, something he does when he's stressed. He's wearing the same tee shirt and loose shorts I helped him put on Monday night, when he was sick of the hospital gown.

His pale eyes meet mine as soon as I cross his threshold. "You came back," he says, sounding surprised.

"I did." I cross the room and deposit our coffee and food on the bedside table.

"Where did you go?"

"You told me to leave," I remind him.

"But where did you go?"

"The hotel."

He frowns. "You checked out of the hotel yesterday at five in the morning."

"No, I changed rooms. I'm on the sixth floor now, in a wing that they're renovating."

"They don't have you listed in the computer," he persists.

His third degree is becoming annoying, especially since I left at his insistence, and I huff in frustration. "Call them and ask for the VIP guest's room. I'm in 642."

His eyebrows raise. "A VIP room? You upgraded?"

I shake my head. "It's just like the room we had. It's a long story." I change the subject, watching his face. "My phone battery went dead, and I lost my charger changing rooms. I didn't get your messages until this morning."

He closes his eyes briefly. "I'm sorry, Charlie. I'm having a harder time with this than I expected."

I move to sit down beside him on his uninjured side. "Are you hurting? Do you need a massage?"

He shakes his head. "It hurts, but the meds help. I meant I'm having trouble with..." He gestures toward his leg.

"Why?"

He shakes his head. "This was supposed to make things better. It was supposed to fix me so I'd stop being a useless cripple. I look even more freakish now than I did before."

I frown. "First of all, you've never looked like a freak, so stop saying that. You look like a warrior who fought like hell and has the battle scars to prove it." His eyes tighten, and I raise my voice, frustration creeping into my tone. "No, Mark. You'd never say that garbage about Stubbs, and I'm not going to listen to you say it about yourself. No more 'half a man' bullshit, no more 'useless cripple' nonsense, none of it. Quit focusing on what's not there and focus on what is."

He sits silently, and though I'd like to say I've gotten through to him, I'm pretty sure he just doesn't want to argue. His stubborn expression doesn't relent at all.

I don't want to argue either, so I reach for the bag of food. "Here. Let's have breakfast and then I'll help you into the shower."

"I can't get my dressings wet."

"You won't. I have a plastic bag and medical tape. This isn't my first rodeo."

An hour later, he's fed, shampooed, and bathed. I help him settle back in the bed and glance at the clock. "You've got a couple of hours before your chipper therapist shows up. You should get some rest."

He startles me by grabbing my upper arms and pulling me down onto his broad chest. His hand slides into my hair as he cups my head. "I haven't kissed you in three days. I need you," he says against my lips. I want to remind him whose fault that is, but the feel of his lips is too delicious. My hands slide over the firm muscles of his chest to rest on his shoulders as he plunders my mouth with deep wet kisses that make my body throb. His hand skates over my ribs to knead my breast. I moan softly into his mouth, and he groans as he reluctantly pulls away. "I'd give my left ass cheek to bury myself inside you right now, Baby Girl."

I smile, relieved that he's acting like himself again. "I'd rather you didn't. I'm quite fond of your ass. How much longer until they release you?"

"I'm not sure. Another day or two, I think."

"God, I hope it's just one," I murmur, realizing too late I spoke my thoughts aloud, and he chuckles, kissing me again.

When Shane arrives for Mark's therapy, he's carrying two black canvas bags. He sets them on the sink and claps his hands together. "I'm glad you're here too, Charlie, because today's the big day. Your prosthetics are here." Mark's eyes widen. "I'm going to teach you how to connect them. You can't walk with them until your implant fuses to your bone. We're just going to practice attaching and detaching today."

The process is surprisingly simple. The end of Mark's abutment fits perfectly into a connector on the prosthesis. He inserts an Allen wrench, gives it one and a quarter turns, and checks to be sure it's secure. "Snug, but not too tight," Shane instructs. He has Mark repeat the process several times, connecting and disconnecting. He makes me do it as well. Once he's satisfied, he returns the prostheses to their canvas storage bags and reaches for the footie attachment.

"Twenty pounds for fifteen minutes six times today," Shane announces. Mark maneuvers to the edge of the bed and attaches the rubber footie while Shane readies the walker/ scale. At thirteen minutes, Mark's thigh is trembling from the effort, and he's bouncing between fifteen and thirty pounds of pressure, unable to maintain control. At fifteen minutes, Shane tells him to relax. Mark sinks onto the bed, his chest heaving.

Shane frowns. "When's the last time you had anything for pain?"

"Last night."

His frown deepens. "I know you don't like the meds, but you've been down this road before. If you're hurting too badly to participate, you won't make progress, and you'll have a slower recovery. If you want to walk sooner, be smarter." He returns the walker to the corner of the room and glances at the clock. "I'll be back at eleven. Your goal today is to prove you can do these exercises on your own. If you do well enough, you may be able to discharge tomorrow. And take the damn meds." He gives him a stern look on his way out, and it's such a sharp contrast to his usual perkiness that I laugh when the door closes.

"Your surfer-boy therapist just chewed your ass," I grin, and Mark scowls. "He's right, though. I could see your thigh muscles quivering."

"Fine," he mutters, pressing the button for his nurse.

He's not happy about it, but he's cooperating, at least for now.

Dr. Walters comes by later with a nurse in tow. "We're going to change your surgical bandage and teach you how to care for your stoma. That's where your fixture exits the skin," he explains. He removes the dressing, exposing a bruised but clean incision with a neat line of sutures across the tip of the limb.

Mark watches, his jaw flexing. It's not difficult – washing it daily with water and baby shampoo, followed by a surgical scrub. In between, he can cleanse it with saline and a gauze pad. His sutures can come out in ten days. In the meantime, he can cover them with a nonstick dressing or leave them uncovered.

His jaw clenches tighter the longer he's forced to view his leg. Mark read everything he could get his hands on about this surgery. He knew – we all knew – he'd have a rod protruding from his leg. That was the entire point of this surgery. I can't understand why the sight of it is so upsetting. Part of the pre-op visit at the VA included a consultation with a psychiatrist to discuss body image. Surely even a moderately-skilled professional could see Mark's self-loathing.

Then it hits me. He wasn't honest with them. Mark said what he thought they wanted to hear so he could have this surgery. He was convinced it would make him "normal", whatever the hell that's supposed to mean, so he said whatever he needed to say to make it happen.

He'll get used to his implant. Looking at a picture in a book or a plastic model in an office isn't the same as seeing it on your own body. It's just a shock. He'll adjust. He just needs time.

Right?

MARK

A freak. I'm a goddamned freak.

I look like a shish-kabob, waiting to go on the grill. A shiska-Mark. All I need to do is stick a few veggies on the end of my damn pirate's peg.

I can conceal it, I guess, if I wear pants while my prosthesis is attached. And when the prosthetic was attached, it wasn't so bad. I mean, yeah, it's still an artificial leg, but it looks high-tech, especially with the carbon-fiber and the hydraulic ankle. That should give me an almost-normal gait when I can finally walk on it. The abutment is still creepy, though.

At least I'm on my way to becoming upright and mobile. They say in three months, I'll be crutch-free, and that's something I can't wait for, to walk around like everyone else, and no one will see my shameful secret if I don't share it with them.

The problem is when my prosthetic comes off. That's when the freak show is on full display, my shish-kabob exposed, unable to be hidden. And when is that?

Oh, right... at night. When I'll be in bed.

With Charlie.

I can't be next to Charlie like this. I can't bear the thought of her looking at me with revulsion.

What if I skewer her with this thing?

What the hell am I going to do? I didn't last three days without touching her. Hell, I barely made it twenty-four hours before I broke down and started leaving messages on her phone.

But I can't be with her. She deserves better.

I need to pull back, wall off my emotions, and stuff my love for her into a dark corner of my heart. I have to bury my feelings, because Charlie deserves someone amazing. And a lifetime with a freak isn't amazing. It's a nightmare.

I'd have been better off if I'd died in that goddamned explosion.

We both would.

CHAPTER SIXTEEN

CHARLIE

MARK DOES WELL ENOUGH with his exercises to prove he can manage his therapy at home under Tom's supervision. The next day, Shane hands him a printed schedule detailing the incremental increases for the pounds of pressure and how long to hold them. "If you want to be walking independently by December, this is your golden ticket," he says, meeting Mark's gaze.

Mark nods. "I want that more than almost anything."

I wonder what he wants more than that, because that's been his primary goal since his initial injury. For a half second, I wonder if he's flirting with me, but his face is serious, and he doesn't look my way.

Dr. Walters sets us up with follow-up appointments, discharge instructions, and prescriptions before releasing Mark. A nurse wheels him downstairs while I bring the car around and load his overnight bag and walker/scale contraption into the car. After he's seated and his crutches are stowed away, I glance at him.

"To the hotel for another night, or a long drive today?"

"I'm not sure I'm up for a long drive today," he says, staring out the window.

Today I'm with quiet Mark again, not regular Mark. He's not angry, but he's withdrawn. I stifle a sigh and drive back to the hotel.

I'm unlocking the door to our room when he speaks. "You never told me why you changed rooms. I thought you'd left me."

You told me to leave.

I hold my tongue. I don't look at him as I carry our things in, holding the door open for him with my foot. "I had night terrors and other guests complained about the screaming. I offered to pay for their rooms for the rest of my stay. The night manager was a veteran, and he offered an alternative. They're remodeling this wing, and the other rooms won't be reopened for a few days. This way, I'm not bothering anyone." I don't meet his gaze.

He raises an eyebrow. "He said you were bothering people?"

I shake my head. "He was very kind. He put us in here for free as VIP guests of the hotel. He said you and I had paid more than enough."

Mark's eyes travel over me, and some emotion I can't decipher swirls in them. Then he turns and goes to one of the beds, tugging down the covers before stretching out. "I'm going to lie down. It's been a long week." As soon as he's in the bed, he shuts his eyes without another word. His dismissal stings, but I push it down.

He just needs time to adjust.

He stays in bed the rest of the afternoon, eyes closed, though by the twitching of his eyelids and his breathing pattern, I can tell he's awake. I work on my laptop at the desk across the room, keeping the blinds drawn and the lights low.

I order takeout for us, and he gets up long enough to eat silently and do two PT sessions back to back. I know he should split them up, and so does he, but I say nothing. He's a grown man, and he's the one who'll be hurting later for overdoing it.

By the time he finishes thirty minutes of pressure, he's pale and sweaty, his right thigh spasming. "Come on," I tell him. "A hot shower will make you feel better."

"I'm not sure we should –" his voice trails off.

Oh.

Disappointment spears through me, although the way he's behaving around me today, that's not exactly a surprise.

I keep my expression neutral. "I meant a regular shower. I'll set you up and leave you alone. It's safe for your incision to shower now as long as you wash it gently. I won't intrude." I turn away, my face growing hot, and set out clothes and towels for him.

I'd meant what I said innocently – a hot shower would relax his thigh muscle – but my eyes sting and a lump builds in my throat at his reaction. Ever since his surgery, Mark flips from affectionate to indifferent in the blink of an eye, and I never know which version I'm facing until he opens his mouth. It's a milder version of his behavior at Brooke before he started his antidepressant, though he was much more volatile and angry then. He's not angry now. Not yet, at least. He's just withdrawn.

I sit at the desk while he showers, my mood sinking. He'd looked forward to this surgery for months, and now that he's had it, he's pulling away from me. When he shuts off the water, I straighten his tangled sheets and flip his pillow over.

He emerges from the bathroom dressed in shorts, his hair still damp, and goes straight to the bed. "I'm going to turn in."

"Do you need your pain medication or a muscle relaxer?"

His jaw tightens. "I guess." I bring them to him, and as soon as he swallows the tablets, he climbs into bed and pulls the covers up.

Apparently, I don't even warrant a "goodnight" now.

A sigh escapes before I can stifle it. I turn away and gather my own clothes and head to the shower. Maybe he'll really be asleep by the time I come out. A large part of me hopes he is. I wonder what that says about me.

About us.

I stay in the shower until I turn pruny, then find excuses to linger in the bathroom, gathering wet towels, lotioning my entire body, blow drying my hair, and packing up the toiletries I won't need tomorrow morning.

When I leave the bathroom, he's pretending to be asleep, lying on his back as still as a statue.

This is the same man who said yesterday he'd give his left ass cheek to get me back to the hotel and have his way with me.

Screw this. His head may be pushing me away, but I'll bet his body can't.

I check the locks on the door before turning off most of the lights, leaving one lamp on across the room so it's not totally dark. Then I peel back the covers on my side of the bed, strip off my clothes, and crawl in next to him, facing the door. I wriggle into place, pushing the leg of his shorts up with my hip so my bare ass rests on his thigh, skin to skin.

I hear his sharp intake of breath behind me and smile. "Good night, Big Guy," I murmur.

No answer.

That's okay. I can wait. He stiffened as soon as I touched him. After a few minutes, I shift my upper body away, angling my hips so that instead of my ass, it's my womanhood against him.

He's silent, but the tension radiating from him ratchets up a thousand percent. His entire body is on high alert.

I smile, letting my body relax into his as though I'm getting sleepy.

Ten minutes later, I roll toward him, tossing my left thigh over his waist and nestling my breasts into his muscled chest. I tuck my head into the crook between his shoulder and neck, purposely breathing into the curve of his neck. He sucks in a deep breath. His cock is rock hard beneath my leg. I sigh softly, relaxing into him, and his entire body tenses.

I let him suffer a couple of minutes, feeling his chest heave and his fists clench and unclench.

When I decide I've tormented him enough, I kneel beside him, pulling the covers back but keeping his right leg covered so he won't feel self-conscious. I press my lips to his chest, kissing my way south, over his abs, down his happy trail. His entire body freezes when he realizes where I'm headed.

"Charlie?" His voice is rough with desire.

I don't answer. Instead, I tug at the waistband of his shorts. After a split-second's hesitation, he raises his hips so I can remove them. When I reach my destination, I kiss down the length of his hard shaft before swirling my tongue around the head. When I take him into my mouth, he inhales sharply.

I work him over like my life depends on it, licking, swirling, and sucking without letting up. His hands fist the sheets as he groans and pants. I take him all the way to the back of my throat again and again, hollowing out my cheeks. It's a heady power, watching him fall under my spell.

His breathing turns harsh as his fingers tangle in my hair. "Christ, Charlie, I'm gonna come. If you don't want me to, stop now."

I slide my hands beneath him, my nails digging into his ass as I pull his hips forward, urging him on.

"Fuck, Charlie." His body stiffens as he comes with a growl, his orgasm ripping through him as I watch his face, gripped in ecstasy. His seed shoots deep into my throat in waves, and I swallow every drop.

He relaxes the hand in my hair, and I crawl back up the bed, nestling into his still-heaving chest and tugging the covers over us.

"Charlie?"

"Good night, Mark."

"But I haven't touched you."

I shake my head. "That was just for you."

He grabs my chin, capturing my mouth in a searing kiss. "Do you have any idea what you do to me?"

I grin. "I know what I did a minute ago. Does that count?"

"Come on. It's your turn," he urges, but I shake my head.

"There'll be plenty of time to make it up to me later." I kiss him again, slowly, tenderly, before snuggling back into his chest. His arm comes up to pull me against him, and I smile.

Seems there's one sure-fire way to improve his mood.

MARK

I'm awake long after Charlie's gone to sleep, her breathing even, her body melted into mine. I can't stop inhaling her scent and stroking her soft skin.

The things she does to me... It's both incredible and terrifying.

It's incredible because I never expected to experience anything like what I feel when I'm with her. All of my adult relationships have been casual, short-term fun. I've never had someone who knows me the way she does, who reaches me the way only she can, who cares more about my needs than her own.

It's terrifying because I'm in way over my head, especially now that I know I'll never be normal. I'll never be able to be what she deserves.

Because Charlie deserves perfection, not some cyborg-looking freak.

With each passing day, my mood spirals lower and lower. I was counting on this surgery to fix things. Instead, it's made them exponentially worse.

Reality is like being dropped naked into an icy pond. It clutches my body with its frigid fingers, leaving me gasping at its brutal harshness.

But I can't let her see it. After my injuries, I was an emotional mess, and Charlie bore the brunt of my turmoil. It culminated in a verbal explosion I'd give anything to take back, a day when I crushed her intentionally because of my inner demons.

I can't bear to hurt her like that again. I love her too much for that.

And there's the crux of the problem. Charlie's my drug, the person I need more than life itself, but I love her enough to admit she's entitled to someone who can give her more than I ever can.

To give Charlie the type of future and happiness she deserves, I need to let her go. Holding onto her because of my desperate addiction is wrong.

But like most addicts, my willpower is weak when it comes to giving up my drug.

I tried in the hospital to send her away. That lasted about twenty-four hours before I broke down, and as soon as I saw her, she immediately bewitched me again. This morning, I doubled down on my resolve to put distance between us. All she had to do was snuggle her sweet ass against me, and I was done. Charlie deserves nothing less than perfection, and I need to pull back, but my body and my heart betray me at every turn.

I'm also not sure when I lost the upper hand in our sexual relationship. When she and I started this "friends with benefits" arrangement, I was confident. I set the pace by giving her the power to select the limits and then working within them to show her what a sexual goddess she really was. She just needed to remember how to access that part of herself. But I was in charge then...wasn't I? I was the one who'd slow things down, keeping her safe from her own desires, making sure things didn't progress to something she'd regret.

At some point, being in charge went out the window. I've lost control, and I don't know how or when. I only know that Charlie owns me, heart and soul. I'm as addicted to her as surely as if I were addicted to heroin. She's in my blood, seeping into every part of me, and I can't get enough of her.

I could never get enough of her.

CHARLIE

I wake up to soft whiskers nuzzling my neck, and I shiver at the scent and feel of Mark.

"Good morning," he murmurs into my skin, and I shiver again.

"Is it? Morning, I mean?"

"I don't know. I couldn't wait any longer, though."

My giggle quickly becomes a moan as his mouth moves down to fasten on my breast. His hand reaches for its twin, rolling the nipple between his fingers to match the tempo his tongue and lips are setting. He nips my peak with his teeth, and electricity fires straight to my core, flooding me with damp heat.

I want him. Now.

Right now.

His erection presses into my thigh, and I snake one hand between us to grasp it. The bead of liquid on him tells me he wants me as badly as I want him. I stroke his length and feel his body shudder as he draws a ragged breath.

"I don't want to hurt you," I whisper.

"Roll to your side, Baby Girl. We'll go slow."

He spoons behind me, his thick cock perfectly positioned at my slick entrance. When he pushes into me, I can't stifle my moan. It's only been five days, but it feels like an eternity. He shifts my leg, driving deeper, stroking that place just inside me with each movement.

It's heaven.

Every thrust is pure pleasure, and that deep ache inside me is building quickly. I clench my inner walls tight around his shaft until he gasps.

"Fuck, Charlie, I'm so close."

I'm panting, unable to answer, my body hovering on the edge as I desperately clutch his hip, pulling him deeper. That's when he sinks his teeth into the sensitive spot where my neck and shoulder meet. It's primal, animalistic, like he's marking me as his own.

Like he's claiming me forever.

His bite and my thoughts nudge me over the edge. I come apart in his arms, barely managing to keep the words "I love you" from flying out of my mouth. Stars explode behind my eyes as my entire body shakes from the force of my climax. It ripples through me in huge waves, and Mark follows immediately, gripping my hip tightly, his teeth still sunk into my flesh as he growls out my name.

I want him to claim me forever.

The thought intrudes, but I push it down. Now is definitely not the time to talk about feelings, not with Mark's moods running hot one minute and cold the next. I need to focus on this moment, on enjoying the right now instead of dreaming about a possible someday.

We lie together skin to skin in the afterglow. I've missed this so much these past few days, being in his arms while he absently strokes my body or plays with my hair. Most of the time, he doesn't even realize he's doing it.

Maybe he's more connected to me than he knows.

God, I hope so.

CHAPTER SEVENTEEN

CHARLIE

WE HAVE A NEW client at work, sent to us from the VA shortly after his discharge from Walter Reed. Kip Kramer is a sweet kid, scarcely twenty-one, with dirty blond hair, bright blue-green eyes, and a smile that reveals dimples on both cheeks. His boyish face contrasts sharply with his powerful body. Like many of the vets we get, he's all muscle. His physique is similar to Tom's. They've both got thick arms and a bulldog-like broad chest that narrows into a trim waist and hips. Kip sustained a traumatic left lower leg amputation following a military vehicle explosion. My heart hurts when I look at him. After all my years as a medic, you'd think I'd be used to it, but seeing a life-altering injury in one so young saddens me. He's barely old enough to order a beer, but he's already battered by the unfairness of the world. I feel it emanating from him, though when he comes in, he's usually grinning and chattering up a storm. Like a magician subtly distracting his audience so they only see what he wants them to, Kip disguises his pain with a smile. I don't fall for it. I've pulled that routine too many times myself.

Kip ends up on my client list. Unlike most of my clients, he doesn't lie quietly and relax during his massages. He talks the entire time. Kip was raised by a single mom who worked two full-time jobs to provide for him. His dad was never in the picture. After his injury, her church took up a collection to fly her to Walter Reed; otherwise, he says, she'd never have been able to afford it. When he was discharged, she'd begged him to come home to live with her, but he'd refused. "I love her, but she'd smother me," he says, running a hand through his hair. "I've killed people, been shot at, and been blown up, but to her, I'm still that same little kid who cried when she dropped me off at kindergarten." Instead, he shares a first floor, two-bedroom apartment with his best friend from high school, Kyle. The landlord added handrails in the bathroom for him.

One afternoon, Kip comes in early for his session and stops at the desk where Lila and I are sitting. It's a rarity – no ringing phones, no appointments for either of us, no stacks of phone messages demanding attention. He halts at the desk, leaning heavily on his crutches, and his normally-chipper expression is missing.

Lila jumps to her feet. "What's wrong? Are you alright?"

He purses his lips. "My girl broke up with me last night." I study his face – the dark circles under his eyes, the unshaved stubble, the scent of stale alcohol. He looks like he's grieving the death of a loved one. I fumble through my brain, trying to remember what he's said about his girlfriend. I remember her name is Jennifer – there was a girl in high school whom I couldn't stand with the same name, and hearing it still makes my hackles go up. She and Kip have been dating for about a year and a half, but he was overseas for most of that. He's only been back home with her for a month. And she's beautiful. He showed a picture to Tom and Lila one day, and apparently she's model-gorgeous, with jet-black hair and big blue eyes. Tom wrinkled his nose when he told me that. His supermodel ex-wife has left him with a bitterness he rarely lets anyone else see.

Lila comes around the desk and folds Kip into a hug. "I'm sorry. What happened?"

He looks away, not meeting her eyes. Then he makes a sweeping gesture down his body toward his missing limb.

She broke up with him because of his injuries? My temper flares to life.

Lila immediately ushers him into a chair and tosses me a get-your-ass-over-here-and-help-me look. Lila sits beside him. I squat on my heels in front of him.

"Hey," I say, waiting for him to meet my eyes. "If Jennifer broke up with you because of your injuries, she's a bitch, and you're better off without her." My voice is even, my gaze unwavering.

Kip's eyes widen, but he doesn't object to my name-calling. Lila frowns, though.

"What Charlie meant to say is that any woman shallow enough to end a relationship because of your injuries isn't worth your time or energy. You dedicated yourself to serving our country, and you paid a heavy price. Anyone who would fixate on scars or injuries and overlook all the wonderful things about you doesn't deserve you. You're sweet, and thoughtful, and handsome, and you deserve someone equally kind and loyal. Nobody's perfect, Kip, certainly not that –" she catches herself before echoing my assessment, and Kip's lips twitch despite his misery – "that woman. All people are flawed, but two people can still be perfect for each other."

"And in case I was unclear, the perfect woman for you is not that callous bitch," I add. The corners of my mouth turn up a bit, and he gives me a sad smile, catching me off guard when he sighs and leans his forehead against mine. I don't panic, because Kip's like a big, sweet, muscle-bound puppy – a soldier version of Tom's dog, Bella. Lila leans against him, one arm around his shoulders, the other gripping his upper arm.

Tom chooses that moment to poke his head around the door. "I feel excluded," he grumbles. "Someone should have called me. I'm a hugger."

I glance sideways at him, Kip's head still pressed to mine. "I'm sure Kip will hug you if you ask nicely."

The mood lightened, Kip pulls back. "I need to get to PT," he says. "But thanks. I needed that. My buddy Kyle said the same thing, but he's a guy, so..."

"While I'll admit it's rare, men do occasionally have a few words of wisdom," Lila teases, glancing at Tom. She tips her head in his direction. "Tom will tell you the same thing we did. Although hopefully," she frowns at me again, "he won't use profanity to express his opinion in a clinical setting, unlike some people I know."

I smile angelically. "I have no idea what you're talking about."

LILA

My period is late.

I'm *never* late.

I've peed on the stick, and now I sit here, unable to stop bouncing my leg up and down, counting down the seconds.

I'm not going to get my hopes up. The hormone shots have probably just thrown off the timing of my cycle. Besides, I'm not very late, not even a week.

Hell, I'll probably have a negative pregnancy test and then get my period this afternoon, so I can have two crushing defeats in one day, because, yay me.

And then of course, I'll cry and rage and take it out on Tucker, who's had to deal with my godawful mood swings from these hormone injections. I constantly feel like I'm at the mercy of my emotions, like they're controlling me instead of the other way around, and that's never been me. Not until very recently, anyway.

My heart is in my throat as I look at the timer on my phone again. Thirty seconds until I see just how badly my day is going to go.

Twenty seconds.

Ten.

Time's up.

But I can't bring myself to look. I don't want to see that single line, telling me I've failed again. I sit on the closed toilet, my head in my hands, my legs shaking.

Suck it up. You're stronger than this. You were a battlefield medic. You've seen all manner of horrors. This is nothing. It's a stick. You can look at a pink and white stick.

I grab the test before my bravado can fade away and stare down at it.

Two lines.

Two lines.

Oh my God.

"Oh my God!"

I don't realize I'm screaming until I hear feet flying up the stairs. Tucker grabs the bathroom door handle, but it's locked, and he pounds on the door.

"Lila! Lila! Are you okay?"

I open the door and he rushes in, looking me over from head to toe, scanning for injuries. When he sees nothing, he glances around the room before looking back at me.

I've gone from shrieking like a banshee to completely mute.

Tucker grabs my upper arms and squeezes. "Sweetness? What's wrong?"

I hold out the test with shaking hands. "Nothing's wrong. It's right."

He stares down at the test. I watch as comprehension slowly falls over him. "Two lines? Is that – did we – are you – pregnant?"

TUCKER

I'm downstairs pouring myself a cup of coffee when I hear a scream from upstairs.

"Lila?"

There's no answer. My mug shatters on the floor as I bolt up the stairs two at a time, rushing into the bedroom. "Lila?" The bedroom is empty, but the bathroom door is closed. I race to it, but the door is locked. "Lila! Are you okay?" I pound the door with my fist.

I'm about to rip it off its hinges when she opens the door, pale and tearstained, a pregnancy test in her hand.

Dammit. Not again.

Then a stunned smile appears on her face, and she holds the pink plastic test out to me.

It has two pink lines.

I'm not entirely certain what that means, but I've seen Lila's reaction to finding out she's not pregnant several times now, and this isn't it.

So then...

"Two lines? Is that – did we – are you – pregnant?"

Lila nods and throws her arms around my neck. "Yes."

I snatch her up and spin her around before setting her down and looking into her stunning eyes. "Pregnant?"

She nods again, and it feels like everything is moving in slow motion for a minute. Then my brain catches up with my body.

"Oh my God – we did it!" I cup her face in my hands and kiss her long and hard, until her body molds itself to mine and we're both breathless. "I can't wait to see you carrying my baby."

Lila wrinkles her nose. "Stretch marks and cankles?"

"Badges of honor, Sweetness, badges of honor." I pick her up and sling her over my shoulder caveman-style as she squeals. Then I take her back to our bed and spend a very long time worshiping every part of her incredible, newly-pregnant body.

CHARLIE

Mark and I gradually resume a routine at home. He sees Tom daily to evaluate whether he's ready to increase the pounds of pressure on his footie-tipped implant or if he needs to maintain his current regimen for another day or two. He's making fast progress, which surprises me – not because he isn't driven and determined, because he is, but because it was such a struggle to get his bones to fuse after the explosion. I'm glad he's healing faster now, because every bit of progress he can make is a good thing. I'll do anything to remove the shadow that clouds his eyes.

He's regressed to concealing his residual limb and abutment when he isn't actively exercising with the footie, something he hasn't done since he first came home. Instead of wearing just shorts, he tops them with pinned-up sweats. He removes his sweatpants for PT, then quickly dons them again, even wearing them to bed. I'm not sure if he's hiding his leg from himself or me.

We still have group workouts and dinners three days a week, often with Tom and Maya. Mark is pleasant but quiet. He answers when spoken to, but doesn't voluntarily engage. None of us mention it. We're trying to wait it out. When it's just the two of us, the silence is deafening. He finds ways to escape, cutting his time with me as much as possible. Each day twists the knife in my heart a little more, because he's pulling away, and there's not a damn thing I can do about it.

Not in the daytime, at least.

At night, it's a different story. He knows I have night terrors when I'm not with him, though I'd never use that to manipulate him. However, because he knows firsthand how bad my night terrors can be, he sleeps beside me, and I have no qualms about using his proximity to my advantage. I go to bed wearing silky barely-there camisoles or chemises, or if he's exceptionally withdrawn, nothing at all. His mind may tell him to withdraw, but his body answers to me.

A few days later, I barricade myself in my office while Mark is in the rehab gym. He'll be in there for close to an hour before spending another hour in hydrotherapy and massage. When I'm alone, I turn on my computer to video chat with the one person who might be able to help.

Stubbs' rich mahogany skin and shaved head contrast against the bright sun streaming in the window behind him. He flashes me his brilliant smile, and when he speaks, the deep timbre of his voice rolls over me. "Missing me already, Green Eyes?"

I grin. "Hey, Stubbs. Did you get your exam results? Are you official yet?"

He beams. "As of this morning, I am an officially licensed mental health counselor."

"Congratulations! So what now?"

He shrugs. "I have a couple of offers I'm reviewing. The VA from Pueblo is one," he adds.

My breath catches. "You know we'd love to have you here."

He nods. "I'm considering it. Moving is a pain in the – " He clears his throat, and I smile. "I've lived in Texas a long time now. I've got roots, you know?"

"I understand. Our offer isn't going anywhere. And if you decide you want it, Lila and I can fly down one weekend to help you pack."

He laughs. "Is that a job perk? I didn't see that in the paperwork."

I laugh, too. "It's in the fine print."

He grins, then his eyes turn more serious. "You said you needed to talk. What's up?"

I fold my hands together, my fingers suddenly cold despite the warmth of the office. "What was your osseointegration surgery like?"

He shakes his head and blows out a deep breath. "Rough. I had both legs done at once. They wanted to do them one at a time, but I told them I was a badass motherfu – uh – that I was tough enough to handle it."

I laugh at his attempt to control his swearing. "You know, you're not going to offend me with profanity. There are days my language could make you blush."

Dark eyes meet mine. "Mark won't answer my texts or voicemails. How's he doing?"

"He's not answering you?" That surprises me. "He's... struggling."

He frowns. "Physically? Or up here?" He taps his temple.

"Emotionally. He went into the surgery happy and hopeful and came out completely different. Distant." I swallow hard. "Since the surgery, he's been withdrawing. He spends most of his time pulling away from me now. After your cryptic warnings on the camping trip, I was hoping you'd give me some insight."

He leans back, running a thick finger over his lips. "It's hard," he finally says. "You survive devastating injuries and go from being in prime condition one day to flat on your back and damn near helpless the next. You push yourself and push yourself and finally come to grips with who you are post-injury. Then the docs offer you this surgery, and it feels like a lifeline, because even though you know in your head it won't make you who you were before, some part of you can't help hoping. Waking up to see metal rods hanging out of your body hits you hard, no matter how prepared you think you are. Some damages can't be seen. We all choose that surgery to recapture what we've lost. Realizing you look like a cyborg knocks you on your ass."

"You had a difficult time, too?"

He nods slowly. "Worse than with my initial injuries."

My eyes widen. "Really? Why?"

"I was angry after the explosion, and I used that anger to drive me. By the time I had the surgery, I wasn't angry anymore. All I had was hope, and that's a lot more fragile than anger."

"So what did you do?"

"Support group. A shrink. Reality checks from other guys who'd been in my position were what helped most." He smiles, but there's pain behind it. "Never leave a man behind, you know?"

I frown. "I'm not sure I can convince Mark to talk to anyone. If it hadn't been mandated at Brooke, he'd never have agreed to go."

"He sees needing help as a sign of weakness, and because of his injuries, he already feels weak. Asking for help isn't something he'll do willingly." He purses his lips, scrutinizing me. "What if he thought he was going to support you? Would he do that?"

I pause. "If I found a support group for vets with body image issues, I think he'd come along, as long as he thought it was for me." My cheeks grow warm. "I have a lot of scars." He merely nods, and I wonder how much of my story he and Mark discussed that awful day Mark exploded on me and Stubbs jerked a knot in his ass.

I frown, thinking over his words. "You said people have surgery to regain what they've lost. Mark's said all along that he couldn't wait to be normal again. We've argued several times about his bullshit belief that he's not 'normal' now." I pause, biting my lip. "I went out with one guy for a while, and when he saw my scars, he freaked out and said – well, it's not important what he said, but he was cruel." I pause. "It wasn't exactly that he hurt me – we hadn't been dating long enough for that. It was mostly that his reaction to my scars made me believe people would always see me as damaged. But Mark kept telling me that my scars didn't define me."

Stubbs' glower speaks volumes about his opinion of Blake, though his tone is mild when he speaks. "Pretty Boy's right."

"It's the same argument I've been making to him about his own body, but I'm not getting anywhere. What am I doing wrong?"

The huge man shakes his head. "Nothing. There's none so blind as one who will not see, right? Mark's got to see it for himself." He pauses. "That day in Texas when he lost his shit was a turning point for him. That was the catalyst that made him realize he needed help."

My heart sinks. "So there's got to be another catalyst."

"Maybe," he agrees, "but I don't think he'll lash out at you again. He was too upset afterwards by how he'd behaved toward you."

I hope Stubbs is right. That day was one of the worst of my life. "So what do I do?"

"Keep doing what you're doing. His reality has changed again, and he needs time to deal with it. Once he's off his crutches, he should be in a much better frame of mind."

"I hope so," I murmur. But he won't be off his crutches till December.

It's currently September.

"For now, look for a support group, and broach the subject of seeing a psychiatrist. I'll be happy to talk with him if he'll take my damn calls, but if he needs his meds adjusted, he'll need to see someone local. I'm sure the VA can recommend someone. I'll keep reaching out to him."

"Thanks, Stubbs."

The huge man blows me a kiss. "Anytime, Green Eyes. Call if you need anything."

The following day, I drive Mark to Pueblo for Dr. Walters to remove his sutures. "Everything looks good," he says. "I'll see you next week. Bring your prosthesis when you come. You'll most likely be wearing it when you leave." Mark beams from ear to ear upon hearing that.

A week later, he leaves his appointment with his shiny new carbon-fiber prosthesis in place. He's on crutches, and he's only partially weight-bearing, but he's making strong progress.

"I'll be walking around like a normal person by Christmas," he says in amazement.

His words hit me all wrong. I'm stressed from his continued emotional withdrawal, and I feel like a broken record repeating the same phrase over and over. "You are normal, Mark."

"You know what I mean."

We're sitting in the car, but I'm still in park, so I turn to him. "Actually, I don't. Why don't you explain it to me?"

"Not a freak. I can wear jeans, and no one will know I'm fucked up if I don't want them to."

I close my eyes and massage my forehead. "There's so much wrong with what you just said that I don't even know where to begin."

He raises an eyebrow, honestly puzzled, because he actually *believes* that bullshit.

"People with disabilities aren't freaks, Mark."

"No, they're not," he agrees immediately, "but I am."

"Why? What makes you so special that your injuries lessen you as a person?"

He stiffens. "I'm not special to you?"

"That's not even remotely what I just said. I'm asking you why you're okay with disabilities in everyone but yourself."

"Because I don't want to be disabled," he snaps.

"I doubt anyone who's disabled does."

"People look at me differently now."

"Which people?"

"People."

"Do I?"

He rolls his eyes. "That's different."

"Do Tucker and Lila?"

"Again, that's different. We were close before."

"How about Tom or Maya? They didn't know you before you moved here."

He huffs, pursing his lips. "Tom works with people with disabilities for a living, and he's raised Maya to think disabilities aren't a big deal."

"So if it doesn't matter to your friends, who does it matter to?"

"People," he says again.

I cock my head at him. "Has someone actually treated you differently because of your amputation, or do you just assume they will?"

"Two people, actually, and Tucker can verify them. He and I went to a sports bar when you and Lila were in Pueblo one weekend. One woman was all over me until she found out I was an amputee. Then she couldn't get away fast enough."

"So a couple of drunk strangers had a problem with your amputation, and you decide the problem is you, not the shallow morons who didn't like you because you were injured in battle?"

"The second woman hit on me *because* I'm an amputee," he retorts. "She had a stump fetish."

I blink, hoping my expression is neutral as irrational jealousy flares. "And that's a problem because..." I prod.

"She only wanted me for my amputation."

"Women have thrown themselves at you your entire adult life because of your looks, and I don't remember you objecting before. Why is it suddenly a problem?"

"It was okay when I was worth looking at," he snarls.

Something inside me snaps. "That's the entire problem with your attitude in a nutshell. You thought you were worth more before because of the way you looked. Now that your body's changed, you've decided you're worthless. That's bullshit, Mark, complete and total bullshit. Your looks were never what defined you, not then and not now. You're defined by who you are and by how you treat others, not by strangers you'll never see again whose opinions don't mean jack shit. And for the record, you're fucking sexy as hell, and I don't give a damn if you have one leg or four. You're worth everything to me."

Silence falls over the car. I didn't use the L-word, but I might as well have.

I reverse rapidly out of the parking space and peel out of the lot, driving far too fast down the curvy mountain roads. My hands are shaking, and I'm on the verge of tears.

"I don't want you to be angry," he says quietly, reaching over and placing his hand on mine. It's the first time he's touched me outside of our bed in over a week.

I shake my head. "I'm not angry. I'm upset."

"Why?"

The tears I've been fighting fill my eyes, and I try to blink them away, but I'm not quick enough. "Because nothing I say gets through to you. You've put this wall up to keep everyone out, even me, because you can't see your own value."

He reaches for my face, wiping away a tear with his thumb. "You're closer to me than I've ever let anyone get. You know that, Charlie."

"Then why does it feel like you keep pushing me away?"

He doesn't answer. He doesn't have to.

Because he is pushing me away, and we both know it. The likelihood of me losing him escalates daily, and the thought is unbearable. Tears trickle down my face for most of the long drive home, but Mark never says another word.

CHAPTER EIGHTEEN

MARK

I HAVE A NEW workout partner in rehab. Terrell, who's been with me since the beginning, moved to an earlier slot after getting a new nine-to-five job managing a shipping company. My new partner is a kid named Kip. His injury is similar to mine, except his amputation is on his left lower leg.

I can tell you a lot about Kip.

For example, I can tell you his amputation happened when a bomb destroyed the truck he was in. A stranded vehicle on a desert road meant his humvee had to go off-road to pass it. A buried IED went off beneath them when they did, and he and another soldier were ejected from the vehicle. The other two soldiers in the humvee were badly burned in the resulting fireball. The second ejected soldier ended up with a broken neck and a traumatic brain injury. Now he's a quadriplegic with no memory of who he or anyone else is. He doesn't even recognize his own mother.

I can tell you Kip spent two months in the hospital, that he broke every vertebrae in his back between L3 and S2, that he fractured his right shoulder blade, multiple right ribs, and his right hip. I can tell you he has a titanium hip replacement on that side and that he struggled with his crutches until his ribs healed. I can tell you the explosion ripped his left ankle off, but the surgeons refined his amputation to just below his left calf.

I can tell you his now-ex-girlfriend's name is Jennifer, and that she has black hair that falls to her tiny waist, huge blue doe eyes, and has had – and wrecked – three new cars in the past two years – a Mustang, a Camaro, and a Miata. Her favorite color is gold (the twenty-four karat variety), and she loves gifts. I can tell you she dumped him, but he believes it's temporary. Just a rough patch, is how he's put it.

Repeatedly.

I can tell you his best friend's name is Kyle, and they share a ground-level apartment. Kyle doesn't think much of Jennifer, but he tries not to say much about it around Kip. Kip overheard him on the phone with his mom, though, and now she won't stop coming over to check on him.

I can tell you all these things because for the love of God, Kip. Just. Won't. Shut. Up.

Today's topic is the car he's thinking about getting Jennifer. A nearby dealership has last year's model convertibles on sale for twenty percent below sticker price because the new inventory is in. He thinks he can swing it, though it'll cut his own budget painfully thin. But it might end their "rough patch" and help Jennifer see he's worth a second chance.

Thankfully, Tom doesn't mind talking to him, leaving me to focus on getting my exercises done and escaping. Kip's a good kid, but I don't have the emotional energy to feed his desperate need for approval and acceptance. It takes all my effort to keep my foul moods from leaking out onto Charlie like I did in Texas, though that was less "leak" and more "steady stream".

Charlie is the best thing that ever happened to me. I know that. But I've also known since I woke up with this fucking pirate peg leg that she deserves something better than I'll ever be able to give her. I know I need to let her go, but I'm weak, and she knows it. She uses her perfect body to pull me back in, and my willpower shatters like glass. She's my heroin, and I'm completely addicted.

A week or so after I finally get to start wearing my prosthetic, Tucker and I go out to his usual sports bar. It's packed to the gills, too loud to even hear each other. After a couple of beers, we call it a night. When I get home, Charlie's in my shower. "Knock, knock, Baby Girl," I call from the doorway, not wanting to startle her.

She opens the glass door a crack, and I catch a glimpse of creamy skin, gorgeous curves, and bright eyes. "I wasn't expecting you home so soon. Want to join me?"

She draws me in like a moth to a flame, and despite knowing I ought to decline, I'm powerless to resist. "I thought you'd never ask."

I scurry back to the bedroom and divest myself of my jeans far enough to use the Allen wrench to remove my prosthesis. I yank it out of the leg of my jeans before peeling them the rest of the way down and off my body. I finish stripping quickly before attaching my flesh-colored shower leg with its non-slip foot, then grab my crutches and hurry to the bathroom.

A couple more months and I won't need these damn crutches at all.

I leave them outside the shower, using the handrails and my good leg to limp to her, still only partially bearing weight on my prosthesis. She faces me, her wet hair slicked back, her eyes luminous. "Hi," she murmurs.

I lean closer, gripping the handrail with my right arm and bracing my left arm on the shower wall, caging her body. My lips close over hers. "Hi," I answer against her lips.

Soft sighs. Softer flesh. Quiet groans and loud moans. Hard planes. Lush curves. Slick skin. Heat. I devour her with my mouth before spinning her around to face the wall. My mouth finds the place where her neck meets her shoulder, grazing her with my teeth. My left hand cups her breast before moving lower to stroke between her legs. My erection juts out, and I thrust lightly against her pussy from behind, sliding from her entrance to her clit and back, and she moans, chasing my cock with her body.

That's all the encouragement I need.

I wrap my arm around her waist, guiding her hips back as I sink into her. She gasps, moving forward slightly before pushing back against me, her inner walls gripping me.

God, she feels good.

I try to hold back, but she's so responsive, pushing back, pulling me in further. I growl deep in my chest before gripping her hip tightly with my left hand, hanging onto the shower rail with my right hand for more powerful thrusts. She's braced with her hands against the wall, and I release her hip, capturing her wrists to slide them higher up the wall, straightening her body and changing the angle at which we fit together before slamming into her.

In a split second, everything shatters.

Charlie turns ferocious in the space of a single breath. She jerks free from me and whirls, elbowing me below the ribs hard enough to double me over. A second elbow catches me in the face, followed by a shove that knocks me back onto my ass, skidding across the wet floor of the shower. I stare at her, confused as hell.

She's panting, snarling, wild-eyed and fierce, but she's not... *here*. She's somewhere else, another time, another place. She scoots backwards on the bench, backing into the corner, pulling her knees to her chest as she stares blankly, breathing hard.

Oh fuck.

"Baby Girl?"

There's no response from her, none at all.

She's having a flashback.

I replay the last couple of minutes and suddenly feel sick.

Fuck. What was I thinking?

Guilt washes over me, thick and sour. When I rescued Charlie from that cell, they'd suspended her by her wrists and raped her from behind God knows how many times.

And I just held her wrists above her head and fucked her hard in that exact position.

"Baby Girl? Baby Girl, it's me. You're safe."

But she just stares, wordless, unblinking. Broken.

I stand carefully, backing away to the rear wall of the shower. I check the temperature to be sure the water's warm before angling the shower head toward her. I'm not sure how long it might take me to get through to her, and I don't want her getting chilled. Then I brace myself on the rail, limping toward the shower door. Cold air rushes into the steamy space when I open it, and she shivers. I reach for a bath towel and drape it over her, careful not to touch her. She doesn't move. Warm water soaks into it immediately. Hopefully, it will keep her warm. I leave the shower door open so I can monitor her without encroaching on her space.

I'm pretty sure a naked man isn't something someone reliving a rape should see, so I dry off quickly and drag on shorts, leaving my shower leg attached. I hobble back into the bathroom.

Charlie hasn't moved an inch, and her eyes are glazed. It reminds me of her expression when they summoned me from Afghanistan to Walter Reed. She was catatonic then. It was so bad, they were considering placing her in a psychiatric hospital.

I drop a towel onto the floor in front of the shower, mopping up the excess spray from the shower before sitting down. I'm in her line of sight, but still far enough away that I'm not a threat, and she has the high ground.

"Hey, Baby Girl. You're safe. No one's going to hurt you. I've got you, Baby Girl. You're safe." I repeat the same phrases over and over as I observe her, my stomach clenching at my thoughtlessness. As minutes pass, her breathing slows and deepens. I'm watching when her arms tense around her knees and her eyes widen.

"You're safe, Baby Girl. You're at home, in my shower. No one's going to hurt you." She jumps visibly, her eyes tracking for the source of my voice before she freezes.

"Oh, God," she whispers.

"Tell me where you are," I prompt her.

"Cedar Ridge. My house. Your shower."

"Tell me four things you can see."

"Water all over the floor, a wet bath towel, you sitting on the floor, and a bruise coming up on your face. I know where I'm at. Oh, God, Mark, did I do that?"

"Do what?"

She throws off the saturated towel and flings herself toward me, nearly slipping on the wet tile. I catch her in my arms as she lands on me, wrapping her wet body around me, her legs around my waist and her head on my chest.

"I'm so sorry, Charlie. I wasn't thinking. I didn't mean – " My throat gets tight at the thought of scaring her, of hurting her.

She shakes her head. "I'm sorry. I – I hit you, didn't I? And shoved you. Are you okay? Did I hurt you? I wasn't – I didn't see you. I only saw them. Him." She trembles violently against me.

I stroke her wet hair. "You're safe now. They can't hurt you ever again."

But I did, because I got too caught up to think about how my actions might affect her.

Again.

Charlie curls closer to me, naked and wet. I lean back and reach for a towel on the wall rack. I wrap it around her, rubbing her through it to dry her damp skin. When her back is dry, I slide a hand between us, gently drying her front, not letting myself linger over her curves.

"Come on. We'll go sit on the bed and I'll dry your hair," I murmur.

Wide eyes flicker to mine. "You'd do that?"

I grin. "I'm a man of many talents, Charlie, and believe it or not, I can operate a blow dryer."

She clambers to her feet and offers me a hand. I hesitate, and she rolls her eyes. I scowl and accept her help, balancing on my left leg until she passes me my crutches. I turn off the shower and follow her, watching the sway of her perfect ass.

Not now. You've done more than enough tonight.

She glances at me. "I got your shorts all wet crawling onto your lap. You might as well pull them off." Then she reaches for a wide-tooth comb and bends at the waist, her luscious ass in the air as she combs the tangles from her hair.

Naked.

I swallow hard as my cock comes to life.

Not now, asshole. You've done more than enough.

Instead, I toss the blow dryer onto the bed. I yank off my wet shorts and detach my shower leg before plugging in the blow dryer and surreptitiously covering my erection with a pillow. She straightens up, and I pat the bed in front of me.

"Come here, Baby Girl."

She sits in front of me, her wet hair falling onto her back, making her shiver. I turn on the dryer and go to work, running my fingers through her hair as I dry her thick tresses. The light from the lamp illuminates the red and gold strands in her light brown hair. I slide my fingers higher, massaging her scalp, and she leans into my touch.

I keep going, long after her hair is dry, just because I like the feel of her silky hair, and because she's melting against me from the warmth and white noise of the dryer. When I finally turn it off, she groans.

"I like you rubbing my head."

"I can do it with both hands if I'm not using the dryer," I point out.

"Less yapping, more rubbing."

She seems like herself again, so I chuckle and do as requested, my long fingers working from the base of her neck all over her scalp. She moans, tipping her head back, and before I can stop myself, I fasten my lips on her throat.

When I realize what I'm doing, I pull away, returning my attention to her massaging her head.

She angles toward me, her eyes questioning. "Why did you stop?"

"What?"

"Kissing me. Why did you stop?"

My jaw tightens. "I'm pretty sure I've done enough tonight."

She frowns. "Because I had a flashback?"

"Because I caused your flashback," I correct her.

Her eyes narrow. "No, those assholes caused my flashback."

My emotions erupt out of nowhere, words and feelings I've buried for years boiling out of me like molten lava. "No, Charlie, I did. It's my fault. Every single bit of it, everything you went through, it's my fault. Don't you get it? I made the call for you guys to go help those villagers. I sent you into a trap. Six men died and two women's lives were destroyed because of me. Me, Charlie. Everything that happened to you is my fault, and I'll never forgive myself. Never."

She stares at me, her mouth agape. "You can't really believe that."

I'm silent.

She kneels in front of me, cupping my face in her hands. "Mark, what happened wasn't your fault. You'd never have sent us in if you'd thought anything like that would happen. Leave the blame where it belongs – on the cruel bastards that committed those atrocities. I wouldn't be here now if it weren't for you. You saved my life, and Lila's, too."

Her mouth closes over mine, and though I kiss her back, when she tries to deepen it, I take her upper arms and gently ease her back.

"I don't think this is a good idea."

"Why not?"

"Because thirty minutes ago you were catatonic in the shower."

Her gaze sharpens. "So you don't want to kiss me anymore because I had a flashback?"

I frown. "Don't be absurd."

"Then kiss me, dammit."

"Charlie," I begin, but before I can say another word, she pushes me back. She stretches out over me, her breasts pressing into my chest, one exquisite leg sliding between my thighs. My cock surges, and she smiles before bringing her lips to mine, stopping just before she touches them.

"Kiss me, Mark. Please?"

The uncertainty in her plea is my undoing. All of my restraint dissipates as my hand slides into her hair, cradling her head as I pull her lips to mine. It's like always – instant fire, immediate passion. Her tongue chases mine. Her hips arch against me. My hands skim lightly over her body until she groans in frustration. "Touch me, Mark. I'm not breakable. I need to feel you."

I roll, taking her with me, positioning myself above her, giving her what she wants, my hands all over her, my lips and teeth and tongue everywhere. She writhes beneath me, her arousal coating both our thighs as she moans and wraps her legs around my waist.

She opens her eyes then, staring into mine. "Take me from behind."

"What?"

"I'm not going to let them win."

"I – I don't think that's a good idea," I say, licking my lips.

"Why not?"

"Because it didn't go well earlier."

"Please," she pleads. "I need this, Mark."

My mind flips through possibilities at light speed. "Fine, but you take me. That way, you're in charge."

She gives me a quizzical glance. "How?"

I roll off her and slide to the far edge of the bed before standing and taking two hops to the chaise. "Come here." I lean back in the arched chaise, my upper body angled, my hips low, and my knees slightly elevated from the S-curve of its design. Charlie crosses the room without hesitation. "Tell me your safe word, Charlie."

"Daffodil," she says immediately, and I nod.

"Sit on my lap and lean back against me."

She follows my instructions, her legs on either side of me, her body perfectly sandwiching my cock, and I groan in appreciation. I reach for her ankles, bending her legs beneath her to provide leverage. "Put my hands where you want them so I can help you move." No way am I grabbing her hips like I would if she were facing me. This is already against my better judgment.

She turns her face to mine. "You talk too much," she murmurs, leaning close and licking across my lips before sliding her tongue inside my mouth. Her kiss ignites a fire that burns straight to my cock, and I grind against her, making her gasp. I palm her full breasts, plucking her nipples, and she arches into my hands.

She lifts her hips, slowly sinking down onto my cock, taking me fully inside her. "Oh, God," she moans. She reaches back, gripping my arms, using them for balance and support. She moves above me, gently at first, gradually going deeper. Harder.

She reaches for my hands, lacing her fingers with mine before guiding them to her hips.

I remember Tucker's advice about making sure she's fully present. "Say my name," I murmur. "I need to know you're with me."

"Please, Mark. Please." Her voice is ragged.

I lift her then, sliding our linked hands beneath her thighs, helping her rise and fall, slowly at first, then faster.

"Fuck, Baby Girl, it's so deep like this," I bite out, trying to slow my raging body. She bows back against my chest, moaning my name over and over. As I help her move, I shift her to a more back-and-forth rhythm, swirling my hips up each time I lower her, feeling her body pulsing right on the edge.

"That's right, Baby Girl. You're so close, so fucking close. I can feel it. Take what you need." She moans, and her pussy throbs. She likes it when I talk dirty.

I sit up, changing the angle, and from this position, it's easier for her to lift and lower herself. She gasps at the fullness. "Oh, Mark," she moans, her words drawn out, her movements becoming more frantic.

"That's right, Baby Girl. Take me. Feel me," I growl, my lips just beneath her ear. She shivers, then grabs my hands and plants them on her hips.

"Faster," she begs, and I oblige, helping her move, rocking with her, feeling the tension within her rising higher and higher. The familiar pressure builds low in my pelvis, and I'm right on the edge, but I have to make this good for her first. I have to.

"Fuck, Baby Girl," I hiss as she grinds down into me. She lifts herself one more time, and as she comes down, I hold her in place and roll my hips as I sink my teeth into her collarbone.

Charlie wails my name as she detonates around me. Her inner walls clench and grip my cock, and I explode inside her. My body pulses, and my vision goes dark for a moment.

We're both breathing hard, damp with sweat and thoroughly sated. I kiss the place where I bit her and feel her chuckle.

"Mmh?"

"The biting. I love it when you do that."

"I know. It tips you over the edge."

"Does it do that to all the women you've been with?"

I frown, not liking this turn in conversation. "I've never done that with anyone else."

"It's very primal," she murmurs. "Like you're a wolf. Like you're claiming me."

I claimed you long ago. You're mine, Charlie, always. Only mine.

"Maybe I'm secretly a vampire."

"Then you're not a very good one," she teases, "because I haven't bled once."

"Clearly, I need more practice," I say, nipping her lightly.

"Practice to your heart's content," she purrs, arching into me.

We've driven a little more darkness out of Charlie's soul tonight.

Unfortunately, I'm pretty sure my soul absorbed it, because when she sleeps, all I can think about is how much it's going to destroy me to let her go.

CHARLIE

Despite moments of closeness, like after my flashback in the shower, the distance between us continues to grow. Mark seems okay when Lila and Tucker are here, but noticeably less so when Tom visits. He's not rude – he's just more withdrawn. In fact, lately he seems to leave me alone with Tom at every opportunity, and afterwards, he's always silent.

When it's just the two of us, the silence yawns between us, a gaping hole that small talk can't fill. And deeper talks? Meaningful talks? Those are a thing of the past. Oh, he's willing to listen if I want to talk, as long as it's not about us or him, but he won't discuss anything about himself, his leg, his thoughts, or his feelings. Conversation is limited to light-and-fluffy, inconsequential topics, like what movie to watch or what's for dinner. The tension inside me builds, because I can feel the distance between us expanding, and I don't know how to fix it. My unease is unrelenting. The more I reach for him, the further he retreats.

The only time I feel anything from him is in bed. He pointedly resists emotional closeness, something we had long before any physical relationship. The loss of our bond guts me. Still, in bed, his need for me overpowers his intentional distance. He can avoid connecting with me during the day, but at night, his body betrays him. His heart and mind may not want me, but his body does, and I use that to my advantage, even knowing it will be more painful for me in the long run. The weighty emotion in his touch every night leaves me feeling like he's preparing to say goodbye, and I have no idea how to get him to love me the way I love him.

The only bright spot in our lives is Lila's positive pregnancy test. She and Tucker kept it quiet for a little while, just to be sure. She was afraid I'd be upset when she told me, but I was ecstatic. I screamed and hugged her, and we both cried happy tears. If anyone deserves a baby, it's Lila.

The rest of my life feels like complete and utter shit. Mark's disgust for his changed body is discoloring everything in his world, and by extension, our relationship. He keeps pulling further and further away, and I keep striving to draw him back in.

But I'm fighting a losing battle, and deep down, I know it.

I cry when I'm alone because I don't see a path forward for us. Nothing I say to him changes how he sees himself. Lila keeps reminding me that the only person who can change Mark's opinion of himself is Mark, and he's not interested. Stubbs encourages me to stay the course, though he's frustrated as well, because Mark still won't respond to his calls and texts.

My fear and despondency flourish unchecked, and I can't even talk to Mark about it, because the topic is off-limits. It's not "light and fluffy". I'm constantly on the verge of tears, headachy and tense, barely sleeping, barely eating, feeling the sword of Damocles dangling over my head.

The following Wednesday is exceptionally challenging. I end up at the VA in Pueblo, courtesy of Dr. Martinez's invitation when he dropped by to see me and met Stubbs. I spend my morning in a boardroom full of doctors, detailing the services our clinic currently offers and gleaning input on options they'd like to see while (shamelessly) drumming up business. They're intrigued when Dr. Martinez discusses offering Stubbs a position as a counselor based out of our clinic. He describes Stubbs' history and his resume, and their feedback is overwhelmingly positive.

The morning goes smoothly, even though I abhor schmoozing. This is Lila's area of expertise, but she coerced me by promising to cook tonight. She caught me when I was distracted, or I'd never have fallen for it, because it's Wednesday – a group workout/ dinner day – and she'd likely have been cooking anyway.

I'm dressed like an actual professional for once, wearing a dark red skirt and blazer with an army green silk camisole beneath. The camisole is high enough in front to conceal my scars, but dips almost to my waist in the back. It doesn't matter, because the blazer covers my back. I've climbed out of my SUV in my entirely-too-high-for-a-gravel-parking-lot heels and grabbed my rarely-used briefcase when I glance at the white van parked next to me. It's disability-friendly, operating entirely via hand controls. Kip's mother's church bought it for him when he got home from Walter Reed. Kip sits inside the van, his head down on the steering wheel.

I pause for a second before circling the vehicle to knock on the driver's side window. Kip raises his head, and I'm startled to see tears running down his face. Without even asking, I pull open the door and touch his arm. "What's wrong?"

He shakes his head, unable to speak, and I react automatically. "You. Me. My office. Now."

Sometimes dealing with soldiers is more effective when you adopt the tone of a commanding officer. There's a certain bark that often instinctively makes them comply. Lila and I mastered the technique as medics. It almost always worked, even with wounded officers who outranked us. Tom already possesses a natural air of authority. This approach serves us well when we're trying to get a client to keep pushing, or in this case, tell me what's troubling him.

My assertiveness has the desired effect on Kip, who raises his eyes, mumbles, "Yes, ma'am," and follows me into the building. I march around the front desk past Tara's raised eyebrows and down the hall to my office, Kip trailing behind.

"Have a seat," I tell him, pointing to the sofa. "I'll be right back."

I stop by the desk, tell a curious Tara I'll be indisposed for a bit, let Tom know Kip will be late, and grab two bottles of water. I return to find Kip glancing around my office. When he looks at me, his eyebrows pull together in surprise.

"You're dressed up."

"I had a business meeting with several physicians at the VA. I usually make Lila go, but she connived me into handling it today."

"You look nice," he says. "I've never seen you in real clothes before."

I hide a smile. "Thanks, Kip." I tilt my head. "How about you tell me what's going on? What's got you so upset?"

He sighs heavily. "I saw her last night. Jennifer. She was with a guy, and they were pretty cozy. It's only been a couple of weeks. When she saw me, she turned and walked away. Didn't even say hello. She acted like she didn't know me and kept going." He pauses. "I was sure we'd get back together, but she's already moved on." Hurt flares in his blue-green eyes.

I open a bottle of water and pass it to him, then open mine and take a long drink, gathering my thoughts. "So you were together about a year and a half, right?"

"A little less. Almost two months before I shipped out, then eleven months over there and two in the hospital, and I've been home six weeks."

"Did she visit you at Walter Reed?" He shakes his head. "So you two were only in the same location for the first two months?"

He frowns. "So because she's creeped out by hospitals, you think she didn't care?"

I shake my head. "I didn't say that. I'm just trying to understand the timeline in my head. Did she keep in touch with you while you were deployed?"

He nods, then hesitates. "Well, at first. Emails and packages. But they kind of dropped off. She's busy, though. She works for a sales company and she travels a lot."

I can see it, even if he can't, or more likely, won't. He and Jennifer dated briefly. She may have said she loved him before he shipped out to give him something to hold on to when things got rough. Or maybe she never said it, and he just assumed she shared his feelings. I've seen it happen more times than I can count. Soldiers in stressful situations sometimes cope by clinging to memories of people they care for. Occasionally, they build a casual relationship into something monumental in their mind. It doesn't matter if it was barely a relationship when they deployed, or if they likely wouldn't be together now if they hadn't shipped out. The old saying about absence making the heart grow fonder is often true for servicemen and women.

I keep all that to myself. Whether their relationship was solid or not, Kip's reeling from its loss. "I'm sorry things didn't work out the way you wanted them to."

Even if he's clearly better off without her.

Kip explodes without warning. "This goddamn leg ruined everything!" As he speaks, he hurls his crutches. One knocks the lamp off an end table, and it falls to the floor with a crash. The other crutch smacks the front of my desk before clattering to the floor.

Footsteps rush down the hall just before Tom bursts in. "Charlie?" His eyes scan the room, landing on the broken lamp and scattered crutches.

"We're fine, Tom," I assure him.

He gives Kip a stern look. "Are we good here?"

Kip is immediately remorseful. "Yessir. I'm sorry."

As soon as Tom leaves — and it doesn't escape my notice that he's left my office door slightly ajar — Kip turns to me apologetically, but I shake my head. "I don't care about the damn lamp. I'm worried about you."

He shakes his head, his practiced mask slipping back into place. "I'm fine," he mutters. "I just let shit get to me for a minute, that's all."

I'm not fooled for a second. "Your life's not ruined, Kip, I promise you. It sucks right now, but your life's not over."

He snorts. "No woman wants someone like this." He gestures down his body the same way he did a couple of weeks ago when he said Jennifer dumped him because of his injuries.

"That's not true. The right person won't care about superficial stuff. We're all damaged, Kip. Some people just hide it better than others."

He scoffs at me. "You don't understand. You have no idea what it's like."

I study his face. "I may not be missing a limb, but I understand more than you might think."

He shakes his head stubbornly. "Don't insult my intelligence." He flips his hand in a sweeping motion from my loosely curled hair to my skyscraper heels. "You could never understand what it's like to feel less than. To not be good enough."

I tilt my head, waiting for him to meet my eyes. "Do you know why I left the military?" It's rhetorical — of course he doesn't. "I spent some time at Walter Reed myself. My team was on a medical assistance mission in Afghanistan when we were attacked by insurgents. I was captured. They took turns torturing me until my unit located me eleven days later." His horrified expression means he's got some idea of what I endured. It's no secret that prisoners aren't treated particularly well in that part of the world.

There's a short pause before his eyes harden. "At least your injuries aren't visible."

I bristle at his intimation that unseen damages are less painful, but suppress my feelings, instead removing my stacked bracelets. Thick pink scars encircle both of my wrists, and I hold them out toward him, staring at them. "They wrapped barbed wire around my wrists and hung me by my arms over an exposed pipe in the ceiling of my cell. The wire chewed all the way into my bones. They beat me. Broke my nose, my cheek, a bunch of ribs, and my tailbone. They kicked me with steel-toed boots hard enough to injure my liver and spleen."

I stand up from my couch and move to sit beside him, giving him my back. I take a deep breath before slipping off my blazer, knowing the low-backed camisole exposes the wide purple rope-like scars mingled with the thin lavender ones, all criss-crossing the flat white swoops and curls that spread from one side of my back to the other. "They used a homemade whip made of leather straps and razor wire. The flat white scar is from a brand they used. It says 'stupid cunt whore'. And they mutilated my chest and –" I falter – "and my internal areas with a rusty knife." I swallow hard, then pull my blazer back in place and return to the opposite couch, not looking up until after I've put my bracelets back on, concealing my scars once more. "You're right. I keep my scars hidden so most people can't see them. But we're all damaged, every one of us," I repeat. "You just have to find the person whose brokenness fits yours."

Blue-green eyes meet mine. "I'm sorry, Charlie. I didn't know."

I smile. "You're in a very elite group. Only my four best friends have seen them, plus one asshole that I dated briefly. We broke up because he saw my scars and freaked out. He said someone with scars like mine belonged in a horror movie." I purse my lips. "So when I tell you someone who can't handle your injuries isn't worth your time and energy, you should listen."

"If you don't show people, why did you show me?"

"Because you needed to know that even people who don't look like it are still broken."

He pauses. "Jennifer's not broken."

I snort. "Bullshit. She's more broken than either of us."

His eyes flicker with curiosity. "What do you mean?"

"Think about it. What kind of person breaks up with someone because they're wounded? She's superficial and shallow. She's after arm candy, someone who'll shower her with gifts and compliments. She might be pretty on the outside, but on the inside, she's a swamp beast. She'll never have an honest, meaningful, deep relationship as long as she's only focused on what people can do for her. I'll bet you a hundred bucks that when she's all alone, she's not happy."

He sits quietly, considering my words. "No, she's not. She's never satisfied, always wanting more. A newer car, a bigger apartment, better clothes." He purses his lips. "It's how she tries to feel better about herself, isn't it?"

I nod. "Exactly. And you deserve better."

I can't say I've convinced him, but at least he looks more thoughtful than when he came in. He looks down at the floor. "I'll replace your lamp," he says.

"I told you, I'm not worried about the lamp."

But he shakes his head. "I like making stuff. I have something in mind. I want to do this for you." Then his expression turns sheepish. "Will you hand me my crutches? Tom's gonna chew my ass as it is. I don't want to be any later."

I chuckle and retrieve them. "C'mon. He won't yell at you in front of me."

"Thanks, Charlie. What you said – what you did – it means a lot."

I simply nod. "Anytime, Kip. We're here to help you however we can."

I have an appointment with Linda after work, my first one in a while. Linda spent a month vacationing in Japan, and when she returned, I was leaving for Aurora to take Mark for his surgery. Between work and his recovery and – I admit, my reticence at discussing what's going on between me and Mark – time's gotten away from me.

I'm not ready to talk to Linda about my relationship with Mark yet. Last time she and I talked, he and I were still firmly in the friendship-only camp. Now we're – I don't know what we are. I only know that everything between us is too raw and painful to talk through with Linda today. I do plan to talk about Mark, though. Him and Kip.

I settle into Linda's overstuffed couch. I'm almost always her last appointment of the day, partially because of my work schedule and partially because I'm more forthcoming when I don't feel pressured to hurry and wrap things up so she can move on to her next client.

"I love the business attire," she says. "Those are fantastic colors on you. Interesting, too. A military medic wearing a blood-red suit with an army green camisole." Linda, a fashion maven in her own right, is wearing a body-skimming black one-piece jumpsuit with a deep neckline and her trademark stilettos.

I grin. "It's a coincidence. I'm an autumn. These are my colors. Ask Lila. She spent hours discussing it while she dragged me all over Pueblo to find appropriately-colored clothing."

Linda smiles. She knows about my reluctant participation in Lila's marathon shopping trips, aka her Acquisition Expeditions. "What would you like to talk about today, Charlie?"

"Your Japanese kintsugi saucer. The black and gold one."

She stands and retrieves the saucer from her bookcase, passing it to me. Kintsugi is an ancient Japanese art form. The saucer is a glossy, inky black, with lines of rich gold highlighting where the piece was shattered and repaired. Rather than concealing the damage, the Japanese choose to accentuate the flaws, turning a simple saucer into a stunning masterpiece.

I examine the piece, turning it over in my hands. "I have a new client," I tell her. "He's young, barely old enough to walk into a bar. A huge, muscular kid who lost his leg. His girlfriend dumped him because of his injuries, and all he can see is that he's ruined, that his life is over. And Mark –" My voice cracks, and I have to clear my throat. "Mark had his osseointegration surgery, and he was convinced it would make him 'normal'." I make air quotes with my fingers at the word "normal". "But as soon as he woke up from surgery and saw the metal rod sticking out of his residual limb, he went right back to loathing his body."

"Was there a time after the explosion when Mark didn't loathe himself?"

"I'm not sure," I admit. "I thought he'd seemed better, but he kept making comments about being normal again, so maybe not."

"And you think the kintsugi analogy might help the two of them to see things differently?"

I sigh. "Mark's stubborn as hell. I've been saying the same things for months, and I feel like I'm beating my head against the wall with him. But I might be able to get through to Kip." I meet her gaze and hold it. "I showed Kip my scars. I told him we're all broken to some degree."

Linda smiles. "I'm proud of you. How do you feel about that?"

I consider it. "I'm okay with it. I chose to do it to reach out, to support him." I grin, remembering what she'd told me before. "I chose intentional vulnerability. And it went a lot better with him than it did with Blake." I frown. "Asshole," I mutter.

"Blake's drunken rant wasn't about you or your scars. It was because he saw a side of himself he didn't like." I cock my head at her in surprise. "Blake reacted poorly when you revealed your scars. He knew it was hard for you to show him, and he knew he'd responded badly and felt guilty. He didn't like that feeling, so he sat outside your house all night to prove to you and to himself that he was a good person. When you chose not to continue seeing him because of his reaction and his statements, he saw himself through your eyes, and he didn't like it. He responded by lashing out at you."

I stare at her. "You came up with that right off the cuff?"

She smiles. "No. We just haven't had a chance to talk for a while. And the fact that you shared your scars with Tucker and now Kip following such a negative reaction is something to celebrate. You're breaking free from the urge to hide them."

"I've been wearing tank tops and camisoles lately," I admit. "Only around the house and with my friends, but I've been leaving my back exposed more."

Linda beams. "You've come a long way, Charlie."

"I want to help Kip and Mark accept themselves, too."

"You can lead a horse to water..." she says, raising one perfectly arched brow meaningfully.

I sigh. "I know, I know. You told me the same things for years, but I had to accept them for myself. I just wish there was a way I could – I don't know, fast track their progress."

Linda chuckles. "If you only knew how many times I've wished that for my clients."

"So no suggestions?"

"You keep beating the dead horse," she says promptly. "It will keep rattling around in their subconscious until hopefully, it takes root. Keep planting the seeds."

My words may have gotten through to Kip, but I'm still beating the dead horse, per Linda's directions, with Mark. At bedtime, Mark insists on wearing his prosthetic to bed under the pretense of "getting used to it".

I almost tell him how full of shit he is. Getting used to it, my ass. We both know he's doing it because he hates seeing the metal abutment extending from his residual limb. Instead, I count to ten in my head and strive for a calm, reasoned tone.

"Are you sure that's a good idea? It might get caught in the blanket."

"It'll be fine," he says dismissively.

I don't argue with him because my head is pounding. It's throbbed like a toothache ever since I got home, and neither aspirin nor ibuprofen have helped. I wasn't planning to seduce him tonight, but it's irrelevant. Wearing his prosthetic boosts his confidence, and he pulls me against his chest and closes his mouth over mine. My headache pales in comparison to the passion between us. Mark hasn't initiated sex with me since I had my flashback in the shower – though he hasn't turned me down when I do – and my need to bond with him is too strong to decline because of a headache. I'm addicted to him, and for one brief moment, it feels like he's addicted to me, too. We lay in each others' arms afterwards, my head on his chest and a leg slung over his waist. I fall asleep to the gentle stroke of long fingers down my spine.

He sits up first when my alarm goes off in the morning. I'm still rubbing my eyes and stretching when he climbs out of bed.

I watch it happen in slow motion, like an impending car accident.

Mark doesn't notice his prosthetic foot tangled in the comforter. He stands and takes a single step, reaching for his crutches. The prosthetic twists, and he tumbles forward, landing hard on the floor. I gasp and scramble across the mattress, kneeling next to him.

"Oh my God! Are you okay?"

His face flushes a dull red. "I'm fine." He pushes me away with one arm, but I ignore him.

"Is the abutment okay? Did you hurt your –" I catch myself before I blurt the word "stump" – "yourself?"

"I said I'm fine," he snaps.

I reach for the comforter, unwrapping it from his prosthesis, running my hands up the smooth carbon-fiber prosthetic to his warm flesh. "Does anything hurt?"

"Jesus Christ, Charlie, I said I'm fine! Leave me the fuck alone."

I freeze at the anger in his voice, abruptly reminded of his icy rage in San Antonio. I drop my hands, unable to meet his eyes, and exit the room without a word, my stomach knotting.

No matter what I do, no matter what I say, I can't get through to Mark.

I refuse to be in that same position with Kip.

When I get to the office, Tara, Tom, and Lila are already there, even though we don't open for another half hour. "Group meeting in my office," I announce, holding up a bakery bag and a tray of coffees. "Raspberry-filled mini-doughnuts and coffee for four."

Tom takes the tray of coffee cups from me and passes them out, and the four of us settle on the plush furniture in my office. "What's up?" he asks.

"We need to talk about Kip," I reply, and I fill them in on what happened yesterday, from finding him in the van to his outburst to our discussion of brokenness. Tara glances at me when I mention showing him my scars, but doesn't ask about them.

Tara's eyes turn sad immediately. "That poor child," she murmurs. Then she dips her head, her auburn hair falling in front of her shoulders. "I mean, I know he's not a child. He's a foot taller than I am. But my kids aren't much older than he is. I could be his mother."

"I'd like to give that shallow bitch a piece of my mind," Lila mutters.

I cock an eyebrow at her. "What happened to avoiding profanity?"

She purses her lips. "That's only in front of clients."

I shrug. "I don't usually curse in front of clients, but she'd made Kip feel like he wasn't good enough for her because of his injuries. I did it intentionally to shock him into listening."

"He told me what you did for him yesterday," Tom says. "He said you helped him see things more clearly."

"For the moment, maybe. But I don't know if it will make a difference long-term." Hell, I've been beating the self-worth drum with Mark for months, and I've gotten nowhere. Hopefully, Kip's not as stubborn as Mark.

Lila turns to me. "I got the name of a local psychiatrist that specializes in wounded veterans with body image issues."

"You did?"

She nods. "After you and I talked, I asked some of our clients. Three of them recommended this guy." She doesn't mention that she was researching it for Mark.

"I can call his office and see if he has an opening," Tara offers. "Do you think Kip would go?"

"I'll go with him, if he'll agree. Not into the actual appointment," I add hastily, "but I'll gladly drive him. Two birds with one stone, you know? Being supportive while making sure he gets the help he needs."

"I think he might do it for you," Tom says, eying me thoughtfully. "You've made quite an impression on the kid."

"I think we should contact his primary care physician, too," Lila adds. "An antidepressant might help. He didn't have one on his medication list when he transferred here."

"Kip's pretty cheerful," Tara said. "On the outside, anyway. I'm guessing he doesn't let his mask slip around the VA docs."

"I'm worried," I admit. "He was already dealing with losing his leg and all the body image issues that go along with that. That superficial bitch made things a thousand times worse."

"I'll call his doctor this morning," Lila promises, "and Tara will see if we can get him in with the psychiatrist."

Tom squeezes my shoulder. "I'll talk to him this afternoon and see how he's feeling."

I nod. "I'll try to swing by PT when he's there this afternoon."

Despite my best intentions, Tara ends up leaving with the stomach flu shortly after making Kip's appointment, and I end up covering her afternoon massages. I'm busy until long after Kip is gone. After work, I go home to a silent house. Mark hasn't spoken to me since he yelled at me after his fall this morning, not even to offer a half-assed apology for yelling. He ignores me for the rest of the day and most of the next as well. I'm miserable.

I never knew I could feel so alone with someone I love right beside me.

When he does speak to me Friday night, it's to flatly refuse to go to dinner at Tom's house. Maya invited us Monday night after Lila and Tucker announced they were having date night on Friday. Maya and Skyler are making pasta (naturally) and we're bringing the salad and wine.

"I'm not going," he says when I poke my head in his room to see if he's dressed. He doesn't bother looking up from his tablet.

"What do you mean, you're not going? Maya invited you. You told her you'd come."

He turns and stares, sending chills down my spine. "I said I'm not going."

I put my purse down and turn toward the kitchen to put the salad in the refrigerator. "Fine. I'll call and cancel."

"You can't cancel this late. It would be rude."

It takes every drop of my self-control not to point out that's exactly what he's doing.

"Besides, I'd rather be alone. I need a break," he continues.

My throat tightens. I leave the house without another word.

I make it through dinner without letting Maya or Skyler see my mood, but Tom can tell. I'm helping him clean up when he stops in front of me and takes the lasagna pan from my hands.

"Want to talk about it?" he asks, his brown eyes soft.

A lump forms in my throat, and I shake my head.

"Would a hug help?"

I shake my head again. "I'll cry if you hug me."

He lifts a bear paw-sized hand to my cheek. "I'll dry."

I hug him then, and he pulls me against his chest and rubs my back while I try not to cry and fail miserably. I lose track of how long I stand in his kitchen bawling all over him, but when I pull away, the left shoulder and chest of his gray tee shirt are wet with my tears.

"I've got a spare room if you need a place to stay," he offers quietly.

I shake my head. "Going home may not fix things, but not going home will make them worse."

Then again, maybe not. Mark did say he'd rather be alone and that he needed a break.

After I leave Tom's, I find an empty parking lot and cry for two hours. When I go home, Mark's sitting in the living room. The TV is on, but the volume is turned down.

I strip off my jeans and crawl into his bed in my panties and the same shirt I wore to dinner, lasagna smudges and all. I study the framed photo of us on my bedside table. It's one Tucker took on our group camping trip, when Mark and I were sitting on the log together. I'm holding his shirt front, and he's cupping my face in his hands. It's beautiful and loving and tender, and it's so far from where we are right now that it makes me cry again. When I feel Mark come to bed much later, I curl against him. He tries to push me away, but this is the only place I can make any headway with him. His head and heart may reject me, but his body overrides his emotions. We end up tangling together, but even then, our passion is fraught with silent anguish.

Something's got to give, and soon, because we can't keep going like this. I just pray I'm able to get through to him, because I'll never survive losing him.

MARK

My mood has grown steadily worse over the past few weeks, though I try desperately to keep it from Charlie. I need her more than life itself, but I keep trying to put distance between us. Just yesterday, she watched me fall on my ass getting out of the damn bed. She deserves someone who can pick her up when she falls, not the other way around. I've got to let her go, let her find someone who can be everything she needs.

My foul mood bleeds into every corner of my soul. Friday, Tom leaves work midday for Parents' Day at Maya's school. Charlie and I are supposed to have dinner at his house later, but I'd rather endure a root canal. I like Tom and Maya, but I just can't. Not today.

My oily darkness leaches out of me while I'm working beside Kip. He's having a rough time lately, and because I'm not exactly the most cheery person to be around, I've avoided engaging with him. Tom's usually here to talk with Kip and encourage him.

But Tom's not here today.

Kip's unusually excited today. The reason becomes clear when he starts blathering.

"Doc's setting me up to go to the VA next month. I'm going to get that osseointegration surgery, too, if my bones look strong enough to support it."

I give a noncommittal grunt.

"That'll show Jennifer." He glances over, his bluish-green eyes shining. Sweat beads his blond hair as he works his quads. "My ex, you know? She dumped me because of my leg. Well, she said it was because her feelings for me changed while I was gone, but she told her friend Taylor the thought of having sex with a guy with a stump made her want to puke."

I grunt again.

"Of course, Taylor told me that when she came over and hit on me, so it might not be true." He bares his teeth, fiercely pushing through his last few reps before flopping back on the mat and turning his head toward me. "I think she's telling the truth, though. But I'll show Jennifer."

"Really?" I mutter as if I care.

"Hell, yeah," he boasts. "Get that surgery and get my prosthesis and show her who's fuckable and who's not. I'll be on top of the world then."

I shoot him a look. "You think so?"

He nods excitedly. "Pull on some jeans and nobody'll know. All they'll see are muscles and ink." Kip's upper body strength is impressive. He's powerful and broad-chested, with military tattoos decorating his entire upper body.

One arm lists the names of friends who didn't survive their deployment. The list runs from his shoulder to his elbow.

I don't have enough space on my body to list the names of all the people I've lost.

And the one I regret losing most, as selfish as it is, is me.

Those cowards on the side of a road stole everything from me, everything. My team. My career. My leg. My future with Charlie.

And no fucking prosthetic on the planet can restore what I've lost.

I glare at Kip, my words coming out in a low snarl. "Nobody'll know, huh? What happens when you get her alone? What then? Gonna fuck her with your clothes on, kid? Sooner or later, your jeans come off, and you still won't have a leg." I sit up, whirling toward him and gesturing to my abutment. "Take a good look, because this shit turned me into a goddamn freak. If you're counting on that surgery to get your life back, you're in for a real disappointment." I grab my crutches, leaving him staring open-mouthed as I storm out.

I refuse to go to dinner at Tom's that night. It pisses Charlie off when I cancel at the last minute, but she has to go anyway, because it's too late for both of us to bail without being rude.

That's okay. I'm fine with being rude.

I can't spend my night watching Charlie with Tom and Maya. Not tonight. My emotions are too raw. Watching them together rips me apart, because Tom is exactly the man she needs. Kind. Dependable. Strong. Handsome. Trustworthy. Loyal. He's a genuinely good person, and those are rare. He and Charlie already care for each other. Plus, Maya absolutely worships her. Tom is perfect for Charlie, and she could be a mom to Maya. Her ready-made family is right there. All she has to do is reach out and take it.

Charlie's been sensing the changes in me the more I try to pull away. She's always been able to read me like a book. Not this time, though. She thinks I'm upset with her.

But I could never be upset with Charlie. Not for this.

I'm upset with myself, for letting myself hope. Letting myself dream.

The only one who fucked up my life this time is me.

And the only way to make Charlie happy, truly happy, is to let her go.

CHAPTER NINETEEN

LILA

THE PAIN WAKES ME, sharp, severe, and unrelenting. It doubles me over, making me gasp with its intensity. I clutch Tucker's arm. He wakes immediately and sits up.

"Sweetness? What's wrong?"

"I don't know. It hurts." Stabbing pain hits me, and I cry out. "Tucker, it hurts."

Tucker leaps from the bed and stuffs his bare feet into running shoes. He scoops me up, wraps a quilt around me, and carries me, half running, down the stairs and out to his truck. I don't realize I'm crying until he wipes my tears away. "I've got you, Sweetness. I'll take care of you."

It's my right side. It must be my appendix. I've broken out in a cold sweat, yet I feel feverish. "My appendix," I say weakly, and he guns the motor, weaving in and out of the light traffic as he races to the hospital.

In the emergency room, they start an IV, draw blood, and give me pain medication. The doctor looks at the nurse and orders an ultrasound when Tucker tells them I'm a few weeks pregnant.

Another sharp pain hits, and I cry out. Tucker grips my hand and rubs a damp cloth over my forehead, wiping away the tears still trickling down my face. The nurse gives me something else for pain, and I drift off to an uneasy sleep.

CHARLIE

The call wakes me from a dead sleep. Mark and I rush to the hospital. Tucker's in the waiting room with his head in his hands.

Lila's in surgery. She has a ruptured fallopian tube from an ectopic pregnancy.

Mark keeps a hand on Tucker's shoulder while I grip his hand and other arm. "She'll be okay. Lila's strong," I tell him. But he never raises his head. The misery on his face rips at my heart, and I know Lila's will be even worse.

We sit silently, just the three of us, alone in a deserted waiting room. Two hours later, we jump to our feet when the surgeon comes out, a tall man with pale blond hair and sad eyes. He keeps a hand on Tucker's shoulder the entire time. Before he's even uttered the first word, I know it's bad news because of his hand bracing Tucker's shoulder. He's trying to reassure him, but there aren't any reassurances he can give. Not really.

"I tried to repair your wife's fallopian tube, but it was too damaged. She still has one functional ovary and fallopian tube. However, this will make it much more difficult for her to conceive. It's not impossible, but given her history, natural conception is very unlikely."

Tucker is devastated. He collapses in tears when the surgeon leaves. I wrap my arms around his waist, and Mark throws an arm around his shoulder, looking miserable.

I can't stop crying. It's bad enough that I'm infertile. But Lila?

Please, not Lila too. She wants a baby so badly. She needs a baby. Please, please don't take that chance from her. I'm not sure who I'm praying to, but I pray with everything in me that she's still able to conceive.

An hour later, a petite blond nurse with pink streaks in her hair comes to get Tucker. "Mr. Maxwell? I can bring you back to your wife now."

We all stand. Tucker hugs Mark first, then holds onto me for a long time. His voice is hoarse. "You guys go home. I need to be with her."

"Of course," I say quickly. "If you need us – if Lila needs me – for anything at all, call me."

He nods. "I will." Then he swallows hard. "Thank you for being here. I –" He breaks off, and I hug him again.

"Take care of each other," I whisper, and he nods.

They need to be together, to grieve together.

My soul aches for them.

With them.

I drive home, silently crying for the losses that never stop coming as Mark stares wordlessly into the darkness.

MARK

Charlie's absolutely devastated by Lila's loss. It dredges up her sorrow over her own infertility.

It's something Charlie rarely talks about because it can't be fixed, a pain without relief, a wound that can't be healed. After the initial period after the doctors told her she'd never be able to conceive, she's only talked about it twice, and both times, she cried silent tears.

The shit those goddamned bastards did to my Charlie sickens and enrages me every time I think about it, and her torment at their hands has been in the back of my mind ever since her flashback in the shower.

She healed from their burns and mutilations and torture, though she bears the scars. She's still healing from their psychological torment, from her nightmares and panic attacks and flashbacks, but she's come such a long way.

But there's no fixing her infertility. The damage they rendered was too severe.

Now Lila's potentially facing the same diagnosis. Charlie feels Lila's pain because they're like sisters, and Lila's situation reinvigorates Charlie's own pain. It reminds her of the losses forced upon her, the things she wanted that will forever be beyond her reach.

She has a difficult weekend.

We both do.

I know Charlie deserves better than I can give her, and I ought to distance myself from her, but seeing her despondence, I can't. In the end, I sit with her and pull her onto my lap, holding her while she cries off and on for most of the day. Neither of us says anything.

Neither of us has to.

CHARLIE

It's an awful weekend. Lila's loss reminds me of my own infertility, and my pain is compounded by the increasing distance between me and Mark. I spend most of the weekend in tears, staring into the gas fireplace that I've turned on despite the warm weather. When he sits beside me and pulls me into his arms, it's both agony and a relief. I need him, and I'm comforted by his touch and the fact that he sought me out, but even as he holds me, I feel the chasm between us.

The next crushing blow comes Monday morning. Lila's going to be out for a few weeks, and Tara and I are covering the clinic. I'm scrambling to rearrange appointments when a police officer steps inside our lobby. When I hang up the phone, I turn to him. "Can I help you?"

His steady gaze and neutral expression give nothing away. "I'd like to talk with you about one of your patients. Kip Kramer."

"We actually refer to them as clients to empower them. Most of them have been patients far too long for their liking. I'm afraid I can't give you any information without Kip's permission."

He observes me carefully. "Kip's dead, ma'am."

My mind immediately fills with images of bright blue-green eyes and a boyish grin, of a kid who was dealt a shitty hand but was trying to make lemonade from lemons. I grip the edge of the counter as my vision blurs with tears. "What happened?"

He hesitates. "He shot himself."

"No. Kip wouldn't do that. Are you sure? There must be a mistake." I hear the shrillness of my tone, but I can't stop it, and my chest tightens. I fight to slow my breathing.

Please no. Not Kip. He was just a kid.

Tom appears, hearing my agitation, coming instantly to my side. "What's wrong, Charlie?"

All I can do is shake my head. I can't speak. Tom looks at the officer, his expression angry, as though the officer has done something to upset me.

Tom guides me into a chair and keeps his hands on my shoulders. At some point Tara comes out, and her face drains of color. The officer's words hang like poisonous gas in the air. Gunshot wound. Inside his mouth, so there wouldn't be any mistake. Gunpowder residue on his hands, his thick index finger caught in the trigger. A suicide note, and a note addressed to Jennifer. They believe it happened Friday night. His roommate and best friend, Kyle, had gone out of town for the weekend and found him when he came home last night.

"Jennifer's his ex-girlfriend," Tom says soberly. "She broke up with him because of his injuries. Or at least, that's what Kip believed."

"His poor mother," Tara murmurs, her hand over her mouth.

Dear God. His mother.

The woman who still looked at him and saw the little boy who cried when she dropped him off at kindergarten. The woman who'd tried to persuade him to move in with her so she could take care of him. My chest tightens further at the anguish she must be feeling.

The officer shakes his head. "Her brother came as soon as he heard. He's taking care of her. She's... struggling."

My heart breaks a little more.

Tara calls our clients without giving details, and we close the clinic for the day. We're all too shattered by the news to function, and among veterans who already struggle with depression, suicide can be contagious. Tom reaches out to the VA, and they agree to send a counselor for a couple of days to discuss Kip's death with our other clients and help them. He calls Tucker, too, giving him the godawful task of breaking the news to an already-devastated Lila.

I sit alone in my office, staring at the lamp Kip brought me just this past Friday before his PT appointment. He made it for me himself, he'd announced, his beautiful eyes shining with pride. It's industrial-style in its design, with a raw-edged reclaimed oak base. The body of the lamp is constructed from a straight section of cast-iron pipe with two ninety-degree elbows branching from it, both facing down. Edison-style bulbs attach to sockets emerging from both elbows and the vertical shaft, casting a soft orange glow. The pipes conceal the inner wiring from view.

"The outer bulbs take a full one-eighty turn from the main pipe, see? Like life. I thought my life would go this way, and so did you," Kip had explained, tracing a long finger up the straight central piece of cast iron. "But life had other plans." He'd pointed to the elbows branching off the main pipe. "Doesn't mean we can't still shine, though." I'd hugged him impulsively, something I could never have done a few months ago.

A lump forms in my throat. I wonder if Kip knew he was going to kill himself that night when he gave me the lamp. I wonder if I could have said or done anything to make a difference.

I replay our conversation on the couch just a few days ago, when I showed him my scars.

When I thought I'd helped him.

Tears stream down my face. I'm no help to anyone anymore, not Kip, not Mark, not Lila.

Tom comes down the hall, and I quickly dry my eyes. I thought he'd left when Tara did. I'm sitting with my socks and shoes off, curled up on the couch, when he comes in.

He looks awful. He's pale, with shadows beneath his haunted eyes. I pat the spot on the couch beside me. But instead of sitting, Tom lays down on the sofa, resting his head on my leg.

"Is this okay?" he asks.

I reach down and run my fingers through his soft hair. "Yeah."

He's silent for a long time, and I finally notice my lap is damp from his tears.

Tom's baby sister Dana committed suicide when she was in high school, and he's always blamed himself for not being able to help her when she needed it most. Now we've lost someone else who was struggling. I lay one hand on his softly-stubbled cheek and stroke his hair with the other.

My tears fall again, and I don't bother hiding them this time.

I'm not sure how many more hits our makeshift little family can survive.

MARK

When Charlie comes home early Monday with swollen red eyes, I think she's still struggling with the reminder of her infertility. I'm on the couch, getting ready to head over for my rehab appointment. She sits beside me and lays her head on my shoulder.

I stiffen when I smell Tom's cologne on her.

Why has Tom been holding Charlie?

"We closed the office today, but if you want to take the keys and go work out alone, you can." Her voice is small, tinged with pain.

Closed the office? They almost never close the office, aside from major holidays. Our group camping trip was a rare exception. Charlie spent three months in Texas with me, and Lila never closed the office. "Because Lila's out for a while?"

She shakes her head. "Kip –" She breaks off, unable to speak for a minute, and I wait for her to explain. Maybe the kid got hurt on their equipment or something.

Her voice breaks when she speaks again. "Kip killed himself, Mark."

I hear her words, but they don't make sense. "What?"

"Kip committed suicide over the weekend."

"What?" I repeat myself as ice settles in the pit of my stomach.

"An officer came by this morning to interview us. Kip shot himself. Left a suicide note and a letter for his ex."

"When?"

She swallows hard. "Friday night, after his roommate left to go out of town."

Friday night.

After I had my fucking outburst in rehab.

After I told him the surgery he was all excited about wouldn't make him any less of a freak.

That night, he went home and killed himself.

It can't be a coincidence.

I killed that kid as surely as if I'd pulled the trigger myself.

I hold her again all evening, ordering pizza from my phone. She doesn't eat. At bedtime, she cries herself to sleep on my shoulder.

When she leaves for work the next morning, I find the police officer's card she left on the table yesterday. Officer Richards is at the precinct when I call, and I arrange an Uber to go speak with him in person.

I check in with an officer at the front desk, who sends me to a bench to wait. Officer Richards comes to find me, leading me back to his corner desk.

"What can I do for you, Mr. –?"

I shake his hand, noting his firm grip and squared shoulders. I'd bet money he served, just based on his posture, attitude, and presence. "Mark Chandler. Call me Mark."

He nods and motions for me to have a seat. "How can I help you, Mark?"

I clear my throat, trying to figure out the best way to begin. "You were there at Kip's house, weren't you? Kip Kramer? The suicide?"

He nods. "Were you a friend of Kip's?"

I shake my head. "More of an acquaintance. He was my workout partner at the rehab clinic." I gesture down to my prosthetic leg. "We had similar injuries."

He nods again, waiting for me to go on.

"The thing is, I – I think maybe I made him do it."

He leans back in his chair, studying me. "How so?"

I launch into my story, giving far more detail than I'd intended, explaining how I myself had been excited about having the surgery and how I'd believed I'd be normal afterwards. I detail how having the surgery had done exactly the opposite, making me into a freak, and how now I wasn't good enough for the woman I love. I describe my outburst during PT and how I'd stormed off, leaving Kip staring at me, his mouth hanging open, just a few hours before he went home and ended his life.

"I was in a bad place," I admit, meeting his eyes. "I still am. But I was speaking of myself and my situation. I never meant to push Kip into giving up. God, he was just a kid." My eyes burn, and I swipe at them, embarrassed at my sudden flood of emotion for a boy I didn't even bother to get to know.

Officer Richards leans forward. "Don't blame yourself. Kip had been planning this for a while."

That surprises me. He'd always seemed so upbeat. Annoyingly so, in fact.

"We looked into his daily habits. He'd only been home six weeks, but every single day, he'd purchased a bottle of over-the-counter sleeping pills. He'd hit a different place each day, sometimes grocery stores, sometimes pharmacies, sometimes convenience stores. He'd emptied all the pills into one large container. He had over two thousand sleeping pills. We also found several versions of the suicide note on his laptop. He'd started writing them while he was in the hospital. Even the letter to his ex had several drafts started two weeks ago."

I stare at him. "Sleeping pills? I thought he shot himself."

"He did. But he'd attempted suicide already, and both previous attempts were with pills. He didn't take enough to be fatal either time." His expression is grim. "He'd decided he wasn't going to make that mistake a third time and shot himself through the roof of the mouth. Even if you were in a bad place on Friday, this isn't on you. Kip had planned to end his life for a long time.

He was just waiting for an opportunity, and when his roommate left town, he took it."

The officer may say it's not my fault, but I disagree. Taking pills gives you a brief window to reconsider, to call for help and get your stomach pumped. A gunshot to the head leaves no room to change your mind. Kip's death is one more unforgivable sin on my ledger.

I've screwed up so many lives, poisoned so many with my presence.

Everyone on the medical mission I sent Charlie and Lila on, the one that got six of my team killed and the two women who mean the most to me tortured and raped by a bunch of savages.

Everyone on my team when we got hit by the IED, when more than half the guys didn't make it back, either dead or critically injured.

Charlie's life, in more ways than I can count, from being at fault for her trauma to dragging her into this relationship to knowing I have to let her go.

And Kip, who ended his life the same day that I told him he'd never be normal, that he'd still be a freak.

My ledger of sins is ready to burst.

Charlie's subdued the rest of the week, and I find her crying daily. I hold her and console her, and although I know I need to pull back, I can't, not when she's in so much pain.

Being close to her, knowing I have to let her go, is ripping me apart, but Charlie's hurting more than I am, and she needs me. I selfishly steal every second of physical contact I can, hoping one day, when I'm alone and missing her, I'll have this memory to draw on, her soft body curled against my chest, her arms around my neck.

Maybe it'll be enough to pull me through.

Or maybe it'll be what destroys me.

CHAPTER TWENTY

CHARLIE

MARK'S EMOTIONS RUN SO hot and cold, I don't know what to think anymore.

No one in my life has ever cared for me the way Mark has. No one's ever reached me like he can. No one's ever been there for me as much as he has, through things most people can't even imagine. The depth of emotion between us, even before we tried "more", was like nothing I've ever seen between two other people. The closest is maybe what Tucker and Lila have, but they're married, and in some ways, I think Mark and I were closer than they were.

But that was before.

Things have been off since his surgery, and I know it's because of his poor body image, but I can't fix that, no matter how much I want to. I can't force him to see himself clearly. I've talked to Stubbs three more times, including once after Mark's fall. He keeps telling me to stay the course, to keep beating my dead horse. He says I'm the best shot at getting through to him, because Mark still hasn't answered a single one of his calls or texts since surgery.

Since Lila's emergency surgery culminating in a likelihood of infertility, things between Mark and I have been even worse. It's so much worse, it's got me wondering if Lila's failed pregnancy has Mark thinking about a family. About kids of his own.

About the babies I can never give him.

He's never mentioned children before, but he'd be a great dad, the kind who wrestles in the floor with little boys and loses on purpose at hide and seek. The kind who has tea parties in the floor with his daughter and her stuffed animals, who hires a manicurist to come over and give her and all her friends pedicures for her fifth birthday. The kind who stays up late on Christmas Eve assembling a bicycle from Santa and makes love to his wife in the wee hours after the little ones are asleep.

The kind of man I'd love to have kids with.

No... *The* man I'd love to have kids with.

Except, of course, I can't.

And maybe that's why he's been so distant. Because he wants and deserves something he'll never be able to have with me.

No matter how hard I try, I can't escape my brokenness.

LILA

The pain is unbearable.

Not the physical pain – I've dealt with much worse than this.

It's the emotional pain stabbing my heart, twisting, slicing, ripping me open from the inside out. My chances of conceiving are virtually impossible now.

Tucker deserves a woman who can have his babies.

I look at him beside me on the sofa, his golden brown hair touched by the afternoon sun, the light playing across his strong features. He's sitting with me, just sitting, the way he's done for the past several days. I've seen the haunted look in his dark blue eyes. He wants more. He needs more.

He needs a family.

And that's the one thing I can't give him, no matter how much I want to.

"I'll understand if you want to divorce me. I won't contest it. We'll split everything evenly. You keep your business, and I'll keep my part of the clinic. We can sell the house and land and divide the profits down the middle."

My words are quiet and unemotional, so I'm stunned when Tucker whips toward me, his face furious. "I don't care about a damn baby!" he explodes. I shrink away from him, but he grips my arms and pulls me forward, making me look into his eyes, at the intensity in them. "I love *you*, Lila. All I care about is you. I don't need kids. I just need you." He hauls me to him and kisses me fiercely, desperately, his pain palpable. "All I need is you."

I wrap my arms around his neck and kiss him back, and my tears blend with his as we cry and hold each other. "I'm sorry," I say, but he silences me with his kiss.

"No apologies."

We kiss for long moments, then hold each other even longer. "I love you, Lila," he says, his voice rough.

My heart swells at the emotion behind his words. "I love you, too." He pulls me tighter against him, and I nestle my head into his muscled chest. A minute later, still wrapped in his strong arms, I smile. "How do you feel about baby goats? Like, a lot of them?"

The laughter deep in his chest rumbles against my cheek, and he kisses my head. "Anything for you, Sweetness. Anything at all."

CHARLIE

All day Sunday, I'm completely on edge. Mark and I have no plans, and when we're alone lately, things don't go well. We don't fight, but he withdraws and becomes silent, and it hurts me, and we both know it. Knowing we're facing an entire afternoon and evening together has me dreading the inevitable pain.

I decide to break out the wine after a nearly silent dinner. We both have some, and for a change, he relaxes with me on the couch while music plays quietly in the background. His hands trace my spine lightly, and I lay my head on his chest.

I feel him drag in a shuddering breath beneath my cheek just before long fingers tilt my face up to his. "Charlie," he whispers, his voice a sigh. He moves toward me, hesitating just above my lips, and I hold my breath, terrified he'll change his mind and pull back.

But he doesn't.

He kisses me tenderly. Gently. His mouth is almost reverent as his lips claim mine over and over, his fingers lightly touching my face, slipping into my hair.

"Come to bed with me," he murmurs.

He undresses me like it's the first time, his eyes memorizing my body, his hands mapping my curves. It's exquisite. Slow, deep kisses, cupping my face like he can't get enough of me, but at the same time, there's no rush to his touch. We lose track of time as he lingers over my body, tasting and caressing, making love to me in every sense of the word. It's the most tender, most gentle, most loving he's ever been. He says with his touch the words he won't utter, and I feel them in my heart, hear them in my soul.

I've never felt so cared for, so worshiped, so *loved* in my entire life.

I'm curled against his chest, my arm snaked around his neck and my fingers twined in his hair. I'm fully sated, physically and emotionally. His arms hold me close, his lips in my hair. That's the last thing I remember before I drift off to sleep in his arms.

MARK

I'm lying there in the afterglow with Charlie, staggered by the perfection of the chemistry we have. She's nestled with her face against my chest, utterly spent. Her breathing slows and becomes more even. I smile and brush my lips across her forehead lightly. "Love you, Baby Girl," I murmur, not sure my words will even register.

She stirs lightly and mumbles, "I love you, Mark."

I freeze and glance down at her. Her breathing is slow and steady. She's half-asleep.

And she said she loved me.

There was no hesitation, and she didn't use her nickname for me – Big Guy. She called me Mark. And half-asleep – that wasn't the usual "love you" we've exchanged for years.

Panic rises in my chest. Has Charlie fallen for me?

No. She can't.

This was just supposed to be adding a physical aspect to our relationship. We agreed not to go into this looking for any romantic entanglements. The plan was to keep our friendship, and add – well, it turned out to be sex, though originally, it was just to see what developed between us.

Sex is not the same as love.

What the hell is she thinking?

What the hell was I thinking?

I run my hand through my hair in frustration. I should have known better than to go down this path. Intimacy for Charlie is so much more involved because of everything she went through. It isn't something she could achieve with just anyone – it took trust, deep trust, the kind built over decades. How could I have thought we could work through her past without her falling for me?

Jesus. This can't be happening!

I lay there, trying to quell the overwhelming anxiety building in my chest. It seems like ages before she rolls to her side and I'm able to slip out of the bed without waking her. I jump up, desperately needing to pace, to expel some energy. Back and forth across the room I march on my crutches, from the door around the foot of the bed to the chaise, over and over.

This can't happen.

Charlie can't fall for me. She can't spend her life saddled with a fucking cripple, a guy with a metal rod sticking out of his stump like a skewer and a body as scarred as a patchwork quilt. She deserves someone strong. Someone virile.

Someone whole.

Back and forth I pace, growing more agitated with each passing hour.

By morning, I'm resolved. I know what I have to do.

I have to let her go.

I've known it since my surgery, but I resisted when the only one getting hurt by my inaction was me. If she's falling in love with me, the clock's run out.

Charlie needs to be free to find someone as perfect as she is, someone beautiful and caring and whole, another pure soul. That sure as hell isn't me. But she'll never listen. She insists on seeing me through rose-colored glasses. I know if I tell her I'm letting her go because she deserves someone better, she'll buck me. She's downright mulish at times.

Charlie needs to think it's what I want for me. She needs to believe I don't want her.

I just have no idea how to pull that off.

When she stirs in the morning, I lean over and kiss her swiftly on the head, my eyes burning as I realize this is the last time I'll be able to do that. "I'm getting in the shower," I murmur.

Her green eyes fly open. "Want some company?" she asks, but I shake my head.

"Not this morning. I have a few things I need to take care of. What time is your last massage today?"

Her face scrunches as she tries to think, still half asleep. "At two, I think."

I nod. "I'll see you then." I can't stop myself from pressing my lips gently to hers for a split second before heading to the bathroom.

Thankfully, she doesn't follow.

CHAPTER TWENTY-ONE

CHARLIE

I SPEND THE EARLY part of Monday drifting through my day in a dreamlike trance. Endorphins still flood my system, and I find myself smiling for absolutely no reason. Last night was beyond description. I've never felt so loved, so desired, so... cherished. I'm floating on a cloud of joy and wonder.

So this is what it feels like when two people are in love.

I finish my last massage just before three and head into my office to make a dent in the ever-growing mountain of paperwork on my desk. With Lila out, I'm spending more time doing massages and less time doing paperwork, and my desk reflects it. Stacks of insurance claims to file, physicians' progress reports to fax, and invoices to pay cover every inch of the surface. It's nearly seven before I lock up and head across the walkway to the house, still cocooned in bliss.

Mark meets me as soon as I come in the side door. "Where have you been?" he barks, his expression terse.

I raise my eyebrows, startled by his sharp tone. "Work. The same place I usually am when I'm not here." I look at him, noting his dark jeans and white dress shirt. "You look hot. Did I forget we had plans?" I ask, moving closer and wrapping my arms around his waist. "Mmm. You smell nice. New cologne?"

Mark snatches my arms loose from his waist and quickly backs away, positioning his crutches forward. The move forces space between us, and I blink, unsettled by his reaction.

His unmistakable attempt to physically distance himself combined with his unwelcoming body language and tone of voice bewilder me, and my blissful state evaporates rapidly as the mood in the hallway turns frigid.

"We need to talk," he says abruptly.

Details begin to register with me. It's Monday, but he's in a dress shirt and jeans, not workout clothes. His lightly-stubbled beard has been trimmed. He's wearing a new cologne.

Mark looks like he's going out, but he doesn't want me touching him.

A prickle of anxiety runs through me. I put my purse down on the washing machine, regarding him carefully as I try to quell my rising uneasiness. "Okay, let's talk. What's up?"

"Last night, you said you loved me. Before you fell asleep," he adds pointedly. His face is tense, his jaw muscles tight.

My stomach tightens, though I keep my face impassive. "I tell you that all the time. You say it to me, too. Actually, you said it first last night, if I recall," I reply, disquieted by his agitation.

He shakes his head. "Last night it was different. You said it like... like you're falling for me." He stares at me, waiting expectantly.

I swallow hard and my heart pounds. Mark's figured out I'm in love with him, and he certainly doesn't look pleased.

This definitely wasn't the reaction I was expecting after the emotion he showed last night. He looks... Angry? Upset? Stressed? I'm not exactly sure, but his expression doesn't bode well.

Do I tell him what he wants to hear, or come clean and confess my feelings?

I watch him closely, waiting for some clue to how I should proceed. But he just stands there staring, waiting for my answer, like he's made an accusation that demands my response.

Finally, I meet his gaze deliberately. "Yes, Mark. I'm in love with you."

My spirits plummet as he shakes his head vehemently. "Charlie, you aren't in love with me," he argues. "You just think you are because we're together all the time. I'm convenient, and we've been intimate, and you're confusing that with love."

"No, Mark, I do love you, and I'm pretty sure you're in love with me, too."

He flinches – *flinches* – then shakes his head again. "Things will never work out between us like that, Charlie. You deserve someone who's whole and healthy. Someone better than me."

Bells are ringing like fire alarms inside my head. I study Mark carefully, examining his appearance again in combination with what he's saying.

His clothes, his cologne, his freshly trimmed beard – those things weren't for my benefit. He was waiting to confront me about my feelings, and not in a good way. So why is he dressed up? And for whom?

An icy chill skates down my spine and settles in the pit of my stomach. *No. Surely not.*

I speak slowly, praying I'm leaping to the wrong conclusion. "What are you saying, Mark?"

His light blue eyes meet mine and hold them steadily. "I think we should see other people."

An unseen fist grips my heart and squeezes the air from my lungs. "You're breaking up with me?"

This can't be happening.

His gaze doesn't waver, his voice resolute. "I'm not the right man for you, Charlie. You deserve someone better," he insists. "This is for your own good."

"I don't want anyone else. I love you, Mark," I say, pushing between his crutches to stand in front of him, looking up into his eyes. "And you love me, too."

"You don't love me. And I'm not in love with you. We need to see other people," he repeats firmly. His beautiful blue eyes suddenly turn cold and detached, and it hits me.

That's why he's dressed up.

The fist around my heart tightens so much I can scarcely breathe, but I somehow manage to keep my expression neutral. Unable to stop myself, I reach forward and smooth the front of his crisp white shirt, feeling the solid planes of his chest beneath my hand. "We need to see other people, or you do, Mark?" I ask quietly.

He doesn't answer, which is, of course, my answer.

I feel the blood drain from my face. "So that's why you're dressed up? Because you're already seeing someone else?" My voice sounds distant and hollow.

He has enough decency to look ashamed. "My date will be here in a few minutes."

Spots dance in front of my eyes, and I feel myself starting to hyperventilate. I snatch my hand off his chest and back away, horrified.

Not now! Pull it together!

I have to get out of here.

Breathe.

Breathe.

The spots fade from my vision and I'm able to maintain my calm expression, though my insides are raging like the sea in a hurricane.

"You've always had a gift for efficiency, but this is impressive, even for you. You didn't waste a single night. I'll change and leave so I don't cramp your evening." I push past him and hurry upstairs, my heart hammering furiously as I will myself not to cry yet. I make it to the safety of my room and wrench off my work clothes, leaving them where they fall as I yank on the jeans and black sweater lying across my chair from yesterday.

Mark is dumping me, not even twenty-four hours after making me feel more loved, more cherished, than I've felt in my entire life. And if that weren't bad enough, he'd already lined up a date before he even bothered to tell me we were through.

Mark did this to me. *Mark.*

My friend. My protector.

The man I love more than my own life.

He blindsided me. Stabbed me in the back.

No. In the heart.

Shock battles with pain, but pain is quickly winning. I've got to get out of here. I can't be here when another woman shows up for him. I'm not strong enough for that.

My feet pound down the stairs, and I snatch my purse off the washer.

"Where are you going?" he calls from the living room. His voice sounds concerned. He's probably just trying to figure out how much time he and his date have before I infringe on their evening. He needn't trouble himself.

"Don't worry about it. I promise not to interrupt your evening." I jerk the front door open, slamming it shut behind me. I run to my car, throwing my purse onto the seat and racing out of the driveway. I'm in tears before I reach the corner.

I drive to Lila's, forgetting until I pull in and see their darkened house that she and Tucker went to an infertility support group meeting. *Shit.* Now what? They'll be home later, but after what's sure to be an emotional, painful evening, they don't need me intruding on their grief.

There's no way in hell I can take a chance on finding Mark in bed with someone else tonight. Images of Mark making love to a faceless woman flash rapid-fire through my mind, slashing my heart like a fiery whip.

No.

Not like fire.

Like leather and razor wire.

I drop my head onto the steering wheel and cry, sobbing my eyes out in Lila's driveway.

I can't see Mark with someone else. I'll never survive a discovery so painful. My old darkness will consume me for sure. I need somewhere to lick my wounds.

I find myself at a hotel without remembering driving there. I've stayed here before, not long after Lila and I moved here, while we were waiting for an apartment to open up. I mop my face and make myself presentable enough to rent a room and check in. I collapse on the bed, turn off my phone, and dissolve in tears.

How can this be happening?

This is Mark, *Mark*, the only person on the planet I've ever completely and wholeheartedly loved and trusted. How could he *do* this?

I mean, if he wanted to slow things down or take a break or assess the relationship, fine, let's talk. But running straight into another woman's arms?

Fuck, this hurts.

My eyes fill with fresh tears at the thought of him with someone else, and once again, I'm left struggling to breathe. Obviously, I grossly misinterpreted last night and read feelings into it on his part that were never there.

My heart physically hurts inside my chest, a stabbing, relentless pain that only worsens the more I think about him. I didn't know I could hurt this badly. It's worse than anything I've ever experienced, even worse than the shit I survived in Afghanistan.

At least that pain was inflicted by people who hated me.

This was intentionally inflicted by someone who loved me.

Or at least, I thought he did.

And he did it because I told him I loved him.

I ugly-cry for three straight hours before I surrender. I have to numb this pain, this horrible, soul-crushing, knife-in-my-chest pain, and the one sure-fire way to accomplish that is to get so drunk, I can't even remember my own name.

Is it responsible? Hell, no. A bad idea? Absolutely. But dark thoughts from my past have resurfaced, threatening to drag me under. I have to find a way to forget, at least for a few hours.

I know. It's a terrible coping mechanism. But right now, I don't care. I have to stop this pain.

I have to.

The hotel has a bar right next door, one Tom and I have been to a couple of times after work or when we're hanging out while Maya's with friends. I glance in the mirror, scrub the mascara trails from my face, and move my handgun from my purse to my belly-band holster.

I tuck my ID and debit card into my pocket and turn my phone back on. Unsurprisingly, I have a slew of texts and missed calls from Lila. Nothing from Mark, though. He's probably occupied with his date. Tears flood my eyes again.

Fuck it. I turn my phone back off and walk next door to the bar. I sit down at the counter, ordering a shot of tequila. I drain it and set the glass down. "Keep them coming," I tell the bartender, an older fellow with a timeworn face and somber eyes. "I'm not driving anywhere."

Four shots later, the tequila has blunted the sharp edges of my pain.

A few more shots, and maybe I won't feel it at all.

MARK

I watch from the window as Charlie peels out of the driveway, slinging gravel everywhere. My heart aches at her distress, even though I know I'm doing what's best for her in the long run. She deserves someone perfect, not a scarred-up, useless cripple.

But I hate that she's driving in her frame of mind. It's not safe. And I hate I've upset her this badly.

I pace on my crutches for a solid fifteen minutes before I call Lila. She and Tucker only live five minutes away. By now, Lila's listening to Charlie curse me. She's probably joining in. I deserve it, even if this is for Charlie's own good.

Lila finally answers on my third call. "Hey, Lila. I need to talk to Charlie."

Even though I know my reasoning is sound, I've hurt Charlie, something I never wanted to do. Ending things will be painful for her now, but better for her in the long run, so she can find someone whole. Healthy. Better.

"Charlie's not with me," Lila replies.

Irritation flares. "I know she's there. Tell her to come home so we can talk."

I hear other voices in the background before Lila speaks again. "Tucker and I went to an infertility support group meeting. It just ended. Did you check the clinic? Maybe she's there."

"She's really not with you?"

"Hang on a second," she says, and I hear things gradually getting quieter on her end. "Sorry. I had to walk outside because of the noise. What's going on?"

"Charlie really isn't with you?"

"No." She gets very quiet. "What's going on, Mark?"

I hesitate. "I broke up with her."

She gasps audibly. "What the fuck, Mark?"

"It's a long story."

"I've got all goddamn night," she snaps. "What the hell is going on?"

"She's in love with me, Lila, and she deserves better. She needs someone whole, someone who can make her happy."

There's several seconds of silence before she snarls, "This had better be a fucking joke, Chandler, or I'm going to cut your balls off myself."

I'm taken aback by the ferocity in her tone. I thought Lila would understand. She should want what's best for Charlie, too.

"Are you goddamned kidding me?" Lila demands.

"I told her we should see other people, and she got upset and left."

"Of course she got upset," she retorts. I fall silent. Her voice is razor-sharp when she speaks again. "What did you say to her?"

"I - I needed her to know I was serious."

There's another silence. "Do not tell me you're seeing someone else," she hisses.

"She had to see I meant it," I insist, though when I hear myself say the words out loud, they make much less sense now than they did when I was pacing around my room last night.

She's quiet for long moments. "Who is she?" Her voice is low, feral, and I'm stunned by the venom in her tone. "Who the fuck did you leave her for?"

"There isn't anyone else. I just needed Charlie to believe there was."

Her anger pulses through the phone, and when she speaks, I wish she hadn't. "So you lied, just to fucking crush her, all because you can't pull your head out of your own ass."

"It's not like that," I protest.

Except it's exactly like that. Well, the first part, anyway.

"I love you, Mark, but you're a real asshole."

"Lila," I say, but the line has gone dead, and I know she's hung up.

I lay my phone down on the table slowly. Breaking up with Charlie was the right thing to do for her, but I've gone about it all wrong. Lila's right. I hurt Charlie on purpose. And I lied to her. I can't remember ever lying to her before.

The problem is, I don't know how to fix this without giving her false hope. She deserves better, and I have to let her go for her own good, no matter how much it hurts.

LILA

I'm so emotionally wrung out after losing our baby and sitting in a support group crying with other women in similar situations that I don't have the emotional energy to coddle Mark. A better person would tell him his true value has nothing to do with physical abilities or disabilities. Not me. I call him an asshole and threaten to cut his balls off, and I mean every word of it.

Charlie's got to be devastated, and since she's not with me and not with Mark, I'm guessing she's somewhere getting drunk.

Tucker comes outside to find me pacing furiously. I've called Charlie's phone, but she's not picking up, and I've sent a dozen texts that have gone unanswered as well.

"What's wrong?" His eyes are instantly worried.

I tell him what Mark's done, and his jaw drops. "Are you fucking kidding me?"

"I wish I were. I swear to God, I'm going to kill him."

Tucker looks dumbfounded. I lay my hand on his chest. "We need to find her."

He nods. "Let me take you home. You're supposed to be resting. I'll go look for her."

"She's probably getting shit-faced somewhere," I say worriedly, and his expression mirrors mine. Charlie drunk, upset, and armed could go sideways in a heartbeat.

"Don't worry. I'll find her," he promises, but he drives faster than normal in his race to drop me off.

As soon as he walks me into the house, he kisses me on the head and jogs back to his truck, promising to update me. I dial Tom's number. "What's up?" he greets me.

I don't give him specifics. I just tell him Charlie left her house really upset, and she's probably getting drunk somewhere and I'm worried.

"I'm on it," he says. "Maya's at my sister's house all week for fall break. Either Tucker or I will find her. We've got this, Lila. Try not to worry."

Easier said than done.

If anything happens to Charlie, losing his balls will be the least of Mark's worries, because I'll rip him limb from limb. And that's not the hormone shots talking – that's my sister-rage, and I mean every damn word.

TUCKER

I consider calling Mark, but I'm too pissed to do this over the phone. I burst into Charlie's house without bothering to knock. Mark's sitting on the steps, elbows on his knees, crutches leaning against the wall.

"What the fuck, Mark?" I demand.

He doesn't look pissed, merely resigned. "I can't talk about it."

"The fuck you can't. What the hell is your problem?"

"Not now, Tucker. Please, just find her and make sure she's okay."

I glare, fighting the urge to punch him. "Yeah. Because people are perfectly fine after they've been betrayed by someone who claimed to love them," I snap.

He recoils at my words, but I don't care. I spin on my heel, slamming the door so hard it rattles.

LILA

Tom calls me a couple of hours later, after I've worn a path in the carpet and called Charlie another dozen times without an answer. "She's at a bar on Seventh."

"Is she okay?"

I can hear the frown in his tone. "She is, but the long-haired cretin sitting way too close to her may not be when I get to her."

"Put me on speaker and don't hang up."

He does, but the bar is so loud, it's difficult to decipher what's happening. Then I hear Charlie explaining to someone in a loud, slurred voice that she's no longer broken, and that she can have sex now, but Mark doesn't want her anymore.

Oh God.

I hear Tom's voice, quiet but determined. "If you make so much as one crude comment or hit on my friend here, I promise you'll spend the next two months in traction."

"It's her choice, asshole," a raspy voice says.

"And whether you leave in an ambulance is yours." I hear a rustle, and I know Tom's taking off his jacket, ready to fight over Charlie.

I swear to God, I'm going to fucking kill Mark.

"Nice talking to you," Tom says then, and I grin. I'd bet money as soon as the cretin got a look at Tom's muscles, he reconsidered his life choices.

"Hi, Charlie," I hear Tom say.

"Well, hey, Tom." Charlie stumbles over her words, and I groan. She's drunk off her ass. "What're you doing here?"

"I was in the neighborhood. How about you?"

"I'm here to get drunk," she announces. "Very, very drunk."

"I think you've succeeded," Tom says, and she giggles.

He takes me off speakerphone. "I've got her," he says.

"I'll call Tucker. We'll come get her."

"It's okay. I'm guessing she's going to need you more tomorrow."

"Are you sure?"

"Positive. I'll call when I get her settled. She can sleep it off at my house."

"Thanks, Tom. I appreciate this."

"I'm just glad I got here when I did. The vultures were circling."

When he hangs up, I call Tucker and tell him to come home.

I swear to God, I'm going to find my rustiest razor blade to castrate Mark if he hurts Charlie any more than she's already been hurt.

CHARLIE

Everything's spinning. The room, the weird man next to me, the lights. The weird man asks why I'm here tonight. I'm explaining how Mark no longer wants me when he disappears without a word. Tom slides into the weird man's now-empty barstool next to me.

"What're you doing here?" My words sound strange, and my tongue is thick.

Tom catches the eye of the bartender, and I raise my empty shot glass. "Another one," I crow, but the bartender looks at Tom.

"How about a cranberry juice for my friend?" he says.

"With tequila," I call after him. The bartender nods, returning with a glass of icy red liquid. I take a sip and turn to Tom, nearly sliding off my stool. "He's a good bartender. The good ones make drinks so you can't taste the alcohol. It just sneaks up on you."

"You just sip on that," he says, and I see him hold out his credit card. "Settle her up."

I frown. "I can pay my own bill."

"I know. This is my bill," he says, and though it doesn't sound right, I don't argue with him. He's pretty smart.

The bartender returns with Tom's card, eying me. "She's gonna hate herself in the morning."

"Probably before then," Tom says, as I chase my straw around the rim of the cup with my lips. Damn thing keeps moving. "I need to take you home," he says to me, pulling his jacket on.

No!

I can't go home.

He's there. With her.

I don't know who she is, but I can't go home.

Panic rises in my throat. "I can't go home. They're having sex. I can't go home."

"Okay, okay," he says quickly, looking confused. "I'll take you to my house."

I shake my head and nearly topple off the barstool, but strong arms steady me. I reach into my back pocket and drag out my key card. "I have a room next door. See?"

Tom takes it from my hand. "Fine. Let's get you back to your hotel." He helps me off the barstool, and I nearly fall, but he steers me through the bar and into the chilly night air. I stagger again. Everything around me is rocking like a boat in the ocean. Tom grips my arm as I wobble.

"You're going to break an ankle," he says. "Hang on. I'm picking you up." He sweeps me up in his arms and walks through the parking lot toward the hotel.

I lean my head back and giggle at the whirling kaleidoscope above me. "The stars are spinning."

"I'm sure everything is." He stops by his car and grabs a backpack, then carries me through the hotel lobby. I wave at the desk clerk, who grins and winks her heavily-mascaraed false eyelashes at me. I shut my eyes as the elevator whirs and lurches before jerking to a halt. Tom carries me down the hall and unlocks my door without setting me down. He shuts it behind him and deposits me in the center of the bed. I flop back, and everything spins again.

Tom looks at me and hesitates. "Um," he says, then pauses. "I'm going to take your shoes and socks off," he says, reaching for my feet.

I close my eyes. "Okay."

"Do you want to sleep in your jeans?"

"Nope," I say, shaking my head. The room spins crazily again.

I hear him sigh. "Okay. Can I help you take your jeans off?"

His brown eyes look worried, but I'm not sure why. "Okay." I reach for my holster. "You should take this," I say, handing him my gun. His eyes widen before he takes it from me and places it on the dresser. I unbutton and unzip my jeans, trying to slide them down, but I can't seem to lift my hips and fumble with my clothes at the same time.

I hear him chuckle. "Sit still," he says. He scoops me up, turns down the sheets, and puts me down again, covering me with the sheet before reaching for me.

"What are you doing?"

"Keeping you covered," he explains, sliding my jeans down my legs beneath the sheet.

"That's sweet," I mumble. He just shakes his head.

"Are you okay sleeping in your sweater?"

I make a face. "It's too hot." He turns and rifles through his backpack. I sit up and yank off my sweater, but my bra clasp isn't cooperating. I'm struggling to unhook my bra when he produces a soft gray shirt and sighs.

"Be still," he says again, sitting down behind me. Warm fingers unclasp my bra, pushing the straps off my shoulders before pulling the shirt over my head. "Slide your bra off and put your arms through the sleeves," he instructs. I get the bra off, but can't find the damn armhole. I hear him chuckle again before guiding my arm through the sleeve.

"Thank you," I murmur.

"You're going to have a rough morning, kiddo."

Tears fill my eyes. "It was going to suck anyway. Now it'll just suck with a headache."

Tom folds my clothes and places them on the dresser beside my handgun. He's lowering himself into the chair by the door when I stop him. "Please don't leave me."

"I'm not leaving, Charlie. I'll be right here."

I bite my lip. "I need somebody beside me. To keep the nightmares away."

He studies my face. "Then I'll stay beside you." He sits down on top of the covers next to me, leaning against the headboard. I sit up, frowning.

"What's wrong, Charlie?"

"You have to be under the covers, or I can't turn over."

"Fine. Let me change clothes first." He digs through his backpack before stepping into the bathroom and changing into shorts.

I frown again. "You didn't change your shirt."

"I gave my shirt to you."

"Oh. Do you want it back?" I reach for the hem to pull it off.

He shakes his head with a grin. "No, Charlie. You keep it." He gets into the bed next to me. I scoot over so my back is against his side while I face the door, closing my eyes.

"Please keep me safe," I whisper, and tears fill my eyes.

"I promise, Charlie, you're safe with me."

I reach for his bear paw-sized hand and drag it under my head, tucking it palm up against my cheek. I hope he doesn't mind tears dripping into his hand. "Thanks, Tom."

That's the last thing I remember.

LILA

My phone buzzes with a text in the middle of the night. It's Tom.

"She's at the hotel on Seventh Street. She's asleep, and I'm standing guard."

"Is she okay?" I text immediately.

"She's had a lot of tequila. A LOT. It's going to be a rough morning."

"Bring her to my house when you head in to work. Tara's going to cover her patients."

"I'll text you in the morning when I see how she is."

"Call if she needs me," I type, and a thumbs up comes back almost immediately.

I'm going to fucking *kill* Mark when I get my hands on him.

CHAPTER TWENTY-TWO

MARK

Fuck.

I can't let Charlie be with me. I can't let her think she loves me. She deserves so much more than a scarred-up mess who's half a man. She deserves someone strong. Virile. Perfect.

Telling her I didn't love her was awful. Lying, faking a callous expression. Intentionally hurting her. The look in her eyes made me want to drop to my knees, beg her forgiveness, and tell her the truth: that I do love her, with every part of my being.

But I did the right thing. The hard thing.

I let her go.

But it doesn't feel right. Lying. Hurting her on purpose. Telling her I'm seeing another woman.

I thought the end would justify the means. That as long as she ends up with the right guy in the end, it will have been the right thing to do.

Then she didn't come home.

She wasn't at Lila's. Tucker went looking for her. I texted Lila, asking her to at least let me know if Charlie was okay. She told me to go fuck myself and suggested positions in which I could do so.

Hours pass. Nine o'clock. Ten o'clock. Eleven o'clock.

I text Tucker and ask if he's found her. He replies with a curt, "No."

Charlie was so upset when she left. Telling her I was seeing someone else was wrong. I'm willing to concede that. And I shouldn't have let her drive off in the state of mind she was in. I should have convinced her to let me get her an Uber to wherever she was headed.

Midnight comes and goes. Anxiety is making my imagination run rampant. What if she's been in an accident? What if she's lying in a ditch somewhere and no one knows she's been hurt? It'll be entirely my fault if anything happens to her.

At one o'clock, I call every police station and hospital within two hundred miles to see if she's been in an accident. No one's seen Charlie. I do the same thing at four o'clock. Still nothing.

Fuck.

What have I done?

CHARLIE

I wake up around five, disoriented. When I sit up, everything spins. My eyes fall on Tom, sitting in the bed next to me. He's leaning against the headboard, shirtless. I glance around. My sweater and jeans lie folded on the dresser.

"Nothing happened, Charlie," Tom says. "I'd never do that."

"I know." I could be drunk off my ass, naked as a jaybird, and horny as a moose in rut, and I'd be safe with him. "I trust you. I just have some blank spots in my memory." I cock my head. "Why were you at the bar last night?"

"Lila called. She said Mark was being a dumbass and you were upset, and she was worried you'd be getting drunk with people who would take advantage of you."

"So you came to protect me?"

He nods. "Always." Then he looks at me. "So what do you remember about last night?"

"You showed up at the bar and made that guy leave." Tom grins. "I was having trouble walking and you carried me. And you helped me change clothes and were very respectful."

"You remember that?"

"Yeah. Thanks."

He shrugs. "You're my friend." Then he studies me. "Do you remember anything from before I showed up?"

I swallow against the lump growing in my throat as I scoot up to lean against the headboard beside him. "I remember Mark breaking up with me because I fell in love with him."

He stares, too stunned to speak at first. "What do you mean, he broke up with you?"

I close my eyes, trying not to cry even as my voice cracks. "I came home from work. He met me in the hall and accused me of falling for him. I admitted I had, and I said I was pretty sure he loved me, too. He told me I wasn't really in love with him and said he didn't love me. He said I deserved someone whole and healthy. Then he said we should see other people. Turns out, he already is."

Tom slides an arm around my shoulder, and I lean against him. "I'm sorry, Charlie," he says quietly. "I don't know what to say."

"Me, either."

We sit silently for a long time. "I'm shocked you aren't hung over," he finally says.

"I'm pretty sure I'm still drunk."

"Want me to go find coffee?"

"Please. And aspirin."

As soon as Tom closes the door behind him, I scramble to my feet. I regret my rapid movement immediately as the room whirls around me. I drop to my knees and close my eyes, waiting for it to pass. After a minute, I get up slowly and dress, balancing against the bed. I stumble to the bathroom, thankful to find a toothbrush and toothpaste.

It's almost dawn when Tom returns with two giant cups of coffee, a bottle of aspirin, and apple-cinnamon danishes. "Get some food in your stomach. It'll help sober you up and keep the coffee and aspirin from making you queasy."

I sit at the table with him and nibble on the danish as I sip coffee. I'm not hungry, but I definitely have to sober up before work.

"Tara's covering your clients today," he says, reading my mind.

I shake my head, wishing I hadn't as a wave of dizziness hits. "I'm not sick."

"Call it a mental health day. Lila arranged it last night."

"I need to be at the office. Mark's at home and I –" I break off. "I need to be at work."

Oh, God. What if his date spent the night? She might still be there. I close my eyes and suddenly feel sick.

"Work in your office." Tom interrupts my misery. "I saw the piles of papers on your desk yesterday. I know you couldn't possibly have finished it all."

"I didn't. I can do that, assuming my head stops throbbing enough for me to read."

"I've been thinking about what would make Mark would react like he did. I think he's scared."

I study his gentle brown eyes. "Scared of what?"

"How much he loves you."

I shake my head. "Mark doesn't love me. He was very clear about that."

He shakes his head, too. "He does, Charlie. Trust me. He's been in love with you for a long time. He just doesn't want to admit it, to you or to himself. If you guys maintain your relationship as merely friends, there's no risk. You'll always be a part of each other's lives. Love isn't like that. It carries an enormous risk. What if he falls for you and you don't love him back, or you leave him? It's scary for him."

I stare glumly at the table. "I know the feeling."

"Charlie, Mark *is* in love with you. He just needs something to make him realize it."

We're both quiet in the early morning light, the silence broken only by the occasional sip of coffee or the crinkle of the paper wrappers from the bakery.

I study Tom, my chin in my hand. "What would make him realize how he feels?"

"He needs to feel something stronger than his fear," Tom answers. "Jealousy is the oldest play in the book."

"What do you mean?"

He shrugs. "If a guy sees another man with his woman, it stirs something visceral in him."

I sag back in my chair. "I'm not sure Mark is the jealous type."

Tom chuckles. "Trust me, he is. I had to work to drag him off Blake that day he was pounding the shit out of him."

I frown. "He didn't do that out of jealousy."

"No, he did it because Blake hurt you. Even then, Mark loved you."

He did. But that was a different kind of love.

I sit quietly for a few minutes. "I wouldn't even know how to make him jealous."

"Spend time with another guy, and do it in front of him."

"I don't know, Tom. What if he really doesn't love me? Then I'm just using some poor guy for no reason."

"Use me," he suggests. I raise startled eyes to his. "Seriously," he says, shrugging his broad shoulders. "I want you to be happy, Charlie, and you two belong together. Let me be your catalyst."

"How?" I ask warily.

"I'll spend more time at your house. We'll be affectionate in front of him. He knows we're close, so he'll assume we took things to another level. I promise you, that big green jealousy monster will rear its ugly head in no time."

"It seems dishonest and unfair to you."

Tom shakes his head. "I'll be spending more time with one of my closest friends. Besides, Mark's very much in love with you. If it takes a little sleight of hand to make him realize it, well –" he grins, "all's fair in love and war."

I wrestle with the idea for several minutes. Then I remember Mark's repeated growls when we would kiss or make love, when he'd claim, "Mine."

Maybe we *could* make him jealous.

I look up at Tom with the faintest glimmer of hope. "When do we start?"

He grins. "This morning."

My eyes widen, and he nods.

"Why waste this perfect opportunity? He knows you didn't come home, and he knows you weren't with Lila. I'll drive you home, walk you to your door, and you'll stroll in wearing my shirt instead of the clothes he saw you leave in last night. He'll think you and I spent the night together. Which we did," he adds, "but not like he'll assume. After work, I'll bring you here to pick up your car, and we can go back to your house. The idea is to make him wonder what's going on between us, to encourage him to jump to conclusions. You need him to be unhappy about you being with someone else, and I'm a perfect option because he knows you're comfortable with me."

The idea has merit. I don't want to be dishonest with Mark, but if I have to mislead him a little to get him to realize he loves me, I'm pretty sure he'll forgive me after the fact. Besides, he's behaving like an idiot, and if this will make him come to his senses, I'll throw myself into the act wholeheartedly.

He'll come to his senses.

He has to.

Tom pulls out his phone and sends a brief text to Lila, letting her know I'm heading home to change and that I'll be working in the office today. Lila fires off a slew of texts, until he finally says we'll explain in a little while, that I'm still not feeling great but that he's taking me home. In the meantime, I change back into Tom's shirt. I try to fix my hair, but stop when I decide a little bedhead might help sell things.

I'm still unsteady when he helps me into his car, putting his jacket around my shoulders when I shiver in the frosty October air. The hotel isn't far from my house, and before long, we're pulling into my driveway. Tom glances up at my front door.

"Game face on, Charlie," he says, seeing Mark glaring out the window. "We've got an audience."

He hops out of the car and comes around to the passenger side, where he opens my door and tucks me tightly against his side, trying to disguise the fact that I'm still tipsy. "Look happy," he murmurs, and I laugh and lean into him.

We're still on the porch when Mark snatches open the front door. "Nice of you to call last night," he snaps.

I raise an eyebrow. "I said I'd leave so you and your date could have the place to yourselves," I reply coolly. "I assumed you'd be too busy with her to pay attention to your phone."

"Like you were?"

I pull out my phone and glance at it. "Must have turned it off," I say breezily. I look at Tom. "It's chilly. Come inside."

Mark's jaw tightens, and I feel Tom brace for a punch. I know he won't release me to block it because he's having to support my wobbly legs. But the hit never comes, and we walk past Mark and into the foyer.

"Come upstairs," I say throatily, and even to my ears, it sounds sexy.

He helps me up the stairs and closes my door behind us. When he releases me, I fling myself onto the bed, making it bang noisily into the wall while I giggle. I immediately regret the idea, clenching my eyes shut while I wait for the room to stop spinning.

Tom sits on the bed beside me. "I think you can dial it back a little."

"Too much?" I ask, my eyes still tightly shut.

"He's got the idea. No need to rub his nose in it. He's already jealous."

I open one eye. "You think so?"

He chuckles. "I know so. I was pretty sure I was going to get punched downstairs."

I frown. "I don't want you to get hit."

He grins. "I get punched for fun all the time, Charlie."

I sit up. "Thanks, Tom," I say quietly. "This means a lot to me."

His eyes soften. "You're special, Charlie, and I don't want Mark to make the biggest mistake of his life." He squeezes my hand. "I need to go home and shower. I'll see you at work."

I take a hot shower and dress quickly, feeling slightly more human as I slip downstairs and out the side door without having to see Mark. When I get to work, Lila's waiting in my office. She shuts the door and pulls me close for a long hug.

"Why aren't you resting? You aren't supposed to be back at work," I protest.

"I'm not working. I'm checking on you. Mark called me last night." She guides me to the sofa. "I already heard his half-assed version of things. What happened?"

I shake my head miserably. "I told him I loved him before I went to sleep the other night, the same way I always do, but it was right after we'd made love and –" I break off for a second, remembering how cherished I'd felt, closing my eyes against the haunting images that stab me in the heart. "I've been in love with him for a while, Lila, and he heard it in my voice. When I came home last night, he accused me of being in love with him, and when I admitted I was, he said it would never work. He said I needed someone whole and healthy and –" I swallow hard, "and that he didn't love me. He said we needed to see other people. I guess he'd planned to tell me earlier, but I came home late. When I realized he was dressed to go out, I asked if he was already seeing someone, and he said his date would be there in a few minutes."

"Oh, Charlie," Lila says sadly. "I'm so sorry."

"What did he say when you talked to him?"

Lila places her hand on mine. "He said he broke up with you because you were in love with him, and that you deserve someone better, someone whole. He said he'd told you he had a date, and I went ape shit on him. But he didn't actually have a date. He said he'd just wanted you to know he was serious."

"Message received," I say sadly, but the knowledge that Mark didn't really spend last night in another woman's arms helps untwist my stomach a tiny bit.

"So what now?"

I sigh. "If he's too stubborn to listen to reason, I'll attack his primal instincts and use Tom to make him jealous."

Lila raises an eyebrow and settles in. "Details. Now."

"It was Tom's suggestion. He said sometimes reminding a guy what he's missing can be really effective. So he brought me home wearing his shirt and jacket and walked me into the house with his arm around me. Mark was pissed. Said I should have called him if I wasn't coming home, and I reminded him I'd told him he and his date could have the place to themselves. He looked like he wanted to punch Tom when we went upstairs together."

A slow smile spreads across her face. "That might be exactly what you need. Let Mark see Tom as an available, sexy guy ready to swoop in if he doesn't come to his senses."

My faint hope wavers. "What if he doesn't, Lila?"

"He will," she assures me.

I wish I had her confidence. "What makes you so sure?"

"You two have been in love with each other for a long time. Tucker and I have seen it for years, but you guys had to find out for yourselves. You're meant to be together. If there really is such a thing as soulmates, it's you and Mark. He's just scared of his feelings for you."

"That's what Tom said."

"He's right. Mark loves you. He just needs to come to grips with it. His body insecurities are his biggest obstacle. Sure, he's got his permanent prosthesis now, and he'll be walking without crutches soon, but he still sees himself as damaged goods. I think Tucker said the term he used was 'half a man'. Until he truly accepts himself, he won't be able to fully commit to you."

I'm not sure Mark will ever accept his changed body. A chill settles over me, because that doesn't bode well for us.

Tom stops by my office later to check on me. "How are you feeling?"

"Like there's a marching band competition inside my skull," I confess, "but to be fair, I earned it after that much tequila."

"I have aspirin at my desk."

I open my top drawer to reveal a large bottle. "Got it covered, but thanks."

"I'm going to head out a few minutes before four. I've got my boxing class at four-thirty. I can give you a ride to your car when I head out."

I don't want to go home. Actually, I'd love to go home and lick my wounds, but I don't want to see Mark. I can't yet. I'm feeling too fragile. "Can I go with you and watch your class?"

"Of course. The boys love showing off. I should warn you though, they're pretty loud and the gym echoes, so if your head hurts, it might not be the best idea."

My face falls. "I don't want to face Mark yet," I admit.

He thinks for a minute. "I have an office at the center. You can turn off the lights and rest in there. Then we'll get dinner and go to your house when you're ready."

I hesitate. "Are you sure you don't mind?"

He grins again. "It's dinner and hanging out together. We do that all the time. I'm pretty sure I can handle it."

Despite my attempts to make a dent in the paperwork that afternoon, my mind keeps returning to getting Mark to acknowledge his feelings. He did seem mad when I came home with Tom, but maybe that was because he'd worried when I didn't come home last night. *Good*, I think grumpily, then feel a brief twinge of guilt.

I push the guilt away. Mark needs something to make him realize he loves me.

I'm still not entirely sure he's capable of jealousy, though. Both before and after Blake, he'd encouraged me to get back on the dating horse. In all fairness, though, that was before we engaged in a physical relationship.

Before he started claiming me as *his* when we'd make love.

He did give Tom a pretty nasty look this morning when I showed up arm in arm with him, sporting his shirt and smelling of his cologne.

I can definitely up my game in the Tom department. Maybe that will knock some sense into him.

It has to.

TUCKER

Lila tells me we can't all take Charlie's side, at least, not openly. She says that will only make Mark dig in his heels and be that much more stubborn. Besides, we need to keep an open line of communication so we can influence him. So here I am, in the middle of the day, knocking on his door while Charlie's at work.

Mark pulls it open, watching me with wary eyes.

"You look like shit," I blurt. He's pale, wearing wrinkled clothes that I'm pretty sure he was wearing when I stormed in last night, and his hair's sticking up all over the place. He looks like he hasn't slept or eaten in days.

He scowls. "Nice to see you, too."

"You gonna let me in, or are we gonna do this in the doorway?"

Mark sighs and opens the door wider, and I step inside.

"Sorry I barged in here and yelled at you last night," I say. "Lila and I had just come from an infertility support group meeting, and it was pretty emotional. Lots of people crying. Lila was crying. It was rough. I shouldn't have taken it out on you."

Even though I meant every damn word of it.

Mark's scowl fades. "I'm sorry. I didn't know. How's Lila?"

"Physically, she's improving. Emotionally... that's another story." I hesitate. Maybe if I share some actual, honest emotions, he'll do the same, and I can get inside his thick skull. "She offered to divorce me, so I could find a woman who could give me children. Said she'd split everything evenly and wouldn't contest it."

He gapes, open-mouthed. "But you two belong together."

"Sometimes people can't see themselves clearly," I say, but he either misses the insinuation or ignores it. "Lila thinks I'd be better off with someone who can give me kids. I told her the only thing I give a damn about is her."

"Did she listen?"

"I think so, for now."

"What does that mean?"

I sigh. "Every month when she gets her period, it's another loss. She blames herself. The hormone shots make her more emotional. So she may offer to divorce me again, or worse, she might actually try."

"Why would Lila blame herself?"

"She once described her uterus like a garden. She said I was planting plenty of seeds, but her soil wouldn't let anything take root."

"But you two are meant for each other. Can't she see that?"

I look at him pointedly. "Like I said, sometimes people can't see themselves clearly. They think their partner would be better off without them because they're fixated on things that don't matter."

Mark's jaw tightens. "Did you just make all that shit up to prove a point?"

I shake my head. "Call Lila if you don't believe me. She'll tell you. She damn near broke my heart over something that doesn't matter to me."

"This isn't the same thing, Tucker."

"I'm not arguing with you, Mark. I don't agree with your decision, but it's your life."

His eyes harden. "You think I'm making a mistake."

Damn right I do. The biggest one of your life.

I shrug. "It doesn't matter what I think. You two tried the physical thing and had some fun, and it's run its course. No strings attached, right? Just friends with benefits."

Hearing myself say those words about Charlie turns my stomach, but I persist, hoping to get through to him. "I mean, it's not your fault she got attached. You had ground rules in place. No romantic entanglements – that was the rule you both agreed to, and she broke it. That's on her, man, not you."

His pale blue eyes turn icy, but I pretend not to notice. "Anyway, I stopped by to apologize for busting in here last night with an attitude. If you need to get away for a beer or need somewhere to crash, call me." I gesture toward him. "And take a shower. You really do look like shit."

I drive off, praying Mark will stop what he's doing before he makes the biggest mistake of his life.

CHARLIE

My headache has improved to a dull throb by late afternoon, so I watch Tom's boxing class. He's managing the large group of kids by himself. I didn't realize he hadn't gotten another assistant coach to help since he fired Blake. Well, technically, I suppose he didn't "fire" him, since Blake was a volunteer. Either way, he informed Blake – apparently using his fists for emphasis – that his services were no longer required.

Tom's good to me, even when it causes him problems, like managing an entire herd of hyperactive boys alone or nearly getting punched in the face by Mark.

Thirty boys ranging in age from about eight to sixteen gather around Tom. He calls out directions, putting them through their paces and warming them up before dividing them into pairs to spar on padded mats. He walks between them, instructing them and correcting their form. At the end of the class, each pair gets into the ring to box one round with their partner, with Tom in the ring guiding and encouraging them.

After his class, he showers and comes out in jeans and a soft olive shirt, smelling of fresh soap with his hair still damp. "Ready?"

I nod as he tosses his backpack over his shoulder.

"Where would you like to go for dinner?"

"Somewhere with soup. I owe my stomach a serious apology."

"I know a place nearby with excellent soup and sandwiches."

"Perfect."

He nods. "Follow me."

I drive behind his SUV, parking beside him in a lot that is surprisingly uncrowded. The restaurant is warm and cozy, half-full and quiet. I order a turkey sandwich on toast and chicken soup. When the waitress brings it, pain echoes in my chest. I realize I've ordered the same meal Mark made for me when I was distraught over the cruel things Blake said.

The restaurant's food is good, but Mark's was better, because he'd made it for me with love.

Sappy much?

I need to redirect my focus. I glance at Tom. "Are you going to get another assistant? It looked like you had your hands full out there."

He shrugs lightly. "If I add any more students, I'm going to have to. There are a couple of guys I spar with that might be good with the boys, but I'm going to do a better job of vetting them in the future."

I cock my head at him. "It's not your fault Blake was an asshole, Tom."

He frowns. "I vouched for him."

"Well, I'm not planning on dating any more of your assistant coaches, so as long as they're good with the boys, that should be the only thing that matters."

He shakes his head. "I won't put anyone else in a position of authority if I can't trust their character. Kids are easily influenced. I'm responsible for making sure they learn the right things, not just in the ring, but out of it."

I smile. "Those boys are lucky to have you."

He rolls his eyes. "They mostly just want to pound each other. I try to teach them how to channel their emotions and roll with the punches, literally."

I shake my head at him. "Do any guys see themselves clearly?"

He laughs. "Actually, I think the majority of us overestimate things and think far too highly of ourselves."

"Some do," I agree, "but I don't think guys have cornered the market on that. A lot of women suffer the same affliction." Tom's ex-girlfriend, Whitney, for example, or his ex-wife, Chele.

Tom studies me from across the table as he consumes a massive triple-decker club sandwich and a bowl of potato soup. "So as far as you and I trying to make Mark jealous, have you thought about the PDA angle?"

I tilt my head. "Public displays of affection?"

He nods.

I reach for my tea. "No. Why?"

"I mean, it's a foolproof way to make him jealous, but..." He glances at me worriedly. "Don't take this the wrong way, but you're like a sister to me."

I blink. "Is that a bad thing?"

He laughs. "I'm just saying, if you decide we should try something hot, it'll be weird."

I laugh, too. "You're saying you don't find me the least bit sexy."

He shakes his head. "I'm not falling into that trap. I'm saying I find you sexy in a brotherly way. You know, sexy, but for other men."

I lean my chin on my hand, thinking. "Should we set limits?"

"I mean, hand-holding, cuddling, things like that are no big deal. That's being affectionate, and we already do that. It'll bother him, but it's not pushing the envelope. Kissing and things like that?" He rubs the back of his head, frowning. "I mean, actors do that with other actors, right? They make it look convincing, even if they aren't into it. I guess we could, if we had to."

I laugh out loud. "Your romantic side knows no bounds."

He grins. "I can be very romantic. Just not with you." Then his eyes widen. "I'm sorry. I didn't mean –"

"I'm not offended," I assure him, still laughing. "The feeling's mutual. How about this? We stick to the affectionate stuff and hope that works. Maybe we won't have to do anything else."

He chuckles. "So you aren't into me either, huh?"

I sigh. "Things might be a lot easier if I were, but no."

I stare into my soup, and it makes me think of Mark again. Pain swells inside me, but I catch myself. He loves me. On some level, he always has. The way he loves me has deepened and changed, that's all. I just need to help him realize that.

After dinner, Tom follows me home. I glance at him and reach for his hand as we walk inside. "We're home," I call.

There's a pause before Mark answers, his voice strained. "In the living room."

Tom and I round the corner hand in hand as the opening credits for a movie scroll across the television. "Hey, man," Tom greets Mark cheerfully, as though there's nothing at all awkward about this. "Mind if we join you?"

Mark stares at us. There's a lengthy pause as he zeroes in on our intertwined fingers. "No, that'd be great," he answers stiffly.

Tom and I settle comfortably on the adjacent couch. Tom relaxes in the corner, reclined with his legs up on the footrest. I lean against his side with my legs stretching the length of the couch. He slides an arm comfortably around me, his hand resting on my hip. I catch Mark glaring at us out of the corner of my eye and have to suppress my smile.

After an hour or so in that position, I reposition myself, sliding further down the couch and laying my head on Tom's lap. His arm slides along my side, his hand coming to rest on my ribs. I hear a sharp intake of breath from the other couch. Mark drops the remote, fumbling to catch it and accidentally muting the volume during an intense action scene. Tom and I both glance at his red face, and I hide another smile.

Determined not to waste this opportunity, I slide my hand up and link fingers with Tom, our hands splayed across my abdomen. I chance a quick glance across the room.

Mark repeatedly clenches his jaw as he stares intently at the screen. He leans down to the mini fridge and pulls out a beer, which he downs, followed by a second and a third in rapid succession. By the time the end credits roll, he's finished a full six-pack.

When the movie ends, Tom looks down and smiles softly, tugging on a lock of my hair. "I should get home. Walk me to my car?"

I give him an equally soft smile. "I'd love to."

Tom holds my hand as we walk around his SUV. It sits between us and the front of the house. He opens the driver's door, causing the car's interior light to come on.

"Lean against the back door and face me," he murmurs.

I lean back, and Tom braces his left arm above my head and leans in, his face close to mine.

"Don't worry. I won't do anything, but to a jealous mind, you can imagine how this looks."

I slip my arms around his neck and pull him down against my shoulder. "I'm not worried. I trust you. But this really does seem like I'm using you."

He chuckles. "I spent my evening cuddling a beautiful friend. I think this is a sacrifice I can make. Besides, it's getting to him."

"You think so?"

He chuckles again. "I know so. He couldn't take his eyes off you."

I grin. "Good."

We stay like that for a couple of minutes before Tom pulls away. He glances toward the porch, and sure enough, Mark is staring out the window. "We have an audience."

"Excellent."

He kisses my forehead and hugs me tightly. "He'll come to his senses, Charlie. You're too good a woman to lose."

I see Mark's shadow moving behind the drapes as I walk back to the house. I steel myself as I climb the steps, unsure if he will be angry, cold, or hopefully, proclaiming his undying love.

But it's none of those things. As I open the front door, his bedroom door closes, and I hear the lock click.

Fine.

Go sulk.

But I know I'm getting to you, because you locked your door for the first time ever.

MARK

I don't believe this shit. I stay up all night, worried sick, afraid Charlie's lying dead in a ditch somewhere after she flew out of here so upset. Instead, she strolls in this morning with Tom like nothing's happened.

With his arm around her.

Wearing his fucking shirt.

Then they go upstairs to her room, and I hear bed springs squeak, followed by the sound of Charlie giggling.

Something hot and fierce surges in my chest, but there's not a damn thing I can do. She's doing exactly what I told her I wanted her to do. She even picked the guy I thought was perfect for her.

Maybe she's been harboring that thought all along, too.

Then tonight, they come in hand in hand and snuggle on the sofa, watching a movie with me. I couldn't tell you what the movie was about if my life depended on it, but I can describe in exact detail everything they did.

Charlie leaned against his chest with his arm down her side, touching her hip.

Then she laid her head on his lap, much too close to his groin.

Tom settled his hand possessively right beneath her breast.

At that point, I'd dropped the remote and accidentally pressed the mute button, so they realized I'd been watching them.

Of course I was watching. I couldn't take my eyes off her.

With him.

Because I want her to be with me.

She walks him out, and they linger, locked in an embrace for several minutes while I peek through the curtains like a damn pervert. Two minutes. Three. Five. Seven.

Jeez, get a room, I think, but I definitely don't want them to do that.

When he finally starts his car, I head for my room before she comes back inside. I pause, then lock the door.

Because if Charlie comes in here, I can't trust myself not to tell her how I really feel.

CHAPTER TWENTY-THREE

CHARLIE

I SPEND TUESDAY NIGHT lying on the sofa with my handgun. I keep the TV on low, too anxious to sleep upstairs and halfway hoping Mark will come out to make sure I'm not on the bench. But he never does, and I never sleep. Around five, I go upstairs and shower before making coffee, which I drink alone at the table. I go to work before daylight because I have no reason to hang around the house.

Lila's insisted on coming in to work this week, though I've made her stay confined to the desk, answering phones, scheduling appointments, and helping with paperwork. She's still healing from her laparoscopic surgery, and performing massages really works your core. I've just gotten myself a second cup of coffee from the kitchen when I find her escorting one of my clients down the hall.

"Thanks for showing him to the room, Lila," I say. "I'll be right with you, Paul."

Paul has no sooner closed the door than I round on her to scold her. Before I can open my mouth, she rolls her eyes. "Don't you think you're being a little overprotective?"

I snort. "Says the woman who threatened to remove Mark's testicles with a rusty razor blade."

She grins. "I'd do it, too, and he knows it. Frankly, it's still not off the table."

Tom finds me in my office as soon as I finish with Paul. Lila is there too, sorting papers into somewhat manageable piles. Both are undeterred by Mark not changing his mind yet.

"Be patient," Lila encourages me. "You know how stubborn he is. He's not going to cave immediately, even if he wants to."

Tom agrees. "Absolutely. We've barely gotten started."

I nod, but in my heart, I'm worried. Mark *is* stubborn. He won't back down when he truly believes he's right. He'll dig in his heels like a preschooler in a cereal aisle. It's a great trait in the military when persistence is needed, but in situations like this, not so much.

I stay late in my office Wednesday, working till long past seven. Tom stopped by earlier and offered to take me to dinner, but I told him I was too tired. With the exception of being passed out drunk for three hours Monday night, I haven't slept in days.

Fatigue eventually lets my anxiety level drop low enough for common sense to kick in. If I want Mark to realize he loves me, then he and I need to talk. I work out what I want to say, gather my courage, and head home to face him. But when I get there, he's already in his room with the door closed.

I stand outside it for a long time, debating whether to knock. In the end, I surrender and spend another sleepless night on the couch.

At four, exhausted yet wide awake, I go upstairs, completely miserable.

How did things get to this point between us? Mark won't even stay in the same room with me. He's avoiding me like the plague, all because I fell in love with him.

How could I have been so wrong about his feelings for me?

I start to wonder what the point even is anymore as despondency soaks into my soul.

In my bathroom, I turn on the shower and sink to my knees, praying the drumming water will muffle my sobs. I cry for a solid half hour kneeling in the tub, then get stiffly to my feet and wash my hair and body in water that has long since turned cold.

I don't know what to do. Should I wake Mark and tell him we need to talk? Should I redouble my efforts with Tom to make him jealous, or will that make things worse? I honest-to-God have no idea, and I'm hanging on by my fingernails.

I meet Lila at the clinic door as soon as I hear her. "Has Tucker said anything about Mark?"

She studies my swollen eyes and tucks my hair behind my ear. I know I look terrible. Dark circles loom large in my pale face, emphasizing my red-rimmed eyes. I've not had a decent night's sleep since Sunday, and the last time I ate was soup with Tom a couple of days ago.

"He's not said a lot," she answers gently. "Mostly that Mark feels like what he's doing will be better for you in the long run."

"It's so frustrating that I don't even get a say in this. He's decided for both of us. And he's avoiding me. We live together, but I haven't laid eyes on him since Tom left two nights ago."

Lila gathers me into a hug. "Things will work out. You just have to be patient."

"I'm not sure I have any other option."

Tom bounces in a few minutes later, full of energy and determination. "You and I are going out tonight," he announces. "I'm picking you up while he's there and bringing you back home, and there will be actual public displays of affection in his presence. We need to step things up."

I'm not sure I have the energy to manage it. I'm weary all the way to my soul.

But Lila nods enthusiastically. "He was obviously jealous the other night," she points out. "Tom's right. Mark needs to be more jealous than afraid." She studies my face and squeezes my hand. "It will work, Charlie. Boys are stupid and easily manipulated." She grins at Tom. "Present company excluded, of course."

He smiles easily. "I know we're stupid and easily manipulated. That's why I suggested making him jealous. It's effective because at our core, we're all a bunch of dumb, possessive cavemen." He turns to me. "Pick a restaurant."

I suggest somewhere quiet, and Tom makes reservations.

I take more care than usual with my appearance, partly because I want to remind Mark what he's missing, and partly because my fatigue and stress levels demand it. I dress per Lila's explicit instructions, donning the fitted black pants that she swears makes my ass look fantastic and a plunging silk blouse that matches my eyes. The black lace push-up bra beneath it definitely accentuates my assets, and I'm wearing a matching thong in case Mark comes to his senses. Plan for the future you want, right?

I style my hair in loose waves and apply makeup, including Lila's strongly recommended smoky eye. I add jewelry and skyscraper heels and send a picture to Lila, getting her immediate approval. When Tom pulls up, I decide to make Mark answer the door.

I'll make an entrance he won't easily forget.

I hear him open the door, and I wait for stilted conversation to filter up the stairs before I descend, adding a little extra shimmy to my walk. I glance innocently at Mark and watch his jaw drop.

Literally, his mouth falls open, and he gapes at me.

I have *never* had that effect on a man before.

Best. Compliment. Ever.

Tom sees Mark's reaction as well and steps forward to greet me with a kiss on the cheek and a hand on my waist. "You look amazing," he murmurs.

"Thank you," I answer, smiling up at him as I run my fingers down the front of his shirt. Mark whirls on his crutches and disappears.

Tom is opening the car door for me when he chuckles. "You really do look amazing. Mark obviously agrees, because his jaw nearly hit the floor."

The thought makes me smile, my first genuine smile in days. "That was my goal."

"You nailed it," Tom winks.

Tom and I have a nice dinner. Conversation is comfortable as we talk about work, clients, Lila, Tucker, Maya and Skyler – anything and everything except Mark. It's only when we head back to my house that I feel the familiar tightening of my stomach, dreading what's to come.

Tom notices my change in demeanor. "Relax. We've got this under control."

"Are you sure? Because nothing about this feels 'under control'."

"It's like Lila said. Boys are stupid. Despite our attempts to become more emotionally evolved, at heart, all men are neanderthals."

"So Mark wants to club me over the head like a seal and drag me back to his cave?"

He laughs. "No. He wants to club *me* over the head and drag *you* back to his cave."

"I'd rather no one got clubbed."

Tom grins. "I'd prefer it myself, but I'm willing to take a hit."

"You've not done anything to get punched over," I protest.

He winks. "The night is young. I told you, we need to step things up. You alright with that?"

I nod. "Actors do it all the time, right? Eye on the prize and all that."

Tom laughs. "That's the spirit."

We enter the house hand in hand again. Mark is in the living room again, this time with the television on a music channel. Tom waves with our entwined hands as he leads me into the kitchen. He's facing away from Mark, but he's clearly within his line of vision.

"Dance with me," he suggests as a slower song comes on.

I smile. This is familiar territory, because he and I have slow-danced together before. I slide my arms around Tom's neck as he wraps his around my waist, crossing his wrists and letting his hands dangle loosely above my backside. I catch a glimpse of Mark's dark expression. He can't see Tom's hands, but he obviously thinks they're cupping my ass. I hide a smile. We sway slowly to the music, my head on Tom's chest as he rests his chin on my head. When the song winds down, Mark turns off the television.

"You guys can have the television. I'm going to read." I hear the squeak of the couch, and Mark moves to the chair by the window where he has a direct view of us.

"Stay right where you are, but stop dancing," Tom whispers, and I do. I lean into him, tightening my arms around his neck as Tom dips his head, tilting it and resting his cheek against mine. I wonder what Mark thinks and hope he's jealous enough to decide I'm worth fighting for. Finally Tom pulls back, looking down at me and brushing my hair back from my face. "Walk me out?" he asks loudly enough for Mark to hear.

"Yes," I say immediately, taking his hand and leading him into the hallway, passing the living room without giving Mark so much as a glance before going out the front door.

Tom props himself against the porch column, and I lean into him. He wraps his arms around me, pressing his face to my hair in a comfortable embrace. "Mark hasn't taken his eyes off you."

I look up. "You think so?"

"I know so. He's watching from the window."

I steal a quick peek. I can see Mark in the chair – a chair which, to my knowledge, he's never sat in before tonight – but I can't tell for sure if he's watching.

"So what now?"

"Now you go in and block the door to his room so you can talk to him."

"You think it will work?"

Tom smiles at me. "He loves you, Charlie, and I can feel his eyes burning a hole in me. I think you've got a pretty good shot." He kisses my forehead. "You do look amazing tonight. Now get in there and work your magic."

I can do this.

I can get Mark to admit he loves me.

I don't have any other choice.

MARK

As far as shitty weeks go, this is one of the shittiest. The only time worse than this was when those bastards took Charlie from me and I didn't know where she was or if she was still alive.

I thought telling Charlie Monday night I didn't love her was the worst I could feel. Then she didn't come home.

Of course, she did the next morning, after spending the night with Tom.

Tuesday night was their snuggle session on the sofa. I downed an entire six-pack in an hour, trying to dull the monster raging in my chest, but it didn't work. I escaped to my room while they were outside doing things I can't let myself think about.

Wednesday night, I knew I couldn't face her. It's too much to ask from my battered heart. Instead, I holed up in my room with the door closed, but I kept cracking my door open and peeking to be sure she's not sleeping on the damn bench with her gun again.

Not that I have any idea what I'd do if she were. Probably drag her to my bed to let her feel safe and end up proclaiming my undying love for her, saddling her with a useless cripple because she's too stubborn to walk away.

She stayed off the bench, though. She spent the night on the couch, but I don't think she slept at all. She got up this morning long before daylight and went upstairs. I know she got in the shower, because I heard the water running.

But what I heard most were her sobs, her desperate, heart-rending sobs. They ripped my soul to shreds because I'm the cause of her pain. And her sobs went on, and on, and on.

I'm miserable, and I don't know what to do.

Charlie deserves someone healthy, someone whole. I'm not that guy. I never will be. I'm too physically damaged. And even though I'm desperately in love with her, there's no way I can tell her. She deserves so much more than I can give her, and the right thing to do is to walk away so she can find it.

And if the last few days are any indication, she can find it with Tom.

That thought only deepens my despair, even as I know it's for the best.

And then tonight... *Jesus.* Rub my nose in it, why don't you?

She leaves with him, looking like a fucking goddess, all green eyes and lush curves and smiling at him like he hung the damn moon.

They come back here after dinner and slow dance in the next room. I can't compete with that. I'm a fucking cripple. And I can tell he's got his hands all over her – grabbing her ass, touching her face, probably kissing her.

Then she wraps her arms around his neck and pulls him closer, and my heart shatters.

Fuck, this hurts.

It's like there's an anvil on my chest.

I can barely breathe, but despite the pain, I can't take my eyes off them.

I'm almost relieved when they go outside, until I glimpse them through the sheer curtains. She's leaning against his chest, wrapped in his arms.

I turn away and remind myself that this is what I told her I wanted.

This is what's best for her.

But inside, I'm raging.

At her.

At him.

But mostly at myself, for being so goddamn useless.

CHARLIE

Once again, as I enter the house, I hear the click of the lock on Mark's bedroom door. "Nope," I say aloud. "Not tonight."

I stride to his door and knock firmly. There's no answer.

"Unlock the door, Mark. We need to talk."

I'm greeted with silence.

"I swear to God, I'll kick this door in if I have to. Open the door." I kick off my ridiculously high heels, and they clatter to the floor.

"Fine," I hear him mutter, and a second later he opens it. "What?" he barks.

"We need to talk," I answer, pushing past him into the room to face him. His blue eyes are cold. Distant. But I see a hint of something else. Maybe anger.

I can work with that.

Mark remains at the door. "There's nothing to talk about."

"Really? It seems there's quite a bit we should discuss."

He studies me. "You seem angry," he says tartly. "What's the matter? Is Tom not lighting your fire? I'm surprised. You two seemed awfully cozy."

I look at him, observing the hard set of his jaw. Yep, he's mad.

Good. It's getting to him.

"Does it bother you to see me with Tom?" I ask innocently. The muscles in his jaw flex.

"Not a bit."

I tilt my head to one side. "Then why are you gritting your teeth?"

"You know, for someone who claimed to love me, you certainly didn't waste any time," he says, sarcasm dripping from his voice.

What. The. Fuck.

"I beg your pardon?"

"You heard me. Jesus, you jumped straight out of my bed and into his."

I'm tired and overly emotional, and my temper erupts like a volcano. I step closer, invading his personal space, feeling the fire I know is flashing in my eyes.

"You can take your self-righteous bullshit and shove it right up your god-damn ass, Mark Chandler." His eyes widen at the palpable anger in my voice. "Sunday night with you was the most loving night of my entire life. I felt beautiful. Desired. Cherished –" my voice breaks on that word, and tears well in my eyes.

Dammit.

I look away and fight to regain control, gritting my teeth. It's a full minute before I trust myself to speak again.

"You were gentle, and tender, and it felt different between us than it ever had before. Then I come home the next evening and you accuse me of loving you, like I've committed some horrible crime. When I admit I'm in love with you, you end things. And in case it's not shitty enough that you threw me aside like smelly fish for being in love with you, you announce we should start seeing other people, and oh, by the way, you're already dressed and ready for your date with some woman you'd already lined up before you bothered to let me know you'd gotten tired of fucking me. You blindsided me, and you did it on purpose to hurt me and punish me, and that's not okay. After everything we've been through together, I deserved better." I shake my head. "Get off your self-righteous high horse, Mark, because of the two of us, you're the one who didn't waste any time." My voice is barely audible when I finish.

His expression has grown progressively guiltier as I've spoken. "I didn't actually have a date. I just wanted you to know I was serious. I didn't want to hurt you."

"You've got a damn funny way of showing it," I snap.

"I never wanted to hurt you," he repeats.

I move away from him and sit down on the foot of the bed. "Well, you did."

He moves further into the room, leaning against the dresser to face me. "I'm sorry, Charlie," he says quietly.

"Then why are you breaking up with me? I don't understand."

"Because you deserve better. You deserve someone whole."

"You keep tossing that word 'whole' around. What the hell is that supposed to mean, anyway?"

He raises an eyebrow and gestures to his missing limb.

"You're breaking up with me because you're an amputee?" I ask in disbelief. He hesitates, and my temper boils over again. "So you're cool with fucking me, and you're fine with fucking me over, but not with *loving* me, because you're missing half your leg?"

"You know it's not like that," he growls angrily.

"Really?" I retort, venom in my voice. "Because that's how it looks from here." I feign a thoughtful look as I tap my lips with one finger. "Hmmm. I'm no expert, but I'm pretty sure you only had one leg when you first kissed me." I nod slowly. "Yep, same thing when you promised getting involved wouldn't destroy what we had. Just the one leg then, too. And when we made love in your bed. And the shower. Oh, and don't forget the chaise. Repeatedly. Just the one leg then, too." I narrow my gaze at him. "So I was good enough for you to fuck with one leg, but not good enough for you to love?"

"It's not just the leg." His tone is biting. "You deserve someone better."

"Better, as in someone with two legs?"

"Better, as in a real man."

I smack my hands down on the mattress in frustration. "Oh, just stop with your bullshit! So by your definition, someone's only a real man if they have two legs? So what, any guy with two legs is a real man? And anyone without two legs isn't?"

He glares, but says nothing.

"I know," I say, pulling out my phone, "Let's call Stubbs. You can explain how losing half your leg makes you half a man. He's lost both legs. Does that make him a quarter of a man?"

"Stop," he says, his jaw tight. "That's enough."

"No, I need to know these things," I continue, sarcasm oozing from me. "Let's talk about the ratios. What if a guy has both legs, but he loses some toes? Maybe he gets frostbitten. I mean, this is Colorado. It happens. So if a guy loses a few toes, what percentage of a man is he? Does it depend on how many toes he lost, or is it more about which ones?"

He glowers at me. "You're turning this whole thing into a joke."

"Because you're being an idiot," I counter heatedly. "What can a guy with two legs do for me that you can't?"

"Dance with you in the kitchen," he responds immediately.

"First of all, that was swaying, not dancing, and you *can* do that, even on crutches. It's a hug with sideways movement. We can do it right now if you like. And second, you've already had your surgery, and in two months, you won't even need crutches. You'll be walking around like everybody else. So drop your bullshit excuses."

"It's more than just the crutches," he says impatiently. He pushes off from the dresser and levers to the bed, throwing them down angrily as he flops next to me. He shoves the left leg of his shorts up. "I've got one thigh that looks like a cheese grater where I was burned." He pushes up the right leg of his shorts. "I've got ugly purple scars all over this leg, and at the end of my ugly-ass stump is a goddamn metal peg, and it'll still be there every fucking night when my prosthetic comes off." He pulls up his right shirt sleeve to the shoulder, exposing the pink scar on his bicep. "Let's not forget this ugly scar," he says sharply, "or this one," he lifts his shirt to expose the wide one crossing his abdomen, "or the dozens of little ones from the shrapnel. You deserve someone better, Charlie."

"What a bunch of crap," I say angrily. "So being wounded and scarred means someone doesn't deserve love?"

"That's exactly what it means!" he roars. "Good people deserve something better than being stuck with someone who's all scarred up!"

No.

The blood drains from my face as Mark confirms my deepest fear, and I can't breathe.

That's the same vile poison Blake spewed in his drunken rant.

That I'd always be alone because of my disgusting scars, because no one should have to look at them.

At me.

I have to get away.

The familiar band crushes my chest, and my breathing picks up speed. I'm hyperventilating, and I can't stop.

I see Mark's startled expression as I back across the room from him, whirling away.

Breathe in.

Breathe out.

Slow and deep.

It's several minutes before I can speak, and I'm trembling like a leaf in the wind, bracing myself on the bookcase by the window.

"It's good to know how you really feel," I finally say. "In case I ever wondered."

When I turn to face him, tears are flowing unchecked down my face. He looks bewildered by my abrupt change from anger to hurt.

"It's good to know that people who are broken and scarred don't deserve to have someone love them. It's good to know that decent people deserve better than anything I have to offer." He stares at me blankly until I unbutton my blouse.

"I didn't mean –" he starts, his expression horrified, but I cut him off.

"Those were your words. Your exact words," I remind him sadly as I pull off my shirt, then reach behind and unhook my bra, dropping it to the floor.

"I was broken and scarred in battle, too. Not the same way you were, of course, but battle-scarred nonetheless." I trace the scars across my full breasts before turning away again, moving my hair in front of me to expose the thick purple and lavender scars covering my back. I unfasten my pants as well, stepping out of them and pushing my thong low enough to expose where the scars stop across my hips, below the small of my back. "It's good to know Blake was right after all. That I don't deserve love. Maybe that's the real reason you're ending things." I pause. "Maybe that was always the reason." I turn back to find his pale eyes wide with shock.

"How can you say that? You can't possibly believe that."

"How can I not?"

"I wasn't *talking* about you. I was talking about me."

"Scarred and broken is scarred and broken, Mark. Either it applies to both of us, or it doesn't apply at all."

Mark vehemently shakes his head, looking away. "It's different, and you know it."

"Fine. Tell me how it's different," I challenge.

He still won't meet my eyes. "My injuries make me less of a man."

"Being a man has nothing to do with how many legs you have. Those bastards that tortured me all had two legs, but that didn't make them men. It made them cowards. Being a man is about who you are, not how you look."

He stubbornly shakes his head again, and I finally lose my patience.

"Alright, jackass, let's talk about what anthropology and evolution say defines a woman. Female mammals are equipped with breasts to feed their young," I say, cupping mine in my hands and moving to stand mere inches in front of him. "They also have a womb for childbearing. They mutilated me so badly, I can't have children. I'm unable to fulfill my evolutionary purpose."

Mark's eyes remain fixed on something behind my head.

"And my breasts, well, they're all carved up, too." He's still seated on the bed, and I lift my breasts slightly, moving them closer to his face. He swallows, but doesn't move. "I've seen enough movies and magazines to know that my carved-up body isn't attractive or womanly, according to their standards. So by your logic, since my breasts are scarred and my womb is useless, I'm less of a woman."

He presses his lips together so firmly, they're white. "It's not the same thing."

"Yes, it is," I respond angrily. "It's exactly the same thing, because it's the natural extension of your flawed logic. If you being scarred and broken makes you less of a man, then me being scarred and broken in the areas that anthropologically define women makes me less of a woman. So again, I don't deserve to be loved."

"Charlie," he says sadly, finally looking at me, "I'm letting you go *because* you deserve to be loved."

"Then love me," I plead.

"I can't," he says, looking away again.

"You're broken and scarred, and I'm broken and scarred," I say softly. "Maybe together, we wouldn't be broken anymore. Isn't it worth it to find out?"

I take a deep breath as I examine his strong jaw, still turned away from me. I reach out slowly, tracing his jawline with my fingertips. I gently tug until he faces me. I study his light blue eyes as I lift my fingers to run them through his hair.

I beg Mark to love me in the only way I have left.

CHAPTER TWENTY-FOUR

MARK

CHARLIE DOESN'T UNDERSTAND.

I've tried to explain. Why can't she see? She deserves someone better. Someone who's as perfect as she is, who sees her for who she is.

Not someone like me. Battered. Broken. Crippled.

I tried to explain, but I fucked up. I hurt her even more by saying good people don't deserve to be saddled with someone that's all scarred up.

I completely forgot about her scars.

I don't even see them most of the time. They're there, but I don't see them. I just see Charlie, and she's beautiful. She's always been beautiful to me.

She could never *not* be beautiful to me.

The only time her scars even register, they fill me with rage toward the bastards who dared to hurt her, and I'm glad I had a direct hand in meting out justice.

She thinks her scars make her less beautiful, less womanly. Why can't she see that her scars simply prove her strength?

Lila doesn't have many scars, not physically, anyway. There's a tiny ridge on her cheek from a broken cheekbone from being punched, and she sustained a few cracked ribs. Of course, her scars from the capture and repeated rapes went much deeper than what's visible. But physically, compared to Charlie, she escaped with relatively minor permanent damage.

Charlie, though – Charlie fought like a wildcat when she and Lila were first threatened, and it earned her their wrath. She never stopped fighting, in every way possible. That's why her body bears their scars – because of her strength, her fire. The scars only accentuate her beauty, because they show her beauty is more than skin deep. She's a beautiful warrior through and through, and she deserves someone equally beautiful, equally perfect.

Charlie steps in front of me, baring her scarred body to me, pleading with me to love her.

I know I shouldn't reach for her. It will only make it harder to let her go.

But I'm powerless. I know from the moment she touches me that I'm unable to resist her. I'm lost in those sad green eyes.

The eyes of the woman I love.

I fought so hard to maintain control as she undressed before me, baring not just her scars, but her soul. I know she deserves someone better than me, but as I look into her impossibly deep eyes, I can't fight it any longer.

I haul her against me and claim her mouth in a fierce kiss. We make love frantically, desperately, unable to kiss or touch or get enough of each other. The storm of our emotions over the past few days bleeds through our touches, and we satiate each other's fervent desires one final time.

Our unbridled passion leaves me with a deep, hollow sadness, for I know what I have to do.

I have to let her go.

And to do that, I have to truly break her heart.

CHARLIE

We lie there afterwards. I'm curled against his chest, smiling, tracing lazy circles on his chest with my finger.

I got through to him. We're okay.

"You don't need to tell Tom about this," Mark says eventually, breaking the silence.

I raise my head, confused. "Why would I tell Tom anything?"

"I mean, so you can keep seeing him. This was just –" he hesitates, "Closure."

My heart plunges into my stomach.

We're not okay.

I bolt upright, clutching the comforter to my chest. "What do you mean, closure?"

"You know," he says, studying my face.

Talons seize my heart, and my breath catches in my throat. My voice is uneven when I speak. "So you're still breaking up with me."

"I'm letting you go so you can find someone whole who makes you happy. Someone like Tom," he adds.

I close my eyes and shake my head. "Tom and I aren't actually seeing each other. I've been trying to make you jealous, to make you realize you have feelings for me."

"Charlie, I told you, I don't –"

"I know," I snap. "Believe me, I'm painfully aware of your continued insistence that you don't have feelings for me." I kneel on the bed facing him, pulling the comforter tighter around me. "But I know you, Mark, the real you, the part you try to keep hidden. You're only pushing me away because of your self-loathing. I know you well enough to know that you do have feelings for me, deep feelings. You're just afraid to admit them, even to yourself."

I remember what Tom said and push on. "If you and I keep our relationship at a friendship level, then we'll always be a part of each other's lives, and there's no risk. But love carries risk, and it's scary. If you admit you love me and things don't work out, you could lose everything, and that scares you." I pause, looking at him. "I get it. I risked everything telling you that I love you. But if you love me too, neither of us loses."

Mark looks away without speaking.

He's already made up his mind.

Making love didn't change a damn thing.

I'd thought he was finally acknowledging his feelings, but to him, this was simply one last fuck.

Closure, he'd called it.

My chest tightens. "So this really was just about sex for you all along. I hope I was at least memorable."

He blanches. "Don't say that. Don't cheapen what we had."

"Me? You're the one who cheapened it. All those times you'd say, 'Mine, only mine,' while we made love – it was all a lie. You never really wanted me to be yours, so why bother saying it?"

He swallows hard, unable to meet my eyes. "I wanted you to feel special."

I bark out a sharp laugh. "Lying to make me feel special, to keep me from realizing from the get-go that I was nothing but another piece of ass to you. Thanks." The knife in my heart twists, and I close my eyes, fighting back tears.

His hands fist at his sides. "Please don't say that, Charlie. You have to know that's not true."

There's a long silence while I gather my pain and bury it deep in my chest. It's going to take time for me to move past this, but I'll find a way. I draw a slow, deep breath. "Fine. We'll figure out how to just be friends again."

"You know we can't do that, Charlie," he says quietly.

"Yes, we can," I insist stubbornly. "No more hugging or kissing or making love. We'll go back to eating dinner together and cleaning up the kitchen and watching movies and hanging out. On separate couches," I add.

He watches me. "We'll just end up in bed together again."

"Why is that so bad?" I ask desperately. "What's so wrong about you and me being together?"

"I'm not the right man for you, Charlie."

I lower my head, and tears began to fall.

It's really over between us.

And I don't understand why.

I need to know.

I *have* to know.

I take another deep breath. "Help me understand," I whisper, working hard to keep my tone even as I avoid looking at him.

"Understand what?"

I turn away, knowing if I look at him, I'll never be able to get the words out. I feel my chin quiver and my mouth twist as I try to speak without crying.

"I don't understand what I did wrong. Sunday night, you made me feel loved and cherished. I felt like – like I mattered. I don't understand what I did that made you so desperate to end this. To end us." I drop my head and cry quietly, unable to face him.

When I eventually glance up, his eyes are closed, and his face looks like he's in terrible pain. "It's not like that, Charlie," he says hoarsely.

"All I know," I say in a voice barely above a whisper, "is that because of whatever I did, now you're telling me we can't even be friends."

"You didn't do anything wrong, Charlie," he insists.

I shake my head sadly. "Then why did it cost me everything?" I drop the comforter and stand, gathering my clothes to my chest and hurrying for the door. I'm about to shatter into a million pieces. I can feel it, and I have to get away.

"Don't leave like this, Charlie," he pleads.

I turn back to him, tears streaming down my face. "Tell me you love me."

He looks at me, his blue eyes searching mine. "You deserve —" he starts.

I'm on the verge of a full-on meltdown, and my temper flares at his words. "I'm not asking you to tell me what I deserve," I interrupt. "I'm fully capable of deciding who I want and what I deserve. I'm asking you to tell me how you feel."

He swallows hard, his eyes pained. "I can't tell you what you want to hear, Charlie."

I meet his gaze unflinchingly. "No," I reply quietly. "You *won't* tell me. There's a world of difference between the two. I can read you like a book, Mark. You're in love with me, and you know it." I wait, but he remains silent, neither agreeing nor disagreeing with my words.

When it becomes clear he has no intention of speaking, I take a deep, cleansing breath. "More than once, you've asked me not to give up on you. I hope someday you'll figure things out. I love you, Mark."

I turn and exit the room, closing the door firmly behind me, leaving my heart in tattered pieces on his bedroom floor.

MARK

Making love with Charlie has given her the wrong idea. I can tell by her tender touch afterwards that she thinks things are okay now.

But they aren't. I have to let her go.

I have to break her heart.

So I do, feeling worse with each word I speak. Eventually, she looks like she resigns herself to it, though her eyes still shine with tears.

"Fine," she says slowly. "We'll figure out how to just be friends again."

That will never work. My will is too weak. I've just proven that.

"You know we can't do that, Charlie," I say quietly.

"Yes, we can."

She's being stubborn, but I have to put my foot down. I know I'm not strong enough to resist her. I've proven it over and over in the weeks since my surgery. If I'm with her, near her, I'll break down and tell her how I feel, and she deserves someone whole. I shake my head. "We'll just end up in bed together again."

"Why is that so bad?" she cries. "What's so wrong about you and me being together?"

She lowers her head in defeat.

I'm hurting her.

The hatred I have for myself rockets to an entirely new level.

I hate myself for putting her through this.

I hate that I'm too broken to be who she needs.

I hate that I'm half a man.

I hate that I ever kissed her that night in the kitchen, because all I've done is cause her even more pain.

She takes a deep, shuddering breath, her head still down. Her words are so quiet, I can barely hear her when she speaks. "Help me understand."

I'm puzzled. "Understand what?"

She turns away, her shoulders small and hunched. "I don't understand what I did wrong. Sunday night, you made me feel loved and cherished. I felt like – like I mattered. I don't understand what I did that made you so desperate to end this. To end us."

She's crying so silently that if it were anyone else, I might not even know. But it's Charlie, and even if I didn't recognize it in her posture, I'd feel her pain, because we're so interconnected.

I close my eyes, anguish washing over me, her pain and mine combining into one awful searing fire in my chest, slicing through my heart like a hot knife through butter.

"It's not like that, Charlie." My voice is hoarse. I'm struggling to speak over the lump in my throat. I try to explain that it's not her, but she doesn't believe me.

She drops the comforter and gets to her feet, gathering her clothes to her chest.

She's hiding her body from me.

Protecting herself from me.

I want to pull her close, tell her how much I love her, and stop her pain, but I can't. I *have* to let her go, because she deserves the best.

God, this is hard. It's the hardest thing I've ever done.

"Don't leave like this, Charlie," I beg quietly.

It can't end like this, with her believing what we had together meant nothing to me. Believing I saw her as nothing more than another piece of ass. Believing she's the cause of our breakup.

It's not her. It's me.

I'm the one who's not good enough.

The one who can never be good enough.

She turns back to face me. "Tell me you love me," she says, watching me.

I've never wanted to do anything so much in my entire life.

I gaze at her, lost in her tear-filled emerald eyes. "I can't tell you what you want to hear, Charlie."

It's the most heartbreakingly true thing I've ever said.

She looks me squarely in the eye. "No. You *won't* tell me. There's a world of difference between the two. I can read you like a book, Mark. You're in love with me, and you know it."

She's completely right, and we both know it, but there's nothing I can say.

She waits long moments for me to speak, but I remain silent, because while she's right about my feelings, I can't admit them.

Charlie deserves someone better.

Finally, she takes a deep breath. "More than once, you've asked me not to give up on you. I hope someday you'll figure things out. I love you, Mark." Her expression is bleak as she turns and leaves the room, closing the door behind her.

Fuck.

I bury my head in my hands, more miserable than I've ever been in my entire life.

The night is endless. When I finally hear Charlie leave for work, I pick up my phone.

"Tucker, I need help. Can you come over?"

CHARLIE

It's a long night for both of us. On the couch, I toss and turn, my handgun on the table, the television on but nearly silent. I hear Mark moving around in his room, rummaging through his drawers and flipping channels on his television.

Once again, I don't sleep.

Once again, I shower, make coffee, and go into work before daylight, because without Mark to keep me company, I have no reason to hang around the house.

Lila corners me in my office to find out how things are going. I'm too miserable to even speak. I simply shake my head. Lila pulls me in for a long hug just as Tom stops by. Lila shakes her head, and he responds with a disappointed look, leaving her to console me.

"Mark just needs time, Charlie," she says, laying a soft hand on my cheek.

"I don't know, Lila. I think he means it." My voice sounds hollow. "He said people who were broken and scarred didn't deserve to be loved, and that no decent person deserved to be stuck with someone who was all scarred and damaged."

Lila's eyes widen, appalled, because unlike Mark, she makes the connection immediately.

"He was talking about himself, but when I pointed out the fallacy of his argument, he refused to back down."

"This is all about his body image," she grumbles. "I wish he were still in therapy."

"I talked to Stubbs. He suggested a veterans' support group for wounded soldiers. He said if I could convince him to go, thinking he was doing it to support me, it might help him. I found one at the VFW last week, but with everything that's happened, I never brought it up. I doubt he'd be willing to go for himself. He's too busy spouting his half a man bullshit. That psychiatrist, the one we tried to set Kip up with?" My eyes burn at the memory of the sweet kid with dirty-blond hair and blue-green eyes. "He'd probably do Mark a world of good if he were willing to listen, but he's not. Not right now, anyway. Maybe someday, though. Even if −" I swallow over the lump in my throat "− even if he and I never work things out, I want Mark to find peace."

All day, off and on, I recall the determination in Mark's eyes last night, and it's unsettling. Fatigue and misery combine to make my nerves feel raw.

Three o'clock comes and goes, and Mark doesn't show up for PT. "He's just upset," Tom assures me. "Don't worry. He's motivated. He'll be back." But I can't shake the gnawing feeling in the pit of my stomach.

Lila leaves just after four-thirty. I stay a few minutes longer, trying to get through the paperwork I've been unable to focus on. I finally surrender and head home, letting myself in the side door.

"I'm home," I call, but when there's no answer, I sigh. I guess it's back to the silent treatment.

I head for the front door to collect the mail, noting as I pass through the foyer that Mark's door is ajar. At least he hasn't locked me out. Maybe he's had time to think. Maybe we can talk, work this out. I grab the handful of envelopes from the mailbox and come back inside.

I pause in Mark's doorway, my unsettled sensation of the past several hours turning to stunned disbelief. The mail in my hands cascades to the floor.

His room is empty, the bed crisply made. The closet door stands open with nothing but empty hangers inside.

My heart stutters.

I cross to the dresser and yank open the drawers. They're all empty. His bedside table is empty as well, the basket on top holding only the remote controls for the television and fan. The framed photo Tucker took of us kissing the day we went hiking is gone from my bedside table.

I can't catch my breath, and my mouth is suddenly dry.

This can't be happening.

I snatch the bathroom door aside just as my cell phone buzzes. His toothbrush is gone, along with his toothpaste, his deodorant, even his walker for the shower. A bottle of shower gel stands in one corner of the shower, still covered in water droplets. Apparently Mark forgot it in his haste to escape. Even the laundry hamper is empty. The towels are all washed, put away in the linen closet in neat stacks.

Except for the shower gel and dried steam trails down the shower doors and mirror, it's as though he was never even here.

My cell phone buzzes again. I ignore it as I hurry to the living room. His book is missing from its usual spot on the end table. The remote controls are tucked into the basket, and everything has been tidied, the throw pillows and blankets precisely placed.

No. Please no.

I move numbly into the kitchen as my phone buzzes again. My coffee cup from this morning has been washed and dried, and the dishwasher is empty.

Mark's cleaned up like my house was a vacation rental and he's trying to get his deposit back.

My phone buzzes a fourth time, and I pull it out. It's Lila. "Mark's gone, Lila," I blurt. "He left me."

"He's here," Lila says. "With us."

"What?" I ask, bewildered.

"He called Tucker this morning, I guess. He said he needed help. I don't know. I haven't heard the whole story. But he's here, and he's safe. Don't worry," she assures me, "we'll talk some sense into him."

"No, you won't," I murmur. "He's made up his mind. I've lost him."

"Don't say that. He'll figure things out. I know Mark," she says urgently. "He loves you, Charlie."

My chest grows tight, and I struggle to stay upright. "I have to go, Lila. Someone's at the door." I hang up and sink to the floor, utterly heartbroken and completely alone.

A SNEAK PEEK AT SHATTERED PROMISES

CHARLIE

No. No! No!

This isn't real. This can't be happening.

Mark wouldn't do this to me. He loves me.

He promised he'd never leave. He said nothing could make him leave me, nothing.

He promised me.

He promised.

But here I am. Alone.

All alone.

I'm on my knees in the hall outside Mark's room, envelopes scattered across the floor where I dropped them when I realized he was gone. My phone lies on the floor beneath the wooden foyer bench. My fists are clenched beside my ears, my head tucked down so my arms shield my face. My heart slams erratically in my chest. Iron bands surround my ribcage, squeezing ever tighter, making it difficult to breathe. I'm gasping, my breaths coming fast. Too fast. Black spots crowd my vision, and my hands and forearms tingle.

Somewhere inside my head, I hear a gentle voice. *Slow, deep breaths. Slow your breathing down. You're hyperventilating. You're safe. Slow your breathing. Nice deep breaths.*

Lila's voice.

I focus on slowing my breathing, trying to block the stark reality crashing over me. I have to close my eyes to concentrate, to stop seeing the truth.

That I'm alone.

That Mark left me.

That my best friend, the man I love, walked out on me.

Worse, he waited till I was at work to pack up his belongings and leave, sneaking away like I was a mistake, a shameful one-night stand. No phone call. No text. No note.

Just an empty house and my shattered heart.

Lila called to tell me he was staying with her and Tucker at their house. She said not to worry, that they'd talk to him. I'd lied and said someone was at the door and hung up. My phone has buzzed more times than I can count, but I can't talk to her. I can't talk to anyone.

She and Tucker can talk to Mark all they want, but it won't make him love me, and that's what it all comes down to.

He doesn't love me.

How could he? I'm too fucked up for anyone to love.

The sky grows dark as hours pass. Shadows crawl across the floor, reaching for me with long claws, threatening, menacing. My heart thunders in my chest again.

I can't be alone in the dark. I can't handle the darkness.

Somehow I get to my feet, turning on every light downstairs before returning to Mark's room.

To the floor.

His floor.

I remember with startling clarity the night we discussed taking our friendship to the next level. I was afraid I'd lose my best friend if things didn't work out between us. Mark stared at me with intense blue eyes from across my dining room table, his large hands gripping mine.

You won't lose me, Charlie, not ever. You've been the best part of my life for as long as I can remember, and nothing would make me walk away from you. Nothing.

Yet here I sit, crumpled in the floor, because he discarded me and walked away.

I drag his pillow off the bed, clutching it to my chest, hoping to dull the sharp pain slicing through me. It doesn't work. Instead, his scent assaults me, reminding me of the perfection of mere days ago, when he made me feel cherished. Loved. Like I was important to him.

He said he doesn't love me.

He insisted I deserve someone better. Someone whole.

He said people who are broken and scarred don't deserve love, referring to his own war wounds. His amputation. His scars.

I'm still flabbergasted he said those words to *me*, a woman whose entire back is a web of interlacing scars from razor wire, leather strips, and an Arabic-script brand that declares me to be a "stupid cunt whore". He made his declaration to a woman whose breasts and upper thighs bear scars of mutilation, whose insides are scarred from repeated rapes and violations from a rusty knife and filthy metal pipes. A woman whose psyche is most definitely broken.

People who are broken and scarred don't deserve love.

So he took his love away.

When I could breathe again after his harsh words, I recognized he wasn't talking about me. My stunned expression left him confused until I removed my shirt. When comprehension dawned, he was horrified I'd thought he was talking about me. He's seen my scars so many times that he'd stopped seeing them, the same way I don't see his. I only see him. I only loved him.

But it wasn't enough.

I gave him all of me. My trust. My body. My heart. It still wasn't enough.

I'm not enough.

I still don't understand what I did. Sunday night was the most tender, beautiful, perfect night of my entire life. His kisses, his touches, were reverent. He made me feel worshipped. Treasured.

And I knew with complete certainty that he loved me.

The next evening, I came home to find him waiting for me in the hall, telling me we needed to see other people. His sudden one-eighty was a knife in my heart. I told him I loved him, but it didn't matter. I fled the house and got drunk, ending up at a bar until my friend Tom came to my rescue. He took me back to my hotel room and stayed at my side, keeping me safe.

Tom and I attempted to make Mark jealous by having dinner together and being affectionate where he would see us. We needn't have bothered. Mark was already emotionally gone. He had been for weeks. Telling him I loved him only made him more desperate to end things between us.

Last night I thought I'd finally gotten through to him after his scar comment. We made love urgently, frantically, unable to get enough of each other. Our bodies said what our words couldn't. I thought we'd fixed things, that he'd realized how he felt about me.

I was peacefully curled up against his chest when he called our lovemaking "closure".

Closing the door on us.

On me.

I begged him to admit he loved me. I was positive he did. He just needed to let go of his fears and say it. He said he couldn't tell me what I wanted to hear. I argued it wasn't that he couldn't, but that he wouldn't.

He didn't deny it.

Instead, he left me.

Telling Mark how I feel about him has destroyed the most important relationship in my life.

It might destroy me.

This pain is unbearable, ripping through my chest, shredding me to ribbons from the inside.

I can't take this pain.

I can't take this.

I can't.

Make it stop.

I just want the pain to stop.

I spend the night on the floor, knees drawn to my chest, clutching his pillow for dear life as though it will bring him back to me.

MARK

I'm facing a furious Lila, trying to explain things. It's not going well, not that I expected it to. She and Charlie are like sisters.

"Let me get this straight," she says, the heat of her violet stare searing me. "You told Charlie you needed to see other people less than twenty-four hours after what she says was the most loving night of her life." My face burns with shame, but I don't look away. I don't trust Lila not to slap the shit out of me, especially since I've earned it. "Then you tell her she deserves someone whole. You tell her people who are broken and scarred don't deserve love." I swallow hard. "You used those *exact* words, knowing the hell she's been through, knowing that's the shit Blake told her, and knowing that's exactly how she views herself, broken and scarred." I wince. "Then you two make love, and just when she thinks that means things are okay, you tell her it was just 'closure'. Then you call my *husband* –" she turns to glare at him before whirling back to me, blond curls sailing over her shoulder with the speed of her movement, "– to come and help you sneak the fuck out of her house, the house she remodeled to accommodate your needs after you were released from the hospital, the same hospital where she stayed by your side for three months when you were injured. You treated her like shit after claiming she was your best friend, after you swore to her nothing could ever come between you." Her voice has steadily gotten louder, and a vein stands out in her forehead. "Did I miss anything?"

"Lila –" I begin, but she cuts me off.

"Don't," she says, holding up a hand and pressing her lips so tightly together they turn white. "Just don't. I love you, Mark, but you're a fucking asshole, and if you say one more word, I swear to God, I'll knock every one of your teeth out." She rounds on Tucker. "And you? Helping him do this to Charlie? What the fuck, Tucker?"

"He didn't know what was happening, Lila," I interject quickly. "All I told him was that I needed some help."

Lila mutters something that sounds suspiciously like, "you're gonna need help when I'm done." Then she holds up both hands, fingers splayed and shaking with rage. "Take your shit to the guest room at the end of the hall. It has a bathroom, but there aren't handrails in the shower, so use your fucking walker." She turns to Tucker. "You can stay on the couch or with Mark, I don't care which. I can't stand the sight of either one of you right now." His blue eyes widen and he opens his mouth to protest, but reconsiders at her murderous expression.

Tucker waits until her door slams upstairs before he sighs heavily. "Sorry about that. The hormone shots and the ectopic pregnancy – it's been hard." His voice trails off. Lila and Tucker have been trying to conceive, and Lila's been taking hormone shots. Just a couple of weeks ago, they rushed her into surgery for a tubal pregnancy, resulting in the loss of one of her fallopian tubes and effectively halving their already-slim chances of conception.

I shake my head. "No, I'm sorry. I didn't mean to get you in trouble."

He shrugs. "She might calm down in a couple of hours. Sometimes once the anger fades, she gets a little weepy. I might not have to spend the entire night on the couch." He frowns. "Or it could go the other way, and I'll be down here long after you and Charlie have patched things up." He steals a hopeful glance in my direction.

But that won't happen.

It can't.

Charlie deserves someone better. Someone who doesn't have a fucking metal peg sticking out of his stump of a leg for a prosthetic to attach to. Someone whose body isn't a goddamn patchwork of scars from burns, shrapnel, and surgeries. Someone who isn't half a man.

She deserves someone as beautiful and as perfect as she is. Someone who sees her true worth and loves her more than life itself. Someone who would die for her without hesitation. Someone who can do anything she wants, like dancing in the kitchen or going horseback riding or making love without having to worry about skewering her with his fucking peg leg.

Someone like Tom.

The thought makes my chest burn, even though I know he'd be perfect for her. He's strong, good-looking, kind, hard-working. They're already good friends, and his daughter Maya worships Charlie. The three of them hang out together regularly. One small nudge in the right direction is all it might take. The burning in my chest gets worse, and I force the image of the three of them as a happy family out of my mind.

I remember the two of them lying together on the couch a few days ago, his hand just beneath her left breast. Entwined in the dark beside his car. Slow dancing in the kitchen.

The pain in my chest becomes a searing, raging monster, and it takes everything I have to force it down.

Despite my jealousy, I can admit Tom is the perfect man for Charlie.

When I said decent people deserved better than to be stuck with someone who's broken and scarred, I was talking about Charlie deserving someone better than me. Her scars and self-described brokenness never entered my mind. I don't see her as scarred or broken. It's true that she has scars, but they don't even register with me. If I do notice them, it only makes me appreciate her strength even more. She's always been beautiful to me. No matter what those bastards in Afghanistan did to her, Charlie could never not be beautiful to me.

She said last night that she knew I loved her. That it wasn't that I couldn't admit I loved her, but that I wouldn't. I didn't bother to deny it, because I can't. I do love Charlie, more than life itself.

And that's why I had to leave.

Charlie wasn't supposed to fall for me. It wasn't supposed to be like this. We've been best friends for most of our lives. We kissed once, in her kitchen, and it ignited an insatiable fire between us. Once we accepted our mutual attraction, we agreed to explore a no-strings-attached physical aspect to our relationship.

I never stood a chance.

Unbeknownst to Charlie, I fell hard for her when we were teens. I never acted on it because I was afraid her parents would freak out. After all, we lived in the same house. Those buried feelings never disappeared. They simply went into hibernation, and at the first opportunity, they consumed me. I fell for her all over again, and I fell hard. I knew when things ended between us, I'd be crushed, but I wanted to savor every second for as long as I could.

But that love can't be mutual. Charlie can't be stuck with me. She deserves someone better. Someone healthy. Someone whole.

I realize Tucker's still waiting for me to respond. I shake my head. "This isn't something that can be patched up, Tucker."

He studies me. "Give it a few days. Things will look different after a little time and space."

A door upstairs opens long enough for a pillow and blanket to sail over the banister before slamming shut. Tucker sighs and retrieves them, tossing them onto the couch.

"Sorry," I apologize again.

"I'm not the one you should apologize to," he says. "I need a beer. Do you want one?"

TUCKER

It's two a.m. Mark's gone to bed. I'm on the couch. Lila's still awake. I can hear her pacing back and forth across our bedroom. I reach for my phone and text her.

"Can I come talk to you?"

Little dots dance on the screen as she types her reply. "Not without physical injury."

Well, it's not a no.

I try for humor. "Open or closed hand? Face or body blow?"

A solid minute passes before the little dots appear again. "Fine."

I collect my blanket and pillow from the couch, but have enough sense to stash them in the hall. If I take them in with me, she'll think I'm assuming I've won this round, and she'll toss me out and keep my pillow and blanket. Been there, done that. Twice, actually. I'm a slow learner.

I open the door and enter, my hands raised in surrender as I study her expression. She's upset, but not ready to erupt.

"Hi, Sweetness. Thanks for letting me come up."

She frowns. "Charlie won't answer any of my calls or texts."

Thankfully, she seems more worried than mad at the moment. I can work with that.

"Where's your laptop?" I ask, and she gestures to the small desk by the window. "I can still remotely access the camera in her foyer. We might be able to see her, depending on where she is, or you can try to talk to her through the mike."

Last year, Lila and I persuaded Charlie to let us install a camera system that feeds directly to our laptops and phones. Charlie battled severe night terrors, reliving the horrors of her kidnapping. She'd awaken terrified and disoriented, often firing her gun. The system would alert us via motion and noise sensors so we could talk to her and reorient her from here. On rare occasions, we'd have to go to her house to intervene. Thankfully, that didn't happen often, because startling a panicked, paranoid sharpshooter isn't something I'd recommend.

Lila's face relaxes. "That's a good idea." I sit down at the desk and open the security program, and she crosses the room to peer over my shoulder.

The fish eye camera comes to life, looking down into her foyer. All the lights are on, but the area is empty. I frown. "She's not on the bench." I'd assumed that's where she'd be. Charlie used to stay on it every night so she could monitor all entrances to her home. She believed hypervigilance would protect her from being victimized again.

"Can you see into the living room?" Lila leans closer, and her blond curls fall forward and brush my cheek. I inhale her subtle cherry blossom scent.

I swivel the camera and zoom in. "You smell incredible," I tell her, not taking my eyes off the screen.

She ignores my compliment. "Do you see anything?"

Her tone isn't overly friendly, but it's not angry, either. I'm close enough to kiss her, and she hasn't mauled me yet.

I scan what I can see of Charlie's living room. One couch and loveseat are empty. I can only see the back of the other sofa because it faces away from the camera. "She might be lying here," I point to the screen, "but if she is, she's out of view."

She purses her lips thoughtfully. "How about Mark's room?"

I look up in surprise. "You think she'd be in there?"

Her eyes grow sad. "It's the one place she'd feel close to him."

I pivot the camera again, turning it toward Mark's room. "There," I nod, pointing to the screen. Charlie's knees are drawn to her chest and she's rocking, her arms wrapped around something with her face pressed into it.

"She's holding his pillow," Lila says, her expression pained.

I drag my hand down my face. "Should we go over?"

She considers, pressing her fist to her mouth. "I don't know. I wish she'd answer her phone."

I reach for Lila's fist and tug her hand down. "She may want to lick her wounds in private. You know she hates for anyone to see her struggle."

Lila scowls. "There wouldn't be a struggle if Mark weren't being such a dumbass." She yanks her hand out of mine. "I can't believe you went along with this."

"What did you want me to do? Let him take an Uber to a hotel? Leave town and disappear? This was the best option. He's safe, and it gives us a chance to talk some sense into him. He's stubborn as a fucking mule. He's not going to change his mind easily."

Her frown shrinks but doesn't disappear. "I guess."

"You know I don't agree with him. This was the best alternative I could come up with."

"Fine," she mutters, "you don't have to sleep on the couch."

I slide a hand behind her neck and pull her down for a quick kiss, followed by a longer kiss until I feel her smile against me.

"Just because you're a good kisser doesn't mean you're off the hook."

I grin. "Of course not." Then I wink cheekily. "Feel free to punish me."

"I have the perfect idea," she says, leaning closer, her breath tickling my neck as her lips graze my ear. My grin deepens as possibilities race through my mind, but our minds are on very different tracks. "You're doing the dishes for as long as Mark stays here."

LILA

I doze off and on through the rest of the night, curled against Tucker's chest with his arm around me. Every time I glance at the laptop, Charlie's still sitting there, clutching Mark's pillow. She's stopped rocking, but other than that, nothing's changed. Every time I raise my head to check on her, Tucker rubs my back and murmurs for me to go back to sleep, because he's watching her.

Shortly after daylight, I fall into a deep sleep, not rousing until ten-thirty. I jump out of bed. I never sleep this late. I glance over, but Tucker's gone, probably downstairs. When I look at the laptop, Charlie still hasn't changed position.

My heart aches as I watch her. I don't know how she'll cope without Mark.

I've known Mark for years. He's the brother I never had. I've never seen him behave this way, and him acting like this with Charlie, of all people, leaves me speechless.

But even though I'm appalled by his conduct, I know exactly what's driving it.

Mark has loathed his body ever since the explosion.

Nine months ago, he was leading a mission in Afghanistan when an IED blew up, killing half the men on his team and leaving him critically injured. The explosion ripped his right lower leg off and caused flash burns to both thighs. He had massive internal hemorrhaging, a head injury, damaged lungs, numerous broken bones, and a body full of shrapnel. His doctors were worried about permanent brain damage, cautioning us that he might not remember anyone or anything. He spent over a week unconscious and on a ventilator. More than once, we nearly lost him.

Most of his physical injuries healed with time. The doctors stopped the bleeding and treated his sepsis. His burns healed with hyperbaric treatment and skin grafts. Broken bones eventually fused after multiple surgeries. Shrapnel punctures slowly closed, leaving his body peppered with scars. Thanks to his determination, intensive physical therapy with Tom, and strength training with Tucker, he's regained his strength.

But he's still an amputee.

That particular psychological wound continues to plague him. Mark can't accept his changed body. He views himself as half a man. I thought we'd finally gotten through to him, but when he and Charlie took their friendship to the next level, he reverted to calling himself a "useless cripple", a phrase he hadn't uttered aloud since he'd first come home from the hospital. Two months ago, Mark had osseointegration surgery, a goal he'd been working toward since his initial injury. A titanium rod was drilled into his remaining lower leg bone. The rod protrudes from his residual limb, allowing a prosthetic to mechanically attach with a simple Allen wrench. As his bone continues to fuse to the titanium rod, he can bear more weight on his prosthesis, and by Christmas, he'll only need his crutches when he removes his prosthesis to sleep. By then, as long as he's wearing pants, no one will know he's an amputee, which is why he'd been looking forward to the surgery for months.

But Mark's mindset worsened dramatically following the surgery. He was quieter, more reserved. He began withdrawing from Charlie. She was concerned his depression was returning. Like many soldiers, Mark struggled with depression following his injury. With the help of medications, a psychiatrist who specialized in wounded warriors, and an amputee support group at the hospital, he'd improved. When he moved home with Charlie, the combination of meds and friends to keep him grounded seemed to return him to his previously healthy emotional baseline.

That healthy emotional state vanished following his long-anticipated osseointegration surgery.

I hear the front door close, followed by feet jogging up the stairs. Tucker opens the bedroom door, sweat trickling from his light brown hair, his gray tee shirt clinging to his muscled chest.

"Morning, Sweetness." He stops in front of me, pulling me close for a kiss, lightly running one hand over my healing abdominal incision. "How are you feeling?"

"I feel like you need a shower," I tease.

"I think we both do," he grins. "Wanna join me?"

"It's too soon for us to get pregnant yet." My response is automatic, and I cringe as hurt flickers in his dark blue eyes.

He masks it quickly. "Then I guess this will have to be for fun." His lips graze mine lightly. I slide my arms around his neck and pull him in for a longer kiss, a wordless apology for my thoughtless remark.

When we pull apart, I peek up at him from under my lashes. "I like your kind of fun."

He laces his fingers through mine and walks backwards, tugging me toward the bathroom with twinkling eyes. "C'mon, sexy lady. I'm gonna make sure you have fun again and again."

That's an offer I definitely can't refuse.

CHARLIE & MARK'S STORY CONCLUDES IN SHATTERED PROMISES!

If you're enjoying my novels, please visit my website and sign up for my newsletter. When you sign up, you'll get a free bonus intro to the characters in my Shattered trilogy, complete with fun facts and photos! You can sign up here: https://phoenix-wolfe.com/The same page has links to follow me on Facebook, Instagram, and Twitter! Pop in and say hello!

If you're enjoying this series, please stop by and leave a review on Amazon. As an indie author, reviews are the best way to get my story out to other people, and to be honest, there are entirely too many women (and men) dealing with the aftermath of not only sexual assault, but the struggle of self-loathing. I'd love to put this story in the hands of as many people as I can because I truly believe the message is something most of us need to hear on some level. If you're willing to help, I'd appreciate it.

LETTER FROM THE AUTHOR

Dearest Reader,

As an author and survivor of sexual assault, I felt it was important to show a realistic portrayal of the lingering aftereffects of such a traumatic event. The road to recovery is long. It is not linear, and no two people's journeys look exactly the same. It took me many years – decades – to reach what I would consider "recovered", yet even now, specific triggers can catch me off guard and cause me to struggle temporarily.

I understand that not everyone can read about such events without re-living his or her own trauma. As such, I strongly recommend reading the trigger warnings page to see if Charlie's story is a fit for where you are in your situation. You may also view a sample chapter at the following link: **https://phoenix-wolfe.com/sample-of-chapter-one**

For those who have survived sexual assault, I stand with you and support you. What happened to you was not your fault, and despite the lies your inner critic may whisper, you are never too damaged to be worthy of love. For those whose lives have not been shattered by rape, perhaps this book will provide insight into the long-term struggles survivors face.

I urge anyone who has survived any type of traumatic event to seek help, even if your trauma is not recent. Many people cope by trying to forget what happened, rather than dealing with it. I'm one of them. I tried to forget, and in the end, I still had to unearth the past and address it. Repressing and burying pain is merely a stop-gap measure. Eventually, you have to deal with the pain of your past. Talk to someone – a counselor, your health care provider, a psychiatrist, support group, or spiritual leader. You can also contact the **National Sexual Assault Hotline** 24 hours a day by calling **1-800-656-4673**. If you prefer, you can go to **online.rainn.org** and chat with someone online.

Additionally, if you or someone you know is considering suicide, I urge you to reach out for help. **You can call, text, or chat with someone from the Suicide and Crisis Hotline by dialing 988.** You can also **text the word HOME to 741741 for free, confidential support** from a Crisis Counselor 24/7. You can also reach out to the **American Suicide Prevention Foundation at 1-888-333-2377.** Please, seek help. Your life is valuable, and **you matter**.

Recovery is a journey, not a destination. You are not alone.

Standing alongside you,
Phoenix Wolfe